THE GATHERING GLOOM

The Further Adventures of Sherlock Holmes

Craig Janacek

The New World Books

Copyright © 2019 Craig Janacek

All Rights Reserved.

'The Schoolroom of Sorrow' originally published 2018.
'An East Wind' originally published 2019.

This book is a work of fiction. Names, characters, places, and incidents either are the product of the author's imagination or are used fictitiously and are not to be construed as real. Any resemblance to actual events, locales, or persons, living or dead, is entirely coincidental and not intended by the author.

No part of this book may be reproduced, or stored in a retrieval system, or transmitted in any form or by any means, electronic, mechanical, photocopying, recording, or otherwise, without express written permission of the publisher. The only exception is by a reviewer, who may quote short excerpts in a review.

Grateful acknowledgment to Sir Arthur Conan Doyle (1859-1930) for the use of the Sherlock Holmes characters.

Some excerpts of 'The Father of Evil' are derived from 'The Edge of the Unknown,' Chapter VII (1930) by Sir Arthur Conan Doyle.
Some excerpts of 'The Fatal Fire' are derived from 'The Tragedy of the Korosko' (1897) by Sir Arthur Conan Doyle.
Some excerpts of 'The Adventure of the Defenceless Prisoner' are derived from 'The Prisoner's Defence' (1916) by Sir Arthur Conan Doyle.

'The Adventure of the Dishonorable Discharge' first published in 'The MX Book of New Sherlock Holmes Stories, Part XI: Some Untold Cases'; David Marcum, Editor; MX Publishing (2018).
'The Adventure of the Awakened Spirit' first published in 'The MX Book of New Sherlock Holmes Stories, Part VIII: Eliminate the Impossible'; David Marcum, Editor; MX Publishing (2017).
'The Adventure of the Third Traitor' first published 'Sherlock Holmes: Adventures Beyond the Canon, Volume II'; David Marcum, Editor; Belanger Books (2018).
'The Adventure of the Unfathomable Silence' first published in 'Tales from the Stranger's Room 3'; David Ruffle, Editor; MX Publishing (2017).

ISBN-13: 9781691926862

Cover illustration by Frederick Dorr Steele for 'The Adventure of the Three

Students' (1904), in public domain.
Printed in the United States of America
The New World Books

First Printing: October 2019
Second Printing: March 2020
Third Printing: October 2020

To Owen & Danica

*"It is one of the strange discoveries a man makes
That life, however you lead it,
Contains moments of exhilaration:
There are always comparisons which can be made
With worse times:
Even in danger and misery the pendulum swings."*

'THE POWER AND THE GLORY' (1940)

GRAHAM GREENE

CONTENTS

Title Page

Copyright

Dedication

Epigraph

LITERARY AGENT'S FOREWORD TO 'THE SCHOOLROOM OF SORROW'	1
THE FATHER OF EVIL	6
THE ADVENTURE OF THE DISHONOURABLE DISCHARGE	40
THE ADVENTURE OF THE FATAL FIRE	76
THE ADVENTURE OF THE AWAKENED SPIRIT	145
THE COLD DISH	176
LITERARY AGENT'S FOREWORD TO 'AN EAST WIND'	223
THE ADVENTURE OF THE THIRD TRAITOR	228
THE ADVENTURE OF THE UNFATHOMABLE SILENCE	265
THE HIGH MOUNTAIN	292
LITERARY AGENT'S NOTES ON 'THE HIGH MOUNTAIN'	328
THE ADVENTURE OF THE DEFENCELESS PRISONER	330
THEIR FINAL FLOURISH	361
APPENDIX: ON DATES	397

ALSO BY CRAIG JANACEK	406
FOOTNOTES	409
Acknowledgement	431
About The Author	433
About The Author	435
Praise For Author	437
THE FURTHER ADVENTURES OF SHERLOCK HOLMES	439

LITERARY AGENT'S FOREWORD TO 'THE SCHOOLROOM OF SORROW'

> *"Should they in the future join their forces, as seems not unlikely, the financial world may find that Mr. Neil Gibson has learned something in that schoolroom of Sorrow where our earthly lessons are taught."*
>
> *– The Problem of Thor Bridge*

When one considers it, the very business of being a detective is an unhappy one. For while there are certainly the occasional happy outcomes – such as when Mr. Neville St. Clair was returned unharmed to The Cedars near Lee, or when Mr. Grant Munro was reconciled with his wife Effie – there are also many gloomy ones. From the very first, Holmes' cases were tinged with tragedy. Old Justice of the Peace Trevor was fatally struck down by the reappearance of the sailor Hudson. The butler Richard Brunton was killed by the mad maid Rachel Howells. And the tragedies only deepen as the years passed by. A lifetime spent studying the ways of thieves, swindlers, and murderers is enough to turn a man pessimistic and uncertain.

In the Preface to *His Last Bow: Some Reminiscences of Sherlock Holmes*, Watson makes it known that in 1902, Holmes retired to the coast for the study of philosophy. The term is, of course, Greek and literally means 'love of wisdom.' It is the study of those general and fundamental problems concerning the deep matters of existence.

Which leads us to ask: what precisely was the nature of Holmes' philosophy? In his account of their first months together, *A Study in Scarlet* (Chapter II), Watson wrote that: "Of... philosophy... he appeared to know next to nothing." By 1888, however, it was apparent that Holmes had studied the works of certain philosophers. It seems he began with Thomas Carlyle (1795-1881), whose work *On Heroes, Hero-Worship, and The Heroic in History* (1841) propounded the 'Great Man Theory' of history. This postulates that the passage of history can be largely explained by the impact of highly influential individuals, who – through the force of their brilliance or will – alter the course of Time's river. One wonders if Holmes saw himself in the same light? From Carlyle, he moved on to Jean Paul Richter (1763-1825), who was more of a Romantic writer than a philosopher, *per se*. However, Richter's writings contained a worldview that stressed the importance of discarding one's illusions in order to live in a state of humorous resignation.

Finally, Holmes was a great admirer of William Winwood Reade (1838-1875), whose masterwork *The Martyrdom of Man* (1872) is a secular universal history of the Western world. Its final section was an outspoken attack upon Christian dogma. In Chapter X of *The Sign of Four*, Holmes remarks: "A strange enigma is man!" Watson counters with: "Some one calls him a soul concealed in an animal." And then Watson goes on to relate that Holmes said: "Winwood Reade is good upon the subject. He remarks that, while the individual man is an insoluble puzzle, in the aggregate he becomes a mathematical certainty. You can, for example, never foretell what any one man will do, but you can say with precision what an average number will be up to. Individuals vary, but percentages remain constant. So says the statistician."

The dual nature of Holmes' being - who frequently alternated between periods of eager and excitable spirits and fits of the blackest depression – perhaps made him susceptible to dark musings. Considering the misdeeds of Professor Presbury in *The Adventure of the Creeping Man*, Holmes said: "When one tries to rise above Nature one is liable to fall below it. The highest type of man may revert to the animal if he leaves the straight road of destiny." Reflecting on the failings of Mr. John Turner in the *Boscombe Valley Mystery* caused him to rail against the cruel workings of Fate: "Why does fate play such tricks with poor, helpless worms?" After saving Mrs. Eugenia Ronder from terrible self-murder in *The Adventure of the Veiled Lodger*, he consoled her with the words: "The ways of fate are indeed hard to understand. If there is not some compensation hereafter, then the world is a cruel jest." He later told Watson that the life was an extended schoolroom: "The examination of patient suffering is in itself the most precious of all lessons to an impatient world."

And Holmes' contemplations turned even darker. In *The Adventure of the Cardboard Box*, while considering the terrible end of Miss Sarah Cushing, he asked Watson: "What object is served by this circle of misery and violence and fear? It must tend to some end, or else our universe is ruled by chance, which is unthinkable. But what end? There is the great standing perennial problem to which human reason is as far from an answer as ever." Moreover, when confronted with the mad deeds of Mr. Josiah Amberley in *The Adventure of the Retired Colourman*, he told Watson: "But is not all life pathetic and futile? Is not his story a microcosm of the whole? We reach. We grasp. And what is left in our hands at the end? A shadow. Or worse than a shadow—misery."

Despite all of these profoundly negative outlooks, hints of optimism shine through. When asked by Watson in *The Adventure of the Red Circle* why he would continue to investigate a case which provided no thought of a fee, Holmes answered: Education never ends, Watson. It is a series of lessons, with the greatest for the last." Holmes felt that mankind was but a small speck in the vastness of the universe, but that those who understood this universal truth had achieved a form of greatness: "The chief proof of man's real greatness lies in his perception of his own smallness" (*The Sign of Four*, Chapter VII). Perhaps inspired by his study of Buddhism,[1] he thought that man was in fact divine, if only he could see it: "I suppose every one has some little immortal spark concealed about him" (*The Sign of Four*, Chapter X).

In the quintet of Adventures which comprise this collection, we catch further glimpses of Holmes' complex philosophy. How his lack of emotion was forged out of the necessity of armouring himself against the horrific deeds of which mankind is capable. How he considered the world to be an eternal schoolroom. How he endeavoured to permit others to see the errors of their ways and learn a better path. And how he learned that much wisdom comes from the simple capacity to hope and wait.

We should never forget that at the very end of Holmes' Canonical career, we heard him proclaim: "A cleaner, better, stronger land will lie in the sunshine when the storm has cleared." On that happy note, we shall leave Mr. Sherlock Holmes and his faithful biographer, Dr John H. Watson, as if residing in the sun-dappled Elysian Fields. There they stand, shoulder to shoulder, quietly talking in intimate converse, recalling once again the glorious days of the past.

§

The Father of Evil (1875)
The Cardboard Box (1889)

The Adventure of the Dishonourable Discharge (1895)
The Adventure of the Veiled Lodger (1896)
The Adventure of the Fatal Fire (1897)
The Adventure of the Retired Colourman (1898)
The Problem of Thor Bridge (1900)
The Adventure of the Awakened Spirit (1900)
The Cold Dish (1907)

§

THE FATHER OF EVIL

In the many notebooks that comprise the records of my adventures in the company of Mr. Sherlock Holmes reside several tales that are not fit for public consumption. If my editors had thought that the tragedy of Jim Browner was too controversial, they would have had little stomach for the repulsive deeds perpetrated by Dr Edward Purcell or Josiah Amberley.[2] However, none of those was as terrible as the horrors of Landmark Priory. Although I felt an obligation to document them here, so as to ensure that they never fade from the annals of history, I doubt that any man besides myself shall ever gaze upon these words during my lifetime.

More than any man of my acquaintance, Holmes possessed a profound aversion to any form of acknowledgement of his birth-day. We had lived together at 221B Baker Street for many years before I managed to deduce it from certain clues provided by his penchant for citing from the escapades of Viola amidst the Illyrians.[3] I suppose this should be no surprise for those who know Holmes' reticent nature. For it took me a whole seven years to even learn that he had a brother in London, and - to this day - I remain uncertain of his mother's given name. Sherlock Holmes was quite good at keeping secrets.

Once I finally determined the date in question, I joined forces with Mrs. Hudson and we spent the first days of the New

Year conspiring how to celebrate. However, our efforts were met with a cold indifference, and we never repeated the attempt. It was not until several decades later – shortly after my re-marriage – that I determined to spend the day with Holmes. I reasoned that as long as I made no overt reference to the motive for my visit, he would hardly refuse a suggestion for a stroll through the former location of Millbank Penitentiary. This had been significantly improved as the new National Gallery for British Art, and was hosting a Pre-Raphaelite exhibition.[4] A supper at Simpson's, accompanied by a bottle of his favourite Montrachet, followed.

The plan was carried out according to my expectations, and I reckoned it to have been a perfect day, even if Holmes was less effusive than his norm. I was providing Holmes with my thoughts on Millais' *Repose* when he suddenly interrupted me.[5]

"Do you know why I have never permitted you to celebrate my birthday, Watson?"

This interjection surprised me and I stammered something to the effect that I was uncertain to the reasons.

He shook his head grimly. "Do not think, Watson, that I was unaware of your efforts today, nor should you believe me to be surfeit of gratitude. It is simply that the anniversary of this day has always been an unhappy one, and I little wanted to be reminded of it."

"What happened?"

Instead of answering, he reached out his long fingers and lifted his wine glass. He slowly stirred its contents and stared into the vortex within. "You have often accused me of being unemotional, Watson. There is an element of truth to that, of course. I have a hereditary aptitude towards art, as a throwback to my grandmother. However, on my father's side, there is a tendency towards a severe lack of emotional expression. And this leads to the great debate which forms the basis of all philosophy, Watson: how much of our behaviour is intrinsic to our physical being, the hard-wiring of our minds, and how much is a conscious choice?"

"Surely there are men who are born with an inescapable tendency to violence?"

"Tendency, Watson. Tendency is the key word. I agree with you that much of this is inherent in the structure of our brains. The case of Phineas Gage is instructive."

"The man who survived having a steel rod accidentally driven through his head?"[6]

"And who thereby lost his friendly, respectful attitude and became uncaring and indifferent. So, much of our personalities is indelibly written on the map of the brain. However, Gage is an extreme example of the malevolent type. Most men are fortunate enough never to suffer such indignities. Instead, they may have been born with a surfeit of empathy, an utter disregard for the feelings of others."

"You speak of the nature of good and evil."

"Precisely, Watson!"

"We have faced some evil men in our times, Holmes. Grimesby Roylott, Jack Stapleton, Jonas Oldacre."

He nodded. "Indeed, Watson. Evil, or perhaps better, mad. There is a fine line, I suppose. However, it takes a very remarkable type to be both fully rational and truly evil. Charles Augustus Milverton, Mrs. Kirby, and the late lamented Professor are the best examples of the latter whom I have encountered during my active career.[7] These are individuals who are capable of unspeakable cruelties, whose cold calculating hearts wouldn't flinch while perpetrating the most horrific acts imaginable."

"I recall you once speaking of a winning woman who was hanged for just such a thing."

"Oh yes. She had learned to feign emotions, so one might think that she was capable of guilt, remorse, or love. However, they were like a sheep's skin she inhabited, while underneath lurked the wolf. I wonder what Mr. Darwin would say about this matter? It seems to me that humans are simultaneously both the most social and most violent species on this planet, as if both were necessary for our early survival."

I nodded. "That is an interesting theory, Holmes. The duality of our natures, like the expressions of the Brahman. Perhaps a man turns evil when the good portion of their being does not properly balance those instincts? But what does this have to do with your birthday?"

"Nietzsche said it best, Watson. 'He who fights with monsters should look to it that he himself does not become a monster. And if you gaze long into an abyss, the abyss also gazes into you.'[8] He could not have been more accurate. Do you wish to hear the story?"

"If it does not pain you."

He took a sip of his Montrachet. "I suppose – after all these years – I am finally ready to look again into that abyss. I had locked the details away in the darkest corners of my brain-attic. However, I should ensure that the story is not suppressed forever. It began late in 1874, shortly after the events that ended the life of Justice of the Peace Trevor. As you recall, Watson, it was at Donnithorpe where I first determined to utilize the little methods of thought – which I had been working out as I moped about the rooms of my college – in the pursuit of criminal research. I returned from that holiday and began to take full notice of my surroundings, utilizing my skills in a myriad of small ways."

"I should like to hear about them," said I, mentally planning to catalogue these actions for some future sketch.

Holmes shook his head. "I think not, Watson. Students would come to me and ask about the location of some item or another that they had misplaced. A landlady asked me to track down a boarder who had skipped out on his rent. There was even a lost spaniel belonging to an old white-haired professor. Hardly the gripping stuff which has so enthralled your readers in *The Strand*, Watson!" said he, with a barking laugh.

"We all must start somewhere, Holmes."

"Yes, well, I have already told you about my acquaintance Reginald Musgrave. Although he was keenly interested in my methods of observation and inference, we were not very close. In fact, there were rather few individuals whom I felt of sufficient sympathy and character to be worthy of more than a few, brief words in passing. However, I soon discovered the utility of a group of personages with even less official standing in the eyes of the law than myself."

"Surely you don't speak of your irregulars?"

"Indeed I do, or at least a prototype thereof, for the number of street Arabs to be found in Oxford rather pales in comparison to our glorious but cruel capital. Moreover, of course, the 'High Street Irregulars' doesn't quite have the same ring to it. Still, I found them to be of considerable aid in some of my earlier endeavours, for between the lot of them, there was little which took place in Oxford which they missed. I was hardly flush for excess shillings in those days, but I always attempted to reward services rendered with either ready coins or some form of wisdom. One urchin in particular was most noteworthy. His name was Christopher Bean, and he was about eleven years of age, though his small frame made him appear even younger. His brain was especially agile, and when the weather was clear, we would bundle up and sit under the Austrian pine in the Botanic Garden to play chess. Bean rarely spoke of his antecedents, though it was plain that he had been harshly orphaned at a young age, and he had managed to survive on the streets for at least four years. I rather admired his fierce tenacity, and I predicted that, with the right support, he could might a name for himself one day."

"I have never heard you mention him."

Holmes shook his head. "No. You would not have. It is a memory which I usually keep locked away in a stout iron chest in my little mental box-room."

"What happened?" I asked, without thinking. "That is, if you don't mind me asking, Holmes."

He stared into his glass of wine. "It is alright, Watson. It is the question I asked myself on the day when Mr. Bean failed to show for our arranged game of chess. After waiting for over a quarter of an hour – he had never before been even thirty seconds late – I went in search of him. I knew that during the day he and his counterparts often gathered in the shadow of the Carfax Tower, and it was with little difficulty that I found a couple of other lads whose service I had previously engaged. The first was unaware of Mr. Bean's location, but the second proved to be a veritable fountain of information.

" 'He was taken by some blue ladies,' said the lad, these enigmatic words the sum total of his wisdom, though he did make it clear that it was their clothes, and not their skin which was blue in colour.

"Now here was a puzzle, Watson. Who were these blue ladies? If there were two of them, both in identical blue clothing, it was likely that this represented a sort of uniform. Perhaps some special branch of the local constabulary? However, a simple inquiry determined that no woman had yet been permitted to join the police force. I wracked my brains for some time to think of what group of ladies would be engaged in making off with a young boy.

"And then it dawned upon me. I had often spotted gaggles of nuns walking about town, their heads covered by white wimples and dressed in bluish grey habits. I had paid them little heed, but I soon rectified that deficiency of knowledge. Although there was no official Catholic church in the town, Christ Church Cathedral was nearby, and I suspected that someone within would have knowledge of their rival's activities. Sure enough, a rector recognized my description of the nuns as ones belonging to a small order known as the Sisters of Succour.[9] The man explained that the nuns lived in a house abutting the ancient ruin of Landmark Priory, which lay about six miles south of town. This was a former religious house, one of hundreds dissolved by the eighth Henry during his purging of the Roman church. However, it had been recently reincarnated as an orphanage and Jesuit boarding school, assisted by the Sisters of Succour.

"Once I heard that it was an orphanage, Watson, I knew that

I was on the right track. As six miles was not a short distance, and this was before the Rover safety bicycle had been invented, I was forced to engage a ride from a local farmer heading home for the evening."

"It seems a great deal of trouble to take for a boy of only general acquaintance," I interjected.

Holmes shook his head. "I don't know how to explain it, Watson. Nevertheless, I could sense that something was amiss, much like my feeling at Donnithorpe. Therefore, it was less than an hour later when I was let off at the entrance to Landmark Priory. It was clear that it had formerly been a substantial place. Twelve-foot high walls once protected the enclosure from invaders, though today they were so riddled with gaps that they could hardly keep out a drove of goats. In one place, a short brick crinkum-crankum wall had been erected to patch one of the holes. Inside the walls, I spied the ruins of a great Norman church built from Caen stone. The empty shells of a few high narrow windows and arches still reached to the heavens. To the left, tucked against the far wall, were several foliage-overgrown outbuildings. Attached to the far right of the church were the remnants of a former cloister and buildings where the monks once lived and prayed. A small tributary of the nearby Thames had been diverted through the grounds. The two-story former prior's house, to my right as I entered the once-proud gate, was the only structure not in ruins. It had clearly been maintained and expanded to serve as the orphanage and school.

"It was upon the door to this building which I banged my fist. A nun wearing the same blue habit of Bean's abductors promptly answered my knock. Her hair was completely covered by a white wimple, but the lines of her face put her age at closer to sixty than fifty. Her face was pinched, and the flinty gaze of her steel grey eyes bespoke of few tender mercies for the students within.

" 'Yes?' said she, gruffly.

" 'Good evening, Sister. My name is Sherlock Holmes, and I

am a student at Oxford. To whom do I have the pleasure of speaking?'

" 'Sister Mary Vincent. I am the Deputy headmistress of Landmark School.'

" 'I wonder if I may speak to a young lad named Christopher Bean?'

"She peered at me for a moment. 'I fail to see how that is any of your business?' she finally replied in a clipped voice.

" 'I am a concerned citizen, Sister. I merely want to ensure that the lad is well.'

"If I expected a softening of her gaze, I was gravely mistaken. 'He is not here,' said she, simply.

" 'I was told that he was taken here.'

" 'By whom?' she asked, sharply.

" 'That is of little matter. What remains is that I have a witness saying that Mr. Bean was brought to Landmark Priory.'

"She shrugged. 'He *was* here. However, our orphanage was full. He was shipped to another.'

" 'May I ask which one?'

"Her eyes narrowed, surprised by my persistence. 'I would have to check the books.'

" 'I can wait.'

" 'Much good it will do you, sir. I told you that this is none of your business.'

"I decided to take another tack. 'May I ask who the Headmaster of the school is?'

" 'The Reverend Father Benedict.'

" 'And may I speak to him?'

" 'No, you may not," said she, firmly. And then she swung the door closed in my face."

"That was quite a rude welcome, Holmes," I noted.

"Indeed, Watson. However, it went beyond mere insolence. I sensed a deception at hand."

"By a nun?"

Holmes shook his head. "Never judge a book by its cover, Watson. Nevertheless, Sister Mary Vincent had made a grave error. If she had just told me Mr. Bean's destination, I would have left Landmark Priory well alone. Instead, with her prevarications, she stirred up a hornet's nest of suspicions in my brain. Of course, only later would I realize that she could hardly have told me the truth."

"So what did you do?" I asked.

"I went round to the county constabulary. After a series of explanations, I was finally ushered in to the office of Chief Constable Malcolm Festen. Festen was still a young man of some thirty years, but what had once been a big and stalwart frame was tending towards flabbiness. He had a balding pate and a ginger-moustache, in which I could spy crumbles of some sweet. His blue eyes were dull with what I hoped was a temporary postprandial somnolence and not a general state of being.

"'What can I do for you, sir?' the man asked.

"After introducing myself, I explained the disappearance of Christopher Bean and my reception at Landmark Priory School.

"When I had finished, the constable leaned back in his chart and laced his fingers behind his head. 'What is your point, Mr. Holmes?' he asked.

"'I believe that Mr. Bean was taken to the orphanage against his will.'

"'On what grounds do you make such a claim?'

"'He would never have voluntarily missed our chess game.'

"Festen guffawed loudly. 'I will alert Scotland Yard,' said he, the mockery thick in his voice. 'In any case, what the Sisters of Succour did was a mercy. They took a starving orphan off the streets – in midwinter, mind you – and have given him a roof over his head, plus three stout meals a day. On what charge then should I arrest Sister Mary Vincent, Mr. Holmes?' he concluded, with a return of acerbity to his tone.

"'So you will not investigate?' I asked, giving the dull man one final chance.

"'There is nothing to investigate, you young fool. Go back

to your books and leave the real police work to the professionals.'

"With that stinging dismissal, Watson, I made my exit from the police station. Since the door to Festen's office had been left open, the entire building had heard him deride me. It was only with a great deal of self-control that I left with my head held high."

"It is little wonder you have so small a regard for the capabilities of the official police forces, Holmes."

"Indeed, Watson. It was at that moment when I realized I would need to take matters into my own hands if I was to learn what had happened to Christopher Bean at Landmark Priory. However, like King Hal studying the terrain at Agincourt, I realized that I would be best served by approaching the place with a full and complete knowledge of its history. I therefore turned my feet to the Bodleian Library, which was open late for the benefit of the studious. At the start of Michaelmas term, I – like all other students at Oxford – had made my declaration 'not to remove from the Library, nor to mark, deface, or injure in any way, any volume, document or other object belonging to it or in its custody; not to bring into the Library, or kindle therein, any fire or flame, and not to smoke in the Library.' The last rule was the hardest of them all; let me assure you, Watson! However, it granted me access to the vast reams of knowledge stored within. You see, I did not start compiling my own index until I came up to Montague Street.

"The ecclesiastical histories were stored in that circular neo-classical building known as Radcliffe Camera. You recall the place, Watson, where your acquaintance Hilton Soames once interrupted my researches on early charters in order to put before me the absurdly simple case of the Fortescue Scholarship, yes? Well, I was – at the time – rather well known within its walls. For the library's tomes of medieval history were also stored within, and I had become rather interested in palimpsests, those vellum documents whose secrets were once scraped away by pumice stones. The careful scrutiny required to penetrate the obvious words in order to find the hidden under-text felt to me like a magnificent riddle. The Bodleian had a fine collection of such parchments, which had been appropriated from monasteries across the land during the Dissolution. I had also begun my study of British criminal law, and the Bodleian possessed one of the few surviving copies of the *Dialogus de Scaccario*."

"I am unfamiliar with that work," said I, dryly.

"It is an essay, from circa 1200, which comments upon the biannual meeting of the treasurer of England, as well as other matters of taxation and revenue."

I shook my head. "I fail to see the relevance, Holmes."

"Yes, well, it is a dull read to most, I suppose. However, the tenth section is of considerable interest. Did you know, Watson, that in medieval times murder was defined as 'the secret death of somebody, whose slayer is not known.' This came from the Old English word 'murdrum' meaning 'hidden' or 'occult,' which itself derived from the Anglo-Saxon practice of seeking vengeance upon their Norman enemies by killing them in remote places."

"Fascinating, Holmes. But what has it to do with the disappearance of Christopher Bean?"

"It is not directly pertinent, but that book was housed very near the spot where I located an enormous tome by Professor G.H. Wolverley entitled *Abuses and Plunder: A Compendium of the Dissolved Monasteries*. Inside I found the following history, which I hand-copied into an early predecessor of my index." He reached out to his row of index books and plucked down the volume labelled 'E.' Flipping through it until he came to a spot at the end, he removed an old sheet of note-paper which had been fastened there. He handed this to me and I read:

> Landmarke Priory was founded in 632 by King Cynegils of Wessex. Subsequent kings continued the endowment, until its great wealth attracted the attention of the Danes. The original priory was sacked and mainly

destroyed by forces under the loose control of Chief Hastein during the reign of King Alfred. For reasons lost to history, the monks had angered Alfred, and in return he both withdrew his protection and then failed to rebuild the abbey after he vanquished Hastein. However, several decades later, Alfred's grandson Eadred appointed one Aethelware as prior and set him the task of restoring the structure.

Landmarke quickly grew to become one of the centres of the Benedictine Reform. Over a hundred-and-forty charters were granted to the priory by various Saxon kings, and the famous Historia Ecclesie Cippus was written there during the early days of the 12th century.[10] Famous priors at Landmarke included Adhelm, who was physician to King Stephen of Blois, and Edward of Chilton, who was present at the Council of Vienne in 1312.

Unfortunately, Landmarke eventually came under the covetous gaze of King Henry VIII. In 1533, his commissioner John Leland – while personally most interested in the priory's library – had described to Henry the great treasures and reliquaries which had come into Landmarke's possession over the prior nine hundred years. When Rowland Brady, the last prior of Landmarke, failed to acknowledge the Royal Supremacy, he brought down the wrath of Henry. Minister Thomas Cromwell himself was dispatched to see to Landmarke's destruction. In 1540, Prior Brady was hung, drawn, and quartered for his treason. The monastic house was dissolved, and the surviving monks fled to the four corners of the world.

In order to more easily extract the valuable lead of the roof, gutters and plumbing, the main buildings were burned to the ground. Building stone and slate roofs were sold off to the highest bidder as a ready quarry. Having already instigated a campaign against superstitions

> such as pilgrimages and veneration of saints, Cromwell saw to it that all of Landmarke's ancient and precious valuables were grabbed and melted down. Even the crypts of saints and royalty were ransacked for whatever profit could be gotten from them, and their relics were destroyed or dispersed. The tombs of Kings Cenwalh and Aescwine were not spared this frenzy of looting.
>
> The only building that escaped destruction was the Prior's House. This was sold to Sir William Harrington and turned into a great Tudor mansion, which he named Landmark. During the English Civil War the house passed into the hands of the Eastlakes, and later into the Sanderson family. When Robert Sanderson died without heir in 1787, the house sat empty and fell into disrepair. In 1867, Landmark was purchased by the Society of Jesus to be used as an orphanage and boarding school, joining the likes of Stonyhurst in Lancashire (re-est. 1803), Spinkhill in Derbyshire (est. 1842), and Beaumont in Berkshire (est. 1861).[11]

When I finished, Holmes opened his grey eyes and gazed at me. "This was invaluable information, Watson. Of all the orders, the Jesuits were said to be the most cunning. I would need to be especially careful to ensure that my investigations went unnoticed by Father Benedict."

"How did you do it, Holmes?"

"Well, I realized that I could hardly infiltrate the Landmark School when my name and face were already known to Sister Mary Vincent. So I went round to the ramshackle New Theatre on George Street and cajoled one of the music hall girls to lend me a wig, whiskers, eyebrows, putty – all the accoutrements necessary to transform myself into Withers, a groundskeeper and general odd-jobs man. It was, I should say, the first time I professionally employed the skills that I had learned during my time upon the stage. You recall the old master mariner who had once given you and Inspector Jones a bit of surprise?

Withers was an early prototype of him.

"The following morning I presented myself to Mr. Stoddard, who kept the grounds around the school. Stoddard proved to be a rather simple old man of limited imagination. I determined that he was likely to be neither a helpmate nor a hindrance to my investigations. After a demonstration to Stoddard of my stamina and a promise to take a scandalously low wage, I was hired on to help with all of the tasks that he felt were beneath him. In so doing, I procured unfettered access to all parts of the former priory. My exploration ranged over the entire area, from the ruined places to the nooks and crannies of the sole maintained building.

"The outbuildings I found in various states of decay. The former stables were still in use by a few old nags, though they had plainly seen better days. A massive oven, its bricks long grown cold, was all that remained of the forge. The buttery and laundry were so overgrown with ivy that I surmised only animals had managed to venture inside in many long years. Only the former masonry house had really stood the test of time and still retained a portion of its roof, as well as a repaired door. Inside, I found evidence of recent habitation. The ashes of a fire were encircled by a rough circle of broken stones. Beside this lay some battered utensils and a water bucket. There were a few empty tins atop a larger stone, which had been repurposed as a crude table. As I gazed about this poor space, I realized that someone was surreptitiously utilizing this secret bolt hole. However, for what purpose – malignant or benign?

"In the course of my explorations, I also ascertained the demeanours of the various inhabitants of the school. This was no select preparatory school, Watson, like the one run by Dr. Huxtable at Mackleton. A skeleton crew of teachers, all Sisters of Succour, provided the bare threads of a curriculum and a strong dose of discipline. Latin and theology were strongly emphasized, while mathematics and natural history seeming stopped at Euclid and Aristotle. All in all, I counted about sixty children, of ages ranging from four to fifteen. However, Christopher Bean was not amongst them.

"Father Benedict proved to be middle-sized, with a keen, aristocratic, hawk-like face. I first saw him as he strode out of the house to the stables, and the sunlight shone upon the arched bone of his prominent nose. His robe was a peculiar tint of yellow and his head was tonsured. Other than Stoddard and myself, Benedict was the only man at the school, though he never said more than a few words to me, and those were barked orders.

"The students were given little freedom and spent most of their time either indoors or in the immediate vicinity of the school, where they performed a series of crude calisthenics. However, I had been there less than a week when I noted a gang of older children rambling about the ruined stones in the gloaming. I learned that they had no formal instructions on Sunday afternoons, and they were supposed to be confined to their attic rooms for quiet reflection. However, one of the older boys had contrived a rather ingenious rope ladder, with which some of the braver children surreptitiously came and went as they pleased from the attic whenever the weather was mild. One night I followed them and learned that it was they who had made a castle of sorts out of the former masonry house.

"This ringleader was a boy of about fourteen years named Paxton Lindsay. He was possessed of green eyes, a tousle of blond hair, and a face that was bright and keen. His parents had died of an ague the year before, and his spinster aunt – wanting little to do with a child – paid Landmark to care for him. In return, he was expected to write letters of gratefulness once a week and make a daily intercession for her relief from crippling rheumatism. However, from the mourning bracelet upon his wrist, I could see that his thoughts mainly turned to his departed flaxen-haired mother.

"The children had long since explored most of the ruins, so seeing my new face was a novelty in their rather dreary lives. I soon befriended them with small confections as well as tales of Prospero, Oberon, and Falstaff. In turn, from Mr. Lindsay I learned just what sort of school Father Benedict was running. While the teachers' rooms were snug and warmed by high fires, in the attics above, the cold wind whistled eerily through the frail walls and cracked windows. All meat and food of sustenance went to feed Father Benedict, Sister Mary Vincent, and the other teachers, while the students survived on little more than stale bread and thin milk. Save only the absence of a significant number of rats, it was little better than a mouldy convict ship like the *Gloria Scott*. Any words of protest led to their mouths being washed out with carbolic soap. To make matters worse, the most minor infraction garnered a brutal beating administered with an India-rubber of the size and shape of a thick boot sole. All of this I witnessed with my own eyes, including the plethora of bruises upon their little bodies.

"My anger grew as I learned what was transpiring unchecked within these walls. And I grew ever more anxious as to the fate of Christopher Bean, for Lindsay and the other children knew nothing of him.

"I soon learned, however, that Lindsay was also a master story-teller. To help the other children – and himself, I may presume – escape from the dreadful reality that they inhabited, Lindsay told stories of ghosts and other terrors in the night. Perhaps by facing these imagined demons, the real ones would seem a shade less dreadful. The following Sunday night, I came upon the group as Lindsay was telling them of the wicked Marquis de Armentières. 'Slowly, slowly, the door turned upon its hinges,' he declaimed, 'and with eyes which were dilated with horror, the wicked Marquis saw…'

"I never learned what the wicked Marquis saw, for my arrival accidentally interrupted the story and prompted stifled shrieks of terror that I might be the Marquis. Instead, I became a sort of Lord of Misrule. For I broke every regulation which had been set forth by the Sisters. On that night, I had smuggled in a sack-load of pies filled with roast beef, along with some watered cider, and plum pudding. When our tiny feast was complete, I encouraged Lindsay to tell us some further stories.

"He cocked his head and considered this request. 'Well, have you heard of Prior Brady?'

" 'The last prior of Landmark?' I replied.

" 'Aye, that's the one. They say that old Henry had him executed just outside his house.'

"I nodded. "That very well might be true, Mr. Lindsay. And what of it?'

" 'Well, they say that the prior's ghost still haunts the grounds of Landmark. You see, Mr. Holmes, the prior had hid some of the treasures of the church in order to prevent their despoiling, and his spirit is still earth-bound on account of his disquiet over these buried relics.'

"I smiled condescendingly. 'That is a fine story, Mr. Lindsay.'

"He shook his head. 'It is no mere story, Mr. Holmes. I saw him myself one night.'

"I frowned at this unlikely fancy. 'And where does Prior Brady show himself, Mr. Lindsay?'

" 'Amongst the ruins of the old church. Near the former altar.'

"On that note, with the sun having long set, the children scampered back up their rickety ladder and attempted to find some warmth under the thin blankets and cracked eaves which confined their dreary existence. However, as I sat there in front of the sinking fire, it dawned on me, Watson, that – despite the preposterousness of Mr. Lindsay's supposed ghost – there might be some element of truth to this account. I decided that the spot in front of the old altar might very possibly be worthy of my attention.

"With a dark lantern, I made my way to what was once the choir end of the former church. I inspected all around the area near the remnants of the altar. There I found a profusion of footsteps flattening the blades of grass, but far too many to discern those belonging to a single individual, or to determine if their makers were set upon a particular purpose. Still, it was something to note, Watson, for why would so many individuals be visiting this particular area of the ruins?

"To settle the question, and despite the falling mercury, I determined to place the area under very close surveillance. All was still and quiet, so I sat upon a weathered stone, and assumed the position of one of those ancient monks. This particular throne sat opposite the altar, but as it was some forty feet away, it was only dimly lit by my lantern. Behind the altar were the skeletal vestiges of the rear wall of the church, its two remaining empty high clerestory window-holes like the sockets of a leering skull. Realizing that nothing was likely to happen by the light of my lantern, I extinguished it. I then removed my disguise and tucked it back into the pocket of my overcoat, for I reckoned that I would need it no longer that night.

"Fortunately, I was still a young man and did not catch my death of cold, but the vigil was a long and bitter one. It was an unhappy way in which to spend one's birthday, Watson, however, I took consolation in the thought that I might soon learn where Christopher had been taken. If I could but recover him from the clutches of the Sisters, then all of these subterfuges and discomforts would not be in vain.

"It took all of my powers of concentration to prevent my teeth from chattering and thereby give away my position. Strange ghostly shadows and illuminations fell across the grass as the clouds passed to and fro in front of the full moon. I sat in the darkness and watched these strange shifting lights coming and going, and the impression was quite ghostly enough for even the most meagre imagination. However, the shifting heavens could not explain all of the forms that I witnessed, and I wracked my brain attempting to elucidate the physical cause. Most likely, I reasoned, some reflection of passing lights in the distance would suffice to create the effect.

"For two hours I had sat in the dark upon my hard seat,

and dimly wondered whether cushions were permitted to the priors of old. The lights still came and went behind the lessened altar, but they only flickered over the top of the high expanse of wall that faced me, and all below down by the altar was pitch black. Then, suddenly, quite suddenly, there came that which no spectre could explain. Roughly twenty feet from me, there was a dull haze of light, a sort of phosphorescent cloud, a foot or so across, and about a man's height from the ground. The light glimmered down and hardened into a definite shape – or should I say shapes – since there were two of them. They were two perfectly clear-cut figures in all black, save only a hint of white that peeked out from their hoods with a dim luminosity. The colouring and arrangement gave me a general idea of cassocks and surplices. For a moment, it seemed as if ghosts did indeed haunt this sorrowful place.

"At first, they were facing away from me, but then they turned and moved in my direction. This allowed me to finally see that they were not misty figures at all, but solid objective shapes. And their names were Father Benedict and Sister Mary Vincent! I watched this amazing spectacle, my mind churning. Where had they come from? There must be a secret trap-door, cunningly concealed within the crumbling masonry. But where did it lead?

"Once the pair had vanished, I re-lit my dark lantern, rose from my hiding place, and searched the area near where they had appeared. One of the great marble pillars of the church still thrust its way upwards, though the roof which it once supported had long-since fallen. I wondered if this column was in fact hollow? A few weathered carvings could be made out on the pillar's face, and it was with a start that I recognized one as a Chi-Rho. I made a sketch of it in case it was needed again.

Holmes handed me a slip of paper, upon which was drawn:

"I knew that ancient symbol had once been used to mark the locations of secret meeting places. I pressed on this stone with all my strength and was gratified to feel it slide back into the column. As it did so, a door ground open to my right. I was amazed that such subtle architecture could survive the rough hands of time, though I supposed that Father Benedict might have repaired its mechanism.

"Rough-hewn stairs spiralled down into the darkness. I had little choice but to follow where this path led. As I descended, I realized that this must be the church's crypt. When I reached the bottom of the steps, I was faced with a branching passage. I took the route to my left and followed it for some time, avoiding the multitude of narrow corridors that intersected it. As I progressed along, I grasped that I had ventured into a veritable labyrinth. I estimated that I was somewhere beneath the former refectory when I realized that I was not alone in this underground warren. Moreover, it was not just the skeletons of centuries' worth of monks. Low moans began to emanate from ahead.

"Eventually I came upon a room blocked by a set of iron bars. As I shone the lantern within, several small dirty faces peered back at me. There were children locked away in this dank dungeon! At first, I was too shocked to move. Then I set down my lantern and shook the bars, even though I knew that they must be locked, with the key residing in the pocket of Father Benedict's robe. Fortunately, one of my earliest interests was in Hobbs' exploits at the Great Exhibition of 1851, where he broke the previously impregnable Bramah and Chubb locks. I devoured every word of his paper 'On the Principles and Construction of Locks,' and was hardly fourteen when I first unbolted my father's wine cellar with a homemade torsion wrench and hook pick.[12] I always carried such tools with me, and was most glad of it that night. In seconds, I had thrown open the door and strode into the cell.

"The children shied away from me, but I soon convinced them that I meant them no harm. The eldest was a girl of fifteen, who shielded a younger boy behind her scarecrow form and asked me my intentions.

" 'I am here to set you free, of course! How many of you are there down here? Bean!' I shouted. 'Bean, are you here?'

" 'I am sorry, sir,' said the girl, shaking her head, sadly. 'But Christopher died. Not six days after he was brought here. The work is hard, sir, and there is barely any food at all.'

"Six days! I thought, full of bitter regret. I had been present at Landmark every day since his disappearance, my feet treading the very area above us, but I had not found this subterranean catacomb in time. My mouth was as dry as the Kalahari and my heart hardened. 'What work?' I asked, attempting to keep the grimness from my tone so as not to scare her.

" 'Why, the digging, sir!' she replied.

"As this answer did little to illuminate the reason why so many children would be bound in this horrific servitude, I bade her show me. It was plain that she wished to flee the place as fast as possible, but after a few minutes of cajoling, along with the promise of my protection, she did as I asked. I bade the other children – of which there were two dozen – to remain in the cell, for they could hardly be asked to navigate the labyrinth of passages back to the surface without my assistance.

"The girl – I learned her name was Sally – led me a short

distance along a passage I had yet to tread, until it stopped at a wall of mortared bricks, which was in a state of being slowly dismantled. A plethora of rusty pickaxes and other mining gear lay scattered about the floor.

"I stared at this blank wall, confused. What possible motive could Father Benedict have to work these children to their deaths, I wondered? 'What is behind it?' I asked.

"Sally shook her head. 'Nobody knows for certain, sir. But it must be gold or jewels is all we can reckon.'

"I turned and looked down at the girl. 'Where did you come from, Sally?' I asked, with as much gentleness in my voice as I could muster.

" 'Reading, sir. I was sent here when my family died,' said she sadly. 'I lived in the school for a while, but when it became clear that no relatives were going to come calling for me, Sister Mary Vincent brought me down here.'

" 'For how long?'

"She shrugged. 'It's hard to tell time, sir, when there is no day and only night. But I think I have been down here for close by two months. I have lasted the longest of anyone. All of the others, like your friend Christopher, were hauled away by Father Benedict when their spirits gave out,' she said, her voice thick with emotion.

" 'And no one noticed them missing?' I asked.

" 'Most of them are urchins, sir,' she answered with a shake of her head. 'From Oxford, Coventry, or Birmingham. No one remarks when an urchin vanishes.'

"I sighed at this cruel truth, Watson. 'Let us go back and collect the others, Sally. I shall lead them to freedom.'

"But when we retraced our steps to the cell where I had found Sally and the others, they were gone. At first, I feared that Father Benedict had returned and absconded with them, but then I realized that they would have little reason to trust my assurances that I would return. Resourceful survivors all, the children had found their own way back to the surface and vanished into the gloomy night like spirits.

"Sally, too, refused any further assistance and bolted from my side. Watching her fading form, I wondered to where she would flee in this harsh world, which cared not a whit for her pale existence?

"But I had other matters to which I first needed attend, Watson. The initial rays of the sun were just beginning to appear over the eastern sky when I turned my steps to the former Prior's House. However, this time I did not cordially knock upon the door. Instead, I once again brought forth my picks and forced my way into the house. It was with little difficulty that I found my way to Father Benedict's room, for it was the largest and most lavish in the house. I had no weapon, but my hands have a rather firm grip, and they were empowered by a righteous anger.

"I burst into Father Benedict's room and seized the groggy man by his night-clothes. I clasped one hand over his mouth and bade him to refrain from crying out, unless he wished to suffer grave bodily harm.

" 'Who are you?' the man stammered when I released his lips.

"I forgot that I had removed my disguise, and he did not recognize my true face. 'I am the Spirit of Vengeance!' I cried.

"Father Benedict shook his head in protest. 'You are no spirit, but a man. And I have done nothing wrong!'

" 'Nothing wrong? What of the children you have imprisoned beneath the ruins?'

" The man paused in surprise, but soon recovered his wits. 'You misunderstand me, sir. I set those children to work not out of hatred, but out of love.'

" 'Love?' I spluttered, incredulously. 'You call that love?'

" 'But of course! For they have been given a chance which few receive upon this earth. They can perhaps wipe away a small portion of the ledger of sin that was created when they were born. With this great work they are one step closer to the Kingdom of Heaven.'

" 'What great work?' I growled. 'For what purpose do you

have them digging in the old crypt? Don't tell me you believe there to be some treasure buried beneath us!'

"The priest smiled, though his icy blue eyes remained cruel. 'Prior Brady was a most determined man, sir. He did everything possible to ensure that the King's commissioners would never find Landmark's most potent relic. He moved it into the *domus tenebris*.'

"I could translate the Latin, of course, Watson, but did not understand the meaning of the words. 'A dark house?' I asked.

" 'An old chamber, located deep underground. Not used since the fifteenth century, when an edict from Rome officially discouraged the practice of immurement – sometimes for years at a time – for monks guilty of sins against the order.'"

"Like Malvolio." I interjected.

Holmes looked at me, askance. "What is that, Watson?"

"Do you not recall poor Malvolio from *Twelfth Night*, Holmes? He begins to act radically different after he reads Olivia's letter with the words: 'Some are born great, some achieve greatness, and some have greatness thrust upon them. Your fate awaits you.' Sir Andrew and Sir Toby thus lock Malvolio away under the pretence that he has gone mad. When Olivia visits him, he complains: 'Why have you suffered me to be imprisoned, / Kept in a dark house, visited by the priest?' "

"Yes, quite," said Holmes, dryly. "I had not thought of that, Watson. In any case, Father Benedict continued his confession. 'Many of the great monasteries and abbeys were built with them,' said he, 'some a simple room, but others much more elaborate. I believe Landmark may have possessed the largest in the land. Most of them were filled in with dirt after they fell into disuse, but the prior of Landmark at the time felt the expense too great. So it wasn't until Prior Brady's time that the *domus tenebris* was finally filled in, this time to seal away the great relic of the priory.'

" 'I read that the priory was stripped of its relics?' I asked.

"Benedict waved his hand. 'Mere baubles left behind in order to distract Richard Layton, the foolish and greedy commissioner of the fat fool Henry.'

"'So the real treasures are still to be found behind the wall? And you would do all of this for a few pieces of silver?'

"He snorted in derision. 'I leave the worldly treasures for lesser souls. I have but one goal.'

"'And what is that?'

"'The Crown of Lucius.'

"I shook my head. 'That means nothing to me.'

"'Ah, but that is because you are clearly a heathen, sir. To the true believer, it is the most glorious relic to be found on our shores, save perhaps only the *Sangreal* itself, should it still be secreted at Glastonbury.'

"'You are delusional.'

"'No, sir, I will soon be heralded as the man who restored the English lands to the arms of the True Church. For Lucius was the Briton king who first introduced Christianity to these shores. Once I bring it forth, it will be a symbol of Catholicism's power over the pitiful Anglican heresy, and the earthly kings and queens who pretend to rule a Church. The masses will abandon them and flock to our banner.'

"'All because of some shabby old crown? I think not.'

"A ghastly smile stretched the skin taut over the bones of his face. 'Ah, but there you have it wrong, my friend. No mere coronet of corroded iron. For when the Normans came in 1077, they too were sceptical that the relics of Saint Lucius had truly been entrusted to the care of Landmarke Priory. It was commonly believed that nothing survived from his day, other than a fading inscription at the church of St. Peter-upon-Cornhill, which Lucius founded in the year 179. However, if you trace his legend back through the ancient annals – from William of Malmesbury, to Geoffrey of Monmouth, to Nennius, to the Venerable Bede, to Nothhelm of Canterbury – eventually you discover that his relics were brought here to forlorn Landmarke. Why else would I have come to such a forsaken place, eh, sir?'

"'Some might claim that it was a calling.'

"Benedict smiled zealously. 'A calling indeed! I have been called to restore the Crown to the world. The Conqueror's friend, Archbishop Lanfranc, was also unconvinced of the Crown's powers and suspicious of a pious fraud. Therefore, he ordered a trial by fire. After a three-day fast, the seven penitential psalms were sung and the appropriate litanies chanted, while the sanctity of the crown was tested. Into the flame it went, and do you know what came out, sir?'

" 'A slag of molten metal?'

" 'No! The crown had been turned to gold,' said the priest, his eyes shining with rabid fervour.

" 'Better than burnt flesh, I suppose. That is what normally happens when you Jesuits light a fire. At least, poor Bruno got to spend a few good years here in Oxford before you cooked him.'[13]

" 'Do you mock me, sir?' growled the priest.

" 'You are several centuries too late, Father Benedict. The time of unreason has passed, and the Enlightenment has triumphed.'

"He shook his head. 'It is never too late to turn back the clock on the secular filth which has infected our society.'

" 'Back to the rubbish of the Dark Ages, I presume? That sounds rather dreadful. And who countenances your work here, Father Benedict? Do they know what you have done? Using children as your chattel?'

" 'They are street urchins, sir. Or those born out of wedlock and into sin. They come and go all of the time, and no one notices.'

" 'I noticed.'

" 'Yes, well, you are unusually observant, I suppose.'

" 'And the ones who don't survive?'

"Father Benedict shrugged. 'Flesh is weak. Ashes to ashes, dust to dust.'

" 'So you burn them?'

" 'Not all. The old groundskeeper Stoddard might grow nosey if we used the furnace too much. The old graveyard hadn't been used since the last days of Prior Brady. There is plenty of room for those too frail to continue our great work.'

"I said no more. No words could penetrate his armour of false belief. He would not abandon his quest willingly. If Father Benedict was to be stopped, it would only be by the influence of a higher power. I threw him against the wall and stormed out of the house."

§

"He sounds like the Father of Evil himself, Holmes," said I.

"Oh, no, Watson. He was but the hand of Evil, and Sister Mary Vincent the midwife. For – by her passive facilitation of the children's mistreatment – she was equally culpable. But there was someone higher to blame."

"Who?"

"The true Evil emanated from Rome. For they were the ones who actively covered up the crimes at Landmark Priory."

"What do you mean?"

"Well, I first took my case to Constable Festen. My first impression of the utility of the provincial constabulary, as gleaned from a reflection of the failures of the Hampshire force in the Beddoes case, was a poor one. To an even worse degree than our friends at Scotland Yard, Watson, they are usually out of their depths when confronted by a crime with even the slightest degree of complexity. But nowhere – even considering the scandalous state of those individuals purporting to police Devon country – was there the level of rank corruption which I noted that day in the office of Malcolm Festen."

"What happened?" I asked.

"With much cajoling, I led the reluctant constable back to the priory. I showed him the entrance to the catacombs by the altar. He agreed to descend into them with me, however – since I had already freed the children – there was no direct proof remaining of their past captivity."

"Surely there must have been evidence that the rooms were

recently being used to house slaves?"

Holmes shook his head irritably. "This was before I had honed my particular methods of observation for the fine details left behind at the scene of a crime, Watson. Even if I had thought to bring along a magnifying glass and located items belonging to children, Festen would never have undertook a deductive leap from such small clues. When I pointed out the area of active digging, he shrugged and said that he would look into it. When I inquired later, he told me that Father Benedict had hired some local labourers to expand the tunnels so that they could be used for storage for the school. Benedict had even produced receipts – faked, of course – to corroborate his story. I accused Constable Festen of being overly credulous, at which point he had me thrown out of the constabulary station.

"Only later did I realize that the local Roman church gave generously to the Police Benevolent Fund, thereby purchasing their implicit trust and cooperation. It was then, Watson, that I realized – despite my burgeoning passion for ensuring that guilty parties would be brought to justice – my methods would be best employed by remaining a strictly unofficial member of the nation's policing body.

"Having exhausted the limits of secular law, I therefore turned my steps to the one person whom might be able to influence Father Benedict on a more spiritual plane. I travelled down to London. From Euston Station, it was a vigorous twenty-minute walk through the university grounds and along Howland Street until I reached the gothic church of St. James's at Spanish Place.

"There, after much pleading with minor functionaries, I was finally shown into the office of Cardinal Boccanegra, the apostolic nuncio.[14] He was an elderly man with grey hair parted in the middle and topped with a red skullcap. Behind golden pince-nez, he had cruel black eyes with drooping, contemptuous lids. His face was drawn and gaunt, like someone who had risen from the grave. He wore a black cassock and red cape buttoned up to his neck. His deep-lined brow furrowed when he heard that I came to tell him of a great crime at the Landmark School. He did not offer me a seat, but instead murmured for me to proceed with my tale.

"I put the whole story to him. When I had concluded, he paused for a moment, I thought to consider the terrible implications of Father Benedict's actions. He then reached out for a J pen and scribbled a note upon a piece of royal cream paper. 'It has been taken care of,' said he.

"'In what fashion?' I asked.

"'I have just had Father Benedict transferred.'

"'Transferred?' I spluttered, incredulous. 'To where?'

"The legate shrugged. 'What does it matter?'

"'What is there to prevent him from simply repeating his foul deeds?'

"'We will keep an eye on him, I assure you, Mr. Holmes. And there is little treasure to be found in the Fens, I think.'

"'But he will not be punished?'

"'Perhaps in another world. Unless, of course, he first sufficiently repents of his sins. Then he will be forgiven.'

"'But not in this one,' said I, bleakly.

"'No. For though his methods were unsound, his cause was a great one. As a countryman of mine once said, sometimes the ends justify the means.'

"'I am afraid that is not good enough.'

"'It will have to be, Mr. Holmes,' said the man, his voice like a blade of steel. 'The arm of Rome is long. I would hate to see it have to deal with you, should you persist in making trouble.'

"I knew a threat when I heard one, Watson. 'Those days are past, *signore*. You cannot treat me like Bruno or Galileo.'

"He shook his head. 'You are pitifully naïve, Mr. Holmes. The Church no longer stoops to do such dirty work ourselves. We have associates who are more than happy to assist us when asked. I assure you that the Red Circle has many followers in Saffron Hill.'

"'Then it is well that I left instructions with my solicitor on what actions he should take should I ever meet with a violent end. He will mail copies of my report on these atrocities to *The Times*, the *Daily Telegraph*, the *Evening Standard*, and many other such worthy organizations. You cannot suppress them all.'

"He smiled cruelly. 'We shall see. Good day, Mr. Holmes.'

"It was clear that there was nothing else to be said. Here was a man who actively facilitated evil. Call it ambitious, Watson, but I determined then and there that I would henceforth make it my task to combat such malevolence wherever I encountered it. When I stepped back outside onto George Street, I was glad that the sun had broken through the clouds, for a needed a ray of warmth upon my face after the inexorable chill of the legate's office."

§

"I am surprised, Holmes, that you ever worked for the Vatican after such an encounter."

"Do not forget, Watson, that four years after my meeting with Cardinal Boccanegra, there was a conclave in Rome and the ascension of a new man.[15] He is hardly infallible, but when the little affair of the Vatican cameos arose in '89, I saw my opportunity to wring some particular concessions from the current occupant of Peter's chair. The London papers did not cover it in great depth, but several highly placed men suddenly decided to retire shortly afterwards, including Cardinal Boccanegra. I wish I could have achieved a greater punishment for him, but I suppose it sufficed. He at least paid a small price for his wicked deeds."

"And the sudden death of Cardinal Tosca in '95?"

"I discovered that it was well-deserved. I made certain that the perpetrator of his execution was safely conveyed to the Americas."

"So there were ulterior motives to those consultations?"

He smiled wanly. "Try as I might, I have – from time to time

– allowed my judgement to be biased by personal qualities. I have never claimed to be entirely without feeling, Watson. There is a vast chasm between actively suppressing one's emotions in favour of the sharp edge of true cold reason, and lacking them entirely."

"And after your meeting with the Cardinal? What then?"

"I am afraid, Watson, that this was the first example of an instance when I felt that it was morally justifiable to take the law into my own hands. In so doing, I stepped outside the ordinary boundaries of legality and subjected myself to the risk of becoming liable to life imprisonment.[16] Though, as you can see," he waved his hand over his chest, "I am still here."

"What did you do?"

"I removed Father Benedict's impetus for further digging. Since long before the days of our association, Watson, I have been most interested in the practical applications of chemistry. At the time, I had free reign over the chemical laboratories in the basement of Balliol College. Having read the technical monograph of Mr. Abel, I learned that it is a rather simple three-step process, as long as one is careful. First cotton is treated with two-parts concentrated sulphuric acid and one-part seventy-percent nitric acid, and then it is cooled to freezing temperatures. Finally, after repeated washing and drying, it is ready for use."

I shook my head. "I am unfamiliar with the product of this method."

Holmes smiled ruefully. "Guncotton.[17] The dominant explosive in our naval mines and torpedoes until it was recently replaced by Lyddite."

"By Jove, Holmes!" I exclaimed. "What did you do with it?"

"One night, by the dark of the moon, I placed a great supply in a broad circumference around what I calculated to be the subterranean location of the dark house. And then, after ensuring that no living soul remained beneath the ground, I set it off."

"No! You purposefully destroyed the Crown of Lucius?"

"It brought me no pleasure, Watson. By and large, I would vastly prefer to see such treasures safely ensconced behind glass in the British Museum. Nevertheless, I saw little other recourse. With the Crown destroyed, there would be no reason for Benedict's minion, Sister Mary Vincent, to maintain her childhood abduction scheme, nor he to continue work children to their deaths."

"I am surprised that I did not hear of this, Holmes, and that you were not caught. Surely Father Benedict would have pointed a finger at you?"

He shrugged. "Given that no one was injured, it received little press at the time. I fortunately managed to situate my charges in such a way that the walls of the Norman church were not destabilized. Constable Festen rather was suspicious given my prior complaints against the school, but I had previously laid out an ironclad alibi for my whereabouts on the evening in question. Several students vouched for my presence at an un-staged performance of Verdi's *Destino* at the Sheldonian." He barked a bitter laugh. "I have said before, Watson, that I would have made a highly efficient criminal had I turned my energies in such a direction! Ultimately, the constable was forced to conclude that the explosion was due to the combustion of methane, hydrogen sulphide, and other gases that had built up in the old cesspit, which had also been destroyed in the explosion."

"So Father Benedict and Sister Mary Vincent got away with their crimes?" said I, shaking my head in dismay.

"Oh no, Watson! You see, the explosion also unearthed a section of the old graveyard. Even to the rather dull mind of Constable Festen, it was abundantly clear that many of the bones found therein came from individuals far too small to have once been monks. He brought in a local palaeontologist, Professor William Hindshire, who determined that the smaller bones – a sad admixture of boys and girls – were interred several hundred years more recently than to those belonging to the adult males who once lived and died at the old priory. Festen could hardly ignore the evidence any longer, and the long arm of Rome could not shield the perpetrators of that great evil from meeting their just fates. Both are long since dead, for the rank atmosphere of Holloway Prison is not one conducive to long life. May Father Benedict and Sister Mary Vincent serve as a lesson to those who would replicate their foul deeds."[18]

I sat in silence for a moment, finally understanding Holmes' reticence to celebrate his birthday, for it only served as a reminder of the day in which he learned that he had failed to locate poor little Christopher Bean in time. "And you, Holmes?" I asked, quietly.

"I first shut myself up for three months and read the annals of crime for twelve hours a day. After that, Watson, I realized that Oxford was too small a place for me. I could walk from the Castle to the Water Meadow in twenty leisurely minutes. I therefore moved down to London in order to take up rooms in Montague Street. There, I used my profusion of leisure time to begin an exacting study of the great hive of sorrow and wickedness that is this vast and terrible metropolis."

" 'It is not a pleasant place; it is not agreeable or cheerful or easy or exempt from reproach. It is only magnificent.' "[19]

He smiled again. "James is always pithy. You see, Watson, I learned that day that we may each be born with certain natural tendencies, but we also all have a choice of how to live our lives. And I decided – in my own small way – to combat evil wherever I encountered it. In that fashion, I hope to leave this world a little better for my existence. What more can we ask, Watson?"

He then turned the conversation to merrier matters, but the horrors of Landmark Priory stayed with me throughout the rest of the evening, and for many years to come. Still, if I were asked, I was glad that I had heard the tale that he related to me that night, for it gave me another sliver of insight into the nature of the great heart beating deep within Holmes' exterior façade of a cool, calculating machine.

§

"I have hitherto confined my investigations to this world," said he. "In a modest way I have combated evil, but to take on the Father of Evil himself would, perhaps, be too ambitious a task."
– *The Hound of the Baskervilles*

THE ADVENTURE OF THE DISHONOURABLE DISCHARGE

The first weeks of January 1895 found my friend, Mr. Sherlock Holmes, in fine spirits. His successful conclusion of the distinctive case of Dr Lowe had temporarily satiated his passion for the unusual which kept burning the fires of his mental engine. He had consulted on a few trivial problems for private individuals, none of which were of a sufficiently remarkable nature to warrant more than a few lines in my notebook. However, he was also in the throes of one of those fits of energy which came upon him from time to time. He spent many hours hunched over his chemical bench working upon an ill-smelling distillation of carbolic acid, which he thought might prove to explain the strange preservation of the body pulled from the Wash near King's Lynn. The following day he spent organizing the various papers littering his desk, followed by him dusting off his old typewriter in order to peck out a monograph upon the role of microscopes and magnifying lenses in the investigation of crimes. I watched this burst of dynamism with weary amusement and one night finally turned in, despite the fact that he had not quite concluded his composition of Variations on a Theme of Campion for violin.[20]

On the morning in question, I awoke and had just sat down at the breakfast table to enjoy Mrs. Hudson's excellent eggs, black pudding, and oatcakes, when Holmes marched into the room with a cudgel tucked like an umbrella under his arm.

"Good morning, Holmes," said I, mildly. "I note that you have retired as a pugilist."

Holmes stopped in his tracks and looked at me with puzzlement in his eyes. "Whatever gave you that impression, Watson?"

"When a man skips breakfast three days running and returns carrying a singlestick, it is not difficult to conclude that he has re-dedicated himself to the art of *canne de combat*."

"I might be carrying it for protection rather than practice."

I shook my head. "Unlikely."

"Why?"

"For two reasons. First, you would have told me if you were on a case, especially one that might involve the threat of violence. For I hope that I do not flatter myself when I note that you still rely upon me in such circumstances. Given that my service revolver is at the moment safely nestled in my desk drawer, I conclude that you are not presently in need of the singlestick for protection."

His right eyebrow rose with interest. "And the other reason?"

I pointed. "The evolving purple bruise upon your right wrist, just visible under your shirt cuffs. Clearly, your opponent is a man of considerable skill if he managed to disarm you."

Holmes smiled ruefully. "Mr. Castle is the top expert in London. I fancy that I am the equal of virtually any other man alive, however Castle still has a few tricks to teach me. But tell me, Watson, why the reference to my boxing days?"

I shook my head. "Last month, I saw you practicing the

sabre, and now it is the single-stick. However, it has been some seven years – since before the Norbury case – when I last saw you enter the ring. I therefore concluded that you have abandoned your plans to join the Fancy."

"Yes, well, there is little doubt that the pugilistic arts are an attractive study, for they require a scientific level of precision. Furthermore, a high level of proficiency with one's fists comes in handy from time to time for a man with my chosen profession. However, Watson, do you recall McMurdo?"

"Bartholomew Sholto's bodyguard? How could I forget him? What of him?"

"I ran into him at Alison's rooms a few months back. He was a pale shell of the man who once blocked our way at the entrance to Pondicherry Lodge some seven years ago."

"What was wrong with him?"

"McMurdo was always known as a man who could take a hit or two. Have you ever heard the term 'punch-drunk'?"

"Of course. It refers to the state when a man can hardly walk under his own power after repetitive blows to the head. It wears off eventually."

"But what if it doesn't?"

"Doesn't what?"

"Wear off."

I shook my head. "I have never heard of such a phenomenon. Surely such a thing – if it did exist – would be the subject of an examination in *The Journal of Psychology* or the *British Medical Journal*?"

"Perhaps not. Not if it had yet to be recognized. However, after encountering McMurdo, I have made the rounds to call upon several of my former opponents. Some are seemingly fine, but others share certain of McMurdo's features. Tremors, slow movements, confusion, and speech problems." He shook his head and a look of horror passed over his face. "You can imagine, Watson, how greatly I fear the permanent loss of my mental facilities. Without them, I am no longer Sherlock Holmes. As such, I have determined to refrain, whenever possible, from engaging in further activities which actively encourage unnecessary blows to my brain."

I shrugged. "That seems a wise course, if perhaps a trifle overly cautious."

However, the look upon Holmes' face made it plain that his thoughts had moved on from this conversation regarding the best method of self-defence. "Unless I am mistaken, we are about to be consulted upon a case," said he.

I frowned in confusion, but before I could ask how he came to that conclusion, there was a brief rap upon the door and the page boy brought in a telegram for Holmes. I can only presume that Holmes' preternatural sense of hearing allowed him to note the boy's light footsteps. Holmes opened the telegram and glanced at it with a look of interest forming upon his face. He glanced over at me with a smile. "What do you say to a jaunt out of London, Watson?"

I shrugged. "I see no impediments. Where did you have in mind?"

"I have here a wire from Inspector Lestrade. It seems that he is currently in the west of Scotland in connection with the Lochaber tragedy."

"That name is unfamiliar to me, I am afraid."

"I share your ignorance, Watson, but it promises to be an interesting one if Lestrade is asking for our assistance."

I reached over for my Bradshaw's. "I see an express train leaving Euston at quarter-past nine. It is due at Glasgow at four o'clock. From there we should be able to find a local to wherever your services are required."

Holmes glanced at his watch. "That will do nicely, though it gives us only half an hour to pack."

Fortunately, Holmes was even faster than I at gathering up his few and simple wants, such that twenty minutes later we were situated in a hansom cab with our valises upon our laps, rattling away to Euston Station. I was amused to find my friend had changed from his typical city attire into his long grey travelling cloak and ear-flapped travelling-cap. When we arrived at the platform, Holmes instructed me to secure some corner seats in a first-class carriage, while he vanished in order to purchase the tickets. However, upon his return, he also carried with him an immense pile of newspapers.

We had the carriage to ourselves, and Holmes spent the time rummaging about and scanning the papers, with intervals of note-taking and meditation. Once we were past Carlisle, he suddenly folded them all into a gigantic wad, and tossed them under the seat. I should note that Holmes had jealously guarded the papers and I was forced to be content with spending my time reading Mr. Stevenson's further adventures of David Balfour.

"I am most happy to have you with me, Watson. You are by now well aware of Lestrade's limits, and from my perusal of the papers, it is clear that the local aid will range somewhere between worthless and actively obstructionist. While you are not yourself brilliant, you have a remarkable ability to direct light into the dark corners of a case. Have you heard anything of the Macpherson murder?" he asked.

I ignored his unintended slight and shook my head. "Very little. The name sounds a bit familiar."

"Yes, well, it was poorly covered by the London papers, but I know a man who carries *The Glasgow Herald*, *The Scotsman*, the *Aberdeen Journal*, and most of the other Scottish dailies. Shall I summarize for you?"

"I would be much obliged, as you have rather monopolized the papers."

A sheepish look appeared on his face. "I apologize, Watson. Surely, you are accustomed to my habits by now?"

"Indeed I am, Holmes. Which is why I have not taken offense, but rather waited patiently for your explanation."

He smiled. "Lochaber is a province in the western Scottish Highlands, centred upon the town of Fort William, where we shall need travel in order to meet Lestrade. North of that town are numerous lochs, all of which are ringed by various old castles and estates. The one in question, Gleannlaithe Castle, belongs to a certain Lady Emma Abercromby.[21] Three days ago, two shots were heard by members of the household emanating from the palm house situated upon the estate. One of Lady Emma's guests, a Mr. Rufus Macpherson, was found dead. Macpherson was a local landowner who had called upon Lady Emma and had been staying at her castle for the last fortnight."

"I believe that I have heard his name before in some other context," I interjected.

"You very well may have, Watson. According to the papers, Mr. Macpherson was once a member of London society, but he had been exiled due to some scandal at the St. James's Club, the details of which have not been made public."

"Perhaps that disgrace was the reason for his death?"

Holmes waved his hand. "It is certainly worth looking into, Watson, however, it is far too early to form any theories which might distract us from an unbiased observation of the facts. It seems that Mr. Macpherson was in the habit of a vigorous morning walk around the estate, followed by taking his tea alone in the palm house. On the day in question, he appears to have followed this routine, but was fatally interrupted during the later activity."

"And do they know by whom?"

"The local police have a man in custody."

"Then what is our role?"

"That is precisely the interesting part, Watson. It seems there may be a difference of opinion between the local force and the C.I.D., or Lestrade would not have wired for my assistance."

"And what is Lestrade's opinion?"

He shook his head. "Neither the papers nor his wire relates that information. In fact, the papers are universally certain that the arrested man is guilty. Their major concern, of course, is not this particular man, but rather how Parliament plans to prevent others of his like from murdering every country gentleman at his table."

I snorted in wry amusement at such hysterics, which reliably sold bushels of papers. "How can they be so certain?"

"At Macpherson's feet was found a hand trowel. Upon questioning of the staff, this item was promptly recognized as belonging to one Donald Scott, who is employed on the estate as a gardener and labourer."

"You said that Mr. Macpherson was shot to death. Most gardeners do not go around armed with pistols."

"Very good, Watson. In fact, a gun was found at the scene and was quickly identified as Macpherson's own weapon. It had clearly been recently fired. Now we must ask why Macpherson would need to carry such a thing on his morning walk?"

"Perhaps he was afraid for his life?"

Holmes nodded. "That is an excellent hypothesis, Watson, and one into which we must hope Lestrade has thought to inquire. The local police believe that Scott came upon Macpherson from behind, seized the murdered man's gun, and fired a shot into him when he turned around."

"For what reason?"

"Ah, there indeed lies our problem. The papers have concluded that robbery does not appear to be the motive, for some French coins were found in Macpherson's pocket."

I raised my eyebrows. "Why would a man residing in the west of Scotland be carrying about French coins?"

Holmes smiled happily. "You are scintillating this afternoon, Watson! I asked myself the very same question. It is an anomaly which I am willing to wager has escaped the attention of Lestrade and the local authorities."

"And if robbery was not Scott's motive, what was?"

Holmes smiled. "The police are at a loss. However, the papers are certain that it was a fit of homicidal madness."

"And what does Scott have to say about the matter?"

"Unfortunately, Scott was born a deaf-mute, and is rather simple. He communicates with the estate's keepers through a crude sign language, and is plainly not up to the task of answering the interrogations of the police."

I shook my head. "If such a man is innocent, his advocate will have a hard time proving it without the actual guilty party being conclusively identified."

"That thought had occurred to me, Watson," said Holmes with an immodest smile. "It is thus a good thing that I will soon be on the scene."

§

At Glasgow we changed trains, and soon passed over the remarkable new viaduct – constructed only eight years prior – on our way to Fort William. The twenty-one arches spanned a hundred feet over the valley floor, blessing us with a fantastic view. Even Holmes, typically immune to such things, seemed stimulated by the scenery. I was moved to break out in song:

> " 'Oh, you'll take the high road, and I'll take the low road,
> And I'll be in Scotland afore you;
> But me and my true love will never meet again,
> On the bonnie, bonnie banks o' Loch Lomond.' "

Holmes glanced over at me with surprise. "Wrong lake, Watson."

I shook my head at my friend's lack of poetry – save only his singular gifts upon the violin. "It's a metaphor, Holmes. The 'low road' is the fairy-folk's route back to Scotland. When a true Scotsman dies, the *daoine sith* will transport his soul back to his home."

"Fascinating," said Holmes, dryly. "I will endeavour to forget that fanciful belief, Watson, rather than allow it to unnecessarily clutter my little brain attic. I can state with reasonable confidence that such knowledge will not advance us during this case."

It was nearly seven o'clock when we at last found ourselves at the highlands town of Fort William. Inspector Lestrade was waiting for us upon the platform, a shoulder bag clutched to his chest. He had thrown off his typical city clothes in favour of the light brown dust-coat and leather leggings which he wore whenever he ventured to more rustic surroundings. With him, we drove northeast some thirteen miles to the crofting hamlet of Gairlochy. A room had been engaged for us at the White Rose. We brought our valises into the common room and Lestrade motioned to a table and chairs.

"I apologize, Mr. Holmes," said Lestrade. "For the hour is rather late, and the way is dark. I know well your dynamic nature, but I fear that we must postpone our visit to the scene of the crime until tomorrow morning."

I could detect a strain upon Holmes' face at this pronouncement. However, he quickly shrugged it off and slumped into one of the chairs. "Macpherson has been dead three days now. Any evidence that existed at the scene has surely been thoroughly trampled by this late juncture. I suppose a few hours more will matter little."

"If you ask me, the case is as clear as crystal," Lestrade continued. "Still one cannot refuse a lady. Lady Emma is distraught at the thought that Donald Scott is guilty. She has heard of you, Mr. Holmes, and insisted that you be consulted. I told her it was a waste of your time and her money, but she would not be put off." He spread out his hands in a supplicating fashion. "Though to be fair, I suppose I once said the same at the Boscombe Pool and was ultimately proven wrong. I would hate for there to be a miscarriage of justice, especially when the poor fool can hardly defend himself."

Holmes nodded. "Your concern is well-warranted, Lestrade. Someone who cannot speak or write is the perfect scapegoat for a crime committed by another."

Lestrade shrugged. "Yes, well, there aren't many others for you to question, Mr. Holmes."

"Who else was present at Gleannlaithe Castle during Mr. Macpherson's demise?"

"The castle maintains a staff of butlers, footmen, maidservants, and the usual servants. I suppose that any of them could have shot Macpherson, though why they would want to is beyond me. And there are the estate groundskeepers and stable staff, of course, but it has been verified that none of them were in the vicinity of the house on the morning in question, save only Donald Scott. There is Lady Emma, of course. But she may be discarded as a potential suspect."

"Why is that?"

"She was having her hair combed by her confidential maid at the time the gunshots were heard."

Holmes shrugged, as if he did not consider such an alibi to be air-tight. "And is there a Lord Abercromby?"

Lestrade shook his head. "Not for many years now. The lady was widowed when her husband died in the Soudan. There is also Lady Honoria Murray, who is visiting from Broughton. She is Lady Emma's spinster sister."

"And where was Lady Honoria at the time of the murder?"

"Reading in the library."

"Any witnesses who might confirm her location?" Holmes inquired.

"None," said Lestrade with a frown. "But what reason would Lady Honoria have for murdering Macpherson?"

Holmes held up a hand. "It is far too early to begin to assign motives, Lestrade. We must seek the facts and then fit theories to them rather than your widdershins approach. Who else?"

"There is also Mr. Carruthers. He is a Scotsman visiting Lady Emma from Dumfries."

"For what purpose?"

"A social call, I presume," said Lestrade, offhandedly.

"To the Scottish Highlands in January? An odd time of year, don't you think, Lestrade?"

The inspector shrugged. "I hadn't really thought about it."

"Of course not," replied Holmes, acerbically.

"Mr. Carruthers has been most helpful," said Lestrade, his tone bristling.

"In what way?"

"It was his evidence which sealed Donald Scott's fate. He

saw the man enter the palm house around the time of the murder."

"Oh?" said Holmes, his eyebrows rising with interest. "He volunteered that, did he?"

"Not at all. In fact, it took a great deal of skilful questioning to bring it out. Mr. Carruthers did not wish to unfairly implicate Mr. Scott. It was only with a great deal of pressure did he reluctantly admit to seeing Scott lurking in the garden that morning. It's all in his deposition."

"Do you have an account of the inquest?" asked Holmes.

"Of course," replied Lestrade, reaching into his bag in order to extract a pile of papers. "Is there something particular you are interested in?"

"The surgeon's deposition."

"Page seven, I believe," said Lestrade, handing over the file.

Holmes turned to the aforementioned page and read through it carefully. In several parts, his eyebrows rose suggestively. Finally, he handed it back to the inspector with a smile upon his face. "Most instructive."

"In what way?" asked Lestrade, suspiciously.

"Well, we will need to examine the scene in order to put everything into its proper context. What about the coins found in Macpherson's pocket?"

"What of them?"

"The newspaper account reported that they were French in origin."

Lestrade shrugged. "Yes, we believe that is why Donald Scott didn't take them. He must have realized that they were not British coins and therefore held no value to him."

"May I see them?"

"They are with Macpherson's effects at the local constabulary. But there is a drawing of one of them at the end of the report."

Holmes flipped ahead until he found the page in question. "This is a Louis d'Or," said Holmes, with some surprise. He passed the sketch to me, which I reproduce here:

Lestrade shrugged. "Yes?"

"These haven't been minted since before the days of the first Napoleon."

"So the man collected old coins, what of it?"

"Perhaps nothing, but it is rather curious. We shall make note of it."

"Is there anything else, Mr. Holmes," asked Lestrade, the irritation apparent in his voice.

"No, nothing else," said Holmes, mildly. "Though, pray see to it that Mr. Macpherson's effects – including the coins and his gun – are all brought round to the castle so that we may reconstruct the scene."

Lestrade nodded. "Well, then, the trap will bring us around to Gleannlaithe at eight o'clock tomorrow." He took his leave of us, and I stood up in order to inspect my room for the night. I paused when it became apparent that Holmes was not stirring.

"Go on, Watson," said Holmes, with a wave of his hand. "I will see you in the morning."

I was surprised that he planned to remain awake, as there seemed little to accomplish at the moment. "It's a little premature for a ratiocination session, don't you think, Holmes? Certainly you are not yet in possession of all of the facts."

"I concur, Watson. I do not propose to seek the solace of my old black pipe, but rather the company of men. We passed a country public house on the way into the village, if I am not mistaken. I think a glass or two of beer is in order."

I stared at Holmes in amazement, for he was much preferential to a fine Beaune or Montrachet when he was in a gregarious mood – which was rarely. I had not seen him order a beer since we paid a call upon Mr. Windigate at the Alpha Inn some six years prior. "Do you require my assistance?"

"No, no, Watson. Off to the Land of Nod with you. I promise to share with you in the morning any local gossip which I manage to acquire."

Finally comprehending Holmes' sudden and atypical interest in socialization, I turned in for the night. However, shortly after I turned out the light, a heavy wind arose, bringing with it a wild beating of rain. I was much used to enduring such tempests while comfortably surrounded by ten miles of man's handiwork upon every side of me. But out here in the countryside, under leaking eaves which had likely been laid before the days of the Usurper, the elemental forces of Nature seemed most awesome in their power.[22] I never felt more conscious of my insignificance, and sleep was long in coming.

§

By the following morning, the storm had passed and the sun was bright in the sky. It was as fine a January day as the Highlands ever witnessed, and despite a briskness to the air, I felt reinvigorated and confident that the day would prove to be a fruitful one in the search for Mr. Macpherson's true killer.

When I repaired downstairs, I found that both Holmes and Lestrade were waiting for me. I quickly partook of some toast and coffee, and then we were off. I wished to know what Holmes had learned in the public house, but knew that – with his reticent nature – he would only share his news when he gauged the moment proper. Fortunately, he was in a garrulous mood this morning.

"Did you know, Lestrade, that Loch Arkaig is the home of a water-horse?" said Holmes, suddenly, as we rode along in the trap.

THE GATHERING GLOOM

"Excuse me?" said the inspector, plainly startled by this strange pronouncement.

"Also known a *kelpie,* it is a shape-shifting water spirit known to devour unwary folks who linger at the water's edge. According to some of the local men, the Loch's water-horse was even witnessed by one of our foreign ministers, the Earl of Malmesbury, less than four decades ago."

"Whatever could a *kelpie* possibly have to do with the death of Mr. Macpherson?" Lestrade spluttered.

Holmes smiled and shrugged. "One never knows."

The ride from the White Rose was a short one. All around us we were surmounted by rugged hills, and as we approached Gleannlaithe, which lies rather low, I noted that it was surrounded by some very fine trees. Dappled by sunlight, the tangled woods could even be termed luxuriant, though I suspected they took on a more sinister nature under a moonless sky. The grey-stone castle, no longer fortified against invasion from the south, was now better described as a manor house. Its window were no longer barred, and its turrets were now more whimsical than menacing.

"Straight on to the palm house, if you would, Lestrade," commanded Holmes.

"You don't wish to talk to Lady Emma?" asked the inspector, with some surprise at Holmes' flouting of societal niceties.

"No, no, that can wait," said Holmes. "Enough time has passed that I fear most of the clues have been long ground to dust, but we live in hope."

"Very well. I had the room sealed," Lestrade noted, as he led the way around the back of the castle.

"Capital!" cried Holmes, beaming. "You have outdone yourself, Lestrade."

The palm house proved to be a fine greenhouse of white-painted metal and glass grafted onto the rear of the ancient castle. A series of walled gardens extended beyond it. Lestrade unlocked the door with a key and we stepped inside,

53

though Holmes bade us pause at the entrance. The interior was considerably warmer than the outside temperature, and I thought about removing my coat, but did not wish to set it down atop some critical piece of evidence. Holmes stepped along the cobblestone paths, taking care to not disturb the dirt areas around the palms and other tropical plants. Each of these locales he inspected for signs of footprints, though I saw him shake his head with disappointment and heard him muttering 'elephants' under his breath. When he reached the far edge of the room, he stopped at a small white-painted wrought-iron table and chair. Situated upon the table was a small tea service for one, collecting both dust and a smattering of insects in the days since Macpherson's death.

After studying this tableau for a moment, Holmes straightened up. "And now I think we are in a position to undertake a thorough examination of the room. First, did you bring Mr. Macpherson's gun, as I asked, Lestrade?"

The inspector nodded and reached into his bag. He brought forth a revolver and handed it to Holmes. Holmes carefully stepped over to the table and glanced about. "The gun was found here, I presume?" He pointed to where a small yellow flag rose from the ground.

"That is correct," confirmed Lestrade.

"Capital!" said Holmes, placing the gun upon the ground. He then proceeded to stand in various spots about the room and stared at the windows and trees around where the man's body had been found. I noted that he paid especially close attention to the man's teacup, even going so far as to lift it up and sniff it.

Lestrade snorted in disbelief at the apparent absurdity of this action. "Earl Grey or Prince of Wales?" he called out with some derision.

Holmes shook his head. "Neither. A simple English breakfast blend."

"And does Macpherson's choice of morning tea tell us who killed him?" asked Lestrade.

Homes turned to him with a smile. "Not immediately.

Though it has no small bearing upon the case, I assure you. As does the peculiar matter of the broken glass."

Lestrade frowned. "But there is no broken glass."

"That is what is so peculiar. Now, then, Lestrade, I believe I read in the papers that there were two shots fired?"

"Yes," said Lestrade. "Every member of the household confirmed that detail."

"Then why did the surgeon's report note that there was only one bullet hole in Mr. Macpherson?"

The inspector shrugged. "Obviously Donald Scott is hardly an expert shot. I expect the first one sailed wide."

Holmes nodded. "That is a reasonable hypothesis, Lestrade. Let us attempt to verify it." He walked about the table until he stopped in front of the chair. "According to the report, Macpherson was shot directly in the heart. Therefore we may presume that his assailant fired from directly in front of him, on or about where I am presenting standing. Do you agree?" When Lestrade and I concurred, Holmes continued. "Now, if I raise my finger at a man sitting in the chair, you may see the potential avenues the bullet may have flown. In fact, it is rather remarkable that the wayward bullet did not shatter any of the panes of glass in front of me." He waved his hand at the spot he indicated. "So, now, where then is the second bullet?"

Lestrade frowned as his gaze followed the direction indicated by Holmes. "Perhaps it is buried in the ground?"

"It is not," Holmes declared.

"How can you be so certain?" the inspector protested.

"Because it is right there," said Holmes, as he performed an about-face and pointed towards one of the palm trees behind him.

"What?" exclaimed Lestrade. He strode forward to verify Holmes' claim for himself. Once he had done so, he stepped back from the tree with a confused look upon his face. "However did you think to look there, Mr. Holmes?"

"I looked because I expected to find it there." He pointed to the gun on the ground. "That is an Adams Mark III. It fires a .450 calibre bullet. However, the surgeon was most clear in his report that the bullet he pulled from the chest of Mr. Macpherson was a .476 calibre, such as used by the Enfield Mark I. Therefore, Macpherson's gun did not fire the fatal shot, yet fire it did, for it was found in a recently discharged state. I presume he fired it in turn upon the man who shot him."

"This changes the complexion of the whole crime," said Lestrade with a hint of wonderment in his voice.

"That is but the first item you overlooked, Lestrade," said Holmes, calmly. "The second is of far greater importance."

"Which is?" asked the inspector, crossly.

"Only that Mr. Macpherson's tea was poisoned."

§

Holmes strode out of the palm house, leaving a bewildered Lestrade in his wake. I hurried after him as he rounded the house, heading towards the front entrance. "Holmes!" I exclaimed. "You cannot be serious."

He shook his head. "I never jest, Watson. There was something added to Macpherson's tea, of that I am certain. I would, of course, need access to my chemical bench in order to identify the exact substance."

"But who would do such a thing?" I cried. "To shoot a man after having just poisoned him? It's disgraceful!"

"I am not certain, Watson. However, I believe that this finding may be the key to the whole thing."

Holmes reached the door, where he pulled upon a massive knocker. When the butler opened the door, Holmes presented his card. The man glanced at it, and said, "You are expected, Mr. Holmes. If you would please follow me, sir."

We trailed the man through a series of old stone corridors and halls. In one of them, we encountered a short man passing the other direction, walking with some degree of a limp. He was some fifty years of age, with lion-like hair and beard. He had a stiff spine, and his lined face carried an air of authority.

He wore a hunting outfit with baggy pants and carried a Penang lawyer in his left hand. The man met us with a respectful smile, though did not remove his bonnet.

"Ah, you must be Mr. Holmes," said the man. "I heard rumours of your arrival. Alistair Carruthers at your service."

"Well, Carruthers, you've served in the army," said Holmes, suddenly.

"Aye, sir," the man replied, a wary look entering his eyes.

"Not long discharged?"

"Aye, sir."

"A Highland regiment?"

"Aye, sir."

"An officer?"

"Aye, sir. I was a colonel in the Lennox Highlanders."[23]

"Stationed at Barbados?"

"Aye, sir. If I may ask, how could you know all of that?"

"I noted that your pants are rather baggy, and your loosely-laced boots far larger than typical for a man of your height," said Holmes, motioning to the man's feet. "I concluded that your lower extremities are afflicted by swelling. Since you have none of the plethoric nature of a man with cardiac dropsy, tropical elephantiasis seemed likely.[24] That condition is commonly acquired only in the West Indies, such as Barbados."

"That is most perceptive, sir. I was invalided out of the army because of it."

"Simplicity itself," said Holmes with a dismissive wave. "May I inquire as to the reason for your visit to Gleannlaithe Castle, Colonel Carruthers?"

The man frowned. "As you have already divined the nature of my illness, I suppose it little matters if I reveal all. I have grown frustrated with the failures of the fools at Teviot Place.[25] They had me repeatedly swallowing an everlasting Antimony pill, but that achieved nothing save purging my bowels.[26] Then I heard from a friend that some of the herbs growing in Lady Emma's garden have had success in treating elephantiasis. I knew the lady slightly, having once served with her husband. I wrote to her and was invited to call upon her for a consultation. I must say that I have been glad with the effects. Over the last week, the swelling has diminished by at least half."

"Very good, Colonel. I am most pleased for you," said Holmes, amiably. "Perhaps Dr. Watson here has a thing or two to learn from our hostess, who we are on our way to meet."

"I daresay he might," said the man with a laugh. "I won't detain you any longer."

We set off again after the butler, who had waited unobtrusively for the three of us to conclude our conversation.

"Well, Watson," said Holmes. "What do you make of Colonel Carruthers?"

"He seemed a typical Scottish soldier, though I am uncertain how you knew him to be an officer? I don't recall Lestrade mentioning that fact."

"He didn't. As to Carruthers being an officer, it was most obvious, Watson. He had a strong air of authority and the bearing of a military man. For instance, he had a handkerchief in his sleeve, something no pure-bred civilian would contemplate. He was obviously Scottish and thus likely from a Highland Regiment. The man was respectful, but he did not remove his hat. They do not remove hats in the army, but he would have re-learned civilian ways had he been long discharged. However, it is most unusual that he does not utilize his rank for his honorific, but instead prefers to go by plain old Mr. Carruthers."

"What do you mean?"

"I wonder if it was a condition of his discharge?"

I frowned in confusion. "To be stripped of his title, he would have to be dismissed with disgrace."

"Indeed. And that is a most rare thing. Even Colonel Sebastian Moran, who once made all of India too hot to hold him, never invoked a scandal sufficiently grave to warrant such a fate."

Anything more Holmes was going to say upon the subject was cut short by our arrival at the drawing room, where we were presented to the lady of the house and her sister. The two women were most alike in form and face, though Lady Emma had a graceful figure and presence, while Lady Honoria's expression was more pinched and haggard. Both women had the luxurious dark waves of hair common to the Highlands, and I guessed the former was still a half-decade shy of fifty, while the other was some seven or eight years her elder. Lady Emma wore a loose riding outfit over which was thrown a fine tartan shawl, and her head was bare. Her sister wore a high-buttoned gown with a sequined neckline and a rather unfashionable mob cap.

"I am most glad that you have come, Mr. Holmes," said Lady Emma, waiving us to chairs opposite them. "I am sorely troubled to think that poor Donald Scott could be involved in this terrible matter. I have known him since he was a wee lad. He was the son of our head gamekeeper."

"Was he always so afflicted?"

"Oh, no. He was once a bright little boy. When he was four years old, he developed high fevers and inflammation of the brain. His life was much feared for, and when he finally recovered, his facilities had fled.[27] After that, there was little to be done for him in terms of education, but I saw to it that he was gainfully employed."

"To think that he repaid your generosity so poorly," interjected Lady Honoria.

Holmes shook his head. "I think it rather premature to judge him, Lady Honoria. In fact, from what I have seen thus far, I think it highly likely that he is innocent."

"Really?" Lady Emma exclaimed. "That is wonderful! But if Donald is not to blame, then who shot Mr. Macpherson?"

"It might have been anyone," said Lady Honoria with some rancour.

Holmes turned to her with interest. "You did not care for Mr. Macpherson?"

Lady Honoria sniffed in disdain. "Rufus Macpherson was a Black Saxpence in human form."

Holmes cocked his head. "I am afraid that I am unfamiliar with that term."

"A Black Saxpence is a Scottish term for a silver sixpence which has tarnished to such a degree that it turns black in colour," I explained. "It is received from the devil as a pledge of a person's body and soul. For the person who keeps it constantly in his pocket, however much he spends, he will always find another sixpence beside it."

"And you think Mr. Macpherson sold his soul to the devil, Lady Honoria?" asked Holmes.

"He didn't need to. He was the devil incarnate."

"If he was so awful, then why open your home to him, Lady Emma?"

"My sister is prone to exaggerations, Mr. Holmes," said she, magnanimously. "Certainly, Mr. Macpherson was unpopular in the neighbourhood. He had sold much of his family's ancestral lands to various mining concerns. The locals are rather conservative and do not appreciate such rash changes."

"I am less concerned about the opinion of the locals than I am about your thoughts, Lady Emma," said Holmes. "Unless you think some local nursed a sufficient hatred to warrant shooting him?"

"Yes, well, I suppose such a thing is possible," Lady Emma conceded. "He was a charming sort of rake, but he was also insolvent and owed money to virtually everyone. He had racked up such massive gambling debts in London that he was recently forced to retire from society. This is why I permitted him to call upon me. I rarely get down to London and wished to hear the news which he still received from some of his old friends. He had a most vivacious way of recounting the scandals and foibles of the first families of the kingdom."

"He also wished to steal all of your wealth," interjected Lady Honoria.

Holmes' eyebrows rose with interest. "In what way?"

"Rufus Macpherson was courting my sister," she explained. "He was playing upon her isolation and loneliness, in hopes of acquiring control over Gleannlaithe. As soon as I heard he was paying a call, I came around in order to defend her."

Lady Emma smiled wanly. "Though my sister had little to fear, of course. Not only is the estate entailed upon my son, Malcolm, who is currently in Edinburgh studying law, but I am hardly as naïve as she fears. I was in no danger from the glamor of Mr. Macpherson." She turned and waved to the butler. "I think it is time for elevenses, Campbell."

The butler wheeled around a silver tray containing a tea pot with cosy, cups with saucers, and some biscuits. Our hostess performed the ritual of adding the loose leaves from the wooden caddy to the boiled water, placing strainers over our cups, and then pouring the tea. She handed a cup to both Holmes and I, and then offered us both fresh milk and white sugar.

I took the cup gratefully, but then reacted with surprise. "Green tea?" I exclaimed.

Lady Emma arched her eyebrow at me. "Surely you don't be believe those tales, Dr Watson? Visions of evil monkey spirits?"[28]

I cleared my throat. "There is a well-documented case in *The Lancet*..."[29]

"Adulterations, Doctor. Unscrupulous merchants who add preservatives and dyes in order to bulk up the volume and colour the tea green for those credulous fools who believe the pale leaves look wrong. I assure you that it will not cause you harm."

"You are quite well-versed in your toxicology, Lady Emma," remarked Holmes with a smile.

"Of course, Mr. Holmes. Although the University of Edinburgh has opened its door to women, it is still an uncommon profession for one such as myself. However, I have long been fascinated with the curative properties of plants. Have you not yet visited the gardens?"

Holmes shook his head and reported that he had not partaken of that pleasure.

"Well, you may find it of interest."

"And why is that?" he asked.

She smiled coyly. "I hate to spoil the surprise."

§

We took our leave of the ladies, and Holmes decided to defer the next step of his investigation in favour of taking Lady Emma's advice. We made our way to the rear of the castle, near the palm house, where we found a curious old-world walled garden. Rows of ancient wych elm trees, some carved with strange designs, encircled the walls like a hedge. Inside, a profusion of flowering shrubs and small trees nestled between gravel paths. The whole effect was rather soothing and restful.

We pushed open the gate, and as we walked about, I watched with some degree of satisfaction as a look of amazement crept onto Holmes' face. It was a rare enough sight that I thought it worth savouring, even if I was myself uncertain of its aetiology. Finally, I could not stand the suspense any longer. "What is it, Holmes?"

He shook his head. "Do you know what this is, Watson?"

"It looks very much like a garden."

"Indeed, but it unlike any other garden upon which I have ever set eyes. I read about such a park surviving in Padua, but to find one tucked into the glens of Scotland is quite a surprise indeed."

"And what makes this particular garden so remarkable?"

"Perhaps if I identified these particular plants, you would share my interest. This one here is *Conium maculatum*, better known as Socrates' bane."

"Hemlock?" I cried, with some alarm.

"Certainly. Here is foxglove or *Digitalis purpurea*, which has significant effects on the beating of the human heart. And next to that you can see a prickly shrub. It is Dr Purcell's favourite tool, *Atropa belladonna*."[30]

"Deadly nightshade!"

"And here we have the Laburnum, or Golden Chain tree. All parts of it are deadly to all beings save the *Lepidoptera*. Next to it, I spot the *Ricinus communis*, the castor-bean plant. And here is the Javanese mulberry tree, from which the fabled uvas poison derives. Then there is this little tree, known in some parts by the quaint name of Quaker buttons. Its Latin name is *Strychnos nux-vomica*. From it is produced that substance which I have heard you counsel your patients carries great dangers when taken in excess of two drops."

"Everything in this garden is poisonous!" I exclaimed.

"Indeed," said Holmes, with a smile of pleasure which made me think he found it all rather wonderful. "It is unique in my experience. Few people are brave enough to have so many deadly substances growing within close vicinity to their vegetables."

"Brave or foolhardy?"

"That may be more accurate than you know, Watson. Do you see this?" he motioned to a small tree, with large, pendulous, fragrant orange flowers. "This is the angel's trumpet."

"That sounds benign enough."

Holmes shook his head. "Unfortunately, I know of ladies who enjoy putting a little of its pollen into their tea. A small amount is known to produce the most pleasurable visions. However, it is a rather fine line, since if you consume too much you may hear the angel's trumpet your entrance into the undiscovered country."

"Do you think that Macpherson was poisoned from something obtained here?"

"It seems a reasonable hypothesis, Watson, given the ease of access. However, the question remains… who slipped the fatal dose into his tea?"

His brow furrowed in concentration and he clasped his hands behind his back. He began to stroll about, and I knew better than to disturb the train of his thoughts. I followed him silently as he passed through a gate and wandered into a neglected area of the garden. This un-walled part was considerably wilder, with its shrubs growing unchecked into the pathways. A pillar – which once supported an old sundial – lay toppled over, and a stone bench sat crumbling off to one side. There were some signs of attention, however, with evidence of freshly turned dirt in one corner, along with an attempt to prune back some of the bushes.

"Now this is an odd item," said Holmes, suddenly.

I followed the line of his gaze, and noted an old, gnarled, English Oak. Dozens of coins had been hammered into its bark.

It looked familiar. "Unless I miss my guess, I would say that it's a Wish Tree."

"Pray tell, Watson. What is a Wish Tree?"

"It is an ancient tradition, Holmes. People festoon special trees with coins in order to have one's wishes granted. It is connected with the origins of tree worship, a topic with which I thought you would be well-acquainted," said I, with some feeling.

He turned his head and peered at me for a moment. "I see. Are they commonplace?"

"Not really. They typically occur only in special locations. There is a Wish Tree at Loch Maree which was famously visited by our Queen nearly two decades ago. If I recall correctly, it was situated near a sacred healing well."

"And what is so unusual about the site of this particular tree?" he inquired.

"Nothing that I can see, Holmes."

"No?" said he, with an arch of his eyebrow. "Perhaps not. However, you will note this abrasion here." He pointed to a linear notch where the bark had been freshly rubbed. "What do you make of that?"

I considered it for a moment. "It appears as if a rope was tied around it."

"Indeed, and recently too. And do you see that the earth

around the base has newly been dug up?"

"Certainly, but there has been much work of late in the gardens," said I, waving my hand about to illustrate my point.

Anything further he was going to say upon the matter was interrupted by the appearance of Inspector Lestrade.

"There you are, Mr. Holmes," the policeman exclaimed. "Now, what are you going on about with this poison nonsense? Who in their right mind discharges his pistol into a man whom is already dying? It's nefarious."

Holmes smiled at the inspector. "An excellent point, Lestrade. And one upon which I mean to meditate, as soon as a few other items are checked off my list."

"Such as?" Lestrade inquired.

"First, I plan to avail myself of Lady Emma's fine library. After that, since I am a firm believer in the *genius loci*, I shall stroll down to the Loch and see if the atmosphere of the woods begets inspiration."

§

With little left to do while Holmes was engaged in his act of meditation, I decided to interview the members of the household staff, in hopes that one of them might have noticed something which they were reluctant to mention to Lestrade and the official force. This task, however, proved in vain. They were all prepared to swear that – at the time the shots rang out – the two women were inside the house while Mr. Carruthers in the garden. Only Donald Scott was sufficiently near to the palm house to be capable of carrying out the murder of Mr. Macpherson.

When Holmes finally reappeared several hours later, he was resting his weight upon a rough Scottish walking stick with a hooked head, similar to an Irish shillelagh. His breath was rapid, as if he had just run or hiked some great distance, and he leaned heavily upon the *kebbie*. He asked Lestrade to gather Lady Emma and her sister, Mr. Carruthers, and the butler,

Campbell, in the palm house.

Once this group was assembled, Holmes smiled. "Ladies and gentlemen, if you will spare me a few moments of your time, I would like to demonstrate how and why Mr. Rufus Macpherson was killed."

The five of them, even Lestrade and the unflappable Campbell, simultaneously burst into a series of questions. However, I knew – from long experience – better than to interject. Like a master dramatist, Holmes would reveal the dénouement at his own pace.

"First, let us consider the possible suspects," he continued. "There is Lady Emma. She has a most unusual interest in poisonous plants, and I have established that Mr. Macpherson was poisoned before he was shot."

"My garden is for healing, not for killing, Mr. Holmes!" Lady Emma interjected. "Ask Dr. Watson! He will tell you that most so-called poisons may be beneficial in small doses!"

"Pray hold your protests until the end, Lady Emma," said Holmes, holding up his hand to forestall the woman's angry retort. "Thanks to your maid, you have a rather ironclad alibi, though certainly maids have been known to lie before in order to protect their mistresses." He turned back to Lestrade. "However, Lady Emma also has little motive. And then there is Lady Honoria. Her means and motive are both greater than those of her sister. She has no direct alibi, save only her word that she was in the library. I inspected the library not two hours ago and can confirm that – thanks to a loose sequin from her dress – she visited it at some point in the last few days. Of course, I am unable to corroborate a precise time for her visit. And she plainly hated Macpherson, whom she considered a dangerous ne'er-do-well."

"Not enough to kill him!" exclaimed Lady Honoria.

Holmes smiled and shook his head. "Perhaps not. And then there is the quiet Mr. Campbell. Like Lady Emma's maid and sister, he would be quick to come to her defence if he thought she and the estate were imperilled by an unscrupulous man.

I note that your whereabouts during the murder are unaccounted for, Campbell."

The man stoically shook his head. "I was in the pantry, sir."

"Alone, we may presume?"

"Yes, sir," replied Campbell.

"Pity," said Holmes. "Nevertheless, we also have to consider the case of Colonel Carruthers. Did he have any cause to dispatch Rufus Macpherson?"

"None, sir!" the man protested. "I just met him a few days ago!"

"So you are not a member of the St. James's club? You are not one of those myriad London gentlemen to whom Macpherson owed a considerable debt?"

"No, sir."

"I believe you, Colonel," said Holmes with a smile. "And you were in the garden at the time of the gunshots, were you not?"

"That is correct."

"Where you saw Donald Scott exit the palm house?"

"No, sir. I was too far away for that. But I did see him enter it some amount of time before. However, I don't wish to claim that Scott was definitely involved. I cannot claim to be an eyewitness."

"Your reticence is admirable, Colonel," said Holmes. "But who else could it have been?"

The man shrugged. "As you say, sir. Though that's up to a coroner's jury to decide."

"Indeed. Now, let us turn our attention to one other matter." Holmes reached into his waistcoat pocket and pulled out a small tumbler containing a substance with a deep indigo colour. "This, gentlemen, contains a most potent drug derived from one of the woad plants in Lady Emma's charming garden. It is extremely bitter to the taste and most offensive to the sense of smell, though not poisonous in small quantities. However, I wish for you – ladies excluded, of course – to test it by smell and taste, for it is pertinent to the case at hand." Opening the vial, he stirred the liquid with his finger. "As I don't ask anything of you which I wouldn't do alone with myself, I will therefore taste it before passing it around." He licked his finger and grimaced at the unpleasant taste.

The tumbler was then passed round and with a wry and sour expression, I watched as Lestrade followed Holmes' lead. One after another, Campbell, Carruthers, and I all tasted the liquid, and varied and amusing were the grimaces that were manifested upon our faces. The tumbler, having gone round, was returned to Holmes.

"Gentlemen, I am deeply grieved to find that not one of you has developed his power of perception, the faculty of observations of which I speak so much. For if you had truly observed me, you would have seen that while I placed my middle finger in the awful brew, it was my index finger which actually found its way into my mouth."

Lestrade threw up his hands in protest. "What the blazes was the point of that little exercise, Mr. Holmes? Are you mad?"

Holmes chuckled. "Not at all. I am merely pointing out the dangers of visual evidence. Had you been placed on the witness stand, Lestrade, you would have sworn under oath that I had tasted the tincture of woad. And you would have been factually incorrect, though you believed it wholeheartedly."

"I ask again, Mr. Holmes," said Lestrade, testily. "What is your point?"

Holmes turned to the butler. "Mr. Campbell, you saw Lady Honoria arrive upon the scene of the crime from the direction of the library, did you not?" The man nodded his silent affirmation. "And Mr. Carruthers from director of the garden, correct?" he asked, and was answered with another nod.

"And yet, what is there to prove that either individual was actually at those sites at the time of the gunshots? Either one could have discharged the gun into Macpherson, raced partway back to their supposed locale, and then turned back around, as if summoned by the noise."

Lestrade's anger began to fade. "Yes, I suppose that is true."

"Now we come to the most interesting part of the case. First, if you will all follow me into the garden." Holmes led the group out of the palm house, through the poison garden, and to the old Wish Tree. He then turned to Lestrade. "Inspector now if you would be so kind as to display the coins the police found in Macpherson's pocket?"

Lestrade brought out the French coins as requested. I watched everyone's face as they were displayed, and all appeared only mildly curious, save Lady Emma. For a brief moment, I could have sworn a look of amazed recognition swept across her now placid features. "Here you go, Mr. Holmes."

"Hold onto them for a moment longer, Lestrade. Now then, in Lady Emma's library I found a long, but clear and fascinating, account of the Jacobite uprisings as written by one Archibald Cameron." Here Holmes drew an old volume from his jacket pocket. "It incalculably enriches the piquancy of an investigation, my dear Lestrade, when one is in a state of mindful understanding with the historical ambiance of one's environs. I will refrain from reading it verbatim, but permit me to summarize for you. As you may recall from your schooldays, the English Oak is a tree with great symbolism to the Jacobite cause. For it was in the boughs of the Royal Oak at Boscobel Woods that the future Charles II hid from Parliamentarian soldiers on Oak Apple Day in 1651."

Lestrade was speechless at this apparent tangent. I frowned in confusion. "Whatever do the Jacobites have to do with this matter, Holmes? I thought their line had died out many years ago."

"You are correct, Watson. After the Young Pretender died without legitimate issue in 1788, his brother Henry, a Cardinal of the Roman Church, was the final Jacobite heir to publically claim the throne of England. However, unlike his father and brother, Henry never made a serious effort to seize the throne. He died childless and the claim passed to a lesser branch. As far as I am able to determine, the Princess of Bavaria is the closest successor, though at this late date she is rather unlikely to ever press her claim."

"And how is this pertinent?"

"You have some Scottish roots, Watson. What was often performed during the Loyal Toast?"

I considered this for a moment. "A Jacobite sympathizer would pass their drink over a glass of water upon the table, to symbolize their concealed loyalty to the King over the Water."

"Correct. Here we have an oak, the symbol of the Jacobite King. And here, at our feet, we have the water."

I glanced down at the patch of earth. "What do you mean, Holmes?"

"I suggest that this disturbed earth covers a forgotten well. And if we were to have it dug up, it would reveal a surprise or two."

Lestrade finally grew impatient with Holmes' leisurely revealing of the truth. "Come now, Mr. Holmes, we don't need to be digging up old wells in order to figure out who killed Macpherson!"

Holmes smiled. "But if you do, Lestrade, you may find yourself the recipient of a medal from a certain gracious Lady at the southern end of the Mall."

I had before seen Lestrade completely astonished by some words or actions of my friend, but the look on his face at this moment was beyond compare.

"Here is how I see it," Holmes continued. "Mr. Macpherson and Colonel Carruthers were having a morning walk in the gardens when they came upon Donald Scott digging in the South Garden. By sheer happenstance, Scott had unearthed an old well, and he was likely considering what to do about it when he was joined by the two gentlemen. Macpherson and Carruthers were both true Scotsmen and knew the legends attached to Loch Arkaig. They immediately made the connection of the well to the oak tree, and Macpherson hurried off to fetch a rope. Being the more nimble of the pair, I presume it was Macpherson who climbed down into the well. When he was finally hauled back up, he was several hundred thousand pounds richer. Presuming, that is, that he could remove the contents of the well without arousing the suspicion of Lady Emma, who would have been certain to alert the authorities."

"What is in the well?" Lestrade demanded, hotly.

"The Loch Arkaig Treasure, of course," said Holmes, mildly.

I rocked back upon my heels at the mention of this legendary treasure. But Lestrade was clearly unfamiliar with the name.

"What in the blazes are you talking about, Mr. Holmes?" he spluttered.

"As I learned today from my researches, in 1745, Bonnie Prince Charlie was raising troops in Scotland with the goal of overthrowing the Elector of Hanover, George II, from the throne of Great Britain. The Spanish, the French, and Pope Benedict XIV all contributed money to the cause, and a large fortune in French livres was sailed to Scotland and unloaded near here at Loch nan Uamh. However, by the time the gold arrived aboard the ships *Mars* and *Bellona*, the Battle of Culloden was already lost, with the Prince in hiding and his army scattered. There was no immediate use for the money, so it was sent to be hidden away by his trusty lieutenants. Its precise location has been lost to the history books for over a hundred years... until now."

Lestrade took in all of this information with increasing incredulity apparent upon his face. "And you believe it to be buried under our feet?" he spluttered.

"I am certain of it," said Holmes. "After instructing Donald Scott to rebury the well, Macpherson and Carruthers met in the palm house to discuss their plans over tea. Plainly, neither of them wished to turn over the treasure to the Crown.[31] But it is equally clear that the two men quickly decided not to share between themselves. I believe that Carruthers surreptitiously slipped some ground-up angel's trumpet into Macpherson's tea. However, once Macpherson began to feel its effects, he must have realized what Carruthers had done.

Macpherson pulled out his pistol and shot at Carruthers, but missed in his befuddled state. Naturally, Carruthers returned the favour."

"That is why Macpherson was shot even though he was already poisoned!" I exclaimed.

"Precisely, Watson. And why the bullet found in Macpherson did not match his gun. Instead, it came from the revolver of Colonel Carruthers."

"You will never prove that," sneered the Colonel.

Holmes smiled and shook his head. "Did you know that you have a most distinctive gait, Colonel? With the marks made by your Penang lawyer, it was child's play to track your steps, even after a heavy rain. I followed them along the dark path of interwoven trees down to the Loch. There I paid some local fishermen to retrieve your gun from the spot where you flung it." He reached into his pocket and pulled out a pistol wrapped in a handkerchief, which he displayed for our viewing. "Unfortunately for you, there has been insufficient time for any rust to obscure the markings which will identify its owner. I am certain we shall have no trouble matching it to the service revolver once issued to you."

All colour drained from the man's face as he realized that the noose had just been drawn about his neck. "It was self-defence! You said so yourself. Macpherson shot first."

"Of that I have no doubt. Sadly for you, Colonel, the little matter of the poisoned tea conveys the lie to that particular argument. Nor do I think the jury shall look kindly upon your subsequent action. For not only did you flee the scene, but when you returned, you intended to ensure another man would hang in your place."

"The trowel!" I exclaimed.

"Precisely, Watson. Knowing that the sounds of the gunshots would raise the members of the household, Colonel Carruthers hurriedly exited the palm house into the gardens. There he came upon the gardener's trowel. He slid it into his pocket and dashed back into the palm house, pretending to have been summoned by the noise. While everyone else was distracted by the sight of Macpherson's body, Carruthers surreptitiously placed the trowel where it would be easily found."

As we considered this act of perfidy, Carruthers suddenly sprang into action. First, he swung his Penang lawyer into the head of the butler, Campbell, who collapsed to the ground. As Lestrade reached into his pocket for his revolver, Carruthers changed the direction of his stick and brought it crashing down upon the inspector's arm. I was too far away to stop him, so Carruthers turned to flee. However, before he could make it more than a few steps, Holmes glided forward and raised his *kebbie*. Carruthers turned to ward off the blow with his own stick, but Holmes' initial swing proved to be a feint. With a quick reversal, Holmes swept the man from his feet. Carruthers collapsed heavily to the ground, and Holmes kicked away the man's weapon.

Holmes turned and faced Lestrade, who had recovered his revolver and by now had it trained upon the horizontal form of Carruthers. "Now, then, Lestrade, Watson and I shall stay at the village inn again tonight before our return to London in the morning. You will, of course, lock up Colonel Carruthers and ensure that you enlist some trustworthy men to stand guard over this well until it is properly excavated. It would be most terrible if the gold vanished before it could be properly placed into the hands of the Queen's agents."[32]

§

Late that evening, as we sat together smoking our pipes in the village inn, Holmes gave me a chance to ask any questions which remained.

"So what did the water-horse have to do with the crime, Holmes?"

Hu chuckled. "Very little, Watson. But it was most instructive to learn about the local legends. It was those loquacious gentlemen at Gairlochy's public house who first whispered to me about the treasure. I was merely demonstrating to Lestrade the importance of seeking out all potential information about one's locale."

I shook my head. "I worry that message was lost on the inspector. So when did you begin to suspect Colonel Carruthers?"

"Since the moment we met him, my dear Watson. Other than former members of the Royal Army Medical Corps, such as yourself – who instead utilize the salutation of 'Doctor' – I have never met an ex-officer who did not retain the use of his rank. As I noted at the time, if Carruthers had a reason for doing so, it would have been a grave one. In fact, as Lestrade has learned from a quick wire down to London, Carruthers was drummed out of the army for his role in the questionable death of a native porter. Nothing was categorically proven, but there was a sufficient stain upon his name such that he was unable to obtain an honourable discharge."

"So Carruthers and Macpherson did not know each other?"

"No," said Holmes, shaking his head. "The fact that two such dangerous rogues happened to be present when Donald Scott unearthed the lost Jacobite well is but one of those strange coincidences which conspire to ensure that life does not remain commonplace and dull."

"So, Scott will be released?"

"Oh, yes. Carruthers sealed his fate, and cleared Scott's name, when he struck at Lestrade with his Penang lawyer."

"Who would have thought that Macpherson was both poisoned and shot over possession of a hundred-year-old treasure?"

Holmes smiled. "Certainly audacity and romance have not passed from the criminal world, Watson. But if there is one worldly lesson to be learned from this case, it is that there is no honour among thieves."

§

"My dear Watson, you know how bored I have been since we locked up Colonel Carruthers."
– *The Adventure of Wisteria Lodge*

THE ADVENTURE OF THE FATAL FIRE

One. The Tragedy Of The Korosko

In recording some of the curious experiences which I have encountered during my long friendship with Mr. Sherlock Holmes, I have often been challenged to present to the public a careful depiction of his unique qualities. For a man who was such a precise observer of human nature, at times Holmes' deeper understanding of those emotions was sorely lacking. Nothing exemplified this better than the case mentioned in a telegram which I received one Saturday afternoon as I was considering what adventure to next set down upon paper. It read:

> *Why not tell them of the Korosko Tragedy? One of the most peculiar cases I have handled.*

I cannot say how Holmes knew that I was between narratives, nor what queer whim caused him to desire that I should recount that particular tale. However, even to this day, I laugh when I recall that he considered it 'peculiar.' For I would say that it is an ancient and familiar story, one that the world is doomed to see repeat itself until mankind has learned at last to live with a higher purpose. But I get ahead of myself.

It was, then, in the fall of the year 1897 that Holmes received a potential client. He was a middle-aged man with a sallow face and an exacting cut to his suit. One hand held an umbrella and the other a Rosebery bag. He produced his card, which read:

> Mr. James Stephens
> Hickson, Ward, and Stephens
> Solicitors
> 30 Swinton Grove, Manchester

Holmes waved his caller to a chair and introduced me. "How may I be of assistance, Mr. Stephens?"

"Have you heard of the fate of the passengers of the *Korosko*?"

Holmes shook his head. "No, I am afraid that name is not familiar to me."

The man nodded. "I suppose that should not be a surprise, Mr. Holmes, despite it being an incident of international importance. A version of it did appear in *The Egyptian Gazette*, however, I will note that account should be discredited, for it was highly inaccurate. I have, until now, refused to put my version of the matter into writing."[33]

The name had struck a chord in my brain, and I finally recalled where I had heard it. "The Dervish ambush!" I exclaimed.[34]

Stephens turned his gaze upon me, his face clouded. "That is correct, Dr Watson. I was one of the unfortunate nine individuals who comprised the landing party which was attacked by Dervishes at the pulpit rock of Abousir.[35] Two men were killed and the rest of us were hauled off to either become slaves of the Khalifa in Khartoum, or ransomed for the highest amount.[36] However, things took a turn for the worse in the desert. Only the swift exploits of the Egyptian Camel Corps prevented our bones from littering the Nubian sands. Upon my return to England, I brought a legal action against the organizers of the expedition for taking us to the Abousir rock, as well as the Egyptian Government for not protecting their frontiers. The first was successful, while the latter was not."

Holmes frowned. "I fail to see how my services are required, Mr. Stephens? What you relate is certainly a tragedy, but what can a consulting detective possibly add to the account?"

The man paused for a moment to organize his thoughts. "One of the men with us, a Mr. Belmont, made a comment shortly after the Dervishes were spotted which has stuck in my brain. I have replayed it over and over again every night for over two years. I cannot find peace until I know the truth of the matter, Mr. Holmes. If I recall correctly, Belmont remarked: 'Well, I could imagine parties of Dervishes on the prowl. But what I cannot imagine is that they should just happen to come to the pulpit rock on the very morning when we are due there.'"

"Did he say this to you, sir?"

"No, Mr. Holmes. It was addressed to Colonel Egerton, another member of the party."

"And what was the Colonel's response?"

"He said: 'Considering that that our movements have been freely advertised, and that everyone knows a week beforehand what our program is, and where we are to be found, it does not strike me as being such a wonderful coincidence.'"

"I concur with the Colonel," said I, nodding. "There was always a chance, however remote."

Stephens looked over at me. "Then I put this question to you, Doctor... do you consider the Dervishes great readers of *The Egyptian Gazette*?"

Holmes sat forward with interest. "What are you saying, Mr. Stephens?"

"I am concerned that this was no accident or happenstance. That it was deliberately planned."

"For what possible reason?"

"Two men died, Mr. Holmes. Mr. Brown and Mr. Headingly. Could they have been targeted?"

I shook my head. "It seems a convoluted way in which to have someone assassinated. Why, any of you could have been killed."

The man nodded. "You may be correct, Doctor. However, if you are wrong, then there has been no justice for those two men."

"Perhaps you should start at the beginning, sir?" said Holmes.

"Very good, Mr. Holmes. You will understand when I tell you that I was travelling to shake off the effects of an attack of influenza. A change of scenery and a warmer climate had been recommended by my physician. I considered Madeira, the Riviera, even Bermuda, but something put me in the mind of Egypt. So I booked passage on the *Rock of Gibraltar*, which stopped at Alexandria on its way through the Suez Canal. From there I travelled down to Cairo and took a room at Shepheard's. There I stayed for several days, my health growing ever stronger. I saw the sights of Sakkara and Gizeh, and heard the howls of the jackals by moonlight near the Sphinx. I finally boarded the *Rosetta*, a steamer of the Thomas Cook and Son Ltd. Company, for the week-long voyage up the Nile to Luxor and Assouan.[37] Most of my future companions aboard the *Korosko* were also travelling up on the *Rosetta*. As the accommodations in Assouan were severely lacking, we transferred directly to our boat at Shellal via the railroad line, so as to bypass the First Cataract.[38] The *Korosko* was a turtle-bottomed, round-bowed, stern-wheeler, with a thirty-inch draught and the lines of a flat-iron."

He paused his recitation, his manner dry and precise, and his mode of speech a trifle pedantic. He reached into his bag and drew forth a manila envelope. Opening this, he withdrew several sheets of foolscap.

"I thought that you might wish to have precise information, Mr. Holmes, so I prepared in advance a small digest of the matter. It is drawn from the hardly-legible notes I hurriedly scribbled at the time upon the flyleaf of my Baedeker's. For reasons unknown, the Dervishes failed to confiscate my pocket-watch, which enabled me to track the times with some degree of precision. This is the sum of my recollections," said he, tapping the pile of papers. "A fortnight later, those of us who survived were whisked up to Baliani in a special boat which had been placed at our disposal, and from there we took the express train for Cairo.[39] Eventually, we each went our separate ways back to our homelands."

Stephens handed the stack of papers to Holmes, who glanced at the top one and then passed it to me. I reproduce it here:

> *Re: Korosko Tragedy*
> *Enclosed, please find:*
> *1) Passenger Card for S.W. Korosko, sailing of 13 Feb, 1895, from Shellal to Wady Halfa.*
> *2) Itemized list of dates/times.*
> *3) Letters of Miss Eliza Adams.*
> *4) Sworn statement of Colonel Cyril Egerton.*

Holmes studied the enclosed documents with interest. He handed the Passenger Card to me, and I read:[40]

> *Colonel Cyril Egerton, London.*
> *Mr. Cecil Brown, London.*
> *Mr. John H. Headingly, Boston, Mass., U.S.A.*
> *Miss Eliza Adams, Boston, Mass., U.S.A.*
> *Miss Sadie Adams, Worcester, Mass., U.S.A.*
> *Mons. Octave Fardet, Paris.*
> *Mr. and Mrs. John and Norah Belmont, Dublin.*
> *Mr. James Stephens, Manchester.*
> *Rev. John Stuart, Birmingham.*
> *Mrs. Schlesinger and her daughter Florence, London.*
> *Miss Kay Byrne, London.*

"You were unacquainted with your fellow passengers before the voyage?" asked Holmes, waving to the list.

"That is correct."

"However, undoubtedly on such a small boat one becomes familiar with each other? Even Anglo-Saxon ice thaws upon the Nile, does it not?"

"Of course," said Stephens. "We were fortunate in being without a single disagreeable person, who would have been sufficient to mar the enjoyment of the whole party."

"What was your impression of Colonel Egerton?"

Stephens shrugged. "He is one of those officers you meet everywhere you go, very neat in his dress and precise in his habits, a gentleman to the tips of his trim finger-tips. He had a very self-contained manner. I will admit that I was, at first acquaintance, a bit repelled. However, in time I came to respect his careful reticence."

"Did he speak of the campaigns in which he served?"

"No, he was not effusive about such matters. On board the boat, he seemed to be a rather stand-offish, narrow sort of man. Now, after our adventure in the desert, I know him to be a man of great courage, filled with unselfish indignations whenever anyone is ill-used."

"And the two Miss Adams? Mother and daughter?"

Stephens shook his head. "No, aunt and niece. The former is a little, energetic Bostonian. What some might term an 'old-maid.' She had never been away from home before, but was quite interested in the general plight of the Egyptian natives."

"And the niece?"

"Ah, yes, Miss Sadie," said the man, with a smile. "She was fresh from Smith College. She is a tall and handsome woman, who I suppose looked older than her years on account of the low curve of the hair over her ears, and that fullness of bodice and skirt which Mr. Gibson has either initiated or imitated. The whisk of those skirts, and the frank, incisive voice and pleasant catching laugh were frequent and welcome sounds on board the *Korosko*. I can assure you that she had the singular distinction of being the most popular person upon the boat."

"The Frenchman?"

"Monsieur Fardet is a good-natured, but somewhat argumentative man. I never caught his occupation, though it seemed to involve much frequenting of cafés. He held the most decided views as to the deep machinations of Great Britain, and the illegality of our position in Egypt. At the end, however, he proved to be as brave as a lion."

"Mr. and Mrs. Belmont?"

"Have you not heard of him? It was my understanding that he was rather famous in some circles."

"Not John Belmont, the marksman?" I interjected.

Stephens nodded. "Yes, that is correct, Doctor."

Holmes looked at me good-humouredly, so I explained. "John Belmont is the Irish long-range rifle champion. He has carried off nearly every prize which Wimbledon or Bisley has to offer."[41]

"Belmont is fearless," added Stephens. "As is his wife, who is a very charming and refined woman, full of the pleasant playfulness of her country."

Holmes nodded his understanding. "And the minister?"

"Ah, Reverend Stuart. A nonconformist of some sort – either a Presbyterian or a Congregationalist. He is blessed with a considerable fund of homely humour, which makes him, I am told, a very favourite preacher, and an effective speaker for advancing Radical platforms.[42] He is a noble and constant man."

"Mrs. Schlesinger?"

The man shrugged. "A middle-aged widow, quiet and soothing. Her thoughts were all taken up by her six-year old child. I suppose that is understandable considering the *Korosko* had only an open rail for a bulwark, and the Nile is not bereft of crocodiles. I really did not spend much time conversing with her."

"Miss Byrne?"

"Florence Schlesinger's nurse. She was not expected to socialize with the rest of us."

"Tell me about Mr. Headingly," said Holmes.

"He was a young American, just graduated from Harvard and completing his education with a tour around the world. He had a quick mind, observant, serious, eager for knowledge, and fairly free of prejudice."

"Did he have any enemies?"

"Not that I could tell. He seemed a keen and amiable lad."

"And Mr. Brown?"

"He informed us that he worked as a diplomat in one of the Continental Embassies, and was down to Egypt on leave. He had typical Oxford mannerisms, with a rather unnatural and inhuman refinement, but was full of interesting talk and cultured thought. He had a sad, handsome, face, a small tax-tipped moustache, a low voice, and a listless manner. I remember him reading Walter Pater."[43]

"Do you recall in which Embassy he served?"

Stephens shook his head. "No. I don't believe that he ever said. Does it matter?"

"Perhaps. He may have been targeted because he was the possessor of some diplomatic secret. I will make inquiries."

"Then you will take the case?" said Stephens, his voice rising with hope.

Holmes nodded. "The incident interests me, Mr. Stephens. I am unable to promise that anything will come of it beyond the official verdict of a regrettable accident. However, as I am otherwise between cases, I will look into the matter."

The man's head bobbed up and down. "Just knowing that you have come to the same conclusion, Mr. Holmes, will be sufficient to set my mind at ease."

"I cannot, of course, rely solely upon your notes, Mr. Stephens, even supplemented as they are by the letters of Miss Adams and the testimony of Colonel Egerton. If your suspicions are correct, and this ambush was planned, it is possible that one of the other individuals made a critical observation which you missed. One which is seemingly inconsequential until properly placed into the mosaic as a whole. Where might we locate your former travelling companions?"

"I believe each has returned to their respective homes, sir." He drew out a small pocket-book from his coat and consulted it. "Colonel Egerton may be found at the Army & Navy Club. Miss Eliza Adams resides at 1954 Commonwealth Avenue. Monsieur Fardet is at 11B Rue Balzac. The Belmonts are at Haran House on the Killarney Road in Bray. Reverend Stuart is at 59 Aston Brook. And Mrs. Schlesinger is at 34 Alie Street."

Holmes jotted these addresses down upon his shirt-cuff. "What of Miss Sadie Adams?"

Stephens paused for a moment, and a sight flush rose to his sallow cheeks. "She did me the honour of becoming my wife. She is currently in confinement after the recent birth of our daughter, and thus I would prefer that you do not upset her by bringing back these painful memories."

"I congratulate you, sir," said Holmes, in a tone which suggested the opposite. "You may return to Manchester and I shall be in touch when I have more definitive information for you."

After Mr. Stephens departed, Holmes stuffed his clay pipe with shag from the nearby slipper and sat smoking in his chair for several minutes, studying Stephens' itemized list. He finally set the papers down and turned to me with a smile. "What do you make of it all, Watson?"

"I think the man's imagination has gotten the better of him, Holmes. As I said before, planning a Dervish ambuscade is a rather far-fetched method of accomplishing anything. Surely, it was nothing more than an unfortunate coincidence."

Holmes shook his head. "I cannot agree with you. As you will see, Mr. Stephens' attention to detail is to commended," said he, tapping the pile of foolscap upon his lap. "Rarely have I encountered a client who was so thorough. However, his imagination is completely wanting. I believe there may be some subtle current which underlies this tragedy. From the start, we find several individuals of interest on board the *Korosko*,

Watson."

I shrugged. "Well, if we are to suppose that a crime was committed, then I would put my money on Monsieur Fardet."

"Why is that?"

"He appears to have been deeply opposed to our Egyptian protectorate. He may have engineered a disaster in an attempt to discredit Great Britain."

Holmes shook his head. "It is almost always a mistake to theorize in advance of the facts, Watson, however, I can think of more likely suspects than the Frenchman."

"Such as?"

"Mrs. Schlesinger is an interesting case, Watson. Why would a young widow embark upon a pleasure trip two hundred miles up the Nubian Nile with her young child? It is an odd choice, is it not?"

"I suppose so. Of course, it might have been Brown or Headingly. Their deaths may have been an unintended accident."

"Then they have paid the ultimate price."

"Or, it might not have been any of them."

Holmes' eyebrows rose with interest. "What do you mean?"

"It might have been someone who wished for England to maintain a strong presence in the area. Certainly after an incident like this our forces will have been redoubled?"

Holmes looked at me with frank appreciation. "You have developed a subtle streak of intrigue, Watson. Let us hope that no such international conspiracies are at work here. However, we can only learn so much from Mr. Stephens' dry recitation of the facts. We must hear other interpretations of those events. I believe a trip to Birmingham is in order."

"To interview Reverend Stuart?"

"Precisely. As you will learn when you peruse Mr. Stephens notes, the Reverend was at one point left behind by the Dervishes. This is an item of some interest."

"Why was he singled out?"

"According to Stephens, the Reverend was out of his mind. He was slowing down the party. They supposedly left him in the desert to die. But was that their true intention? Or was it so that he may be rescued? The Dervishes would have known that the riders of the Camel Corps were not far behind. Madness is simple enough to feign."

"But what reason could he have had to arrange such a thing?"

"The Reverend Stuart is a dedicated Liberal, Watson, and as such, he likely favours his party's imperialist policies. When the *Korosko* sailed two years ago, it must have already been obvious that his man Rosebery was on track to lose the General Election later that year to the Conservative Salisbury. Perhaps the Reverend was hoping that an incident abroad would help flame sentiments at home to vote Liberal?"

"Now who is theorizing ahead of the facts, Holmes?"

He chuckled wryly. "Touché, Watson. If you will be so good as to head around to Euston Station and purchase two return tickets to Birmingham New Street, I will meet you there."

"Where are you going?"

"I am going to visit the nearest telegraph office and send some telegrams to Paris and Dublin. Monsieur Fardet and the Belmonts might be situated a bit too far for a quick visit, but perhaps we shall have a helpful reply nonetheless."

§

Once we were comfortably situated in two corner seats of the first-class carriage, Holmes extracted Stephens' envelope of documents. "You may wish to familiarize yourself with the lawyer's account of the situation, Watson. I intend to utilize these two hours perusing the letters of Miss Eliza Adams and the statement of Colonel Egerton."

I took the notes from Holmes and proceeded to read:

<u>13 Feb</u>: Visit to Island of Philae.
<u>14 Feb</u>: Inspection of Nubian bas-reliefs at the Temple of Debod.

THE GATHERING GLOOM

<u>15 Feb</u>: Climbing of Korosko hill.[44]

<u>16 Feb</u>: Visit to hollowed-mountain shrine of Abu-Simbel.

<u>17 Feb</u>: Visited Faras Cathedral
- 1700: Arrival at Wady Halfa, the Second Cataract (three hours late due to mishap in engine-room).[45] I calculate that we made less than five knots an hour even at full steam.
- 1730: Shore party, consisting of the Belmonts and Rev. Stuart, depart to see the town.
- 2030: Announcement of the next day's program by the half-Copt, half-Syrian dragoman, Mansoor.

<u>18 Feb</u>: Expedition to Abousir rock.
- 0645: Mrs. Belmont and Mrs. Schlesinger chose to remain on the steamer.
- 0700: Our departure on donkeys for five-mile ride, escorted by six zouave soldiers of the 10th Soudanese battalion of the Egyptian army (recruited from the Dinkas and the Shiluks – two tribes living to the south of the Dervish country, near the Equator).
- 0900: Inspection of the engraved wall and pillar of Temple of Amon-Ra built by Thotmes the Third (18th Dynasty).[46]
- 1200: Reached the base of the pulpit rock of Abousir, dismounted from donkeys. Inspected graffiti left by Herodotus, Belzoni, and Gordon.[47]
- 1205: Climbed to the summit of the rock, where we found a semi-circular platform with views of the Nile and the Libyan Desert.
- 1207: Approach of approximately seventy red-turbaned men upon camels noted by Miss Sadie Adams.
- 1208: Mons. Fardet suggests that the men may be friendly Bedouins employed by the Government upon the frontier.
- 1209: Col. Egerton noted that: 1) there are no 'friendlies'

on this side of the river; and 2) our party's retreat was entirely cut-off.
- 1210: Escort takes cover behind the rocks upon the haunch of the hill. The corporal gives the order to load their Martini rifles.
- 1212: Mr. Headingly suggests hiding the women.
- 1220: A concealed cairn of stone slabs completed. Miss Adams and Miss Adams squeezed into this shelter.
- 1222: First shot by escort soldier. Dervishes out of range (five hundred yards).
- 1225: First solider killed by shot through head. Mr. Belmont claims the man's rifle and its remaining three rounds. His attempts to pick off Dervish leader fail due to bad light.
- 1229: Mons. Fardet wounded in the right wrist.
- 1230: Mr. Headingly attempts to go to Fardet's aid, but is shot in the stomach and killed.
- 1235: Escort soldiers run out of ammunition. Second man is killed, and the corporal in charge has received a bullet in the thigh. Remaining three men fasten their bayonets.
- 1240: Dervishes slaughter our donkey boys.
- 1245: Fifty Dervishes climb the hill, half of them black, half of them Bagarra Arabs. One of our remaining soldiers is killed, the other two are disarmed.
- 1247: Rev. Stuart suddenly attacks Dervishes with a stick, until he is wounded by a spear-thrust to his leg.
- 1250: Mons. Fardet attempts to appease the Dervishes by praising the Khalifa and the Madhi, but is struck down by the butt-end of a Remington rifle.
- 1252: Mons. Fardet again attempts to appease the Dervish chief using the dragoman as a translator. He is instructed to be quiet on pains of death.
- 1255: Mansoor informs Colonel Egerton that the chief is the Emir Ali Wad Ibrahim. He is reputed to be one of the most fanatical of the Khalifa's leaders. He killed an entire

Nubian village last year.
- 1257: Wad Ibrahim informs the group that we are to become slaves of the Khalifa until we can be ransomed.
- 1300: The villain Mansoor is threatened with death, and buys his life by revealing the hiding-spot of the women.
- 1315: We are all forced to board the spare camels, but only Rev. Stuart is restrained. We begin to ride into the desert. Note: I was permitted to retain my Baedeker's, in which I had drawn a small map. From this I could determine that we were travelling almost due west towards a caravan route which runs parallel to the river, about seventy miles inland. North, it leads to Asyut. South, it leads to Dervish country.
- 1558: I solicit water from one of the Black dervishes for Miss Eliza Adams.
- 1612: Rev. Stuart begins to gabble like a lunatic. Roaring for oranges. Clear signs of delirium from sun-stroke.
- 1742: Sunset.
- 1744: The Emir calls a halt. Half a tumbler-full of hot and muddy water is provided.
- 1804: Col. Egerton observes two Arabs killing Mr. Brown with a knife thrust to his chest as he resisted a search of his pockets.
- 1806: Col. Egerton attacks the two Arabs, but is subdued and restrained.
- 1824: Mons. Fardet reports seeing riders approaching from a distance. He, Mr. Belmont, and Col. Egerton begin to celebrate our rescue.
- 1827: It becomes clear that the thirty newcomers are also Arabs. One carries a small white banner with a scarlet text scrawled across it.
- 1830: I notice that the new band has a female prisoner. She is soon identified as Mrs. Belmont. It is clear that the steamer has also been taken.
- 1833: Mansoor reports that the leader of the new band is the Emir Abderrahman. Col. Egerton notes that the Emir

is reputed to be a monster of cruelty and fanaticism.
- 1837: Mrs. Belmont is permitted to join our group of prisoners. She reports that a boat escaped with Mrs. Schlesinger, her daughter, and the nurse Miss Byrne.
- 1842: The Dervishes lay out their prayer carpets for Maghrib.
- 1902: A bugle rings out the end to prayer. A flat dry loaf of brown bread and a second ration of water is provided to us.
- 1909: The Dervishes begin to mount their camels. Under the sight of several rifles, we follow suit. It becomes plain that the Dervishes intend to travel throughout the night.
- 1910: Col. Egerton notes that no Dervish is assisting the Rev. Stuart. Mansoor reports that the man will be left behind. Egerton protests and receives a rifle butt to his ribs.
- 1912: Rev. Stuart has been abandoned to die in the desert. Even when he has been lost to sight, we can hear him deliriously singing hymns.
- 2115: The desert cold has descended in full force. Miss Eliza Adams begins to shiver miserably. I cover her with my Norfolk jacket. I attempt to provide verbal comfort to Miss Sadie Adams.

19 Feb: The Libyan Desert
- 0619: Dawn. A halt is mercifully called. We are each provided a single cup of water.
- 0637: The two Emirs confer re: the fatigue of the baggage camels.
- 0641: We are addressed by the Emir Abderrahman, with Mansoor translating. We are informed that we must become Moslem forthwith or no longer be worth the extra weight and delay to the caravan.
- 0643: We all refuse.
- 0645: The Emir sends for a pair of scissors. It is unclear what he intends, though he seems intent on harming Miss Sadie.

- 0646: I swear to turn Mohammedan if they will leave the women alone, but Mansoor does not translate my words.
- 0649: Col. Egerton says that we cannot convert without being instructed in the ways of the path of Allah.
- 0653: The Emir accepts this argument.
- 0704: A bugle rings out the signal to mount. We ride west for hours.
- 1040: Our path is blocked by drift sand. The caravan is forced to detour to the north.
- 1112: We clear the drift sand. The tired camels are whipped into a jogtrot. This is exciting for a few minutes. Then a terrible camel-ache seizes us by spine and waist, with a deep dull throb, which rises gradually to a splitting agony.
- 1150: We have come upon the caravan route. It is paved in bones. We begin to follow this track south.
- 1234: The Emir Wad Ibrahim notes a weary baggage-camel limping badly with a strained tendon. With his Remington, he sends a bullet through its brain. This camel was being ridden by one of our wounded Soudanese soldiers. He falls heavily to the ground, and is stabbed to death by a Baggara Arab.
- 1304: We pass the crumbling remains of ancient buildings, and upon the top of a little knoll, a shattered plinth of red Assouan granite carved with the cartouche of the second Ramses.
- 1330: We reach the wells of Selimah, which are located in a bowl-shaped hollow. We receive as much natron-tainted water as we could stomach, and a ration of dates and bread. We are permitted to rest under the shade of an acacia tree and some palms.
- 1654: Col. Egerton informs us that he has conceived an escape plan with several former-Egyptian soldiers serving amongst the Dervishes
- 1703: Six mounted camel-men appear at the lip of the basin. An instant later, the bugle sounds an alarm. The

two Emirs confer with the leader of the patrol. It becomes apparent that the Egyptian Camel Corps is close behind.
- 1716: Utilizing Mansoor as a translator, the one-eyed Moolah attempts to convert us to the law of Allah. Mons. Fardet uses his ingenuity to delay the Moolah with a series of questions.
- 1824: The sun has set, and a bugle sounds. We are told to covert now or be killed.
- 1825: Mons. Fardet requests a sign of Islam's power. The Moolah refuses, and asks for Fardet to produce one of his own.
- 1826: Mons. Fardet amazes the Arabs by drawing a large, shining date out of the Moolah's beard, and then the nostril of a camel.
- 1828: Mons. Fardet's third conjuring attempt fails and he drops the date. He is immediately struck across the shoulders with a spear shaft.
- 1829: The Emir Abderrahman asks us to embrace his faith. We all refuse. He orders our hands to be lashed.
- 1832: The three women are loaded onto camels.
- 1835: The four men are asked who is the richest. We claim that we are equally rich. We are ordered to draw lots. The Moolah holds four splinters of palm-bark of varying lengths. Col. Egerton wins this terrible lottery.
- 1838: The Colonel is loaded onto the last camel. Fardet, Belmont, and I, as well as Mansoor and our last Soudanese soldier, are all to be put to death.
- 1840: We are permitted to take our leaves of the women. They and the Colonel are led away with the main caravan.
- 1855: We are left in the rear-guard with twelve Baggara Arabs and the Moolah. They seem beyond either pity of bribery. We consign ourselves to our fate. Then, shots ring out in the darkness from beneath the trees. They are not directed at us! The men about to murder us have

been killed!
- 1905: After much confusion, we learn that the former Egyptian soldiers who had bargained with Col. Egerton decided to turn on the other Dervishes. These eight men have saved us, though they expect great rewards when we reach civilization.
- 1920: The leaders of the former soldiers inform us that they will not ride in active pursuit of Col. Egerton and the women. Even with the five of us (inc. Belmont, Fardet, Mansoor, and the sole remaining wounded Soudanese rifleman) armed, it makes only thirteen men against over seventy Dervishes. Their math is sound. It would be a suicide mission.
- 1930: They convince us that the best path is to wait out the night in the relative comforts of the oasis and then retrace our steps to the Abousir rock and the Nile.

20 Feb: Reunion!
- 0737: We come upon a black, bulging ridge like a bastion upon the right side of a dry ravine, which rose into a small pinnacle. There we are greeted by a stirring scene. The Dervish band had been caught in an ambuscade by the Sarras and Halfa companies of the Camel Corps and wiped out to the last man!
- 0744: We race our camels for a reunion with Col. Egerton and the women. Even Rev. Stuart is there, looking rather hale, despite supporting his bulk with a thick-lance-turned crutch. He had been picked up by the Halfa Camel Corps shortly after his abandonment.

Upon reaching the end of this fascinating narrative, I glanced up at Holmes. He was looking out the window, an unlit briar pipe clamped between his lips. When he noticed that I had finished, he tossed the wad of letters he had been reading upon the seat next to me.

"Nothing of interest in Miss Eliza's notes, I presume?"

Holmes chuckled. "Not unless you consider a series of diatribes against saddle-galled donkeys, starved pariah dogs, flies hovering around the eyes of babies, naked children, importunate beggars, and ragged, veiled women to be relevant, Watson. Miss Adams seemed to have hardly landed in Egypt before she realized that the country failed to measure up to the standard of Massachusetts, and she promptly busied herself with the self-imposed task of single-handedly reforming the country."

I picked up the letters and skimmed through them. "There is a rather amusing account of her attempting to treat two native children with trachoma of the eyes, Holmes.[48] What of the Colonel's statement?"

"It essentially recapitulates the version provided by Mr. Stephens. Though there are some added details regarding the Colonel's apparent heroism during the hour of the group's rescue. It seems that when the Camel Corps caught up to the Dervishes escorting the Colonel and the women, they set up an ambuscade in a ravine. The Dervishes attempted to flee the gauntlet of fierce fire which was being poured upon them from above. One of them, a Bagarra Arab, had his camel shot out from underneath him nearby where the Colonel and the women had sought refuge. With an exultant shout, the Dervish dashed towards them, his broad-bladed sword gleaming above his head. Miss Eliza Adams was the nearest to him, but at the sight of the rushing figure with its maniacal face, she threw herself off the camel upon the far side. The Arab bounded onto a rock and aimed a spear thrust at Mrs. Belmont, but before the point could reach her, the Colonel leaned forward with his pistol and blew the Dervish's head in."

"Good man!" said I, approvingly.

"There are also some rather harsh assessments of the Frenchman. Before the appearance of verifiable Dervishes, it appears that Monsieur Fardet spent much time doubting their existence. Colonel Egerton made plain his option of Monsieur Fardet's absurd beliefs, which ran counter to that of the officers who have the responsibility of caring for the safety of the frontier. There were words between the two of them when the Colonel later mocked the Frenchman by saying that he hoped Fardet had learned something from this desert adventure. Though they seemed to have patched things up by the end. Finally, the Colonel concludes with some rather bitter self-recriminations."

"For what?"

"He said that he was an infernal fool for not protesting more energetically against an unwise expedition into the lands on the western side of the river which had no fortified base located between their destination and the camps of the Dervishes."

"He was correct."

"It appears so, Watson," said Holmes, nodding his head thoughtfully.

§

We found the Reverend Stuart at his house, which was conveniently situated next to his Congregational church. At first, I thought no one was at home, but eventually the door was opened by the man himself. Stuart proved to be a man of immense stoutness, with large, white cheeks, ox-brown eyes, and a nearly bald pate.

After we introduced ourselves and the purpose for our visit, he motioned for us to come inside. As he led us to his sitting room, I noted that he was rather torpid in his ways. He walked slowly, and with the aid of a yellow wooden cane, each step accompanied by a puff of exertion.

"I am afraid that I can be of little help to you, Mr. Holmes," said he, settling into an oversized chair. "I was only present for portions of the incident."

"Was there anything of note when you departed the boat?"

The man shook his large head. "Not that I can recall. The dragoman had set aside the prize donkey for me, on account of my rotundity. I'm one of those men who carry everything before them," said he, glancing ruefully at his belly, and chuckling wheezingly at his own little joke.

"What about later, during the ride to the pulpit rock?"

"The dragoman stopped us at that heathen temple. He showed us some shocking hieroglyphics of the pharaoh's victorious exhibition into Mesopotamia over three thousand years ago. He had a gaggle of captives tied to his chariot and then he cut off each man's right hand as a sacrifice to the false idol Ammon-Ra."

"What is so shocking about that?"

"Why, that nothing has altered, Mr. Holmes! As poor Mr. Brown pointed out at the time. The East is still the East, with no advance towards peace in over three thousand years. It is a most deplorable thing."

"And what are your memories of the top of Abousir?"

Stuart paused and turned his gaze to the ceiling. A distant look entered his eyes. "It was a view which, when once seen, must always haunt the mind."

"What do you mean?"

"Such an expanse of savage and unrelieved desert might be part of some cold and burned-out planet rather than this fertile and bountiful earth. Away and away it stretched, only to finally die into a soft, violet haze in the extreme distance."

"And what did you do when the Dervishes appeared?"

The clergyman stared at Holmes stolidly and shrugged. "What could I do, Mr. Holmes? I was frightened, of course. I stood there, holding my umbrella against the sun's beating rays, but what defence had I against the guns of a Dervish band? I suppose I froze, like a man in a cataleptic trance."

"Mr. Stephens reports that you strenuously attacked the Dervishes?"

Stuart shook his head. "I do not know what that was, Mr. Holmes. Perhaps the mania of fear, or it may have been the blood of some Berserk ancestor – my mother's family hailed from York, you know - which stirred suddenly in my veins? I honestly have very little memory of it."

"What of the time after you were wounded?"

"My memory is even more spotty. I was conscious for a little while, I believe. But my wounded leg was oozing with blood and I had lost both my hat and umbrella in the scuffle. The burning desert sun was beating down upon my bare head. The savages had tied my hands with a plaited camel-halter and I clutched onto the Makloofa saddle with all of my waning strength in order to prevent my body from swaying dangerously from side to side with every stride of the camel. Colonel Egerton eventually made a turban out of his red cummerbund, and insisted that I should wear it. This relived my torment for some time. I believe that I spoke words about life and death, of the present and our hopes for the future, and how a golden rift can appear even amidst the blackest cloud of misery."

He paused for a moment in his recitation, and laboriously caught his breath. "After that, I remember nothing until after the Halfa boys revived me with their camel ambulance. I was quite myself again by the next day. The doctor said that my wound was a trifle and that a man of my habitus would be the better for the loss of blood. They passed me along to the Sarras group, who took me along with them as we rode out after the band of Dervishes. We came upon the group escorting Colonel Egerton and the ladies first. I am afraid that in my excitement to see them alive, I almost betrayed the ambuscade which the Camel Corps had set for them in the ravine pass."

"Would you care to elaborate?" asked Holmes.

"We were hiding behind a ridge, and at the site of them, I jumped up and began to wave my hand. I was almost shot by a bullet from one of the Dervish's Remingtons. Fortunately, Captain Archer seized the tail of my coat and hauled me down in time. He threatened to have me tried by a drumhead court-martial and shot on the spot if I spoiled any more of their plans, though he later apologized for his harsh words."

"But the plan succeeded nonetheless, did it not?"

"Oh, yes. I watched the entire thing from the safety of the pinnacle. As soon as I was pulled to safety, each side of the cliffs erupted with a long, rippling roar of rifle shots. The Emir Abderrahman – as I later learned he was called – was the first to fall. He sprang back up again, though his long white beard was splotched with blood. He kept pointing and gesticulating, but I think his meaning was no more clear to his followers than to I. Some of them went tearing down the pass to safety, while some from behind were vainly pushing up to the front. A few dismounted and tried to climb up, sword in hand, to that deadly line of muzzles, but one by one they were hit, and came rolling from rock to rock to the bottom of the *khor*.[49] The Emir had fallen again, and this time did not stir from his crumpled heap upon the rocks, like a brown and white patchwork quilt.

"And when about half of them were down, it became evident – even to those exalted fanatical souls – that there was no chance for them. They must get out of those fatal rocks and into the desert again. The galloped down the pass, and it is a frightful thing to see a camel galloping over broken ground. The beast's own terror, its ungainly bounds, the sprawl of its four legs all in the air together, its hideous cries, and the yells of its rider who is bucked high from his saddle with every spring, make a picture which is not soon to be forgotten. I recall that the women trapped below screamed as this mad torrent of frenzied creatures came pouring past them."

"But they were not swept up?"

"No, the Colonel had edged their camels father and farther in amongst the rocks and away from the retreating Arabs. While the soldiers were busy with their tasks, I took charge of what I could, Mr. Holmes. I led two boys carrying baskets and water-skins to the Colonel and the ladies. I made sure that they each took a modicum of water, bread, and meat – not too much, of course. They were despondent at the thought that the others – especially Mr. Belmont – had perished, but I encouraged them to not lose heart. For I too had been abandoned, yet had survived. Surely the others could do the same."

"Anything else of note?"

"I should say so. For it was then that we witnessed something seemingly from another century. The sound of a volley came crackling up the narrow ravine, and then another and another. Colonel Egerton was fidgeting about like an old horse which hears the bugle of the hunt and the yapping of the pack, and asked where we could see what was going on. I led them up the path back to the top of the pinnacle, taking care that the ladies came after me so as to spare them the sight of anything painful. We walked along the side in order to avoid the bodies which were littered thickly down at the bottom of the khor. It was hard traversing the shingly, slaggy stones, but we made our way to the summit at last. Beneath us lay the vast expanse of the rolling desert, and in the foreground such a scene as none of us are ever likely to forget. In that perfectly dry and clear light, with the unvarying brown tint of the hard desert as a background, every detail stood out as clearly as if these were toy figures arranged upon a table within hand's-touch of them.

"The Dervishes – or what was left of them – were riding slowly some little distance out in a confused crowd, their patchwork tunics and red turbans swaying with the motion of their camels. They did not present the appearance of men who were defeated, for their movements were very deliberate, but they looked about them and changed their formation as if they were uncertain what their tactics ought to be. It was no wonder that they were puzzled, for upon their spent camels their situation was as hopeless as could be conceived. The Sarras men had all emerged from the khor, and had dismounted, the beasts being held in groups of four, while the rifle-men knelt in a long line with a woolly, curling fringe of smoke, sending volley after volley at the Arabs, who shot back in a desultory fashion from the backs of their camels.

"But it was not upon the sullen group of Dervishes, nor yet upon the long line of kneeling rifle-men, that our gazes were fixed. Far out upon the desert, three squadrons of the Halfa

Camel Corps were coming up in a dense close column, which wheeled beautifully into a widespread semicircle as it approached. The Arabs were caught between these two fires. The camels of the Dervishes had all knelt down simultaneously, and the men had sprung from their backs. In front of them was a tall, stately figure, who I was later informed was the Emir Wad Ibrahim. We saw him kneel for an instant in prayer. Then he rose, and taking something from his saddle he placed it very deliberately upon the sand and stood upon it.

"I was mightily confused by this action, but Colonel Egerton explained that the Emir was standing upon his sheepskin. You see, Mr. Holmes, every Arab has a sheepskin upon his saddle. When he recognizes that his position is perfectly hopeless, and yet is determined to fight to the death, he takes his sheepskin off and stands upon it until he dies. Soon enough, they were all upon their sheepskins. The Colonel noted that they would now neither give nor take quarter, and he was correct.

"The Halfa Corps was well up, and a ring of smoke and flame surrounded the clump of kneeling Dervishes, who answered it as best they could. Many of them were already down, but the rest loaded and fired with the unflinching courage which has always made them worthy antagonists. A dozen khaki-dressed figures upon the sand showed that it was no bloodless victory for the Egyptians. But then there was a stirring bugle call from the Sarras men, and another answered it from the Halfa Corps. Their camels were down also, and the men had formed up into a single, long, curved line. One last volley, and they were charging inwards with the inspiring yell which the native soldiers have brought with them from their central African wilds. For a minute there was a mad vortex of rushing figures, rifle butts rising and falling, spear-heads gleaming and darting among the rolling dust cloud. Then the bugle rang out once more, the Egyptians fell back and formed up with the quick precision of highly disciplined troops, and there in the centre, each upon his sheepskin, lay the gallant barbarian and his raiders. The nineteenth century had been revenged upon the seventh."

I was thrilled by the Reverend's tale, but Holmes appeared only mildly interested. "There is one thing missing from Stephens' notes, Mr. Stuart. What happened to the dragoman Mansoor after your return to civilization?"

The man grimaced. "Shortly after Stephens and the two ladies left for Cairo, he was put on trial. Colonel Egerton had remained behind at the provincial camp at Assouan in order to give evidence against Mansoor. The dragoman pleaded excuses for his conduct when he betrayed the hiding-spot of the two Miss Adams. He claimed that his own life was forfeit if he had not bargained, and that in the end no harm had been done. But Colonel Egerton was implacable. He saw to it that Mansoor had a rope tied round his neck."

"That seems a harsh punishment," I cried.

"Egypt is a harsh country, Doctor." His big, brown eyes lost their twinkle, and became very solemn and reverent. "We were all upon the very confines of death, Mr. Holmes. It is a miracle that only two of us did not survive."

Holmes' lip curled up at the mention of miracles. "It seems to me that a deity who thrust you into the fire, should expect no thanks for also pulling you out."

"I don't deny the difficulty, Mr. Holmes," said the clergyman, slowly. "No one who is not self-deceived can deny the difficulty. Recall how boldly Tennyson said it in his *Way of the Soul*:

> " 'I falter where I firmly trod
> And falling with my weight of cares
> Upon the great world's altar stairs
> Which slope through darkness...' "

" '...And faintly trust the larger hope,' " I concluded.[50]

The clergyman glanced at me and nodded, before looking back at my friend. "It is the central mystery of mysteries, Mr.

Holmes. The one huge difficulty which the reasoned mind has to solve in order to vindicate the journey of mankind from cradle to grave. But take our own case as an example. I, for one, am very clear what I have got out of our experience. I say it with all humility, but I have a clearer view of my duties than ever I had before. It has taught me to be less remiss in saying what I think to be true, less indolent in doing what I feel to be right."

After these words, delivered with a sort of wounded dignity, I no longer saw before me a somewhat gross and vulgar man, but instead a man who had been transformed by this bitter healing draught. He had found deep within his weak flesh, a calm centre. For a moment, I rather envied him.

§

Two. The Morality Of The Desert

We took our leave of Reverend Stuart, and Holmes was silent for most of the train ride back to London. I knew better than to disturb his thoughts while he was contemplating the details of a case. As we begin rattling through the outskirts of London, he finally looked up at me with a smile. "I have spoken before of your invaluable talents as a companion, Watson. Where do you think that I have been?"

"Upon the Nile – in spirit."

He laughed. "You know me too well. You are exactly correct. While my body has occupied this train carriage, my essence has floated over the dunes of Nubia for the last hour."

"And did you learn anything of note?"

"Perhaps. It may be only a fancy, but there was one thing of note amongst the melodrama of the Reverend's recollections."

"Which was?"

He waved his hand. "No, I will not prejudice your own observations, Watson. For I may very well be premature in my suspicions."

The lamps were being lit along Marylebone Road as we finally made our way back to Baker Street. "We will visit Mrs. Schlesinger in the morning, I think," said Holmes, as we climbed out of the hansom cab. "We may turn in now."

But this plan was not to be. For we found a sturdily-built man with an iron-grey moustache waiting for us in our sitting room. Upon our entrance, he rose from his seat.

"Ah, Mr. Belmont," said Holmes, before the man had even opened his mouth. "This is a surprise."

The man's brow furrowed. "Do you know me, sir?" His voice was strong and thick, like his figure.

Holmes motioned towards a leather case near the rose. "Who else carries with them a long rifle-case when visiting London?"

The man smiled. "Very clever, Mr. Holmes. Well, I was down at Bisley doing some shooting, and was about to return home when I received a telegram from Norah. She had received your note and forwarded it on to me. As I needed to pass through London in any case, I thought I would call upon you."

"I am glad you did so, sir," said Holmes, waving his hand for the man to resume his seat. I fixed a whisky and soda from the gasogene and handed it to our visitor as he lit his bulldog pipe.

"So you've had a visit from James Stephens, have you?" the man asked.

"Indeed. And I have studied his notes about the matter. What is your impression of Mr. Stephens?"

"He is the living embodiment of prosaic law and order. Or at least he was when he first set foot upon that boat. I think the tragedy in the desert opened his eyes, and he began to see that his employment was rather trivial when compared to this wonderful, varied, inexplicable world of which he had been so ignorant, confined in his dry, technical work. Why do you ask?"

"As I said in my telegram, Mr. Belmont, he has suggested that the events of the Nubian desert may not have been a coincidence."

The man shook his head. "I cannot believe that, Mr. Holmes. If you had been there, you would realize that there is a fine line between serenity and calamity out there in the furthest reaches of the Empire. The slightest breeze can upset the balance."

"I have not been in Egypt, but I can say the same is certainly true of the Hindu Kush," I interjected.

Belmont glanced at me and nodded. "It is a singular country, this Nubia. Varying in breadth from a few miles to as many yards – for the name is only applied to the narrow portion which is capable of cultivation – it extends in a thin, green, palm-fringed strip upon either side of the broad coffee-coloured river. Beyond it there stretches on the Libyan bank a savage and illimitable desert, extending to the whole breadth of Africa. On the other side, an equally desolate wilderness is bounded only by the distant Red Sea. Between these two huge and barren expanses Nubia writhes like a green sandworm along the course of the river. Here and there it disappears altogether, and the Nile runs between black and sun-cracked hills, with the orange drift-sand lying like glaciers in their valleys.

"Everywhere one sees traces of vanished races and submerged civilizations. Grotesque graves dot the hills or stand up against the sky-line: pyramidal graves, tumulus graves, rock graves – everywhere, graves. And, occasionally, as the boat rounds a rocky point, one sees a deserted city up above – houses, walls, battlements, with the sun shining through the empty window squares. Sometimes you learn that it was built by the Romans, sometimes the Egyptian, sometimes all record of its name or origin has been absolutely lost. You ask yourself in amazement why any race should build in so uncouth a solitude, and you find it difficult to accept the theory that this has only been of value as a guard-house to the richer country down below, and that these frequent cities have been so many fortresses to hold off the wild and predatory men of the south. But whatever be their explanation, be it a fierce neighbour, or be it a climatic change, there they stand, these grim and silent cities. And up on the hills you can see the graves of their people, like the port-holes of a man-of-war. It is through this weird, dead country that we passed on our way to the Egyptian frontier. And as we travelled, we grew to know and like each other. Such harsh landscapes invite great familiarities."

"So, you do not believe that any of your travelling companions are capable of arranging the Dervish attack?" asked Holmes.

"Absolutely not. On a vessel which is little more than a large steam launch, the bore, the cynic, or the grumbler holds the company at his mercy. But the *Korosko* was free from anything of the kind. Everyone was most merry."

"You have already given me your opinion about Mr. Stephens. What about Miss Eliza Adams?"

"Miss Adams is a hard-featured Bostonian, with somewhat stern and swarthy features, but she is a brave lady, no one could argue otherwise. She was full of conviction that her conscience had been challenged. However, as she could not speak a word of the language, and was unable to make any of the natives understand what it was that she wanted, I am afraid that her passage left the immemorial East very much as she had found it." He snored in wry amusement at the memory.

"I understand that your wife did not accompany you to Abousir?"

"She had a touch of the sun the day before and her head was aching very badly. I recall how she came out upon the saloon-deck and waved her handkerchief. I waved my white puggar-eed hat back to her. For some while, you know, I thought that was the last time I would ever set eyes upon her beautiful face."

"Fortunately that was not to be the case," said Holmes. "Did anything of note occur before you reaching the pulpit rock?"

"Colonel Egerton and I spent the first part of the trip discussing the relative advantages of the Mauser, the Lebel, and the Lee-Meford rifles." Belmont paused and considered this further. "But now that you mention it, Mr. Holmes, there was one odd thing which happened. At the temple, Mr. Brown and Mr. Headingly dropped behind the rest of the party. They were speaking in low tones to each other. I could only make out snatches of words. Something about sacrilege, and ruins, and manslaughter."

Holmes sat forward with interest. "Manslaughter, did you say? Why would they be talking about that?"

Belmont shrugged. "I cannot say, Mr. Holmes."

"Is it your impression that Brown and Headingly knew each other before the voyage?"

"If they did, it was a well-kept secret."

"Anything else?"

"Yes. The Colonel suddenly said that he didn't like the situation."

"This was before the Dervish attack?"

"Yes. I recall that I laughed. I believe that I responded that the expedition to Abousir seemed like a fine idea in the saloon of the *Korosko*, but now that we were there, it seemed like we were dangling upon the end of a fishhook. However, I reassured the Colonel and myself that a tourist party visited the pulpit rock every week, and that nothing had ever gone wrong."

"What was the Colonel's response?"

"He said that he didn't mind taking a chance when on the war-path, as that was a straightforward part of the business. It was having women and other defenceless sorts about which bothered him. However, he declared it a hundred-to-one odds that there would be any trouble. And when we got to the top of the rock, I forgot all about Egerton's premonitions.

"You see, Mr. Holmes, below us on the far side was a perpendicular black cliff, a hundred and fifty feet high, with the swirling, foam-streaked river roaring past its base. The swish of the water and the low roar as it surged over the midstream boulders boomed through the hot, stagnant air. Far up and far down we could see the course of the river, a quarter of a mile in breadth, and running very deep and strong, with sleek black eddies and occasional spoutings of foam. On the other side was a frightful wilderness of black, scattered rocks, which were the debris carried down by the river at high flood. In no direction were there any signs of human beings or their dwellings. On the far eastern side was the military line which conducts Wady Halfa to Sarras. Sarras lay to the south, under a black hill. The air was so clear that we could make out two blue mountains in Dongola, more than a hundred miles from Sarras.

"And when we turned to the west, in the foreground the sand was of a bright golden yellow, which was quite dazzling in the sunshine. Here and there, in a scattered cordon, stood the six trusty native soldiers leaning motionless upon their rifles, and each throwing a shadow which looked as solid as himself. But beyond this golden plain lay a low line of those black slag-heaps, with yellow sand-valleys winding between them. These in their turn were topped by higher and more fantastic hills, and these by others, peeping over each other's shoulders until they blended with that distant violet haze. None of these hills were of any height – a few hundred feet at the most – but their savage, saw-toothed crests, and their steep scarps of sun-baked stone, gave them a fierce character of their own. It was a majestic landscape.

"The dragoman was proudly pointing out due west across the great Libyan desert, where the next house would be found in far off America, when Miss Adams noted men in camels coming out from between nearby hills."

"What did you do?" asked Holmes.

"I first confronted the dragoman. As if that foolish man could do anything about our predicament!" said Belmont, harshly judging his own behaviour under pressure. "The Colonel and I then crawled down to where the Soudanese soldiers were firing from behind the boulders."

"Mr. Stephens' notes report that you used one of their rifles in an attempt to bring down the Dervish leader?"

"It was that confounded light," Belmont cried, his cheeks flushed with annoyance. "It was a shocking bad light for judging distance, and the Martini rifles do not compare with the Lee-Metford when it comes to a low point-blank trajectory. I tried him at five hundred feet, to no avail. Think of my wasting three cartridges in that fashion, Mr. Holmes! If I had him at Bisley, I'd have shot the turban off him, but that vibrating glare caused too much refraction. Once my ammunition was gone, I folded my arms and leaned upon a rock. I suppose you will find it ridiculous, Mr. Holmes, when I say that those three misses and the tarnish to my reputation as a marksman troubled me far more than my impending fate."

Holmes smiled. "Vanity is a powerful emotion, Mr. Belmont."

"After we hid the women, there was little else we could do to resist. Mr. Headingly was dead. I remember that the Colonel, with his hands back in his trouser pockets, tried to whistle out of his dry lips. Cecil Brown stood erect and plucked nervously at the up-turned point of his little prim moustache. Fardet attempted to appeal to the Khalifa and the Madhi, but got the butt-end of a Remington to his stomach for his protests. Only the Reverend really attempted a struggle, as futile as one unarmed man might be against a hoard of armed assailants.

"Once the women had been betrayed and we were surrounded by the Dervishes, we were hurried down the steep, winding path in a miserable, hopeless drove to the cluster of kneeling camels. Our pockets had been ransacked, but the careless beggars missed my little hip revolver. I thought about shooting the cursed dragoman for giving away the women, but Colonel Egerton convinced me that we may have better use for it before all was over.

"Other than Reverend Stuart, the rest of us, including the dragoman and the two wounded Soudanese soldiers, were allowed to mount without any precaution against our escape, save that which was afforded by the slowness of these beasts. Then, with a shouting of men and a roaring of camels, the creatures were jolted on to their legs, and the long, straggling procession set off with its back to the homely river, and its face to the shimmering, violet haze, which hung round the huge sweep of beautiful, terrible desert, striped tiger-fashion with black rock and with golden sand.

"None of us, with the exception of Colonel Egerton, had ever been on a camel before. It seemed an alarming distance to the ground when I looked down, and the curious swaying motion, with the insecurity of the saddle, made me somewhat sick. But my bodily discomfort was forgotten in the turmoil of bitter thoughts within. What a chasm gaped between my old life and the new! And yet how short was the time and space which divided them! Less than an hour ago I had stood upon the summit of that rock, and had grumbled at the heat and flies, becoming peevish at small discomforts. And now humanity, reason, argument – all were gone, and there remained the brutal humiliation of force. And all the time, down there by the second rocky point, I thought that our steamer was waiting for us – our saloon, with the white napery and the glittering glasses, the latest novel, and the London papers. I could see it so clearly: the white awning, Mrs. Schlesinger with her yellow sun-hat, my wife lying back in the canvas chair. There it lay almost in sight, that little floating chip broken off from home, and every silent, ungainly step of the camels was carrying me more hopelessly away from it. That very morning how beneficent the universe had appeared, how pleasant was life! A little commonplace, perhaps, but so soothing and restful. And now!"

"Yes, indeed," said Holmes, his clipped tone indicating that he was completely indifferent to the man's rather poetic descriptions. "And what happened during your first few hours in the desert? Mr. Stephens' notes are rather scant upon the subject."

Belmont considered this question. "Well, I was thinking about my wife, of course, and then I looked over at my companions. It was shocking to see the change in the little Bostonian lady, for she had shrunk to an old woman in an hour. Her swarthy cheeks had fallen in, and her eyes shone wildly from sunken, darkened sockets. Her frightened glances were continually turned upon her niece. I kicked my camel's shoulder with his heel, until I found myself upon the near side of Miss Eliza Adams. 'I've got something for you here,' I whispered. 'We may be separated soon, so it is as well to make our arrangements.'

"By her wail, Miss Adams was plainly unhappy at that thought. I asked her to not raise her voice, for I didn't want that infernal Mansoor to give us away again. I told her that we must be prepared for the worst. For example, they might determine to get rid of us men and to keep the woman. Miss Adams shuddered in response to my words and asked what she was supposed to do. I instructed her to put her hand out under her dust-cloak and, when she did so, I passed her my little hip revolver. I told her to hide it in her dress, and she would thus always have a key to unlock any door. Miss Adams felt what it was which I had slipped into her hand, and she looked at me for a moment in bewilderment. Then she pursed up her lips and shook her stern, brown face in disapproval. But she pushed the little pistol into its hiding-place, all the same."

"Anything else?" asked Holmes.

"It was then that the Colonel suggested that I look back at the river. Our route, which had lain through sand-strewn *khors* with jagged, black edges – places up which one would hardly think it possible that a camel could climb – had just opened out on to a hard, rolling plain, covered thickly with rounded pebbles, dipping and rising to the violet hills upon the horizon. So regular were the long, brown pebble-strewn curves, that they looked like the dark rollers of some monstrous ground-swell. Here and there a little straggling sage-green tuft of camel-grass sprouted up between the stones. Brown plains and violet hills, there was nothing else in front of us! Behind lay the black jagged rocks through which we had passed with orange slopes of sand, and then far away a thin line of green to mark the course of the river. How cool and beautiful that green looked in the stark, abominable wilderness! On one side I could see the high rock – the accursed rock which had tempted us to our ruin. On the other the river curved, and the sun gleamed upon the water. That gleam of river must be somewhere near Halfa, and I thought that my wife might be upon the very water at which I looked. Of course, the wounded clergyman had it worst."

"I wonder, Mr. Belmont, do you think that Reverend Stuart's delirium could have been feigned?" asked Holmes.

The marksman shook his head violently. "Absolutely not. The pink had deepened to scarlet upon Mr. Stuart's cheeks, his lips were crusted, and his eyes were vacant but brilliant. Nature herself had coaxed his mind away into the Nirvana of delirium. He gabbled nonstop as we rode, until it became insufferable to listen to his ravings. When a man begins roaring for oranges, you can be certain that there is no shamming."

Despite the gravity of Belmont's description, I could hardly contain my snort of amusement and Holmes glanced over at me. "What is it, Watson?"

"I was thinking of a world overrun by oysters."

Holmes smiled. "Yes, well, certain talented actors may be able to produce a very satisfying effect of illness, though I doubt that Reverend Stuart would have had access to Vaseline, belladonna, and beeswax. Nor is there any doubt in regards to his leg wound." He turned back to Belmont. "But you did not suffer?"

The man shrugged. "Not to the same degree. I suppose that I was somewhat studier than the younger men, and younger than the old Colonel."

"I wonder if you witnessed the death of Mr. Brown?"

The man shook his head. "No, I was engaged in a series of mental calculations. You see, I was attempting to count times and distances. Our party was due back at the steamer by two o'clock. I thought that if Norah had decisively insisted upon the indolent reis giving an immediate alarm at Halfa, then our pursuers should have already been upon our track. Suppose they started back at two-thirty, they should have been at Halfa by three, since the journey is downstream. The Camel Corps or the Egyptian Horse would travel by moonlight better and faster than in the day-time. I knew that it was the custom at Halfa to keep at least a squadron of them all ready to start at any instant. The prior day, I had dined at the mess, and the officers had told me how quickly they could take the field. They had shown me the water-tanks and the food beside each of the beasts, and I had admired the completeness of the arrangements, with little thought as to what it might mean to me in the future! It would take less than an hour to turn out the Camel Corps and another hour to get them across the river. They would be at the Abousir rock and pick up the tracks by six o'clock. After that I figured it was a clear race. We were only four hours ahead, and some of our camels were very spent. I thought it would be at least an hour before we would all get started again from our present halting-place. That would be a clear hour gained. I was still adding these numbers in my head when the Colonel began to shout about Brown's murder."

"I understand it was precipitated by his resistance against a further robbery?"

"That is correct."

"Is there anything more that you can tell us about it?"

Belmont shook his head. "Not really, Mr. Holmes. You would have to ask the Colonel. He was the only witness."

Holmes nodded. "I will do so. However, all of your elaborate calculations regarding timing were in vain, were they not?"

"Yes," said the man bitterly. "For the blasted Arabs had taken the *Korosko* too, and brought my Norah back with them. At that moment, I thought that our chances of rescue upon which I had reckoned were as unsubstantial as the mirage which shimmered upon the horizon. There would be no alarm at Halfa until it was found that the steamer did not return in the evening."

"But you were wrong?"

"Oh, yes, Mr. Holmes," cried Belmont, with his responsive Irish nature shining through his previous gloom. "The guards held me back for some time, but once I was reunited with Norah, she told us that Mrs. Schlesinger and her child and maid had fled in one of the small boats. The Arabs had fired at them for some time, and by Jove, I knew that the garrison must have heard the shots. By this time, the great red sun was down with half its disc slipped behind the violet bank upon the horizon, and it was the hour of Arab prayer. However, after they rolled up their praying carpets, a bugle rang out, and I groaned when I realized that, having travelled all day, we were fated to travel all night also. I had reckoned upon our pursuers catching up to us before we left this camp.

"My spirit took a greater turn for the worse when they abandoned Mr. Stuart. I remember how he deliriously sung until his voice died away into a hum and was absorbed into the masterful silence of the desert. Colonel Egerton had protested, and received a frightful rifle butt to his ribs for his trouble. I knew that some of them must be broken, for the old solider fell forward with a gasp. He had to be carried, half-senseless, to his camel. I gripped at my hip-pocket for my little revolver, and then remembered that I had already given it to Miss Adams. It is a good thing too, for my heat was up, and if I had clutched it, it would have meant the death of the Emir, followed closely thereafter by the massacre of us all."

"The Colonel appears to have rallied quickly from this blow," remarked Holmes.

Belmont snorted in amusement. "Yes, he only had the wind knocked out of him. But he was not made of iron, rather he was wearing stays to support his military carriage. Please, Mr. Holmes, you must keep this detail to yourself. The Colonel asked me to let it go no further. I even refrained from telling my wife, at his insistence."

"You then rode through the night, did you not?"

The man nodded slowly, his square chin and strong mouth set like granite. "Yes, as we rode onwards, we saw one of the most singular of the phenomena of the Egyptian desert in front of us, though the ill-treatment of Reverend Stuart had left me in no humour for the appreciation of its beauty. When the sun had sunk, the horizon had remained of a slate-violet hue. But now this began to lighten and to brighten until a curious false dawn developed, and it seemed as if a vacillating sun was coming back along the path which it had just abandoned. A rosy pink hung over the west, with beautifully delicate sea-green tints along the upper edge of it. Slowly these faded into slate again, and the night had come. It was but twelve hours since we had breakfasted on the saloon deck of the *Korosko* and had started spruce and fresh upon our last pleasure trip. What a world of fresh impressions had come upon us since then! How rudely had we been jostled out of our take-it-for-granted complacency! The same shimmering silver stars, as we had looked upon the prior night, the same thin crescent of moon – but what a chasm lay between that old pampered life and this!

"It still comes back in my dreams, Mr. Holmes – that long night's march in the desert. It was like a dream itself, the silence of it as we were borne forward upon those soft, shuffling sponge feet, and the flitting, flickering figures which oscillated upon every side us. The whole universe seemed to be hung as a monstrous time-dial in front of us. A star would glimmer like a lantern on the very level of our path. I looked again, and it was a hand's-breadth up, and another was shining beneath it. Hour after hour the broad stream flowed sedately across the deep blue background, worlds and systems drifting majestically overhead, and pouring over the dark horizon. In their vastness and their beauty there was a vague consolation; for my own fate, and my own individuality, seemed trivial and unimportant amidst the play of such tremendous forces. Slowly the grand procession swept across the heaven, first climbing, then hanging long with little apparent motion, and then sinking grandly downwards, until away in the east the first cold grey glimmer appeared, and the haggard faces of my companions shocked my sight.

"Eventually, the long, cold, weary night was over, and the deep blue-black sky had lightened to a wonderful mauve-violet, with the larger stars still glinting brightly out of it. Behind us, the grey line had crept higher and higher, deepening into a delicate rose-pink, with the fan-like rays of the invisible sun shooting and quivering across it. Then, suddenly, we felt its warm touch upon their backs, and there were hard black shadows upon the sand in front of us. A short halt was called, during which time, the Emirs threatened to put us all to death, for the baggage-camels which bore us were plainly worn out with the long, rapid march. They had laid their long necks upon the ground, which is the last symptom of fatigue.

"The terrible old man, Abderrahman, stared at us with his hard-lined, rock features. Then he said something to Mansoor, whose face turned a shade more sallow as he listened. Mansoor told us we have to accept the Koran at once or be put to death. One by one we refused this terrible choice. We were all looking Death in the face, and the closer we looked the less we feared him. I was conscious rather of a feeling of curiosity, together with the nervous tingling with which one approaches something unpleasant. Fortunately, the Colonel had the inspiration of asking for instruction in the path of Allah. The Emir stroked his beard and gazed at us suspiciously, but in the end he agreed. At the wells of Selimah, we would have one more chance to choose whether we were allowed to go on to Khartoum or whether our bones would litter the sands.

"So we were to have a reprieve of a few hours, though we rode in that dark shadow of death which was closing in upon us. What is there in life that we should cling to it so, Mr. Holmes? It is not the pleasures, for those whose hours are one long pain shrink away screaming when they see merciful Death holding his soothing arms out for them. It is not the associations, for we will change all of them before we walk of our own free-wills down that broad road which every son and daughter of man must tread. Is it the fear of losing the I, that dear, intimate I, which we think we know so well, although it is eternally doing things which surprise us? Is it that which makes the deliberate suicide cling madly to the bridge-pier as the river sweeps him by? Or is it that Nature is so afraid that all her weary workmen may suddenly throw down their tools and strike, that she has invented this fashion of keeping us constant to our present work? But there it is, and all of us tired, harassed, humiliated folk rejoiced in the few more hours of suffering which were left to us.

"There was nothing to show us as we journeyed onwards that we were not on the very spot that we had passed at sunset upon the evening before. The region of fantastic black hills and orange sand which bordered the river had long been left behind, and everywhere now was the same brown, rolling, gravelly plain, the ground-swell with the shining rounded pebbles upon its surface, and the occasional little sprouts of sage-green camel-grass. Behind and before it extended, to where far away in front of us it sloped upwards towards a line of violet hills. The sun was not high enough yet to cause the tropical shimmer, and the wide landscape, brown with its violet edging, stood out with a hard clearness in that dry, pure air. The long caravan straggled along at the slow swing of the baggage-camels. Far out on the flanks rode the vedettes, halting at every rise, and peering backwards with their hands shading their eyes. In the distance their spears and rifles seemed to stick out of them, straight and thin, like needles in knitting. Colonel Egerton asked how far we were from the Nile, and I said that I thought it was a good fifty miles. He argued that it was closer to forty, for he reckoned that we could not have been moving more than fifteen or sixteen hours, and said a camel does not do more than two and a half miles an hour unless it is trotting. That seemed to me to be plenty of time for Hamilton and Hedley of the Camel Corps to catch up to us.

"In the meantime, I had gotten my pistol back from Miss Adams, and told the Colonel that I was prepared to sell my life dearly. My wife noted that it was the loneliness of death that made it so terrible. If we and those whom we loved all passed over simultaneously, we should think no more of it than of changing our house.

"From there it got even grimmer, Mr. Holmes. Right across the desert, from north to south, there was drawn a white line, as straight and clear as if it had been slashed with chalk across a brown table. It was very thin, but it extended without a break from horizon to horizon. It seemed incredible, and yet it was true, for as we drew nearer I saw that it was indeed a beaten track across the desert, hollowed out by long usage, and so covered with bones that they gave the impression of a continuous white ribbon. Long, snouty heads were scattered everywhere, and the lines of ribs were so continuous that it looked in places like the framework of a monstrous serpent. The endless road gleamed in the sun as if it were paved with ivory. For thousands of years this had been the highway over the desert, and during all that time no animal of all those countless caravans had died there without being preserved by the dry, antiseptic air. No wonder, then, that it was hardly possible to walk down it now without treading upon their skeletons. I looked at it with a listless curiosity, for there was enough to engross me at present in our own fates. The caravan struck to the south along the old desert track, and this Golgotha of a road seemed to be a fitting avenue for that which awaited us at the end of it. Weary camels and weary riders dragged on together towards our miserable goal.

"There were many things to interest us in this old trade route, had we been in a condition to take notice of them. Here and there along its course were the crumbling remains of ancient buildings, so old that no date could be assigned to them, but designed in some far-off civilization to give travellers shade from the sun, or protection from the ever-lawless children of the desert. The mud bricks with which these refuges were constructed showed that the material had been carried over from the distant Nile. Once, upon the top of a little knoll, we saw the shattered plinth of a pillar of red Assouan granite, with the wide-winged symbol of the Egyptian god across it, and the cartouche of the second Rameses beneath. After three thousand years one cannot get away from the ineffaceable footprints of the warrior-king. It is surely the most wonderful survival of history that one should still be able to gaze upon him, high-nosed and masterful, as he lies with his powerful arms crossed upon his chest, majestic even in decay, in the Gizeh Museum. The cartouche was a message of hope, as a sign that we were not outside the sphere of Egypt. I noted that they left their card there once, and they might again.

"And finally we came upon one of the most satisfying sights on which the human eye can ever rest. Here and there, in the depressions at either side of the road, there had been a thin scurf of green, which meant that water was not very far from the surface. And then, quite suddenly, the track dipped down into a bowl-shaped hollow, with a most dainty group of palm-trees, and a lovely green sward at the bottom of it. The sun gleaming upon that brilliant patch of clear, restful colour, with the dark glow of the bare desert around it, made it shine like the purest emerald in a setting of burnished copper. And then it was not its beauty only, but its promise for the future – water, shade, all that us weary travellers could ask for. The spent camels snorted and stepped out more briskly, stretching their long necks and sniffing the air as they went. After the unhomely harshness of the desert, it seemed to me that I had never seen anything more beautiful than this. I looked below at the green sward with the dark, star-like shadows of the palm-crowns; then I looked up at those deep green leaves against the rich blue of the sky, and for a moment, I forgot my impending death in the beauty of that Nature to whose bosom we were about to return.

"We lay down under the palms, and the great green leaves swished slowly above us. I could hear the low hum of the Arab talk, and the dull champing of the camels, and then in an instant, by that most mysterious and least understood of miracles, I was in a green Irish valley, my spirit wandering back along the strange, un-traced tracks of the memory, while my weary, grimy body lay senseless under the palm-trees in that oasis of the Libyan Desert."

"What happened then?" asked Holmes. "Anything of note?"

"Yes, of course!" Belmont exclaimed, slamming his palm into his forehead. "There was Tippy Tilly!"

"What is Tippy Tilly?"

The man chuckled. "Not a what, Mr. Holmes, but a who. Of course, that was not his real name. He was one of the former black tribesman soldiers of Hicks' shattered army.[51] He had served in the Egyptian Artillery under Bimbashi Mortimer.[52] He was taken prisoner when Hicks Pasha was destroyed at El Obeid and had to turn Dervish in order to save his skin. He began conversing with us when Mr. Stephens had asked for some water for Miss Adams, though the man's grasp of English was tenuous at best."

"So how did you negotiate with him? According to Mr. Stephens' notes, this individual was of some assistance at the end, was he not?"

"Indeed! Colonel Egerton knew a few words in Arabic. He did most of the communication with the man. He thought that Tippy Tilly was inclined to be friendly to us, and would rather fight for the Khedive than for the Khalifa."[53]

"And that proved to be the case?"

"Yes, well, it required Colonel Egerton promising the man that he would be promoted to Bimbashi when we got back to Egypt. That, and one hundred pounds to the old gunner, as well as the same for each of the others – five black men and two fellaheen Copts – who were also willing to turn against the Dervishes and re-enter the service of the Egyptian army. Of course, the Tippy Tilly's original plan soon proved to be less than ideal."

"How so?"

"First, once we reached the wells of Selimah, Tippy Tilly passed a clumsy, old-fashioned pistol to Colonel Egerton, who slipped it into the inner pocket of his Norfolk jacket. Then one of his men, a chap named Mehemet Ali, fastened twelve camels together behind the acacia tree. There were the fastest of all, save only those which are ridden by the Emirs. Tippy Tilly proposed that we mount and make a break for it, thinking that few would be able to overtake us, and even if they did, our new allies would have their rifles ready to defend our party. The man claimed that the water-skins were all filled, and that we may see the Nile again by to-morrow night."

"There is only one flaw with that plan," said Holmes. "Twelve camels minus eight former soldiers equals only four camels for your party of eight."

Belmont nodded grimly. "Precisely, Mr. Holmes. When Colonel Egerton pointed this out to Tippy Tilly, the man shrugged his shoulders and said something which sounded like '*mafeesh*.'[54] He indicated that one of them was old, and in any case there were plenty more women if we ever got back to Egypt! He then actually suggested that Miss Adams, her aunt, and my wife would not come to any hurt, as they would be placed in the harem of the Khalifa! Can you imagine such a disregard for womankind, Mr. Holmes?"

Holmes merely nodded silently, so the man continued. "Of course, Colonel Egerton refused to consider such a plan and the two men argued for some time. Finally, the Colonel promised to increase the reward up to three hundred pounds each, which seemed to do the trick. Unfortunately, during all of this negotiation, a patrol of Dervishes returned from the desert with a report that the Egyptian Camel Corps was not very far off, or so I judged by the great fuss that they were making to the two Emirs. Sadly, this news scuttled our scheme and promptly led to the attempted conversion by the Moolah, where Mr. Fardet did his best to buy us time. Ultimately, he was unsuccessful, and the Emirs made the decision to proceed to Khartoum with just the ladies. I protested vigorously again this separation, but I was quite weak from privation, and two strong Arabs held me by each elbow."

"The account of Mr. Stephens suggests that you were given a chance to go with your wife and the American ladies, but declined?"

The man shrugged. "Share and share alike. All sink or all swim, and the devil take the flincher."

"But you drew the short splinter?"

"Yes, though Colonel Egerton offer to give me his place. He said that he had neither wife nor child, and hardly any friend in the world."

"You still refused?"

"Indeed! An agreement is an agreement. It's all fair play, and the prize to the luckiest. The old Emir had ridden off with the vanguard. The Moolah and about a dozen Dervishes surrounded us. They had not mounted their camels, for they were prepared to be the ministers of death. Mr. Stephens, Monsieur Fardet, and I understood as we looked upon their faces that the sand was running very low in the glass of our lives. Our hands were still bound, but our guards had ceased to hold us. We turned round, all three of us, and said good-bye to the women upon the camels. I recall how my wife was sobbing convulsively, with her face between her hands.

"Once the Colonel and the women were gone from sight past the edge of the oasis, the Arabs closed round Stephens, Fardet, and I. But surely Mr. Stephens account tells of how Tippy Tilly and his men shot the men planning to murder us? I will never forget how, even in death, the malicious eye of the Moolah stared at us. I was most glad to see his grizzled beard splattered with his life's blood."

"And after your rescue, anything else of note?" asked Holmes.

Belmont considered this for a minute. "I remember vividly

sitting on the steamer which was carrying us back to the Continental Hotel in Cairo. It was very soothing and restful up there on the saloon deck, with no sound but the gentle lipping of the water as it rippled against the sides of the steamer. The red after-glow was in the western sky, and it mottled the broad, smooth river with crimson. Dimly, I could discern the tall figures of herons standing upon the sand-banks, and farther off the line of riverside date-palms glided past us in a majestic procession. Once more the silver stars were twinkling out, the same clear, placid, inexorable stars to which my weary eyes had been so often upturned during the long nights of our desert martyrdom. We spoke of not losing sight of each other. Miss Eliza Adams invited us to visit the United States, and my wife laughed at the thought of such a long voyage. I said that we must all meet again, if only to talk our adventures over once more. I thought it would be easier in a year or two, as at the time we were still too near to them."

"And have you all met up?" asked Holmes.

Belmont shook his head mournfully. "No. I find that even though over two years have gone past, the thoughts are still too painful. Do you know that this was my first trip to Bisley since we returned to Ireland, Mr. Holmes? I was afraid to leave my wife alone, as if Bray was about to be suddenly overrun with marauders." He laughed, but there was no joy in it. "I tell you this, Mr. Holmes. For the last two years, I have believed that entire tragedy to have been nothing more than a terrible happenstance of Fate. If you tell me otherwise, I shall personally ensure that the person responsible pays for his crimes."

§

The study Irishman had been seen out, and was even now back on his way home via the rocking rails of the London and North Western Railway line. Holmes indicated that there was nothing more for us to accomplish this evening, so I retired after a long day of journeying to the West Midlands and back.

When I arose the following morning, I found Holmes already situated in his armchair, where he was studying some official-appearing documents. In response to my quizzical look, he noted that they were the Government's inquiry into the matter, which he obtained through the offices of his brother.

"Anything of importance?" I inquired.

He shrugged. "Not much. Though I will note that Colonel Egerton lost his boots in the desert and was forced to resort to wearing puttees."

I laughed. "They may look like bandages, but we found in India that those long strips of cloth were the best support to the leg while marching. Surely you are not suggesting that a long-lost cousin of the Colonel's absconded with his boots in order to set a glowing jackal upon his track?"

My friend's lips pursed as he glanced at me. "You are in a rather pawky mood this morning, Watson," said Holmes, turning his attention to the morning editions.

Shortly after I had breakfasted, there appeared at Baker Street a long telegram from Paris which seemed to only increase the mystery surrounding the events which occurred to the passengers of the *Korosko*. After Holmes had finished reading it, he handed the message to me:

> *Monsieur Holmes –*
>
> *I have received your note. There may have been accusations flung against the good name of Octave Fardet. But let me set the record straight.*
>
> *Perhaps I was premature in my supposition that the Dervishes were an invention of Lord Cromer in the year 1885.*[55] *I am not too proud to admit it.*
>
> *You may have heard that I was conspiring against the English with the American Headingly. This could not be farther from the truth. If only the poor man was alive to corroborate this. Instead, you must take my word as a gentleman in this matter.*

You may have heard that, upon our departure from the boat, I was whispering in French to the traitorous dragoman, but I assure you that – upon my honour – there was nothing to this.

You may have heard that I initially mistook the Dervishes for the Bedouins, such as the Ababdeh or Bishareen, who are known to be employed by the British Government upon the frontier. You may have heard that I stamped around in anger rather than seek cover behind the rocks with the other tourists. This is not a falsehood. For how else did the stinging wasp of the bullet prick my wrist? Sacre nom! You may have heard that Monsieur Headingly was struck down attempting to come to my aid. But did I ask for such a thing? No!

You may have heard that I attempted to bargain with the Baggara chief. That I said that I was a friend of the Khalifa. That I claimed my countrymen have never had a quarrel with the Khalifa and that his enemies are also ours. This is a bald-faced lie!

You may have heard that I sobbed when the perceived rescue instead was revealed to be the arrival of the Emir Abderrahman. If I happened to trip at that very moment and get sand in my eyes, who is there to argue otherwise? You may have heard that the villainous dragoman suggested that we allow the fat, little man – he who had a name among them for converting the infidel and a great pride in it – to bring us into the Mohammedan faith. Was it not Fardet who suggested that we debate with the priest? And when the Irishman suggested that Colonel Egerton pretend to be interested in the priest's religion, was it not Fardet who laughed at the notion? For like most of his countrymen, the Colonel is very wanting in sympathy for the ideas of other people. It is the great fault of the English. There was no possibility that the Colonel could act well enough to deceive such a man as this priest. This task could only fall to Fardet. For I am

THE GATHERING GLOOM

equally interested in all creeds. When I ask for information, it is because in verity I desire it, and not because I am playing a part.

You may have heard that I put my hand to the Colonel's throat when he mocked my anger over the arrival of additional Dervishes. For this, I may only plead that my temper had gotten a bit frayed and thin. Fortunately for him, Monsieur's Belmont and Stephens pulled me off him before I could cause any real harm to the old fellow. For his Upham's dye was wearing off and his grey hairs were returning.

You may have heard that I sat moodily and refused to speak to the Moolah. Of course, Mrs. Belmont alone understood my true nature and that I am incapable of abandoning a lady. Therefore, was it not Fardet who dazzled the Moolah with his ingenuity? Was I not the man who was strongly attracted to the Moolah's faith, and yet has one single remaining shred of doubt? Even as the Moolah countered, was there not always some other stubborn little point which prevented my absolute acceptance of the faith of Islam? Did I not mix my questions with so many personal compliments to the Moolah and self-congratulations that our band should have come under the teachings of so wise a man and so profound a theologian? Did not the hanging pouches under the Moolah's eyes quiver with his satisfaction? Was he not led happily and hopefully onwards from explanation to explanation, while the blue overhead turned to violet, and the green leaves to black, until the great serene stars shone out once more between the crowns of the palm-trees?

Was it not Fardet who staved off the Moolah for a critical five minutes longer with my conjuring tricks? Did this not bring a deep hum of surprise from the ring of watching Arabs? If only my wrist had not been injured, I may have single-handedly saved the day, but alas, I was in-

stead struck down by a spear shaft for my efforts. Who else, I ask you, could have done more?

And perhaps it would have worked, if not for the impractical and obstinate nature of the Irish. Mon Dieu! For was it not the Belmonts who dropped to their knees in prayer and embarrassed the Moolah before his Emirs? And then voila! It was like the camels – one down, all down. For both of the American ladies fell to their knees beside them. Was ever anything so absurd, I ask you?

And then, was it not Fardet who agreed to join his companions on his knees even though he cared not a while for any foolish creed? Sapristi! Did they suppose that a Frenchman would be afraid of them? I myself have no belief in survival after death. My friends in Paris chuckled when they heard that I had almost laid down my life for the Christian faith. To this day, I alternate between gusts of laughter and fury at the thought of how the whims of Fate almost snuffed out the fire of my life.

And when the Dervish chief wished to know which of the four men was the richest, so as to be worth keeping for the ransom, was it not Fardet who suggested that it should be Monsieur Belmont? And when that stubborn man would not go, nor Stephens or Colonel Egerton, was it not Fardet who pointed out the foolishness of allowing the ladies to be carried off alone, and that it surely would be far better than one of us should be with them to advise them? Finally, was it not Fardet who graciously did not insist upon an apology from Colonel Egerton after he left us to die?

You ask, Monsieur, how I spend my days? I spent it petitioning the fools at the Rue du Faubourg to address forthwith the remissness of the British Government in not taking a more complete control of the Egyptian frontier, as we French have done in Algiers.[56]

Please accept, Monsieur Holmes, the expression of my highest consideration,

Octave Fardet
Café Cubat

"What do you make of it, Watson?" asked Holmes, when I had finished.

"He appears to be the epitome of an excitable Frenchman. He seems to bear some antipathy to Colonel Egerton. And there is a strain of defensiveness throughout, which makes me wonder what Fardet is hiding? Perhaps my early supposition was accurate?"

Holmes shook his head. "I cannot agree with you, Watson. Monsieur Fardet tells us many things, but if my theory is correct, only one of his comments is germane."

"Which one?"

Instead of answering, Holmes posed a question. "Here is a pretty puzzle, Watson. Five men, each of whom experienced the same events, and yet, each with a different interpretation of what transpired that day. For Mr. Stephens, a dry recitation of the most basic facts, with little to suggest that the experience changed him, other than gaining him a wife. For Reverend Stuart, the Dervishes were little more than the active hands of a higher power, challenging him to perform more good deeds in the future. For Mr. Belmont, the experience was a personal failure, one in which his greatest powers were unable to keep his wife safe from harm. Furthermore, he required rescue by external forces, which was achieved in no small part by the delaying tactics of the Frenchman and not by any actions by Belmont himself. Finally, for Monsieur Fardet, we have a man whose prior vision of the world was profoundly shaken, but whose monstrous pride imagines that he alone was the saviour of the captured party. Which interpretation is the accurate one? And do any of their observations suggest that a nefarious plan was to blame for their tragedy?"

"You said 'five' men, Holmes. That is only four."

"Ah, yes, but there is also the sworn testimony of Colonel Egerton. It is a brief and concise document, which little contradicts the others, though there are pertinent elements which I believe to be missing. And in order to get to the bottom of this, I believe we must pay him a visit." Holmes glanced at his pocket-watch. "It is now past ten o'clock. Do you think, Watson, that the Colonel will have already entrenched himself at his club?"

§

The hansom cab rolled down the long-drawn hum of Pall Mall and dropped us off outside the Venetian-style domicile of the Army and Navy Club. We had stopped along the way long enough for Holmes to dash into a chemist's shop, but when he returned, he appeared to be empty-handed. My club membership allowed us passage within, and thus we strode into the richly ornamented hall past the Crimean stained glass. A word with one of the footmen pointed us in the direction of the house dining-room. We found Colonel Egerton taking supper at a little round table opposite to the bust of Nelson. He was a sun-darkened, straight, aquiline man, with a courteously deferential manner, but a steady, questioning eye. He wore a grizzled military moustache, and his hair was singularly black for a man of his years. His dress was neat and I could tell that he was precise in his habits.

After Holmes introduced us, the man nodded and waved to the chairs across from him. "Would you care to join me for a hock and seltzer, gentlemen? No? Well, how may I be of service?"

"I have been retained, Colonel, to look into the matter of the *Korosko* deaths."

The man's eyebrows rose with interest. "Retained, you say? By whom?"

"Mr. James Stephens."

Egerton frowned. "What could the solicitor possibly want to know at this late date? There have been inquiries. The matter is closed."

"So you believe it to have been a simple accident?"

"Of course," said he, with a shrug. "Tour groups were going out to that damned rock every week. The Dervishes were sure to have heard of it. They must have decided that they could easily gather up some hostages in order to help finance their cruel regime. And they were almost right, if not for the swift actions of Captains Archer and Hamilton."

"But you do not believe that a member of the party that day arranged for the Dervishes to be present?"

The man snorted derisively. "That is preposterous! To what end? And only a fool would take such a horrible risk. We all came within a hair of shuffling off this mortal coil."

"An excellent point, Colonel. I wonder if you would you care to peruse Mr. Stephens' recollections of the events in question?" Holmes had taken the manila envelope out of his coat pocket.

"Certainly, if it would help in some fashion." Egerton took the envelope and proceeded to skim through the pages. When he was finished, he slid it back across the table to Holmes. "It is an accurate account, though it reveals the bricked up nature of Stephens' soul. To think to reduce such an horrific adventure to a dry little list, as if it were a legal briefing!"

"Are there any points upon which you wish to expound?"

The Colonel considered this. "How much time do you have, Mr. Holmes? There are many tableaus which come to mind. For instance, of all the pictures which have been burned into my brain, there is none so clear as that of Reverend Stuart, his large face shining with perspiration, and his great body dancing about with unwieldy agility, as he struck at the shrinking, snarling savages upon the top of Abousir.

"Or how, after the terrible lottery when I was led away with the women, I could not at the time understand why the throats of my companions had not been already cut? I wondered if it were that, with a refinement of cruelty, the rearguard would wait until the Camel Corps were closer, so that the warm bodies of their victims might be an insult to the pursuers? No doubt that was the right explanation. I had head of such a trick before."

"Where was that?"

The man waved his hand indifferently. "I am afraid that I don't recall the details, Mr. Holmes. One hears many stories around this club."

"Of course," said Holmes, evenly. "One item which was not included in the accounts of Mr. Stephens or Mr. Belmont was the fate of the old Egyptian gunner. What was his name?"

"Tippy Tilly."

"Surely that was not his real name? I believe that was merely his attempt to say 'Egyptian Artillery' in a tongue not his own, was it not?"

"You are correct, Mr. Holmes. I believe his real name is Athon Deng. He is a member of the Dinka tribe."

"And is he now a Bimbashi?"

The Colonel smiled wanly. "Of course not. He is a now a Shawish, and he and his men certainly got the money which they were promised. However, I was unable to convince the Sirdar that Deng – who could barely speak English – was officer material."[57]

Holmes nodded. "You were the only person to witness the death of Mr. Brown, were you not?" he asked, switching topics.

"That is correct."

"Are they any details you would care to share? The other accounts are rather sparse."

The man shrugged. "There is little more to tell. During one of the brief stops, I had strolled over this nearest crest, and had found a group of camels in the hollow beyond, with a little knot of angry, loud-voiced men beside them. Brown was at the centre of the group. He looked pale and heavy-eyed, with his upturned, spiky moustache and listless manner. They had searched his pockets before, but now they were determined to tear off all his clothes in the hope of finding something which he had secreted. A hideous man with silver bangles in his ears, grinned and jabbered in the young diplomat's impassive face.

There seemed to be something heroic and almost inhuman in that calm, and those abstracted eyes. Brown's coat was already open, and his assailant's great black paw flew up to his neck and tore his shirt down to the waist. And at the sound of that rip, and at the abhorrent touch of those coarse fingers, Brown, who I had thought was nothing more than a man about town and a finished product of the modern era, suddenly dropped his life-traditions and became a savage facing a savage. His face flushed, his lips curled back, he chattered his teeth like an ape, and his eyes – those indolent eyes which had always twinkled so placidly – were gorged and frantic. Brown threw himself upon the Dervish, and struck him again and again, feebly but viciously, in his broad, black face. He hit like a girl, round arm, with an open palm. The Dervish winced away for an instant, appalled by this sudden blaze of passion. Then with an impatient, snarling cry, he slid a knife from his long loose sleeve and struck upwards under the whirling arm. Brown sat down at the blow and began to cough – as a man coughs who has choked at dinner, furiously, ceaselessly, spasm after spasm. Then the angry red cheeks turned to a mottled pallor, there were liquid sounds in his throat, and, clapping his hand to his mouth, he rolled over on to his side. The Dervish, with a brutal grunt of contempt, slid his knife up his sleeve once more. I frantically attempted to come to Brown's aid, but was seized by the bystanders and dragged away."

"And the man who killed Mr. Brown? Surely he was not part of Athon Deng's party."

"Of course not. He was an Arab."

"So you do not have a favourable impression of the Arabs?"

"I am not a rich man," answered Colonel Egerton, after a brief pause, "but I am prepared to lay all I am worth that within three years of British troops being withdrawn from Egypt, the Dervishes will be upon the Mediterranean. What would happen to the civilization of Egypt then? Where would be the hundreds of millions of pounds which have been invested in that country? Where would be the monuments which all nations look upon as most precious memorials of the past?"

"You think that the Dervishes would attempt to destroy the pyramids and other monuments?" I asked.

"You cannot foretell what they would do, Doctor. There is no iconoclast in the world like an extreme Mohammedan. Last time they overran that country they burned the Alexandrian Library.[58] You know that all representations of human features are against the letter of the Koran. A statue is always an irreligious object in their eyes. What do these fellows care for the sentiment of Europe? The more they could offend it, the more delighted they would be. Down would go the Sphinx, the Colossi, the Statues of Abou-Simbel – just as all the saints went down in England before the troopers of that monster in human form – Oliver Cromwell."

Holmes nodded. "So, you believe, Colonel, that England is justified in being the order-keepers of the uncivilized areas of the world?"

"Of course! I think that behind national interests and diplomacy and all that there lies a great guiding force – a Providence, in fact – which is forever getting the best out of each nation and using it for the good of the whole. When a nation ceases to respond, it is time that she went into hospital for a few centuries, like Spain or Greece – the virtue has gone out of her. A man or a nation is not placed upon this earth to do merely what is pleasant and what is profitable. We are often called upon to carry out what is both unpleasant and unprofitable, but if it is obviously right, then it is mere shirking not to undertake it."

"But surely other countries have a role in policing the outbreaks of madness in the world?" asked Holmes.

The Colonel shook his head. "I believe that each country has its own mission, Mr. Holmes. Germany is predominant in abstract thought; France in literature, art, and grace. But we have among our best men a higher conception of moral sense and public duty than is to be found in any other people. Now, these are the two qualities which are needed for directing a weaker race. You can't help them by abstract thought or by graceful art, but only by that moral sense which will hold the scales of Justice even, and keep itself free from every taint of corruption. That is how we rule India. We came there by a kind of natural law, like air rushing into a vacuum. All over the world, against our direct interests and our deliberate intentions, we are drawn into the same thing."

"There are men in Parliament who do not share your opinion, Colonel."

"Fools all!" said Egerton heatedly, before emitting a long sigh. "The world is small, and it grows smaller every day, Mr. Holmes. It's a single organic body, and one spot of gangrene is enough to taint the whole. There's no room upon it for dishonest, defaulting, tyrannical, irresponsible Governments. As long as they exist they will always be sources of trouble and of danger. But there are many races which appear to be so incapable of improvement that we can never hope to get a good Government out of them. What is to be done, then? The former device of Providence in such a case was extermination by some more virile stock – an Attila or a Tamerlane pruned off the weaker branch. Now, we have a more merciful substitution of rulers, or even of mere advice from a more advanced race. That is the case with the Central Asian Khanates and with the protected States of India. If the work has to be done, and if we British are the best fitted for the work, then I think that it would be a cowardice and a crime to dodge it."

"There are those who would ask who gets to decide when a country has a fitting case for independence?"

"Events – inexorable, inevitable events – will decide it, Mr. Holmes. Take this Egyptian business as an example. In 1881, there was nothing in this world further from the minds of our people than any interference with Egypt; and yet the year 1882 left us in possession of the country. There was never any choice in the chain of events. A massacre in the streets of Alexandria, and the mounting of guns to drive out our fleet – which was there, you understand, in fulfilment of solemn treaty obligations – led to the bombardment. The bombardment led to a landing in order to save the city from destruction. The landing caused an extension of operations – and here we are, with the country upon our hands. At the time of trouble we begged and implored the French, or anyone else, to come and help us to put the thing to rights, but they all deserted us when there was work to be done, although they, like that fool Fardet, are ready enough to scold and to impede us now.

"And just when we tried to get out of Egypt, up came this wild Dervish movement, and we had to sit tighter than ever. We never wanted the task; but, now that it has come, we must put it through in a workmanlike manner. We've brought justice into the country, and purity of administration, and protection for the poor man. It has made more advances in the last twelve years than since the Moslem invasion in the seventh century. Excepting the pay of a couple of hundred men, who spend their money in the country, England has neither directly nor indirectly made a shilling out of it, and I don't believe you will find in history a more successful and more disinterested bit of work."

Holmes smiled. "I agree with you, sir. I have also considered the possibility that Monsieur Fardet was working with the Khalifa with an aim of discrediting the colonial aspirations of England," said Holmes. I looked over at him in surprise at this statement, but Holmes' gaze was fixed upon the man across the table. "Do not forget that the Khedivate of Egypt was under the influence of France until our victory at Tel El Kebir."[59]

Colonel Egerton appeared interested. "What makes you think that?"

"There are several reasons. One, his strenuous denial of the existence of the Dervishes is too absurd to be credible. Could any man truly believe that the British empire pays to keep its troops in Egypt for no reason at all? Two, what was the man's first action when you encountered the Arab band?"

The Colonel spoke slowly. "He shouted: '*Vive le Khalifa! Vive le Madhi!*'"

"Precisely," said Holmes. "And then he utilized the dragoman Mansoor to converse with the chief. He said he was a friend of the Khalifa, did he not?"

The Colonel shook his head. "But Fardet was struck down and the Emir threatened to feed him to the dogs if he was not silent."

"I ask you, Colonel, could it have all been an act?"

"Impossible! The man was shot."

"Was he?"

"What do you mean?"

"Did you personally inspect his wound?"

"Well, no."

"I assure you, Colonel, that the Borjois company of Paris long ago perfected the art of compounding an artificial blood for use upon the stage."

"I cannot believe that."

"No? Well, I do not insist upon it. It is possible that his wrist was hit by accident. Surely a bullet aimed to miss him could have simply ricocheted off of a rock?"

The Colonel pursed his lips and nodded slowly. "I will have to ponder your words, Mr. Holmes. I wish to review my memories of the entire event, to see if there is anything else which supports your theory."

"It may interest you, Colonel, to learn that I received a telegram from Monsieur Fardet this very morning. Of course, he failed to confess to any such machinations."

"So will you go to Paris to interrogate him?" the Colonel inquired.

"Perhaps," said Holmes. "Though there is one other individual whose motives for being aboard that cruise are also suspect. And they are situated a bit closer."

"Who?"

"Can you not think of anyone?"

The Colonel shrugged. "I hate to think ill of any man."

"What of a woman?" asked Holmes, severely.

He frowned and considered this. "Not Mrs. Schlesinger!" he exclaimed.

"And why not? What do you know of her?"

"Well, very little, I suppose. She mainly kept to herself."

"Yes, that would be an effective cover," said Holmes.

"Surely you don't think that she was some sort of spy?" said Egerton, an appalled look upon his face.

"I cannot say for certain. I have not yet questioned her, as I wished to hear your impressions first, Colonel. But there are indications. One, her name is German. Two, despite bringing a nurse to watch her child, Mrs. Schlesinger still kept to herself and seemed strangely indifferent to the ancient monuments which typically account for the primary purpose of such a tourist cruise. Three, she and her daughter were the only member of the *Korosko* party who suffered no privations at the hands of the Dervishes. Was their painless escape an act of good fortune, or a cleverly staged exit?"

Colonel Egerton nodded slowly. "Your logic is quite profound, Mr. Holmes. Surely the German Government is quite interested in our defence plans for the Suez Canal. And why would they also not be interested in our plans for the Soudan? For is it not the path straight to German East Africa? Which in turn is the only colony standing between the British Empire stretching in a continuous line from Alexandria to Cape Town? To think that they would be so bold as to send a lone woman and child to be their spies!"

"Bold indeed," said Holmes with a smile. I, for one, however, was baffled by the direction the conversation had taken. First Holmes blamed the Frenchman, and now he was considering the idea of German spies being responsible for the *Korosko* tragedy. He must have learned something in the official inquiry which, with his customary penchant for the dramatic, he failed to disclose to me.

"So you will question her next?" asked Egerton.

"That is my intention. Though, if my suspicions are incorrect, it would hardly be seemly for me to do so without a friendly face being present."

"Oh! Do you wish for me to accompany you?" inquired the Colonel.

Holmes chuckled. "No, sir. I was thinking of someone of a more feminine persuasion. Mrs. Belmont is in Dublin, which is, of course, rather far to be practical at the moment. Miss Eliza Adams is across the entire Atlantic, and I doubt she will again soon stir far from the comforts of Commonwealth Avenue. So, I have taken the liberty of asking Miss Sadie to escort me."

"Ah!" said the man. He removed a silver case from his coat pocket and offered a cigarette to Holmes and I. We both declined. I noticed that his hand shook slightly as he struck a wax vesta and lit one for himself. He leaned back in his chair and drew in the fragrant smoke. "A wise choice. Miss Adams is a breath of fresh air. She could see the joy and laughter in any occasion."

Holmes suddenly changed the subject. "I wonder, Colonel, had you been out to Egypt before the *Korosko* cruise?"

" 'Fraid not, Mr. Holmes. I spent most of my career in India. After the British Government decided that I had reached a point where I was incapable of further service, I have amused myself by travelling about. I shot lions in Somaliland, and explored the Atlas Mountains in Morocco."

"So you were not in Alexandria in 1882 after the bombardment put down the massacre in its streets?"

"No," said Egerton, firmly.

"But surely you have spent time there?"

"Not really."

"Enough time to appreciate the especial handiwork of Ionides."

The man's eyes narrowed. "What do you mean?"

Holmes smiled. "I have trained myself to recognize the distinctive features of over one hundred and forty different brands of cigar or cigarette. The one you hold in your hand was hand-rolled by a man in Alexandria."

The Colonel cleared his throat and hummed and stammered. "Yes, well, I did pass through Alexandria on my way to Cairo, of course. I always seek out the best tobacconist in every city I visit."

"But you never served with Hicks Pasha?"

"No."

"Surely though, you have an opinion of the man?"

Egerton shrugged. "Of course. He was the soul of bravery. Sent by a gaggle of fools with a worthless army across a waterless waste in order to attack a force four times his in size. And yet, he went. Magnificent."

"Most of his men were killed, I understand."

"That is an understatement, Mr. Holmes. Hicks led ten thousand men to El Obeid. Only three hundred returned. One was the General's cook, who said that Hicks was the last officer to fall, pierced by the spear of the Khalifa."

"And his head was taken to the Madhi as a trophy."

"Savages," said the man, with a growl.

"It may surprise you to learn, Colonel, that I too have been to the Soudan," said Holmes.

"Oh, yes?" The colonel's eyebrows rose with interest.

"I once paid a visit to the Khalifa himself in Khartoum."

"And you lived to tell the tale?" said Egerton, the admiration in his voice plain.

"I was in disguise, of course. I got the idea from Burton, though my explorations were less geographical and rather more related to reconnoitring the region's defences. I hesitate to boast, however – since we are amongst friends – I can confidently claim that without my intelligence, Lord Kitchener's victories at Ferkeh and Dongola would not have come so easily."[60]

Colonel Egerton nodded appreciatively. "You have done your country a great service, Mr. Holmes."

"Thank you, Colonel," said Holmes, with a smile. He then turned to me. "I believe, Watson, that the answer to the question posed by Mr. Stephens lies in the remarkable allusions

Colonel Egerton made to those campaigns in which he once distinguished himself. Do you remember what Mr. Stephens told us about them?"

I considered this for a moment. "But, Holmes, the Colonel made no such allusions."

"That is what was so remarkable, Watson. It is a most natural tendency, when in such pleasant company, to make much of your past exploits. Unless, of course, there is some strong reason to be more reticent." He turned his gaze back to Egerton. "Is there such a reason, Colonel?"

The man was frowning, and his eyes blazed. "Let us just say, sir, that my campaigns date back to such early Victorian days that I have had to sacrifice my military glory at the shrine of my perennial youth."

"Ah, indeed!" exclaimed Holmes. "You first saw action at the retreat from Kabul, did you not? So says your official record."

The man's eyes narrowed. "That is correct."

"The Massacre of Elphinstone's army occurred in 1842. Therefore, if you had been eighteen at the time, you must have been born in 1824."

"Your mathematical skills are impeccable, sir," said Colonel Egerton, acidly. "What is your point?"

"After I departed Khartoum, I spent some time recuperating at the Winter Palace Hotel in Luxor. I established numerous contacts up and down the Nile. It was from one of them that I managed to obtain the evidence of Captain Archer, of the Egyptian Camel Corps, as given before the secret Government inquiry at Cairo."

"I am certain that Captain Archer's testimony in no way contradicts my own."

"Indeed. Though, he had several interesting observations, Colonel. For one, he noted that when he first came upon you, he did not recognize you. He said, and I quote, that it was as if 'the spruce, hale old solider he knew seemed to have been pounced upon by old age.'"

"That's right," cried the Colonel, testily. "You try a few days with the Dervishes, and see if your friends will recognize you!"

"He also noted that you had lost three inches in the desert."

"My boots were stolen from me."

"Yes, I noted that. Three inches makes for a rather tall heel, do they not?"

"What business of that is yours?" the man exclaimed. He then paused and visibly mastered himself. "I apologize, gentlemen. I have been told that my Indian service left me with a curried-prawns temper, and that my time in the Libyan desert added an extra touch of cayenne."

Holmes smiled. "Most understandable, Colonel. However, risers are the not the only concession to your advancing years, are they? There is also the small matter of the stays you wear in order to maintain your erect posture, as noted by Mr. Belmont. And then there is this," said Holmes, taking a small black bottle with a pink 'Upham's' label from his pocket and setting it upon the table between us. "This is the dye you utilize in order to keep your hair that glossy black colour, as noted by Monsieur Fardet."

Colonel Egerton frowned. "My friends say that I have a young man's heart and a young man's spirit, so that if I wish to keep a young man's colour also, is it not very unreasonable after all?"

"It is if it leads you to murder," said Holmes, severely.

"What do you mean?" the man barked.

"Mr. Belmont mentioned that you had been on a camel before. Reverend Stuart told us about the Dervishes standing upon their sheepskin, a ritual whose meaning he learned from you, Colonel. And where in turn would you have learned it, if not in Egypt?"

The right side of the man's mouth curled up with a sneer. "They have camels in the Nubra Valley of India." He waved his hand about the club. "And look around you, Mr. Holmes. If you spend an hour in here, you are bound to hear a few tales."

Holmes smiled back at him. "Of course. But these little discrepancies were sufficient to induce me to look up your records. You did, in fact, serve with Hicks Pasha at Sennar. Where I suspect that you became familiar with the gunner Athon Deng."

Egerton shrugged. "Is serving under Colonel Hicks a crime?"

"Not in and of itself. But I am curious as to the reason for your reticence about such matters, Colonel? One might think you have something to hide. Perhaps such as conspiring with Athon Deng to bring a small force of Dervishes to the Abousir rock?"

"Preposterous!" the man barked. "Why ever would I do such a thing?"

"Because you planned to fend off the feigned attack, most likely by taking command over the Zouave soldiers. Your mastery of the dangerous situation would have earned you the profound admiration of your companions, and Miss Sadie would have learned to turn to you as a lady naturally turns to her protector. Perhaps this would induce such a young woman to see past your advanced years and develop emotions which she might mistake as love."

"I don't know what you are talking about," said the Colonel, his voice hoarse with feeling.

"No? Were you unaware that Miss Sadie Adams is no more? Or are you simply unwilling to accept the fact that she is now Mrs. Sadie Stephens? But your plan went awry when Deng's superior, the Emir Ali Wad Ibrahim, found out about it. Wad Ibrahim must have seen this as an opportunity to effortlessly capture some hostages for ransom. However, when he in turn told the sterner, more fanatical Emir Abderrahman, the latter decided that you were only worth keeping if you were to forcibly convert to his faith. In this fashion, a simple melodrama turned into a disaster when Mr. Headingly was shot and killed."

"No," said the man, violently shaking his head. "You are wrong."

"And what of Mr. Brown?" continued Holmes, his tone inexorable. "Did he suspect your involvement with the Dervishes?

Is that why you had him killed?"

"No!" cried Colonel Egerton. "I had nothing to do with that! The damned man angered the bloody Dervishes!"

"I have cabled to Egypt, Colonel. Athon Deng would not confess, but the fellahin Mehemet Ali was much more forthcoming. He is still rather annoyed that you broke your promise to make him a Bimbashi."

The man's gaze dropped to his lap. He shook his head, as if in disbelief. "It was an accident. No one was meant to be harmed."

"And what of the dragoman Mansoor? He was hung upon your testimony. I suspect that he was your intermediary between Halfa and the Dervish post at Akasheh. But he suffered mightily in the desert when the Emirs took over the attack. He was almost killed for his efforts. I am sure that he would have been more than happy to spread the tale that he was working under your orders. So you took steps to ensure his silence."

The man could only shake his head silently. All fight had gone out of him. The veins of his face were injected, and his features were shot with heavy wrinkles. He sat with his back hunched and his chin sunk upon his breast. Despite the early hour, I thought I detected a hint of white stubble beginning to obscure the firm, clean line of his chin and throat.

"You were wise to abandon Hicks before El Obeid," said Holmes.

Colonel Egerton looked up. All traces of the former brightness and alertness of his eyes had vanished. "Who says that I did? I was there, Mr. Holmes! I was the only European to escape that massacre! And when I finally made my way back to civilization, I found my youth had been dissipated. And what did I have to show for it? Only a modest pension and a life of solitude, save but a few other rapidly fading companions. I vowed at that time that I would not die alone."

He paused for a moment and took a sip from of his seltzer. "Aboard the boat from Cairo, Sadie's youth, her beauty, her intelligence and humour, all made me realize that she could at best only be expected to charitably endure me, unless something remarkable was to happen which would cast me in another light altogether. Could I trust to Fate to deliver such a challenge at the perfect time? Or should I create my own Destiny? You know, Mr. Holmes, which path I took." He shook his head. "It is not my fault that it did not go precisely as intended. Napoleon once said that no plan survives contact with the enemy."

"The general may plan the battle, Colonel, but when it fails, he must also take the responsibility. Instead, you sought to cover up your crimes."

Instead of answering, he looked over at me. "You served, Doctor?"

I nodded. "Maiwand."

He smiled. "Then you know what it is like. Long days marching under a merciless foreign sun. Desperate battles against a merciless foe. All of my friends lay forever under distant soil. As they fell, one by one, I wondered why Fate had desired that I alone should survive. Perhaps the Universe heard my secret wish. For I always had an idea that I should like to die in a real, good, yellow London fog. Though it now seems as if a piece of me – perhaps the only good piece – died in Egypt, when I asked Mansoor to contact Deng. What is left," he said, gesturing to his chest, "is but a pitiful remnant."

"You will have to accompany us to Scotland Yard now, Colonel," said Holmes.

"Yes, I suppose so," said the man, shaking his head slowly. "Would you give me a moment, Mr. Holmes, to bring my affairs into order?"

"You will make no attempt to escape?"

"I give you my word as a gentleman that I shall not leave the club."

"Very well. We shall wait for you on the pavement."

I followed Holmes out to St. James's Square. We stood there for about three minutes before a shot rang out from within the building.

"Ah," said Holmes, softly. I quickly turned, intending to rush back inside, but he laid a restraining hand upon my shoulder. "There is nothing you can do, Watson," said he, with a sad shake of his head. "I doubt that the Colonel would have made an incomplete work of it. I wondered if he would actually face a tribunal, or if his colossal pride would force him to fall on his sword. It seems we now know the answer."

He turned his back to the club and hailed a hansom. However, I stared back inside the cool passageway for a moment, even though I could not actually see Colonel Egerton in the darkness beyond. I knew that, for once, Sherlock Holmes was wrong. It was not pride which had led to his downfall, rather it was the fatal fire of yearning which had burned deep within the breast of Colonel Cyril Egerton.

§

THE ADVENTURE OF THE AWAKENED SPIRIT

It was a dark and stormy afternoon in early November when an uncommon client called upon my friend, Mr. Sherlock Holmes, asking for help of a most peculiar nature. The new century was almost a year old, though upon the day in question both Holmes and I were feeling like relics of a more ancient era. Holmes was listlessly drawing a bow across the strings of his violin, while I was rather drowsy and dreamy, an old tale by Mr. Irving resting upon my breast. Our repose was shattered when the bell announced a visitor.

I glanced over at Holmes. "Undoubtedly a new client," I opined.

His heavy dark brows rose, and a glimmer of interest appeared in his suddenly sharp, piercing grey eyes. "How can you tell, Watson?"

"Because Mrs. Hudson shut the door quickly. When it is a tradesman, she typically natters with them for a while."

"It might have been an express district messenger," said Holmes. "They rarely have time for small talk. Nothing less than attempted murder will keep the London message-boy from speeding upon his way."

I shook my head. "I heard someone enter. A messenger would not have done so."

"It might be a friend of mine?"

"Except that you have none. In the almost twenty years of our partnership, I can count upon one hand how many social visitors you have received."

He snorted in wry amusement. "You may have missed a few during those times when you deserted our little suite at Baker Street. But, very well… it might be one of Mrs. Hudson's cronies?"

"That is highly improbable, Holmes."

I had the rare opportunity to witness a look of confusion upon Holmes' face. "Why ever not?"

"Because I had a conversation with her at tea, and she specifically noted that she was planning upon a quiet evening with her knitting. She would not have made such a claim if she was expecting the visit of an acquaintance."

Holmes threw back his head and laughed. "Well, even if the case turns out to be a dull one, I have our visitor to thank for your rousing display of my methods at work."

"So you agree?"

"I do, Watson. However, your reasoning remains faulty."

"How so?"

"Pray tell, how do you know that it is not Lestrade or Gregson or some other perplexed member of the Yard?"

I considered this for a moment. "I suppose it could be."

He shook his head. "It is not."

"And how can you tell with such certainty?" I asked, puzzled.

"Because at this very moment I hear our visitor's tread upon our seventeen steps, and it is both distinct and unfamiliar. I would know the presence of Lestrade or Gregson long before they ever opened our door. The man who is about to enter shall be rather unusual. I would wager that he is tall, thin, and endowed with rather large feet."

As Holmes concluded, a knock upon the door was followed

by the entrance of a man who uncannily matched his prediction. He was tall, and exceedingly thin, with narrow shoulders, long arms and legs, and hands that appeared to dangle out of his sleeves, despite the fine cut to his suit and vest. Black leather shoes could not hide enormous flattened sole, and his whole frame seemed to loosely hang together. Contrastingly, his head was small and rather flat, with large ears, bulging brown eyes, and a long point of a nose.

Holmes welcomed the visitor inside and bade him take a seat in the basket chair. "I am Sherlock Holmes, and this is my friend and confidant, Dr John Watson. What can I do for you, sir?"

Once the man was settled, his face quivered with something which resembled fear. He had taken off his bowler hat and was nervously spinning it around by its brim. "My name is Peter Cannon. I come on behalf of my father-in-law, Sir Randolph Russell. Do you know him?"

Holmes shrugged, as if the name meant nothing to him.

"The celebrated jurist?" I interjected.

"The same," answered Cannon.

"Ah, yes," said Holmes. "I remember now. He heard the case of Patrick Cairns, did he not? I recall that the papers reported that he had been unusually lenient in the sentencing."

"Indeed," replied Mr. Cannon. "Sir Randolph rarely allows for a quality of mercy. His judgements on the High Court, while never unfair, are seen by some as harsh. Nevertheless, he is expected to soon rise to become Lord Chief Justice of the Queen's Bench."

"Indeed. I hope to never have to stand in his dock!" laughed Holmes. "And what problem of the Honourable Sir Randolph requires my humble services?" asked Holmes.

"The matter concerns Sir Randolph's home."

"Has it been burgled?" I asked, for I had seen nothing to that effect in the morning edition of *The Times*.

Cannon shook his head. "No. I wish it was as straightforward as that, Doctor. A theft we could simply bring before Scotland

Yard. I am afraid that the problem is rather more complex and peculiar than a mere burglary."

Holmes leaned forward, his interest piqued. "Pray tell, Mr. Cannon. I recommend you start at the beginning."

"Very well. Sir Randolph resides at No. 100, Barclay Square in Mayfair."[61]

"And you are staying with him temporarily upon your holiday from Cambridge?"

The man started in surprise. "How could you know that, Mr. Holmes?"

Holmes pointed to the man's hat. "Your bowler hat has a tag inside which plainly reads 'Ryder & Amies, Cambridge.' It would be a rare London gentleman who would travel to Cambridge simply for a hat which one could easily purchase at any haberdashery on Savile Row. Therefore, I presume that you live and work in Cambridge."

"I see. Very clever," said Cannon, nodding appreciatively. "You are correct, Mr. Holmes. I am a Professor of Philosophy. I was formerly at UCL, but received a Jacksonian Chair at King's eight years ago. However, Penelope and I pay a visit to Sir Randolph every year at this time in order to mark her birthday."

"And where is your wife now?" I asked.

The man appeared stricken and did not answer.

"Watson, it is plain that Mr. Cannon is a widower," interjected Holmes. "And from the location of that golden strand of hair upon your vest, I would estimate that his daughter is no more than ten years of age."

Our visitor composed his face and continued. "That is correct, Mr. Holmes. Penelope was born just over ten years ago. Tragically, my sainted wife Dorothy died shortly thereafter from puerperal fever."

"And the reason for your visit to us, Mr. Cannon? The house?" urged Holmes.

"Ah, yes. Well, the house came into Sir Randolph's possession some twenty years ago."

"Who owned it before that?" I asked.

Cannon shook his head. "It has changed hands several times, Dr Watson. I believe it was originally built by a former Premier, and after he died, it was occupied by an aged spinster. I am told that Sir Randolph bought it from an eccentric gentleman by the name of Thomas. The son of an MP, Mr. Thomas was something of a recluse. He was rarely seen in the neighbourhood, and typically opened the door of his room solely in order to receive food from his servant. At the end, Mr. Thomas was said to be fully mad, rambling about the house making strange sounds."

"I see," said Holmes, dryly. "And the current problem?"

"As you must know, two days ago was All Soul's Day.[62] We therefore visited Nunhead Cemetery. We decorated my wife's grave and lit candles. We brought some soul-cakes and had a bell rung in her memory. However, when that bell rung, I think something happened," he finished, an ominous tone in his voice.

"What?" I exclaimed.

"I believe, Doctor, that we set up a spiritual resonance. On that day – when the boundary between this world and the otherworld thinned – a gateway was opened."

"And what came through?" I asked, with morbid curiosity.

"The spirit of my deceased wife. It followed us home that afternoon."

Holmes sniffed dismissively. "Are you claiming that Sir Randolph's house is haunted?"

"That is correct," said Cannon, nodding eagerly. "However, I assure you, Mr. Holmes, that I am not the only one who believes this to be true. The house has long been considered to be a magnet for spirits."

"According to whom?" I asked.

"Well, Doctor. When you talk to the neighbours, you find that the stories go back to the first days of the house. The house is known for eerie noises, which primarily emanate from the attic room. I understand that many years ago, a young woman killed herself there. She flung herself from the window after being abused by a cruel step-father."

"Threw herself, or was thrown?" asked Holmes, with a grimace. "I am aware of similar tragedies."

Cannon shrugged. "I know nothing more of the matter, Mr. Holmes. Simply what the servants tell me. The young woman's spirit typically takes the form of a brown mist, though upon occasion it can materialize as a white figure."

"Fairy tales," said Holmes, waiving his hand dismissively.

"That is not what my father-in-law's friend, Lord Spencer, said after seeing the apparition himself."

"What happened?" I asked, eagerly.

"This was before I met Dorothy, of course. However, from what I hear, Lord Spencer was intrigued by the house's stories, so he asked permission of Sir Randolph to spend the night locked in the attic. He brought his fowling piece, and during the night, the other occupants of the house heard the gun fire once. In the morning, Lord Spencer appeared to be paralyzed with fear. Although he couldn't speak for days afterwards, there was no sign of anything else in the attic... save only the spent cartridge. Two years later, his health ruined, Lord Spencer hurled himself down the stairs of his London home and broke his neck."

Holmes raised his eyebrows speculatively. "It sounds like the man had a melancholy disposition."

Cannon shook his head again. "That is what Sir Randolph said. He hated the ghostly rumours, and wished to dispel them once and for all. Shortly before Dorothy and I became affianced, Sir Randolph convinced a friend in the Admiralty to loan him a contingent of sailors from the *HMS Bellerophon*. Twelve brave lads went into that attic, and by morning, one was dead. The poor boy had thrown open the door, and in a state of abject fear, tripped upon the stairs. His head was bashed in by the fall. The survivors noted that they had been aggressively approached in the night by the spirit of the madman, Mr. Thomas. They unanimously refused to ever set foot in the attic again, not for all the gold in Threadneedle Street."

THE GATHERING GLOOM

"These are old stories, Mr. Cannon," said Holmes. "However, you speak as if something has transpired recently?"

Our visitor nodded fretfully. "You are correct, Mr. Holmes. After the tragic incident of the sailor, it seemed that the ghosts' lust for blood had been sated. They passed on to the great Beyond. Nothing more was heard from the attic room for many years, save only the standard creaks and groans of an old house. And yet, two nights ago something changed. A ghost returned to the house."

"And you believe this to be the ghost of your deceased wife?"

"I do."

"Have you seen it yourself?"

"I have not, heavens be praised. I could not bear to look upon Dorothy's face again."

Holmes frowned. "Then how do you know that there is a ghost?"

"We began to hear noises. Sounds that could not be produced simply by an aging house."

"Such as?"

"Knocking upon the walls. Furniture moving. Chains rattling."

Holmes shrugged. "All easy to imitate."

"Perhaps," said Cannon, nodding in an unconvinced fashion. "But not the voices."

"Voices?" I asked, my interest aroused.

"Voices unlike anything you have ever heard before, Doctor. Deep and sonorous. Sometimes I think it's almost a song… but no earthly song. Only something that has passed to the Beyond could make such a noise."

Holmes sniffed. "And what, pray tell, is your exact question for me? Do you wish for me to perform an exorcism of some sort? I am a detective, not a priest."

Cannon shook his head. "No, Mr. Holmes. I simply wish for you to determine whether you are in fact able to prove a supernatural explanation, or whether this is some cruel fraud.

If the former, I need to do whatever I can in order to allow Dorothy to pass to her place of eternal rest. If the latter, I would know who is tormenting us so."

"And what does your father-in-law have to say about the matter?"

"Sir Randolph is most displeased, however, he is inclined to ignore the noises. It was with some reluctance that he first permitted me to hire Henry Worth to investigate the case."

Holmes frowned. "I believe that I am acquainted with all of my supposed rivals – both within London and without – however, the name Henry Worth is unfamiliar to me."

Cannon laughed nervously. "Oh, no, he is not a detective, Mr. Holmes. No, indeed. He is the Secretary of the Ghost Club."

"The what?" I exclaimed.

Holmes eyebrows rose with apparent interest. "I have heard of them, but to date have paid little heed to their activities, as they do not typically overlap with our purview." He turned to me. "Watson, if you could reach the G, we might see what they are all about."

Acceding to his request, I took down the index volume in question and handed it to Holmes. He placed a side pillow upon the table, and used this as an impromptu stand to facilitate his rapid scan through the wide and varied cases of his career.

"Genius loci," he read. "Gerard, the Gascony lieutenant. What a vain fool, that one! The German Master's murder. I have a memory that you wrote the case up, Watson, though the product was overly-romantic, as per your typical wont. Geyser of Craig. Terrible death, that! The Ghazi's shamshir. The Ghibelline code.[63] Here we are! Good old index. It will be many moons before someone invents a superior system. Listen up, Watson. Ghost Club. Founded 1855, Trinity College, Cambridge, in order to undertake practical investigations of spiritualist phenomena. Counted Charles Dickens as an early member, dissolved upon his death – though it seems that his spirit most unkindly refrained from coming back and assisting in their research, eh, Watson!" He chuckled at his little humour. "Re-launched 1882 by A.A. Watts and the Reverend Stainton Moses, in parallel with the Society for Psychical Research. The membership roster is a secret, however, the current iteration appears to operate from the 'Established Hypothesis.'"

"What do you mean by that, Holmes?"

"The empiricist, Watson, operates from the 'Null Hypothesis.' That something is not true, unless so proven. On the other hand, the Ghosties – as we shall call them – are already convinced that ghosts are a verified fact. This is a scientifically unsound method. They merely seek to try to convince others, and thus are no different than any other cult or religion."

"So, will you take the case, Mr. Holmes?" asked Cannon, pitifully.

Holmes smiled broadly. "You may be certain of it, sir. Please return to your father-in-law's house and tell him to expect us at eight o'clock tonight."

"You won't come straightaway?"

"No, Mr. Cannon, there is one stop to make first," said Holmes, shaking his head. "However, we shall see you soon, do not fear."

Holmes showed his new client to the door and then turned to me with a shrewd smile. "I presume you intend to accompany me, Watson?"

"I wouldn't miss it for the world! However, it sounds as if this ghost might prove to be dangerous, Holmes. You may need a weapon. There's something of the kind in the drawer at your right, if I recall correctly."

Holmes shook his head. "If Lord Spencer's fowling-piece was of little use, then my Webley revolver won't be either. No, I think my hunting-crop will prove to be sufficient for the matter at hand."

§

"Where are we headed, Holmes?" I asked, as we strolled along Baker Street in the direction of Marylebone Road. The Underground Station closest to us was shuttered for repairs to the platform, and his based on his refusal to hail a hansom cab, I was concerned that Holmes intended a long jaunt despite the dismal weather.

"There are times, Watson, when the great plethora of clubs in London astonishes me. There are political clubs, military clubs, clerical clubs, artist clubs, merchant clubs, adventurer clubs, clubs for the learned and the literary, and clubs for the dissolute. Even clubs for the unclubbable, such as my brother. And now, we shall visit one of the most peculiar of them all.... a club for the imaginary! According to the Index, we shall find it at No. 49 Marloes Road, Kensington."

"So you do not believe that there is any chance we will prove Sir Randolph's spirit to be real?"

"Do not be absurd, Watson. There's as much truth in ghosts as there is water in the Sahara. There will be a man behind all of this, mark my words."

He turned at the corner and led us into the Metropolitan Railway Underground entrance. Any further conversation was limited by the noise in the carriages. When we reached the High Street Kensington stop, Holmes motioned for us to disembark. From there, it was a brief walk to our destination, which I found to be an unremarkable, white-painted, terraced house. There was no sign or other marking to inform the average passer-by that it was the gathering place for individuals of a decidedly-spiritualist bent.

Holmes knocked upon the door, which was promptly opened by a footman. Holmes explained that he wished to speak to Mr. Worth, and we were promptly shown into the library.

The man in question was studying a book when we entered. Worth proved to be an elderly man, only a few years shy of seventy, unless I missed my guess. His hair was receding away from a brow which appeared heavily furrowed. His large flat nose and long arms gave him the appearance of a loose-limed simian, though his dark brown eyes shone with intelligence. His vested suit was rather rumpled, but a golden watch chain bespoke of no want of funds.

"Welcome to the Ghost Club, Mr. Holmes!" Worth exclaimed, animatedly. "I never thought to see you grace our presence. I was under the impression that you were rather sceptical of ghosts?"

"Your impression is correct," said Holmes, tersely.

"And yet, the overwhelming evidence suggests the contrary."

"Is that so?" Holmes asked, mildly. "Perhaps I have yet to examine all of the available evidence?"

"You are welcome to peruse the volumes in our library any time you wish. I will ensure that you are given unlimited access by the warden. Not as a member, of course. Not unless you become convinced and wish to join officially? No? It will be, shall we say, a sort of 'by courtesy' appointment. Herein you may read, for example, the *Diary* of Samuel Pepys. This is someone we universally consider to be an accurate and honest eyewitness to the events of his age... the Restoration and Second Dutch War, the Great Plague, the Great Fire, etcetera. And in those pages you will find his thoughts on the Drummer of Tedworth, a 'strange story of spirits and worth reading indeed.' Do you know it, Mr. Holmes?"

"I do not."

"In 1661, John Mompesson, a landowner in Tedworth, began to be plagued by nocturnal drumming noises after he won a lawsuit against a vagrant gypsy drummer named William Drury. But Mompesson was hardly the only one to hear the noises. It was heard by his children and servants, as well as the philosopher Joseph Glanvill. How do you explain that, Mr. Holmes?"

"Perhaps a *folie à deux*?"

Worth shook his head sadly. "A shared delusion? Come now,

Mr. Holmes. Soon you will have Dr Watson regaling me with tales of exotic powders which stimulate the brain centres in order to create visions."

Holmes smiled wanly. "Nevertheless, I think Sir Randolph would be well served to have a second investigator glance over the scene of the haunting."

"And what do you think that you will find that I missed?" asked Worth, a hint of irritation entering his voice.

"I suspect that we will encounter a fraud. Something akin to the Cock Lane Ghost."

"Scratching Fanny?" said Worth, smiling thinly.

"Indeed." Holmes turned to me. "Are you familiar with the case, Watson?"

I considered this for a moment. "Not that I can recall. Should I be?"

"As a man of letters, Watson, you might have caught mention of it in some of Dickens' work, as he was quite taken with the tale.[64] It is a long and sordid account, regarding how one Fanny Lynes supposedly returned from the dead in order to accuse her lover William Kent of poisoning her with arsenic. It drew great crowds to Cock Lane, but was eventually proven – by a committee composed of Dr Samuel Johnson and others – to be a trick played in revenge by the daughter of Kent's landlord." Holmes turned back to Worth. "Or do you doubt the conclusion to that case, Mr. Worth?"

"It may surprise you to learn, Mr. Holmes, that we in the Ghost Club are not credulous fools. We know that there are more Fox Sisters out there.[65] We take our work earnestly, and are fully cognizant of the fact that false sightings do terrible damage to our cause. They tend to induce people to empty the baby out with the bath, metaphorically-speaking. In fact, one of my first assignments with the Club was to help debunk the spirit cabinet of the Davenport Brothers. However, I also investigated the Brown Lady of Raynham Hall, and I could find nothing that would contradict the notion that the spirit of Lady Dorothy Walpole still walks those halls."[66]

"And the residence of Sir Randolph?" asked Holmes. "What have you concluded from your investigation within?"

A grave look appeared upon Worth's face. "It is a most serious matter, Mr. Holmes. I went round to Barclay Square first thing this morning and inspected the attic chamber. I also questioned all of the residents, as well as the servants. I assure you that the reports were unanimous regarding the sounds of unholy revelry that were heard to issue from the attic last night. This is the genuine article."

"Revelry? I thought Mr. Cannon was under the impression that it was his wife who has crossed the pale, and come back to haunt her father's home? She seems an unlikely sort to be engaged in a loud festivity, does she not? I would think moans, and perhaps chains to rattle, would be more along her line."

Worth's eyes narrowed. "Perchance you would be of another mind if you learned that Mrs. Cannon died shortly after a soiree thrown in celebration of her daughter's birth?"

Holmes shrugged. "No, I assure you that such a snippet of information does not alter my opinion of the case one iota."

"And yet, I find it rather compelling, Mr. Holmes. Mrs. Cannon has returned from the Beyond for some reason. It is our job to determine the nature of her message."

"Why can she not simply tell it to us? Why make us guess?"

Worth shook his head. "I cannot pretend to understand the laws that govern how the universe functions, Mr. Holmes. I only know that – in every case I have investigated – the ghost in question is barred from direct communication."

Holmes snorted derisively. "That seems to be rather opportune for the medium. If I was inventing such a thing, I too would place strict rules upon who is allowed to converse with the dead."

"So you believe it to all be faked, do you, Mr. Holmes? You do not admit to even the slightest possibility of real ghosts?" asked Worth, reasonably. "I find that most of mankind may disagree with you. It seems to me that there are two sorts of men. There are those who at least admit the chance of the existence of ghosts, and who would make some effort to witness one. And then there are those who profess to not believe, but whom are in secret mortally afraid of them."

Holmes chuckled at this modest insult. "Perhaps I am a third sort? I find that there are inherent contradictions which make their existence exceptionally implausible."

"Such as?" asked Worth, frowning.

"For example," said Holmes, "I put to you the question: are ghosts insubstantial?"

The ghost hunter nodded. "All ghost-hunters agree that is the case. There are many reports of them being able to pass through solid objects, even people."

"And yet they can also slam doors shut and throw objects across rooms? To be able to do so would suggest that they are, in fact, material. Unfortunately, the law of physics is such that it must be one or the other. Nothing can exist in both states."

"I appreciate your attempt to explain the essence of ghosts in scientific terms, Mr. Holmes, I really do. You are a one of those folks who only believes in what you can touch – *quod tango credo*. Someone who walks in the narrow path of certain fact, and this is quite reasonable given your profession, I suppose. However, that does not rule out the possibility of the unseen and the supernatural. Things beyond the currently understood laws of nature."

"Then what are your ghosts composed of, Mr. Worth?"

"The common supposition is that they are spirits of the dead who have gotten lost on their way to the Afterlife. All of the great religions of the world tell us that when a man dies, he casts off all the cares and troubles of the world and becomes a pure and ethereal spirit. But it is not possible that a man – or woman, mind you – could be harried from this world with his soul steeped with some single all-absorbing passion, such that it clings to him even after he has passed the portals of the grave?"

"Human souls, then?" asked Holmes.

"If you will."

"And yet they wear clothes? And carry canes? And what of the supposed ghost-animals or ghost-carriages? Does a train have a soul, Mr. Worth?"

"Now you mock me, sir," said Worth, heatedly.

"Not at all. You share your beliefs with many illustrious sorts. Even the Bard himself made much use of ghosts. The murdered victims of Richard III returned to torment him on the eve of his death. Macbeth was haunted by the ghost of murdered Banquo. And without the prompting of his father's ghost, Hamlet would never have been set upon the path to his destruction."

"Those tales all ended poorly, Mr. Holmes. Do you fear something untoward happening to Sir Randolph?"

Holmes shrugged. "That is precisely what I intend to discover. A good day to you, Mr. Worth."

§

Upon our exit from the house, I deduced that Holmes had seen enough of the Underground on this gloomy day, for he promptly engaged a black hansom cab to take us from Kensington to Mayfair.

"You are rather quiet, Watson," noted Holmes as we rode. "Upon what are you reflecting?"

I shook my head. "I am concerned, Holmes, that you are proceeding counter to your typical methods."

"What do you mean?" asked he, sharply.

"Rather than waiting for fuller knowledge of the facts of the matter and avoiding the formation of a provisional theory, in this instance, you do not appear to give any credence to the possibility of a genuine haunting."

"Surely, Watson, you do not think there is anything to the ideas of Mr. Worth?"

"I will admit, Holmes, that I find his theories intriguing. Certainly, I was taken by the idea of a ghost emerging when a person perishes while still possessed by a deep passion. This need not solely be dark feelings of hatred or revenge, but also love, or patriotism, or some other pure and elevating passion. I could imagine such things – even after death – obstructing the poor soul, so that it cannot pass onto the other side. This would account for the many unexplainable things which have happened even in our own time, and for the deeply rooted belief in ghosts which has existed in every age. Odysseus consulted the ghost of Achilles. Pliny the Younger tells of a villa in Athens haunted until the bones of an old man bound with chains were found buried in the courtyard and properly interred. As far back as tales go, the idea has persisted. Can so many be wrong?"

"You will again accuse me of a monstrous egotism, Watson, when I say – with confidence – that yes, so many can indeed be wrong. There is a madness in crowds. Take the South Sea bubble, for example. The Railway Mania, the various 'witch' trials, even the poor souls wanting to join the Red-Headed League."[67]

" 'I can calculate the movement of the stars, but not the madness of men.' "

Holmes smiled. "Precisely, Watson. Newton is always pithy."

"I still think it possible that a psychic residue could remain after a particularly tragic death."

He shook his head. "I, for one, refuse to subscribe to the dogma of purgatory - souls forced to wander the earth for eternity. There is no sound rationalistic principle to support such a fantasy."

"Then what happens to us after we perish, Holmes?" I asked. "Are we simply dust and shadow? Is there nothing eternal?"

He was silent for a moment. "No one knows the answer to that, Watson. Anyone who says otherwise is a liar or a fool. We all have to wait until we cross over to that undiscovered country."

"But surely you must believe in something?"

He shrugged. "I find the standard version, derived as it

is from the Greek Hades and Elysian Fields, unsatisfying. If pressed, I suppose I would say that my time with the great Lama has made it such that I consider the Buddhist concept of eternal re-birth to be the most convincing explanation. Though, secretly, I hope that Poetic Edda is correct. I think that some humble corner of Valhalla sounds like a pleasant place in which to pass eternity."

My eyes narrowed. "Are you mocking me, Holmes?"

"Certainly not, Watson!" said he, his eyebrows rising in surprise. "I would assume that you will join me there! You too have fought your fair share of battles."

I shook my head in dismay at Holmes' flippant tone and, instead of conversation, settled for staring grimly out of the window into the darkening evening.

The driver deposited us next to a lamplighter, who was just extracting his pole from the street light situated immediately in front of our destination. Like many such residences in the area, No. 100 Barclay Square was set off from the pavement by a small wrought-iron fence. I had half-expected some tumble-down old pile, with a garden choked up by rank weeds and girt round by pools of stagnant water. Instead, it proved to be a tidy, four-story, Mayfair, flat-roofed townhouse, constructed of white-grey Portland stone. A series of small flues poked out above, suggesting multiple fireplaces within. The ground floor had a solid black door flanked by two windows, while a small balcony ran along the length of the first floor. However, it was the highest windows which attracted my attention.

"Holmes!" I exclaimed. "The attic windows are bricked up!"

"Indeed, Watson," he replied, studying the front of the house carefully. "That is certainly suggestive."

"Of what?"

"That the legend of the haunted attic is – as Mr. Cannon noted – not a new one. The tales of the house's ghost must be deeply ingrained in all who reside or work here."

"Surely you don't suspect one of the servants of faking the ghost?"

"Why ever not, Watson? It is a perfectly valid explanation for what Mr. Cannon described."

"Why would a servant want to do such a thing?"

He shook his head. "Now you are asking me to theorize in advance of the facts, Watson. Let us first examine the members of the household."

As we climbed the steps, the front door was opened by Mr. Cannon himself. He expressed his gratitude for our visit, and said that he would take us up to see Sir Randolph immediately. He showed us into a great, grey-curtained study. There the eminent jurist awaited us, as aloof, self-contained, and remote as a ruin in a desert. Cannon excused himself so that we could consider Sir Randolph's independent opinion of the matter at hand.

Sir Randolph glared at Holmes. "I have heard good things about you, Mr. Holmes, from Lord Holdhurst. I am surprised to find you wasting your time with such nonsense."

Holmes raised his dark eyebrows with interest. "So, you do not accept a supernatural explanation for the events transpiring in your residence?"

"Balderdash!" the judge exclaimed. "Of course, that was the conclusion of the charlatan we had by earlier."

"Do you refer to Mr. Worth?"

"A credulous fool. Let me tell you something, Mr. Holmes. I have heard a great many terrible things in my forty years upon the bench, and I have sent many a worthy cad to face Jack Ketch. If ghosts were real, it would be one of them haunting my every step. Not my poor Dorothy! She was the treasure of my life."

"But you did hear something the last two nights?"

"Of course!" he cried. "A deaf man could have heard them!"

"And what do you propose it was?"

"It was my mother!" a voice suddenly exclaimed.

Holmes and I turned and found that a young girl had entered the room. She was a striking lass, pale-faced and dark-haired, with piercing, ice-blue eyes. This could only be Mr. Cannon's daughter, Penelope. Her cheeks were red with embarrassment.

"Little girls are meant to be seen and not heard!" Sir Randolph thundered.

Penelope's eyes widened in alarm, and she turned and fled.

"I apologize for my grand-daughter, gentlemen. Cannon is not a bad chap, but he is hardly a replacement for Dorothy. The girl has grown up without a mother, surrounded by mouldy books and impractical professors. Hence, she has little sense of proper decorum."

"Hmmm, yes, I can see that," murmured Holmes.

"In any case," Sir Randolph continued, "there can be no truth to these ghostly rumours. It is a hoax of some sort, I tell you."

"I share your opinion of the matter, and intend to prove it. With your permission, I would like to have a word with your housekeeper."

"Mrs. Bosworth? Why ever do you need to speak to her?"

"I assure you, Sir Randolph, that I intend to investigate this case with the same thoroughness that I do any other. I would be a poor detective if I failed to interview all the potential witnesses."

"Very well," the judge agreed.

"And afterwards, I take it I have your permission to examine the attic room? If so, I will ask Mrs. Bosworth to show it to us. No, no need to get up. I am sure we can find her without difficulty."

Taking our leave from Sir Randolph, we made our way back into the hall. I assumed that Holmes would head for the lower levels in order to locate Mrs. Bosworth, but to my surprise he stopped in his tracks.

He stood there quietly for a minute and then smiled. "You may come out now, Penelope," he called.

Moments later, the little girl that we had briefly seen in the study appeared from behind one of the pillars. "Yes, sir?" said she, shyly.

"You are a clever girl, Penelope. Most people would never have sensed you hiding behind that pillar."

Her eyebrows rose with interest. "How did you do it then?"

"I am not most people." He pointed at a gas jet upon the wall. "That light casts a shadow, and the edge of the pillar was not as straight as it should have been. In fact, it was decidedly curved, much like a human form."

She shrugged. "It might have been a servant."

"Are your grandfather's servants in the habit of hiding behind pillars?"

She considered this for a moment. "No, I suppose not. Mrs. Bosworth wouldn't fit behind a pillar. And Wooten would never think of such a thing."

"Who is Mr. Wooten?"

"My grandfather's butler. He's almost a hundred years old, and has no sense of humour whatsoever."

"And the other servants?" Holmes asked.

She shrugged. "There is a charwoman who comes in early in the morning to light fires, clean boots, and scrub the front steps."

Holmes' eyebrows rose in surprise. "No valet?"

She shook her head. "My grandfather prefers to do those tasks himself."

"Surely a secretary?"

"There is Simon, who comes round from Westminster on days when grandfather doesn't go in, but he doesn't live here."

"So there you go, Penelope," said Holmes, spreading out his hands. "With so few others in the house, who else could it have been?"

"It might have been the ghost!"

"Do ghosts cast shadows?" asked Holmes.

She frowned as she thought about this question. "I don't know. The stories never mention it one way or the other."

"What stories, my dear?"

"Well, there is Mr. Dickens' signal-man.[68] That's a mighty fine tale. Or the ones my daddy's friend from Cambridge likes to tell. Whenever he comes over for supper, afterwards Mr. James tells me all about ghosts and goblins, as well as haunted fields, brooks, bridges, and houses. He knows about direful omens and portentous sights and sounds in the air, and frightens me so with speculations upon comets and shooting stars."[69]

Holmes smiled. "I see. Very good, Penelope. You have been most helpful. I hope to talk with you more later."

"Good bye, sir," said she with a curtsy, before departing.

Holmes watched her go for a moment and then turned to me. "Most instructive, wouldn't you say, Watson?"

"I suppose so, Holmes. It is odd that Sir Randolph has such a limited staff."

"Hmmm, indeed. Well, let us go find Mrs. Bosworth and see what she has to say about the matter."

We found her in the look-out cellar kitchen. As Penelope had suggested, the comfortable-looking Mrs. Bosworth would not have fit behind one of the pillars in the upper hall. After Holmes had introduced himself and explained his purpose in the house, the housekeeper consented to an interview.

"Now, then, Mrs. Bosworth, you have been with Sir Randolph for how long?" asked Holmes.

"Eighteen years."

"And has your employment been a satisfactory one?"

She pursed her lips as she considered this question. "I would reckon so. Sir Randolph is a stern man, but very fair. If you do your job well, he notices and appreciates it."

"And if you do not do your job well?"

"Then your term in this house is limited," said she, with grim finality.

"It must be a lonely house, with just Sir Randolph and the butler?"

"We used to have more, but with just Sir Randolph residing here now, the needs are less. Wooten is a fine cribbage player, and Sir Randolph generously permits me two evenings out with my friends every week. That is sufficient for me."

"Surely it was once more gay, back when Sir Randolph's daughter was alive?"

Mrs. Bosworth's face fell and a glisten appeared in her eyes. "You are correct, sir. Miss Dorothy was the apple of Sir Randolph's eye. And after she died, not two months later, Lady Russell was carried off by an apoplexy." She shook her head sadly. "I always thought that Lady Russell died from sadness."

"Ah, so the appearance of Penelope was the herald of two other deaths?"

"You can't blame the poor lass, Mr. Holmes! She was just a little baby! She is a good girl, mayhaps a touch different. But who can fault her, raised as she has been by her father and a bunch of eccentric old professors?"

"And what is your opinion of the attic ghost?"

She peered at Holmes. "Call me a fool, if you will, but I have heard it with my own ears."

"Since when?"

"Since the day I came to work for Sir Randolph."

Holmes' eyebrows rose with surprise. "Truly?"

"Everyone knows that this house attracts spirits. For a while it bothered me. One of the neighbours told me that a maid had slept in the attic room and was found mad the following morning. An old waiting-maid of Lady Russell's told me that a young man had once been locked in that room, fed only through a hole in the door, until he went mad and died." She shook her head. "After some time, I realized that neither I – nor anyone I knew – was being bothered by the ghosts, and I suppose I simply got used to the noises. Like the passing of the hansom cabs in the street outside."

Holmes smiled and nodded. "You have been most helpful, Mrs. Bosworth. I would very much like to inspect the attic room before it draws much later. I suppose it is locked?"

"Of course. I possess the only key. Sir Randolph is most adamant that no one is to ever enter, though he earlier gave permission to that Worth fellow, so I suppose you too can take a look. Make sure you bring the key right back, mind you. And

THE GATHERING GLOOM

you best take a torch, or you won't see much."

Acquiring the suggested item from a storage closet, Holmes and I found our way up the staircase which led to the attic. As we walked, I asked Holmes why we had not questioned the butler Wooten.

He shook his head. "That would be a waste of time, Watson. You heard Penelope's characterization of the man. Even if – with the carelessness of youth – she exaggerated his age, Penelope noted that he was completely devoid of humour. The young can be surprisingly perceptive, Watson. I doubt such a man would be capable of manipulating such a hoax."

"So you still think it is all a fraud?"

"Let us say that my views upon the matter have begun to shift. I think an inspection of the troubled garret will prove to be informative."

The entrance to that room was located at the right hand landing of the lofty staircase's top floor. The massive oaken door was secured by a padlock. A gas jet was set in the wall next to the door, and its flame shone a fair amount of light into the otherwise dark corner.

As Holmes bent to insert the key, he nodded in the direction of the door. "Observe, Watson, the lack of a hole through which Mrs. Bosworth's mythical young man was fed."

"The door might have been replaced."

Holmes finished removing the padlock, and knocked upon the stout wood. "These houses around Barclay Square were built about a hundred years ago. I suspect this door is no younger."

He pushed open the door and we caught our first glimpse of the terrible place beyond. The room was bare and unfurnished, save only a dilapidated wicker chair. It was a place of undisturbed solitude and darkness. As I had noted upon our arrival, the room was entirely cut off from the light of the outer world by the bricking up of its solitary window. I was about to set foot inside, when Holmes barred the way with his hand.

"Hold a minute, Watson. Although I would recognize your footprint anywhere, it will be easier to observe the dust upon the floor if only one of us enters."

He trotted carefully into the room and – much like the night of our very first adventure together in the Lauriston Gardens – he proceeded to examine the room with the utmost of care. Once his inspection of the floor and chair was complete, he used his tape to measure the walls, and then tapped upon each one with his loaded hunting-crop. Finally, he replaced his glass and tape in his pocket and turned back to me.

"Did you fancy sleeping in your own bed tonight, Watson?" he asked with a smile.

I frowned in confusion. "I was unaware that there is somewhere else I need to be?"

"Yes, your assistance will be invaluable. For we are going to pass the night in this haunted house. And by morning, we shall either have solved the mystery of its spirits, or we shall ourselves – perhaps – be mad."

§

After he replaced the door's padlock, I followed Holmes back down to the study, where he explained his plan to Sir Randolph and Mr. Cannon.

"This is most irregular, sir," the jurist protested.

"I assure you, Sir Randolph, that this is the only way to get to the bottom of the matter. Either your house is truly haunted, or someone is playing a cruel trick upon you. Send Mrs. Bosworth and Mr. Wooten to a local hotel for the night. That will remove them from the equation. I will then personally go around and ensure that there are no secret modes of ingress by which an external party might enter the house undetected. Once we are alone in the house, I shall bunk in with you, while Dr Watson will reside with Mr. Cannon. It is hardly the first time that he and I have held a long sleepless vigil through the night."

Cannon shook his head. "What of Penelope?"

"We shall make certain that she has everything she requires and then – for her own safety – we shall lock her within her room."

Cannon looked troubled at this plan, but Sir Randolph appeared to have been won over. "It is a sound strategy, Mr. Holmes, for proving that this is all claptrap. But when there are no noises tonight, how will we determine the identity of this hoax's perpetrator?"

Holmes smiled. "I assure you, sir, that I too have considered that very question. I will explain further in the morning if the expected course comes to pass."

Sir Randolph rang for his butler and housekeeper, while Mr. Cannon went to inform Penelope of the situation for the evening. Meanwhile, I drew Holmes aside.

"I thought you had excluded the butler, Holmes. So you must suspect that Mrs. Bosworth is involved? But what could be her motive?"

"Ah!" exclaimed Holmes. "That is exactly the question that I asked myself some time ago, Watson. It is the question that shines light where everything else is dark." He nodded. "You will see soon enough, if I am not mistaken. But keep an eye on Mr. Cannon, too, Watson. I have not yet determined whether he is involved in this matter. Oh, and keep that torch. We shall need it later."

He left me to inspect the house, while I pondered his words. I knew Holmes suspected a human agency rather than some force from outside our narrow understanding of the world. However, I could not be so certain. Mrs. Bosworth seemed an unlikely perpetrator, and in any case, she had been banished from the house along with the butler. I was certain that Peter Cannon firmly believed the spirit of his wife had returned from beyond the grave, and it was inconceivable that Sir Randolph himself was involved. Holmes was not infallible. He had been beaten at least four times by men – as well as a woman. Surely his prejudices against the spiritual world could be blinding him to the possibility that the long-standing tales of this house were actually based in fact?

And thus it was with a dreadful foreboding that I settled into my night watch. Mr. Cannon attempted to read, but I saw him nodding off several times. I, for one, was able to wait silently without signs of flagging. Hours by Holmes' side had trained me well. I had pulled out my pocket watch and noted that midnight had just passed when I heard the noise. It was very clearly the sound of a chair being moved, followed by the rattling of chains. Even if I had suspected the unlikely involvement of Holmes or Sir Randolph, I knew these sounds were not coming from the neighbouring bedroom. They were coming from the floor above, where no being resided!

And then came a sound which chilled me to my bones. It was the sound of a human voice, but one distorted beyond one's ken. I could almost make out the words, though the deep roar made it impossible to be certain. The only thing I knew was that it was it was not the voice of a living human being. This horrible sound cut off as quickly as it began, only to be replaced by the chair moving again.

Cannon had startled awake and looked at me with wide eyes. "Now do you believe, Dr Watson?" he gasped. "My Dorothy has returned."

I sprang to my feet and raced for the door. Throwing it open, I stumbled into the hallway at the same time as Holmes.

He looked at me with a deep exhilaration in his eyes. "Watson!" he yelled. "To the attic!"

Sir Randolph and Mr. Cannon had followed us into the hall, and Mr. Cannon moved towards Penelope's door. But Holmes forestalled him. "No, Mr. Cannon, hold a minute. If she had been awakened by the sounds, she would have cried out in terror. We heard nothing, so she is safe. Follow me, if you please."

Holmes led the way up the stairs back to the padlocked door. He rapidly opened the lock with the key which he had retained from earlier, and then he threw open the door. I shone my torch inside, but there was no one to be seen, nor any chains to make that ratting noise. The only thing of note was that the chair had plainly moved from its last location, and was now closer to the far wall. I knew that Holmes had not moved the chair in this locked room, so who had? A shiver passed down my spine.

After Sir Randolph and Mr. Cannon had silently inspected the room from the doorway, Holmes indicated that we should repair back down to the study. However, on the way, he stopped in front of Penelope's door. "I think we should have your daughter join us, Mr. Cannon. Would you unlock the door, please?"

Cannon nodded and did as Holmes instructed. Cannon went inside to rouse Penelope from her bed while Holmes followed him, presumably to ensure her safety. When the two of them returned with the little girl, Holmes wore a satisfied smile upon his face.

The five of us had settled into the study. Sir Randolph took his accustomed arm-chair, I sat in the chair across from him, and Cannon and his daughter took the sofa. Holmes refused a seat and began to pace up and down the Persian rug.

"Your situation is, to my knowledge, unique amongst all others which have come before me," said Holmes. "I have investigated countless cases and never seen its' like."

"So you admit the possibility of a ghost?" exclaimed Mr. Cannon.

"I thought you did not believe in the possibility of the supernatural, Holmes," said I.

He turned his piercing gaze upon me. "That was true, Watson. However, this case has forced me to question those assumptions. First, when we inspected the attic room, both this evening and just now, I noted the complete absence of footprints in the dust. Therefore, we must ask ourselves how the chair was moved. Furthermore, the sound of chains was very clear, and yet I can say with confidence that there are no chains in that room."

Sir Randolph appeared much upset. "I cannot believe it, Mr.

Holmes! Do you mean that the ghost is real?"

Holmes pursed his lips. "I can wholeheartedly assure you, Sir Randolph, that there was no man behind the noises emanating from the attic. In fact, I sense that the spirit behind these apparitions is with us still. It will not rest until it has achieved its goal."

"I shall leave the house at once!"

Holmes shook his head. "I assure you, sir, that this spirit is not confined to the house. It will follow you wherever you go."

"Then what should I do?" said he, his voice trembling with dismay.

"I would ask yourself... what does the spirit want?" said Holmes, severely. "What mistake could you have made in order to have awoken this spirit? Only then will you find peace."

"I do not know!" the jurist wailed.

"Mr. Cannon and your granddaughter believe this to be the returned spirit of Dorothy. If this is indeed the ghost of your daughter, would she be happy to see you shun your own blood?"

Sir Randolph's face quivered and his eyes moistened. He sat there for a moment in silence and then turned to Penelope, his hands outstretched. The little girl shyly moved over to him, and he wrapped her in his arms. Knowing that the great judge would not wish for strangers such as Holmes and I to witness this private reconciliation, it was clear that it was time for us to depart. I sincerely hoped that this small action would sanction a final rest for Dorothy's ghost.

§

As we sat in the hansom back to Baker Street, I shook my head in wonderment. "Holmes, I am thoroughly amazed. I never thought to see you admit to the presence of a ghost."

He looked at me sharply. "Who said anything about a ghost, Watson?"

I frowned in confusion. "Well, you did."

Holmes shook his head. "In point of fact, Watson, I did not. I told Sir Randolph that a spirit that was behind the sounds, and in so doing I spoke the literal truth. However, I never claimed that said spirit had ventured from another plane of existence. Do not you and I have a spirit that distinguishes us from the animals?"

"But you and I watched Sir Randolph and Mr. Cannon the entre time!" I protested. "There was no one else in the house!"

"Watson, you have made the same mistake as Sir Randolph. You have overlooked the most obvious spirit of them all. The spirit of a little girl who has never received an ounce of love from her grandfather because she – through no fault of her own – was the instrument of her mother and grandmother's demise." He reached over and deposited a long strand of dark silk into my hands.

"Penelope!"

"Indeed."

"I don't understand," I exclaimed.

"It is simple, Watson. Like all investigations, this case boiled down to means and motive. The means was relatively easy to determine. First, that room was locked with a single key, which never left the possession of Mrs. Bosworth. And yet, someone was making noises within. Therefore, there must have been a second entrance. When we stood outside the house, you pointed out the bricked-up window. However, I was estimating the width of the building. Once I measured the attic room, I knew that there must be a secret door, a fact I confirmed with my series of knockings upon the wall. I did not bother to trace the passage behind, but I deduced that it led down to Penelope's room. I can only assume it was built upon the orders of one of the first owners – perhaps as a method to facilitate assignations with one of the maids – and the curious Penelope accidentally discovered the other side of the passage."

"I am amazed, Holmes. What else made you suspect a

human agency?"

"Second, for a room that was never visited, it was shockingly free of any dust upon the floor. Penelope must have swept it regularly in order to mask any signs of her visits."

"But the chains?"

"Hidden behind the door, and rattled after she tugged upon that monofilament string, the other end of which was tied to the chair. As I little desired to disrupt her show, I cannot say with certainly, however, I suspect that she tied the chair with a highwayman's hitch or thief's knot, in order to facilitate the rapid untying of the string, should someone investigate either the attic room or her own whereabouts. I found that silken strand in her room and removed it as a souvenir, especially since she will not be needing it any longer."

"So her 'haunting' career is over?"

"Of course, Watson. Penelope has achieved what she desired. Her grandfather has stopped unreasonably blaming her for causing the death of her mother and grandmother. I told you that the motive was the key. Once I knew what the perpetrator wanted, her identity was plain."

I considered this for a moment and then realized the error in his conclusions. "But the horrible voice! Surely, Holmes, little Penelope did not make that noise!"

He smiled wanly. "I confess that I didn't expect that. Even though Mr. Cannon had warned us, I didn't believe it until I heard it with my own ears and – for a moment – I was frozen in my seat. Fortunately, my time in Lhasa gave me the answer."

"What? How can your travels in Tibet have anything to do with it?"

"The monks there have fostered a rather unique form of chanting – though I have determined that it can also be found amongst the Tuvan people of Siberia – in which the singers develop the ability to create sounds from their vestibular folds."

"The false vocal cords!" I exclaimed.

"Indeed. I must admit, Watson, that earlier today, I was starting to think that I had seen it all. Fortunately, Penelope made me realize that there are still surprises in the world."

I shook my head. "But you said that today forced you to question the possibility of the supernatural!" I protested.

"And so it did. For a brief moment, I questioned it. And then I realized that there was a far more human reason for those sounds. We spoke before of Shakespeare, did we not, Watson? Many years ago, before I settled into my chosen profession, I performed the Danish play in Chicago and in New York. I recall how the stage manager had borrowed Henry Irving's idea of burning limelight in order to magnify the ghost's otherworldliness. And even then I was struck by the ghost's power. If the deceased king had not incited Hamlet to move against his uncle, the entire tragic chain of events might have unfolded far differently. Did Shakespeare believe in actual ghosts, or was he merely using it as a symbol of Hamlet's secret regrets? If I may be excused for once more paraphrasing the Bard, men often make their own ghosts from the wicked deeds or intents within their hearts.[70] Surely such was the case of Sir Randolph, don't you think, Watson? Thankfully – due to the actions of a clever little girl – it can certainly be hoped that Sir Randolph will henceforth conduct his life filled with a more charitable spirit."

§

THE COLD DISH

Although Mr. Sherlock Holmes has been in retirement at his small villa upon the South Downs for the last five years, this change in situation has not precluded our continued acquaintance. Many a weekend found me upon a train to Eastbourne for an agreeable visit, and our correspondence was even more frequent. The latter often consisted of my queries regarding the plethora of extraordinary recollections stored in his brain-attic, which I asked in order to help supplement my notes upon cases long-past. Many of these I am currently endeavouring to write up for public consumption in order to appease the loud clamouring of demands for more cases solved by my still-famous friend.

However, upon occasion, our letters centred upon topics of a more immediate nature. Although Holmes was adamant regarding his policy of not returning to London every time the official forces were stumped by an outré crime, I was often unable to refrain from following such events with great interest. One series of communiques between Holmes and I may be dated to the period surrounding a trio of mysterious deaths in London. To this day, Scotland Yard has been unable to elucidate the perpetrator of those wrongdoings, and my notes upon the subject are far too sensitive to publish anytime during the next several decades. However, I suppose that I must eventually give notice for their eventual release – once the principals are beyond the arm of earthly justice. Only then will I be able to assuage my conscience that no more time will be wasted by desperate adventurers in the remote reaches of the Bushveld, futilely pursuing the location of millions of pounds in missing gold. But, as Holmes has often accused me of doing, I am starting this tale he wrong way around.

§

For me, retirement – after several decades by the side of Mr. Sherlock Holmes – was a most strange transition. I liken it to a river… sometimes the surface was troubled and sometimes smooth, but the stream always ran swiftly. The roar of the final falls sounded ever louder in my ears, whenever such cataracts appeared in my path. In many ways, the experience was similar to that period of time when Holmes had absented himself from London following the death of Professor Moriarty. I, of course, retained my deep interest in crime – developed over the years of our acquaintance - and rarely failed to study with close attention the various puzzles which came before the public.

It was one such mention in the newspaper whose features immediately appealed to me, as I was remotely acquainted with one of the peripheral figures. I therefore purposefully set myself upon the trail of this adventure. In a quest for the solution, I attempted to convey both my long-study of the methods of Sherlock Holmes, as well as his remote advice whenever available. At the end, the results proved to be far too fantastic to bring forward immediately, and the general absence of Holmes from the scene made it difficult to record in the fashion of one of my standard narratives.

Therefore, from this point forward, I will primarily follow the course of events as I once did during the Dartmoor case, by transcribing my own letters to Mr. Sherlock Holmes, as well as his scant replies – which lie before me on the table. These are presented almost exactly as written at the time, and show my feelings and suspicions of the moment more accurately than my memory - clear as it is regarding these tragic events.

§

Charing Cross Hotel, *Jul. 3rd*
My dear Holmes:

I am back in London at the moment, wrapping up the sale of my Kensington practice in order to make my final transition to a shingle in Southsea. My solicitor's office is located at Bell Yard, and afterwards, I was passing through the Strand on my way to Charing Cross Station. There I stopped to purchase a copy of the *Daily Telegraph* from the one-legged news-vendor who plies his wares along that stretch. The black-upon-yellow top sheet caught my attention with its lurid account of an unsolved death:

MYSTERIOUS DEATH OF ENGINEER: NATURAL CAUSES OR MURDER?

This seemed like a simple enough case, and I paid the newsman my halfpenny, intending to peruse the story while waiting for my train. However, a familiar name leading the second paragraph induced me to pause in the doorway of a tobacconist's shop while I ran my eyes along the entire account. I retained the relevant page, so in case you are no longer receiving the *Telegraph*, you may see it in its entirety. This is how it ran:

> *We report that Mr. Lewis Gloucester, the well-known mechanical engineer of 25 Upper Brook Street, was found dead last night at his club, the Tankerville. There are no exact details to hand, but the events seem to have aroused the attention of Scotland Yard. Such interest, and the fact that Mr. Gloucester was only two years past forty, suggests to this reporter that foul play is suspected. Major Linwood Prendergast, who was present at the*

scene, reports that Mr. Gloucester had appeared to be in good health and spirits earlier in the evening. The two had played a rubber of whist together, and Mr. Gloucester was noted to have won some £60 in the sitting. This cheerful windfall implies that self-harm is not to be considered. Nor are the gentlemen whose hands failed them against Mr. Gloucester thought to be responsible, for both are respectable members of the House of Lords and departed the club while Mr. Gloucester was observed to be enjoying a post-victory drink at the bar.

Our sources confirm that the conduct of the investigation has been left in the veteran hands of Inspector Lestrade, who is questioning the members and staff of the Tankerville with his accustomed vigor and perceptiveness. Anyone with information concerning the case is urged to come forward to Scotland Yard forthwith.

Although I had tickets for the ten o'clock train, I decided to stroll down Whitehall and call upon Inspector Lestrade at the new Yard in order to see if I could offer any assistance. I thought my years at your side, Holmes, might permit me insights into the case which the official force was missing. Although you and I had rarely visited the headquarters for the C.I.D. – you always preferred to make the inspectors come to Baker Street – my face was recognized by several men whom we had helped out over the years, and I was quickly shown into Lestrade's presence.

The inspector is considerably less-lean than when we first met, though I suppose the same could be said for myself. But his eyes are still bright, and he grinned sardonically as I strode through the door to his office. "I wondered when I might see you, Dr Watson," said he, without preamble.

"Whatever do you mean?"

"This is just the sort of thing that would attract your attention. In fact, if I didn't know better, I might wonder if you were responsible yourself."

"How so?"

He smiled. "Let me lay out the facts for you, Doctor. Perhaps they will be of sufficient interest to lure Mr. Holmes back to London for a few days, eh? Last night, around eleven o'clock, the manager of the Tankerville Club, a Mr. Dennison, discovered Gloucester's body in one of the private upstairs rooms. There had been no robbery, nor is there any evidence as to how the man met his death, for there are no wounds upon the body."

"Poison?" I hypothesized.

Lestrade nodded. "Yes, very likely. Though there are no signs of how Gloucester was induced to swallow it."

"Any witnesses?"

"Plenty of club members saw Gloucester earlier in the evening. As the paper noted, he was engaged in a high-stakes game of whist with Major Prendergast, after which he had a drink at the bar with Mr. James Heath Newton. But at some point he received a note and excused himself."

"What did the note say?"

The inspector shook his head. "That is just the thing, Doctor. The note seems to have vanished."

"Taken by the murderer?"

"We must presume so."

"Therefore, the murderer must have been present in the Club," I reasoned. "One of the members? It would not be the first time that the Tankerville allowed a scoundrel into its ranks. Colonel Moran was a member, if you recall."

Lestrade nodded slowly. "Yes, indeed. I agree that a member or a guest could be responsible. I have one of my best men gathering a list of everyone present last night, but I fear it will be several dozen long. I will send a copy around, if you are interested, Doctor."

"Certainly. Please do so, Inspector. Who were the two men playing against Mr. Gloucester?"

"You can forget about them," said Lestrade, firmly. "Lord Balmoral and Lord Backwater are both above reproach."

"And Mr. Heath Newton?"

Lestrade shrugged. "An adventurer and sportsman of some note. Just back from a stint in Borneo, I understand."

"If he was the last person to drink with Mr. Gloucester, surely he must know something?"

"That is certainly possible, Doctor, and my next stop will be to pay him a visit."

"Were there any clues in the room where the body was found?"

The inspector smiled broadly. "As you are no doubt aware, Doctor, we in the Yard hold Mr. Holmes in the highest esteem, and we nowadays do our best to emulate his practices. But it did not take a careful examination to find a clue of the highest importance. For you see, one wall in the room was naturally shaded from the light of the fireplace and lamps. It was also the only one of the four to display no decoration of any sort. Across this barren space there was scrawled in black letters a single word: '*EINS.*' Now, what do you make of that, Doctor?" exclaimed Lestrade, throwing out his hands. "It reminds you of the Lauriston Garden mystery, does it not?"

"I suppose it does. Is it a name?"

Lestrade wagged his head. "I believe so. 'Rache' may not have been short for 'Rachel,' but I wager this time there is an Einshorn or an Einstein at the bottom of this matter."

I considered this for a moment. "It could be a misspelling, I suppose. There is a Professor Einhorn in Munich who recently invented something called procaine, an anaesthetic with fewer side-effects as cocaine. But it's an alkaloid all the same."

"An anaesthetic, eh? Nice work, Doctor! Anything that can take away pain can also take away life. Why don't you nip down to the mortuary and have a chat with the examiner? I will see Mr. Heath Newton, and we can meet after lunch to compare notes."

I followed Lestrade's instructions and sought out the earthly remains of the unfortunate Mr. Gloucester. An acquaintance of mine, Dr Trepp, was on duty, and he waved me though with a roguish grin, likely at the sight of an old dog like me still poking around at cases of mysterious death.

As noted in the newspaper, the former engineer was in his early forties, tending towards corpulence, with thick straight hair and a full beard. He was well-dressed in immaculate evening clothes. All signs of *rigor mortis* had long since dissipated and his expression appeared serene. I had been expecting a fearsome and terrible contortion of a man struggling to hold off death, and instead found the face of someone who was at peace with his passing. It made me consider the possibility of self-murder, despite the assertion of the man's financial prosperity in *The Telegraph*. Perhaps there was some other reason for Gloucester to believe that there was no reason to continue his existence? It was certainly not the face of a man fighting for his survival against some mysterious foe, nor that of a man suddenly struck down by an internal ailment.

Trepp came in and showed me the list of effects found upon Gloucester's body. This included a gold watch, No. 242, by Breguet, of Paris, and a platinum ring engraved with three interconnected links. These, along with the aforementioned whist winnings, ruled out simple robbery as a motive.

I asked the examiner for his medical opinion. He informed me that the man was completely healthy, other than being dead, of course. There were no signs of pathology in his arteries, no apoplexy in his brain, or tumours of any kind. There was also no evidence of any site of injection, so if Gloucester had been poisoned, it was in something he ingested. However, the man's stomach proved to be empty, suggesting a liquid rather than a solid source. I thought again of the drink which the man had shared with the adventurer Mr. Heath Newton. Unfortunately, all of the standard tests, including the Marsh, Marquis, and Mandelin, were negative.[71]

I will not trouble you, Holmes, with any additional theories, nor too much description, for I know how you hate sensational poetry and believe that all should be nothing but unadorned facts. I would hope to hear some ideas from you regarding my next plan of action. Best of all would be if you could come up to London for a few days. Clara is performing at the Royal Albert.[72] In any case, you will hear from me again in the course of the next few days should further clues present themselves. I have wired by wife in order to explain my delay in London and checked myself into a hotel, where you may reach me.

Very sincerely yours,
JOHN H. WATSON.

§

Even after he concluded his official consulting from Baker Street and had more leisurely time for such things, Holmes rarely wrote when a telegram would serve. In fact, despite his protests that he was retired, I knew first-hand from my weekend visits that Holmes received a remarkable degree of correspondence spanning four continents from a wide swath of individuals hoping to enlist his aid in some matter of consequence. Most of these attempts were largely in vain. However, Holmes invariably answered back with a short telegram, which typically provided some critical insight that ultimately proved to be of assistance to a perceptive recipient. Since his villa was some miles from the closest telegraph station at Eastbourne, Holmes employed a veritable army of young lads, who flocked from the nearby small farms which dotted the Downs in order to carry his messages to and fro.

It was, then, with considerable surprise that I received a full letter from my friend. Although he protested rheumatism as his motive for avoiding the miasmas of London, the writing upon the single watermarked page was firm and clear.

MY DEAR WATSON:
I write these few lines in order to point you in the correct direction. The murder of Mr. Gloucester is not without its

elements of interest, though certainly not sufficient to induce me to sally forth from Sussex. I have been called an omnivorous reader, though I suppose I must say the same for the perpetrator of this little crime, for he certainly appears to be a connoisseur of sensational literature from the monthly serials. I suppose you should be congratulated that your early work is now so popular that it is being imitated, not just upon cheap wood pulp, but in real-life.

Let me first warn you from following false paths. 'Eins' is German for 'one,' Watson. So don't spend too much time looking for a source of Professor Einhorn's anaesthetic. There are very few poisons which act rapidly, are both odourless and tasteless, and fail to be detected by the standard tests. I therefore suspect poisoning by thallium in a mega-dose, for your report contains no signs of chronic exposure - such as hair loss or other reports of ill health - in the minutes before Mr. Gloucester's death.

The second lesson is to discern motive and means, Watson. There are obstacles to narrowing down the means. Thallium is widely available as a rat poison, and even the prodigious resources of Scotland Yard will likely prove to be insufficient to track down every purchase in the last few months. 'Months?' I hear you ask. Yes, months, Watson. For surely few individuals frequenting the Tankerville Club would have kept a phial of thallium in their pocket to be used in the event of a sudden urge to assassinate someone who angered them. No, Watson, this was no heated crime, but something long-planned.

Therefore, in such a case, only by discovering the motive will you be able to move forward. Something in Mr. Gloucester's past was sufficiently sordid as to induce a homicidal instinct in someone present in the Tankerville last night. Find the connection and you will have your man.

Pray give my greetings to Lestrade. Scotland Yard as a whole is a dull lot, and seriously out of their depths when confronted with anything beyond a simple smash and grab. But Lestrade was the best of them during our time together, when we regularly dashed through the crooked fog-bound streets of London in hopes of preventing some catastrophe. Towards the end of my active days, I thought that he had even learned a thing or two. I hope your present case does not disabuse me of that generous notion.

Very sincerely yours,
SHERLOCK HOLMES.

§

I admit to disturbing the patrons of the hotel's dining room when I laughed aloud at Holmes' notion of generosity over my breakfast. I immediately repaired to the nearest telegraph-office in order to dispatch the most critical update from Scotland Yard.

I scribbled the following message for Holmes:

> *Important development. Lestrade has arrested one Simon Ingram, a waiter at the Tankerville who had been seen arguing with Gloucester on the night of the murder. Please advise.*
> *– WATSON.*

While I awaited Holmes' reply, I considered the events of the morning. A note had come round to the hotel from Lestrade. It informed me that Mr. James Heath Newton had mentioned during questioning that there appeared to be a tension between Gloucester and the waiter Ingram. Ingram was well-known to Heath Newton, as he had worked at the club for some years. He was considered to be a hot-headed but likeable lad. Heath Newton had stepped away for a moment to attend to personal business, and when he returned to the table where he was sharing a drink with Gloucester, he noticed Ingram stomping away, his face flushed with anger. Gloucester's brow was furrowed, but when asked, he laughed and dismissed the whole thing as a minor misunderstanding. Heath Newton had forgotten the entire incident until Lestrade's skilled interrogation - his own words! - had brought it to the surface. Lestrade briskly followed up the matter, and discovered that Simon Ingram was engaged to one Clara Becker, an assistant cook in the Tankerville's kitchen. Under questioning, Miss Becker admitted that Mr. Gloucester had made unwanted advances towards her, and when he learned of it, Simon had become furious. Lestrade had further determined that Ingram had left the Tankerville early that evening, and had no alibi for the time of Gloucester's death. Presuming that Ingram had snuck back into the club and murdered Gloucester, Lestrade had summarily arrested the waiter.

However, I was far less certain of Ingram's guilt. Scotland Yard had arrested the wrong person before. John McFarlane, Flora Miller, and John Hopley Neligan were proof positive that the C.I.D. was not infallible. Moreover, I knew that in the annals of the typically magnificent British criminal law, innocent men had upon occasion been condemned by the flimsiest of evidence. I now had a much more pressing motivation than curiosity alone to pique Holmes' interest in the murder of Mr. Lewis Gloucester. If the truth was not revealed, a potentially innocent man would hang.

Eventually, Holmes' terse reply came in to the office. It read:

I revise my opinion of Lestrade. This was no unpremeditated attack. Have you found the motive yet?
– S.H.

Holmes was, of course, correct. If I was to help clear Mr. Ingram's name, I would need to determine why someone else would wish Gloucester dead. Time was ticking.

§

London Library, 4 July 1907
My dear Holmes:

I thought long and hard about your words. Given that your commonplace books and indices have been removed from London, I required an alternate source of information about the antecedents of Mr. Lewis Gloucester. I therefore sought out my old friend Lomax at the London Library. He supplied me with several trustworthy encyclopaedias of reference.

I learned that Gloucester, as had been reported in the newspaper accounts, was formerly a successful engineer. His origins were humble, being the son of a tavern keeper in Forest Row, Sussex. However, he moved to London in his early twenties, where he apprenticed at Chanter and Mason, the well-known firm of Woolwich. After a decade of fairly unremarkable work, Gloucester hit upon a novel method to manufacture a high-density glass with a unique refractive index. Although the text was rather vague, I surmised that this glass was of special interest to certain members of the Royal Navy, and both Gloucester and the firm came into a fair sum. Gloucester had long hence served his required time at the firm, so shortly after the invention he retired from professional activities and became known as a man of leisure. He belonged to several clubs, seemed well-regarded, and had no apparent debts or enemies. There is nothing I can find to suggest a reason why someone would wish to bring about his death.

Any suggestions you might have would be most welcome. Replies will continue to find me at the Charing Cross Hotel.

Very sincerely yours,
JOHN H. WATSON.

§

Charing Cross Hotel, 4 July 1907
My dear Holmes:

I sent off the earlier short note to you via express messenger. I had hoped that you would respond quickly with one of your typically-brilliant insights, but I knew it would take at least several hours. In the interim, I was feeling rheumatic and old, so I decided to visit the baths on Northumberland Avenue. After a relaxation in the dry air of the warm room, and a dip in the waters of the hot room, I retired to the isolated corner of the upper floor's cooling chamber. I lay enveloped in sheets upon one of the divans and enjoyed a moment of pleasant lassitude under the bright Alhambra tiles. I have often found that this cleanser of the system serves as a fresh starting-point for the mental energies required to see a task through to its proper conclusion.

Despite the soft tinkling of the fountain, I was vaguely conscious that the adjacent couch had become occupied by another customer. He was respectful of my meditation, and made no effort to commence an unwelcome conversation. However, when one of the boys came over with a message for him, his noble title was sufficiently curious to induce me to open my eyes and glance over in his direction. His age was hard to accurately place, but roughly in the middle of his forties, with a face lined by great cares. I thought him a man whose fire of youth had died down, but which was replaced with a steady dose of experience. Even wrapped in a robe, he carried himself with a measure of chivalry.

He saw my interest, and turned to me with a smile. "Good afternoon. I trust you are enjoying the baths?"

"Very much so. They are expensive, but most relaxing."

"Indeed," said the man, nodding his head. "Everything in London these days is quite exorbitant. Why, I once partook of a similar bath at the Cemberlitas Hamam in Istanbul for a quarter of the price."

"I have not had that pleasure," I responded. "Sadly, I did not have sufficient time to visit the Mughal baths when I was in India."

"Ah!" his face beamed with gratification. "A fellow traveller! Please allow me to introduce myself. I am the Marquis de Loam. Alexandre Doumer to my friends."

"John Watson," I replied.

His eyebrows rose with interest. "There is an author by that name…"

I smiled. "I have been fortunate to have accompanied my friend Mr. Sherlock Holmes upon a few cases of interest, which I subsequently chronicled in order to lay before the public."

"Well, this is a great pleasure indeed to make your acquaintance!"

I held up my hand in protest. "I assure you, it is my friend who is famous, not I."

"I have heard that Mr. Holmes is no longer in active practice?"

"That is true. He has retired to the countryside."

"Ah, a great loss for the people of London," said the Marquis, sadly. "Though, I must say that I can sympathize with his position. There is a great energy to London, but it also asks much of a man." He waved his hand about the room. "Other than these rare islands of tranquillity, there are few places to escape the constant bustle. I keep a small suite of rooms here, but rarely use it. London is a city for young men."

He said it with such languidness that I laughed aloud. "You will forgive me, Marquis, but I think you must be at least a decade younger than I."

He smiled. "A wise man once said that age is not measured in years lived, but in miles travelled."

"And you are well-travelled?"

"Oh, yes. Not so much in my youth, but recently, since I came into my estates, I have endeavoured to see as much of the world as possible. I have recently returned from Sarawak."

"And where are your estates, Marquis?"

"Near Montpellier."

I started at the mention of that city, as I recalled that you had once spent time there doing research into coal tar derivatives. For a moment I wondered if this was some curious role adopted by you. The man did have your grey eyes, but rather than being shining and mobile, the Marquis' were hard. They matched his grim mouth, half-hidden by his bushy beard. I realized that he must have come from that Huguenot blood which has strengthened and refined every race which it has touched. There was no possibility that this man was you in disguise, Holmes.

"And if I might ask, what brings you so far from home, Marquis?" I asked.

"It is by special invitation to a society ball. I say, Doctor, I wonder if you are already occupied this evening? I would be delighted if you could attend. The ball is being hosted by Sir Thomas Donahue."

I recognized the name. "The shipping magnate?"

"Indeed. He is an old friend of mine."

I shook my head. "I am a simple former army surgeon. I have never been one to run in high society."

The Marquis laughed. "Nonsense! You have journeyed many leagues, Doctor Watson, from the path of a simple army surgeon. How many such men can claim to have rubbed elbows with two Premiers of England and the King of Bohemia?"

"Not on my merits, I assure you, Marquis. All of that was done in the company of my friend, Mr. Holmes."

"Nonetheless, you are no stranger to high society, no matter how much you deny it. I insist."

"But I have no invitation," I protested.

He smiled broadly. "I will guarantee that your name finds its way onto the guest list. You merely need to present yourself to his doorstep and you will be granted access. Say you will come!"

I reluctantly acquiesced to the man's request. He rose and shook my hand enthusiastically before taking his leave. As I slowly dressed and did up the laces of my boots, I wondered why I had consented to such a whim. Surely it could do little to further my investigation into Mr. Gloucester's murder. However, there was something infectious about the French aristocrat, and something he had said had sparked an idea. But as soon as it had flickered in my brain, it was gone. If only I had developed your little trick of the brain attic, I surely would have been able to place my finger upon it. Until then, I would have to ensure that I had with me suitable attire for a ball.

Very sincerely yours,
JOHN H. WATSON.

§

When I returned to the hotel, the desk clerk handed me a note that had been delivered in my absence. I quickly opened it to find the scribbled hand used by Holmes when he was hurried.

> *Dear Watson,*
> *There are one or two points which might be of interest to you. Shortly after Lewis Gloucester invented his novel glass, one of his fellow employees was convicted of treason. Mr. Edgar Virgil had attempted to steal the plans and sell them to an agent of a foreign power. An action which, if successful, would have greatly lessened the strategic advantage the glass afforded our Navy. On the basis of the testimony of Gloucester and two other men - including the firm's owner, Mr. Peter Chanter - Virgil was sentenced to life imprisonment at St. Helena. A wire to that remote island confirms that Virgil died there early last year.*
> *– S.H.*

I stared at Holmes' message, attempting to determine how precisely this information advanced the case. Holmes seemed to be implying that Virgil's recent death was related to the murder of Gloucester. If this was true, then Simon Ingram, the Tankerville Club's waiter, was certainly innocent. But how did I go about proving it?

§

Charing Cross Hotel, 4 July 1907

My dear Holmes:

There have been considerable developments in the case. I am happy to report that Mr. Ingram has been released by Scotland Yard, though I can hardly take the credit. Lestrade had been unable to secure any shred of evidence other than the weak motive. There were no witnesses to suggest that Ingram had ever returned the club that night, and at the time the waiter had departed, Gloucester had not yet received the now-vanished note which had summoned him to his doom. However, there was one other incident which more conclusively suggested Mr. Ingram's innocence. And strangely enough, it occurred at the ball thrown by Sir Thomas Donahue.

I soon discovered that I had neglected to bring with me a seemly outfit for a formal ball, so I was forced to send round to J. Dege and Sons in Savile Row, for a suit, and to Latimer's in Oxford Street, for a pair of shoes. Although it was less than a mile walk along Whitehall, both my unbroken shoes and our social mores suggested that it would be unwise to arrive at the ball on foot. Therefore, the upper attendant at the hotel hailed a carriage to take me round to Sir Thomas's home at 4 Cowley Street.

During the short ride, I reflected on what little I knew about Sir Thomas' rapid rise to prominence. Webster's *Red Court and Fashionable Register* noted that the man had only been elevated to his baronetcy within the last year. He was evidently hosting this ball as a method of displaying the obscene wealth which had facilitated this advancement. I recalled that the gossip columns had been rife with speculation about how a once-humble captain of a merchant ship had suddenly managed to develop a massive shipping empire, though none of the rumours seemed particularly credible.

When I arrived at my destination, Sir Thomas' recently acquired mansion proved to be one of those old-fashioned and secluded homes which lie between the river and the Abbey, within easy earshot of the great bell hanging over the Houses of Parliament. My carriage was but one of many disgorging its occupants for this fashionable event. I was momentarily dismayed to discover that it was a masquerade ball, a fact that the Marquis de Loam had neglected to mention. Fortunately, Donahue's footmen were prepared with a variety of masks for any such wayward guests. I gave my name, which had been added just as the Marquis had promised, and was promptly handed a small gold and silver mask, which I doubted did much to conceal my identity. You will accuse me of vanity, Holmes, however, I fear my moustache and general countenance has gotten far too much exposure in the sketches of Mr. Paget.

When I finally entered, I was struck by the impressive scene. The ball was being held in a suite of six or seven rooms which, unlike the typical straight vista favoured by most houses, twisted and turned their way so that every dozen yards the visitor was obligated to pass into another chamber. Each was decorated in an entirely different fashion, and I would normally describe them in detail, however, I suspect that you, Holmes, would find such flourishes excessive. Suffice it to say that the place easily held some seven score guests, not to mention the musicians, and a small army of servants.

As I gazed about the largest room, I quickly realized that you, with your Bohemian soul, would have loathed this society event. Only a few times did we ever set foot in such circumstances, the most notable being the one held in the unusual setting of a Wapping furniture warehouse.[73] As my wife would well attest, one skill I have never mastered is the waltz. I therefore strenuously avoided the couples crowding the dance-floor and instead busied myself by conversing with those gathered near the tables overflowing with drinks and a wide variety of delectable foods. I soon fell in with Lady Hilda Trelawney Hope, who recognized me despite my mask.

At first, the crinkled around her eyes suggested alarm that

I might indiscreetly reveal the mode of our acquaintance. "Dr Watson," she exclaimed. "I never expected to see you here." She looked around rapidly. "Are you working on a case with Mr. Holmes?"

"No, madam. Holmes remains retired and is out of London. I am simply a guest of the Marquis de Loam."

The tension drained from her face and her eyebrows rose with interest. "I see. The Marquis is an interesting man. How do you know him?"

I shook my head. "By pure chance. We were taking the baths at the same time, and got to talking. I believe he invited me on a whim. But I really know little about him."

"Few do. He is new upon the London society scene. He is said to be well-travelled and is rumoured to be fabulous wealthy. Come, Dr Watson, since you are new to this particular battlefield, I will see that you are introduced to a few individuals."

Despite our concealed past association, that courageous woman was not afraid to serve as my guide, and presented me to a dizzying array of the cream of society. In short order, I had met, amongst others, the Earl of Dovercourt, Sir Cathcart Soames, Lady Alicia Whittington, Lord Eustace St. Simon, Mr. Arthur Holder, Lord Leverstoke, and two women who I knew better by their former sobriquets of Lady Hilda Adair and Miss Edith Woodley. All of these names passed over me so rapidly, that I barely had time to process why they seemed so familiar. I even shook the hand of the Countess of Morcar and managed to compliment her upon the brilliant blue carbuncle which shone out like a star from the dark hollow of her necklace. Little did she realize that this was not the first time I had gazed upon that famous gem, which spent a night under my roof many years ago.

Lady Trelawney Hope was called away, and I stood alone, momentarily overwhelmed by the poignant memories which had come flooding back at the prompt of these individuals. They reminded me of a time when I strode with giants, my actions playing a role, however small, in the fate of the world. A time which had passed me by, never to be experienced again. There was little wonder why I had taken such an interest in this case. If I was to be honest with myself, I was attempting to try to recapture one small speck of my fleeting youth, before such chances were gone forever.

My reminiscences were finally interrupted by the appearance of the man who had invited me to the ball. He wore a very simple black mask, which could not obscure his hard grey eyes or bushy beard. It was plain that the Marquis de Loam was already far along in his cups, for as he approached, his gait wobbled slightly. He shook my hand, his palm rough against mine, and begged me to relate an untold story of one of our adventures. "I have read all of the ones published in *The Strand*, Doctor, but there must be many more in your files which you have not yet lain before the public."

I shook my head. "I could not possibly. I always obtain Holmes' permission before I lay out such narratives."

"I will not squeal, Doctor. You have my word as a gentleman."

Taking him at his word, I launched into the tale of the Barclay Square poltergeist.[74] I had just arrived at the most suspenseful part of the tale – the great roar echoing through Sir Randolph's haunted home - when my recounting was cut short by strident calls for a doctor.

I followed the sounds through several rooms until I finally came upon the source of the commotion. Unfortunately, by the location of the large knife protruding from the man's heart, it was unlikely I could be of much assistance. However, I did note that the currently-jailed Mr. Ingram could breathe easier, for there was little chance that he could have left the note attached to the dagger via a thin scarlet thread. In plain block capitals, this simply read: *ZWEI*.

I didn't need you, Holmes, to tell me the English translation. Mr. Gloucester's killer had struck again.

It wasn't until nearly an hour later, after both Lestrade and

Gregson had appeared on the scene, that I learned the identity of the dead man. He was the Honourable Wesley Hildyard, the younger son of the Earl of Burnley. Lestrade permitted me to inspect the body, which was that of a man nearer sixty than fifty. Beyond the obvious cause of death, there was one other item of note. In the dead man's mouth, I found a half-sovereign coin. I wondered the meaning of such a bizarre ritual, which could only have been performed at great risk by the assassin.

Another anomaly was the absence of Hildyard's wife, who had clearly declined to attend the ball with her husband. When she finally arrived, I found her absence of emotion rather curious. She was a statuesque beauty, much younger than her spouse, and with a face like alabaster. She tersely confirmed the identity of her deceased husband for Lestrade, and then - without a hint of tears in her eyes - departed silently.

Amazingly, the result of Lestrade's questioning revealed that amidst the enormous crowd of ball attendees, no one had witnessed the actual attack upon Hildyard. The catalogue of possible suspects was even longer than the one containing of all the members and guests of the Tankerville Club present upon the night of 2 July. However, I knew that the murderer had made his first mistake. For it would not be difficult to cross-reference the two lists, and when that task was complete, if I was not mistaken there would only be a few names remaining. And one would have a date with Jack Ketch.

Very sincerely yours,
JOHN H. WATSON.

§

I had posted the previous letter upon my return to the hotel, paying a premium to ensure that it reached Holmes by the following morn. When I awoke, I went round to Scotland Yard in order to enact my plan. I explained it carefully to Lestrade.

The inspector listened intently and then sat back contentedly in his chair and interlocked his fingers behind his head. He then smiled. "Surely, Dr Watson, you don't think that we didn't already have the same idea?" He waved his hand to a side table. "The lists are over there."

I paused, a bit surprised that Lestrade - who Holmes had always described as a bit plodding - would have already come upon this tactic. "Well..." I stammered.

"You will be pleased to note, Doctor, that we have already determined the identity of the murderer."

He said it with such confidence and assurance that I failed to mask my feeling of surprise.

"Oh, yes, it was a German Nihilist by the name of Johann Spies. The C.I.D. has been on the lookout for the man for some time, and we recently received a tip from one of our informers that Spies was operating under the alias of George Smith. As Smith, the man managed to get himself hired as a groom at the Tankerville Club. He also was one of the temporary servants hired to wait upon the guests at Donahue's ball."

"And where is Spies now?"

Lestrade shook his head sadly. "As near as we can tell, he went straight from Sir Thomas' house to London Bridge Station, where he took the first train to Dover. He caught passage aboard the *Queen* steamer across the Channel and has by now melted into the vile alleys of Calais."

"Why would Johann Spies target Lewis Gloucester and Wesley Hildyard?"

The inspector shrugged. "The man is an anarchist, Doctor, and as mad as a hatter. If he ever sets foot upon our shores again, we will catch him, and I assure you that we will ask him that very question. But if I had to wager a guess, I would say that the goal of such men is to spread fear and terror amongst our ruling class. It would do little to advance his Socialist aims to strike down a common working lad or two. No, he needed to try to prove to the cream of society that they are vulnerable, not that such a preposterous aim would ever succeed. No, I think the British spine is a bit stiffer than that.

Gloucester and Hildyard were randomly selected, I suspect."

As he concluded this dissertation, a message came in for Lestrade. He glanced at it, and rose to leave. "Sorry, Doctor, duty calls. There has been a robbery at the Post Office Savings Bank. Please feel free to call the next time you are in London. It is always a pleasant reminder of past days." He shook my hand and departed.

I turned to do the same, but my gaze alighted upon the lists of individuals present at both the Tankerville Club and Sir Thomas' ball. I picked them up and ran my eyes down the names. As Lestrade had reported, upon both, under the heading of 'Servants,' was the name George Smith. But I spotted one other name which was common to the two lists. I suppose that finding should have been of no great surprise, given that members of the Tankerville were likely to run in the same circles of society as Sir Thomas Donahue.

I slowly made my way down the staircase and out onto the Embankment. From there I trudged to my hotel. With the case solved, there was no further reason for me to remain in London. I needed pack up my valise and finally buy my ticket home. I would likely jot a few facts into my notebook upon the three-hour journey, merely for the sake of form, as this was not a case worthy of any longer record. It was so unexceptional that Holmes could not even be bothered to stir from his villa.

At least these were my thoughts as I turned into the lobby of the hotel. I asked for my key, and was surprised to find a brief note from Holmes awaiting me. It was short and concise:

Coin = symbol of slander. Hildyard testified against Virgil.
– S.H.

I frowned and considered the meaning of this cryptic message. If Hildyard was the second man upon whose evidence Edgar Virgil was sentenced to transport to St. Helena, then there was a link between him and Gloucester. Lestrade was wrong. This was no random nihilistic act. It was an act of revenge from beyond the grave. If I was correct, the murders were not finished. There was still one more man scheduled to die... Mr. Peter Chanter, of the firm of Chanter and Mason. Suddenly, I knew where I must go.

§

Fortunately, the clerk at the hotel was able, with the help of a telephone call, to quickly determine the location of the residence I sought. The hansom pulled up at 53 Lancaster Gate some twenty minutes later, and I lifted the knocker.

The door was promptly opened by a man of average height, with curly brown hair, and a strange discoloration to the lower half of his bare face. He wore butler's livery and tinted spectacles. I presented my card to the man. Instead of being asked to wait while he took my card inside, the butler bowed. "You are expected, Dr Watson. I will show you to the Marquis, if you would please follow me."

I frowned at this unexpected turn of events. As I trailed the man deeper into the flat, I noted that he walked like a sailor unused to dry land. Any further thoughts about this were driven from my mind at the sight of the room where he had led me, for the Marquis' library was rather remarkable. It looked like a small museum; both broad and deep, with bookshelves and cabinets all round, crowded with objects from around the world.

As I gazed about in wonder, the voice of the Marquis de Loam called out from an easy chair. "Ah, Dr Watson!" he exclaimed. "What a great pleasure to see you again so soon."

"Your man said that you were expecting me?"

He shrugged. "Let us call it a lucky guess, shall we? Of course, your friend Mr. Holmes doesn't appear to believe in something as shallow as luck, does he?"

"No, he believes in cause and effect."

"As do I, Doctor. I assure you that nothing has been further from my mind recently. Please take a seat." He waved to an comfortable-appearing armchair across from him. "But first, I see your eyes studying my collection. Are you yourself a patron of curios?"

I shook my head. "I have kept a few mementos from some of the more remarkable cases which I pursued in the company of Sherlock Holmes. Items that Scotland Yard did not commandeer for its Black Museum."

"Such as?"

I shrugged. "The muzzle from Stapleton's hound, for one."

He smiled broadly. "Ah, yes, perhaps my favourite of your works, Doctor."

"Your interests appear quick broad, Marquis."

"Well, I am no Hans Sloane, to be certain. But I have been fortunate to acquire a few items of note."

"The tiger, for example?" said I, motioning to a magnificent stuffed specimen.

"Yes, I brought that beast down on the shores of the Caspian Sea. Not for sport, mind you, I am no Colonel Moran, depriving the mountain slopes of their heavy game for fun. This one was a man-eater who had haunted the environs of a small village near Baku until I laid in wait for it one night."[75]

"The City of Winds is a long way to travel."

"Oh, I have wandered all around the world, Doctor. I find it enriches the soul. You see my little lion over there?" He gestured towards a weathered sandstone carving of a lion holding a crouching gazelle. "I acquired that in Palmyra, where it was sadly neglected by the locals, who no longer care for the great goddess Al-Lat."

"I have not heard of her."

"No? For many centuries she was worshipped across Arabia, until she was stamped out by the unwashed hordes of greedy monotheists. I suppose I find her to be a symbol of the forgotten."

"And the smell?"

"Ah!" he exclaimed with a smile. "I do so prefer to be surrounded by lovely fragrances. That is the resin of the agarwood tree of Sabah. It is quite rare, and worth twice its weight in gold." He paused for a moment and stared into my eyes. "Would you permit me a question, Doctor?"

"Certainly."

"On whose behalf do you act?"

I frowned. "I am not certain precisely what you mean?"

"Let me be more specific. Did you come to see me today as a representative of the police?"

"Not specifically. I suppose you could say that I am an independent agent."

"Very good. But surely Mr. Holmes must know that you planned to call upon me?"

"I think it likely. It was his idea which suggested I should do so."

"Truly?" said the Marquis, his eyebrows rising. "Is he in town?

"I am afraid not. He is advising me from afar."

"And what, pray tell, was his advice in this matter?"

I shook my head. "It was rather mysterious. He merely said that the deaths of Gloucester and Hildyard had to do with a dead man."

His eyebrows rose with interest. "Oh, yes? And who might that be?"

"Edgar Virgil."

He threw back his head and laughed. "Oh, that is fantastic, Doctor! He is just as clever as billed. I must apologize, Doctor, and plead that I have only been on England's shores for a brief time, when I admit to you that only just in the last few days have I found the time to read your tales from *The Strand*. But once started, I found that I could hardly put them down. A *tour de force*! I was especially interested in a specific handful of the adventures that you shared with Mr. Holmes."

"Indeed?" I said. "Which ones?"

"The tales of Mr. John Turner, Mr. James Ryder, Corporal Henry Wood, Captain Jack Croker, and of course, the anonymous noblewoman who relieved London of one of its worst men."[76]

"You speak of cases in which Holmes did not inform the official forces the identities of those individuals whom his deductions had identified as the perpetrator of a crime."

He waved his hand languidly. "Perhaps. I am curious as to Mr. Holmes' rationale for such actions."

"Holmes has pardoned a crime before when the situation was extraordinary. However, he would never countenance murder." I shook my head. "I am afraid that I cannot permit you to carry out the final step in your plan."

"And what is that?"

"The murder of Peter Chanter."

He smiled. "And I am afraid that you are too late, Doctor. For Chanter is already dead. He blew his brains out this morning. A verdict of *felo de se* is certain."

I frowned. "You must be mistaken."

"I assure you that I am not. It has been verified by a completely reliable witness, even if the news has not yet reached the ears of Fleet Street."

"Why would Chanter kill himself?"

"It seems that Chanter's finances were not as solvent as they appeared. The man was heavily in debt and had speculated all of his remaining credit upon the possibility that the price of gold would increase. When that speculation didn't come through, he took the only remaining course open to him."

"May I presume that you had something to do with his ruin?"

He shrugged. "And if I did? What of it? No one forced Chanter to foolishly gamble away all of his wealth. If I made some rather risky suggestions which unfortunately did not pan out, I can hardly be blamed. In fact, I myself lost money in gold speculation when a mysterious source suddenly flooded the market. I can show you the proof, should you require."

"That won't be necessary."

"All attempts to gain great wealth in a short amount of time are burdened by the possibility of terrible failure, Doctor. It was a lesson that Lewis Gloucester also finally learned, some ten years after the fact."

"And have you had any communique with Peter Chanter today?"

"I may have sent around a little note of condolence at his loss. Though I doubt the C.I.D. men who read it will quite know what to make of it."

"Because it merely says '*DREI.*'"

He smiled. "Very good, Doctor. I must say that of all your masterful works, my especial favourite is the far-reaching revenge of Mr. Hope. Like him in America, when the narrow laws of England turned their back upon me, Doctor, I decided to walk outside the pale."[77]

Anything further the Marquis was about to say was interrupted by an appearance from his butler. The man sauntered over to de Loam's side and bent over to whisper in the man's ear. The Marquis started to wave him away, but suddenly an interested look appeared on his face. "Show him in," said he, nodding at the butler.

We waited in silence for this new player upon the scene. It eventually proved to be an elderly and deformed man, with a sharp, wizened face peering out from a frame of white hair. He carried with him a small wooden box. I studied him with interest, for he seemed strangely familiar.

"You're surprised to see me, sir?" asked the newcomer, in a strange, croaking voice.

The Marquis de Loam frowned. "Indeed. What did you mean by that word you spoke to my man?"

The old man smiled. "Ah, the magic word, akin to Ali Baba's *Sésame, ouvre-toi*.[78] Yes, I thought you might be interested in these." He held forth the box.

De Loam took it hesitantly. He opened it slowly, and I leaned forward to peer inside. It contained three golden coins. The Marquis stared at them for a moment and then began to laugh. He plucked one out and tossed it over to me. Both faces were covered in ornate script, 'EEN POND' upon the face side, and 'ZAR 1902' upon the reverse. I had never before seen it's like, but I reproduce it here:

"It's a *veldpond*, Watson," said a well-remembered voice. I turned and found Sherlock Holmes standing and smiling at me. "Only about five hundred were ever minted, at the very end of the Boer War. It took some effort to scare up three of them, but I thought it the most likely lubricant to loosen the Marquis' tongue."

"Holmes," I finally stammered. "What in the world are you doing here?"

He shook his head. "I am not here, Watson. An old peddler visited the Marquis this morning, nothing more. Sherlock Holmes is still in retirement on the South Downs. The number of pleading communiques has finally died down after all these years. If word was to get out that I was in London, the deluge would commence again. However, I must admit that your letters piqued my interest. I desired to hear this particular story with my own ears, so I travelled up by the nine o'clock train." He turned and faced the Marquis de Loam with an expectant look upon his face.

The Marquis smiled and waved Holmes to a chair. "By all means. It is a great pleasure to finally meet you, Mr. Holmes. Though it seems as if you already know my tale?"

Holmes nodded. "I know that you are in fact Edgar Virgil and I suspect that you are in possession of Kruger's Gold, however there are a few precise details regarding your undertakings of which I remain uncertain."

"Very well then," said the man, spreading his palms out wide. "My life is an open book. As you have deduced, Mr. Holmes, I was born Edgar Virgil."

"How is that possible?" I interjected, shaking my head. "Virgil is dead."

The man's hard grey eyes took on a far-away look. "You are correct, Doctor. Virgil is dead to the world. But he has been reborn in a new form."

"That of a French Marquis?" I said, the realization of the truth sinking in.

"Although my father was English through-and-through, my mother was in fact a French Huguenot. So it is not so far from the truth. But I fear that we are starting in the middle. Shall I take you back to the very beginning?"

Holmes nodded. "Though Watson often fails to abide by such a format, I agree that is the logical method by which to tell a story."

Virgil – or the Marquis, as I shall continue to call him – nodded. "When I began to apprentice for the firm of Chanter and Mason, I was but a few years behind Lewis Gloucester. He appeared to take an interest in me, and I frequently shared with him the new ideas I was working on during my free time. Eventually, I discovered a novel method to manufacture a glass with a very high density and a refractive index. The potential uses of such a material were myriad, but before I brought my invention before Mr. Chanter, I wished to ensure that my technique was reproducible. I showed my equations and formulas to Gloucester and asked him to help me. Instead, he took my idea to Chanter and presented it as his own. To ensure that Chanter would believe his version, Gloucester also forged letters from me which purported to tell of my intention to sell the invention. These were addressed to the German Embassy at Waterloo Place."

"And Hildyard?"

De Loam snorted in derision. "Ah, yes, a fine example of the English peerage. If they are all as rotten to the core as Hildyard, I fear that the foundation of this nation is in grave danger of collapse. You see, as I grew older, I also developed a friendship with Miss Portia Chanter, the only child of the firm's co-owner. The firm was a wealthy one, and she was certain to come with a considerable dowry, though I had no such goal in mind. She had an energetic mind, as well as a beautiful face. The money was immaterial to me. But not to a wastrel like Hildyard. He regularly paid court to Portia. I knew that his sole goal was to prop his flagging fortunes, which had been gambled away in the clubs of Mayfair and spent upon ladies of the night. I like to think that Portia saw through his lofty name and fine manners and preferred me, the simple apprentice. Hildyard must have known that, and Gloucester would have found in him a ready accomplice for his scheme to destroy me. Hildyard's fallacious testimony before the magistrate, in which he told of seeing me slip papers into the little door on the Duke of York's steps, was delivered with an impressive stateliness. Who would doubt such a story from an Earl's son?

"Once my fate had been sealed, Portia was faced with the choice of remaining loyal to a man destined to die in prison, or agreeing to marry Hildyard. I have long suspected that her hand was forced by pressure from her father, who had visions of noble grandsons. Of course, the final straw came when Peter Chanter backed Gloucester's version of the tale." He shook his head ruefully. "In retrospect, I must give Gloucester credit, for he had planned his scheme well. When it was all revealed before me, I was powerless to provide sufficient evidence that would contradict it. But I learned well the lesson that Gloucester taught me that day."

He paused and pursed his lips. "I hold no rancour towards the magistrate. I too would have sided with those cunning men. As you must know, Mr. Holmes, I was spared an execution for my supposed treason, but my crime was considered of such a heinous nature that I was deemed unfit for incarceration in a plain old English prison, such as Princetown or Pentonville. Instead, I was sent to the island of Saint Helena for the remainder of my existence.

"I still recall my first sight of the 'Rock' - as it was called by my fellow prisoners aboard the HMS *Britannic* - rising out of the ocean, bare and rugged. Precipitous cliffs encircled the interior, making it a veritable fortress. Imprisonment upon it offered a gloomy prospect. As it drew ever closer, the feeling grew upon me that this might be my last sight of the outside world, for only the most despised are banished to such places to be forgotten by mankind.

"Unfortunately my quarters proved not quite as hospitable as those provided to Bonaparte. I was held in the maximum security dungeon of Fort James, in a noisome underground hole as capable of stifling a man to death as the Black Hole of Calcutta.[79] I was typically kept in irons and chained to a ring bolt. In summer the heat was intolerable; while in winter, moisture from the nearby stream would seep through the earth and drip steadily down the walls. My only sustenance was rice and fetid water. For the first five years of my exile, I was more corpse than man. I rarely spoke more than a handful of words in a single month. When there is nothing left to live for, there is little reason to bother putting one foot in front of the other."

"What changed?" I asked.

"The arrival of the Boers during the second war against them.[80] The majority were sent out to a specially-constructed camp upon Deadwood Plain. But a handful of the most notorious characters were crowded in with us at Fort James. The great increase in numbers made it such that there was no longer any means of inflicting solitary confinement in any method sufficient to make it efficacious. Instead, each cell - which were roughly ten feet in length and width - became the home of five or six desperate individuals. Although a guard would look in from time to time during the day; at night, it was a free for all. Anything could transpire, without the probability of it being heard by the guards.

"By chance, I found myself crowded in with three fellow Englishman and one Boer. I soon learned that the former were some of the most despicable scum to ever walk the earth, and would have cheerfully strangled their grandmothers for a crust of bread. The latter was different. He was a sunburned, tangle-haired, full-bearded farmer. But in his prime, he was one of those black-veld Boers who were perhaps the finest natural warriors upon earth, a marksman, a hunter, accustomed to hard fare and a harder couch. He was rough in his ways and speech, but I could tell he had once been most formidable, despite his primitive qualities. Unfortunately, he had been badly wounded during his capture, such that the crowded conditions of the boat and the pestilential air of the prison conspired until I despaired for his life.

"Certainly the jackals with whom we shared the cell had no such concerns, and I could tell that it was only a matter of time before they made their move upon his meagre rations. Why I cared is a mystery - other than the fact that I have never been fond of a bully - but I was determined to prevent such an assault. One night, during which the amount food delivered was especially scanty, the three of them decided that they had had enough. They made their move upon the Boer, but in so doing, they turned their backs upon me. Perhaps they believed that I would not intervene. They were wrong.

"Over the years, I had managed to retain enough awareness that when an opportunity arose, I took it. Upon two or three occasions I had been led out of my cell and allowed to breathe fresh air in the prison grounds. The final time, I had stumbled across a slightly-dulled razor blade and managed to pocket it without being seen. Another time I found some wood, and from the tatters of my shirt I fashioned a rough string, for such clothing was a hindrance in the heat of the summer and near-useless in the winter. With these treasures, I managed to improvise a crude shiv, which I hid carefully by wrapping it around my calf beneath my threadbare trousers. At the time I fashioned it, I was unsure of when it might prove useful, for it would never be sufficient to facilitate my escape from the stone walls of Fort James. But now was the time for it to make an appearance.,

"I leapt upon the ringleader of the trio and drove the shiv deep into the side of his neck. He collapsed without a word, and I was on the second man before the shock of my attack had time to dissipate. I finished him off too, thanks to a thrust to his eye, but the third man had gathered enough wits to defend himself. He jumped upon my back and had curled his arm about my neck, such that I was having a hard time drawing breath. As the stars began to spin in front of my eyes, I realized that I was finished.

"However, I awoke a few minutes later and found the third Englishman dead, his head bashed in upon the stone walls. The Boer had managed to rise from his sick pallet to join the fray and he dispatched the man who had near strangled me to death. The Boer shook my hand for coming to his defence, an action which had nearly cost me my life. We became fast friends that night.

"By the morning, the stench of the dead men's blood, brains, and excrement was unbearable, even to men such as us who had already passed beyond the gates of Hell. Fortunately, the prison was so constructed that every facility was afforded for self-destruction, such that these instances were commonplace. We had little trouble convincing the apathetic wardens that the three men had died attacking each other, though such a tale required the surrender of my little dagger."

The Marquis de Loam paused from his recollections and glanced in my direction. "What is your opinion of the Boer War, Doctor?"

I considered this for a moment. "There were many tragedies, of course, as there are in any war. I suppose that later generations will look back and say that man passes like the brown leaves, but the tradition of a nation lives on like the oak that sheds them – and the passing of the leaves is nothing if the bole be the sounder for it."

Our host shook his head. "After hearing the accounts of my new friend, I cannot share your views, Doctor. Kitchener's scorched-earth policy and concentration camps were very close to being called acts of genocide. But I may not be an impartial judge, for I too have been on the receiving end of supposed British justice.

"In any case, I digress from the story of Mr. Egnatius Botha, as I learned he was called. He had been captured at Rooiwal in April 1902 and sent down to Cape Town for trial. From that transit camp, like so many others, Botha was sent out to St. Helena. Although he had rallied during the assault by our cellmates, Botha was a gravely ill man. His wounds were festering and his frame was wracked by enteric fever. I think he knew he was dying, which is why he entrusted his story to me.

"He told me about the fourth of June, 1900. When he, John Hotzhausen, Marthinus Pretorius, and Philip Swartz were ordered to conceal one of the great treasures of the modern age. Are you familiar with the legend, Mr. Holmes?"

My friend waved his hand. "Only generally."

"Then you will permit me to refresh your memory. I believe there may be some subtle connection between the barrenness and worthlessness of a land's surface and the value of the minerals which lie beneath it. The craggy mountains of Western America, the arid plains of Australia, the ice-bound gorges of the Klondike, and the bare slopes of the Witewatersrand veld – these are the lids which cover the great treasure chests of the world. Gold had been known to exist in the Transvaal before, but it was only in 1886 when it was demonstrated that the deposits which lie some thirty miles south of the Boer capital are of a very extraordinary and valuable nature.

"Surely you are aware that a vast river of gold flowed from the hills of the Transvaal between the years 1884 to 1900? I have heard it confidently reported that seven hundred million pounds were pulled from the Rand mines. However, with great wealth comes great lust, and the British Empire desired control over those hoards. And so, in 1899, watchers on the signal station at Table Mountain saw the smoke of a fleet of giant steamers coming past Robben Island and disgorging troops upon the shores of South Africa. The Boers fought stubbornly, but the British still pressed onwards, disregarding all else and striking straight for the head of the nation, much as Blucher struck at Paris in 1814.

"By the end of May 1900, Paul Kruger, the autocratic President of the South African Republic, could sense that the capitol of Pretoria was about to fall before the massed might of the British Empire. So, on the fourth of June, he sent the entirety of the nation's treasury – two million pounds of gold and diamonds loaded into wooden boxes – to be hidden in the distant wastes.[81]

"Botha told me that the four of them had loaded the treasure into the baggage compartment of a train at the orders of Ernest Meyer, Master of the Mint. All of them armed to the teeth, the four men travelled in the passenger compartment guarding both the gold and Mr. Meyer from harm, as the last train flying the flag of the Republic left Pretoria amidst the thunder of British cannon fire. Six hours later, the train arrived safely one hundred and thirty seven miles east at Machadodrorp in the Lowveld, where Kruger had set up a government-in-exile. The treasure then turned north to Pilgrim's Rest and was there loaded onto a boat, which they sailed up the Blyde and Oliphants Rivers deep into the province of Mpumalanga. From the river's bank, they then hauled it an additional fifty miles north into the Ermelo region and hid it in a well-concealed cavern.

"Afterwards, the four of them returned to the front under the command of General Ben Viljoen, but Botha kept track of his confederates. Marthinus Pretorius was killed in action in September 1901. Philip Swartz was wounded at Scheeper's Nek in 1901 and sent to a prisoner-of-war camp in Ceylon. As far as Botha knew, John Hotzhausen still lived, and Botha figured that Hotzhausen was doing everything in his power to claim the treasure for his own, since Kruger was in exile in

Germany.

"Botha was conflicted about who should possess the gold. By this time, the war had already ended. The Boers remained prisoners only while the final terms of peace were being negotiated. There was no longer an independent Boer republic to which the gold might be returned. And Botha had little desire to see it end up in the hands of the British Government, who would only use it to pay their debts amassed while fighting Botha's friends and relatives. So, Botha figured that he was entitled to a share, which he bequeathed to me for my unsolicited aid during the night assault. We had no ability to write or draw, but Botha described the landmarks so well, that it was if I could see in my head a map to that hidden cave, even if I had never set foot in Africa. If you reach over to that table, you will find a map which I later used to trace his journey."

I followed his command and glanced at the rough sketch. Unfortunately, I was unable to take the Marquis' sketch with me, so I instead enclose a professional version below. Of course, the areas of greatest interest, where the cavern was actually located, are cut off at the north-eastern edge for the sake of confidentiality:

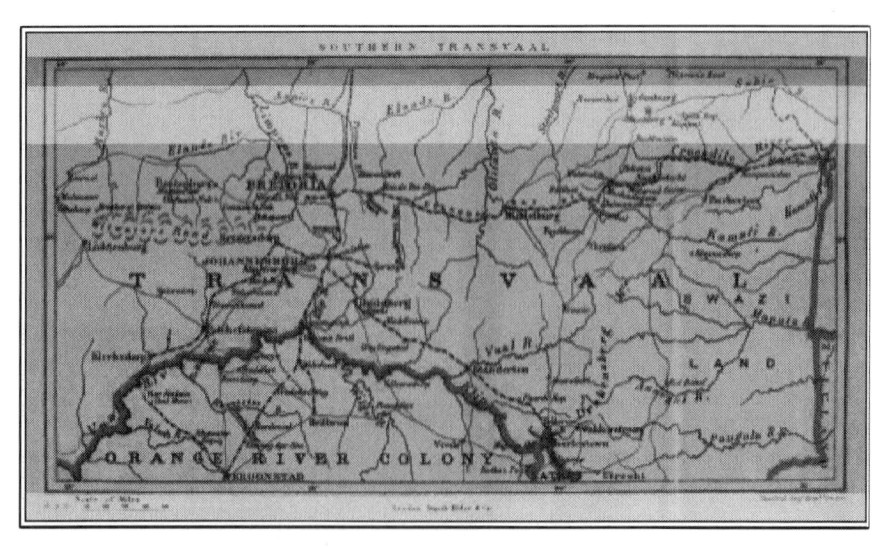

"But how did you escape?" I asked.

The Marquis shook his head. "For many years, I thought it impossible. We had all heard about failed escape attempts. Men who managed to steal boats, only to be caught shortly after by the Navy ships which patrolled the waters. However, one attempt fired my imagination. One enterprising prisoner-of-war, who had more freedom of movement at the Deadwood Camp than we had at Fort James, managed to fashion a shipping crate for himself. He marked it 'Curios Only,' 'With Care,' and 'This Side Up,' and labelled it with a false address in London. He packed it with clothing, matches, a rough map of the Southampton dock, and sufficient food and water to last for twenty days. He then climbed inside and waited for someone to come collect the crate. Amazingly, the crate was loaded onto a passing ship, and the lad managed to hide in his crate for five days before his absence was noted. The authorities wired to Ascension Island, where the ship was stopped and searched. Although the lad had eventually been re-captured, I felt that escape must be possible by the sufficiently desperate, and surely that term described me well.

"I have heard of men who preside over a mass mutiny, overpower the guards, and commit terrible crimes in their break for freedom. I assure you, Doctor, that my hands are clean. I will tell you how I did it. When Botha finally died, I recalled the procedure followed at the time of the deaths of our cellmates. The oft-drunken guards were not trusted with the seemingly-simple task of declaring a man dead, so they always brought in a camp surgeon. The surgeon would assure himself that there were no signs of life, marked down the prisoner's name in a ledger, and then left. The guards would then load the corpse into a rough wooden coffin, and then leave the chamber briefly to fetch nails and a hammer. Once the coffin was sealed they would then haul it out.

"It was a desperate toss, but I had little to lose. Turning my face to the wall and covering my head with the rough blanket they afforded prisoners, I feigned a deep sleep at the entrance of the guards and did not stir when they loaded the corpse.

The minute they departed in search of nails, I sprang from my pallet and pulled poor Botha from the coffin. I placed him on my pallet and covered him with the blanket. I then assumed his place in the coffin, mere seconds before the guards returned. My heart pounded so loudly, it was a wonder that they could not hear it, but they merely hammered home the nails and carried out the box with me inside.

"You may wonder at the laxity of their security precautions, but what fear did the authorities have that someone would carry out such a rash plan? I was counting on being able to break out from the flimsy wood coffin and then dig through the ground before I ran out of air, but who knows how many others attempted such a thing only to suffocate to death? And even if I managed to accomplish that near-impossible task, I was still stuck upon an island over a thousand miles from the nearest shore. Where was I to go?

"But I didn't consider all of those obstacles at the time. I simply knew that I required a route out of that dungeon before I shared Botha's fate. Everything else I was trusting to Lady Destiny. And she finally smiled upon me. What I did not know when I started my attempt was that the guards were too far sluggish to be bothered to dig holes in the ground during the sweltering summer months. Instead they loaded the coffins onto a cart, which was pulled by a donkey to the nearest cliff face. From there, the boxes were simply hurled into the embrace of the rock-strewn Atlantic Ocean. It was a fall that no man was likely to survive. However, Fate smiled upon me again. Providentially, just as the cart reached its destination, a torrential rain began to fall. The guards hurriedly unloaded the cart and carelessly dumped the coffins upon the ground rather than face the onslaught of the storm winds whipping over the cliffs. I suppose that they reasoned that they could return the next day to finish the task and that the dead would patiently wait.

"Once I could no longer hear the wheels of the cart, I strained against the lid of the coffin. I was weak from malnutrition, but I knew that this was my only chance. Fail here, and I would either drown in the ocean or be recaptured, which to me was a fate worse than death. From some secret reserve, power flowed into my limbs and I burst the coffin open.

"I was immediately assaulted by the storm, but the warm rain felt majestic upon my face. I opened my arms to the sky and for a moment luxuriated in the feeling of freedom. I soon realized that there was still the small matter of escaping from the island to overcome, and my celebration withered. But I had come too far; the seed of determination was now rooted in my chest, and I would not quit until I had managed to return to London.

"Leaving an empty coffin would be a signal that a prisoner was on the loose, so despite the winds, I dragged it to the cliff-face and tossed it over. I then set out to make my way to the harbour. There was a goat track winding in and out among the rocks, so I had no difficulty in finding a path down. It stood to reason that such trails in St. Helena would eventually lead towards the water. I began to descend the wet and dark hillside, almost slipping and falling to my death multiple times. But I finally reached the shore, after which I followed it along until I came to some huts, from which I pilfered a bit of food and a slight upgrade in attire. I am not proud of having to resort to stealing, Doctor, but desperate times called for desperate measures.

"Feeling somewhat restored, I continued along the shore until I reached the port. There was no hope of reaching a ship that night, so I sought shelter further up the hillside and slept the sleep of the dead, untroubled by howling winds and pounding rains. By the time I awoke, the storm had passed, and though I was wracked by a ravenous hunger, I laid low throughout the daylight. As soon as the sun was down, I crept back down to the harbour and scanned it for options.

"I quickly spotted a large steamship. The name *Botany Bay* was painted on her stern. My plan was to swim out and climb aboard her. I would then keep under the hatches until the next port. I had a few coins in my pocket from my act of thievery, and I figured I could use them to pay some poor sailor to smuggle a sufficient amount of food and grog to last me the duration of the voyage.

"To my amazement, my plan actually worked, at least for some time. I managed to stow myself in the hold of the ship and waited until we were far out to sea the next day before making my presence known to one of the sailors. The man was willing to fall in with my scheme, and for several days, I traded my Saint Helena stone cell for a ship's cramped wooden closet. But I cared not, for I felt the ever-closer taste of freedom. Alas it was not to last.

"One of the companions of my bribed sailor noted that he was sneaking away from the mess with food and followed him to my hiding place. I was soon discovered, my arms were tied behind my back, and I was hauled before the captain. By rights, he could have had me tossed into the middle of the South Atlantic, and that would have been the pitiful end of Edgar Virgil. Instead, I was able to convince him that I could make it worth his while to keep me alive. I told him both my tale of injustice, and the story I had heard from Botha. I promised to share with him half of the Kruger gold if he took me to South Africa."

"The captain listened carefully to my saga, and eventually agreed to assist with my possibly-foolhardy quest. Unfortunately, the trade winds were carrying us away from the Cape, and the captain could hardly abandon his cargo to go in search of what might be nothing more than the fictions of a dying man. So, it was some time before I finally got a chance to search for Kruger's millions.

"I was never a good sailor. I recall that the trip out to St. Helena was misery incarnate. But something was different about that return voyage. The fresh air revived me, and from that time onward I accommodated myself to the motion of the vessel. As I grew stronger, I learned to pull the ropes which hoisted the sails, and also to haul the long sticks to which they are attached. I also befriended one of the sailors, a chap named Gil Hughes. We originally bonded over our somewhat similar appearance, and later he left the sea life in order to remain in my employ."

"Your butler!" I exclaimed.

"Indeed. Mr. Hughes was always a popular chap, in no small part due to his remarkable ability to mimic the voices of others."

"He impersonated you at Sir Thomas' ball, didn't he?" said I, accusingly. "I suppose the masquerade was your idea?"

"Guilty as charged," the Marquis replied with a smile. "Eventually, in October 1906 we docked at Durban with sufficient time to mount an expedition into the interior. My major concern was that either Swartz or Hotzhausen could have gotten there first. It turns out that I had reason for alarm. Swartz had bragged in a letter about his days of financial insecurity coming to an end once he was released from prison and returned to South Africa. This letter was intercepted, and Swartz was released and his movements watched by the authorities, who hoped that he would lead them to Kruger's gold. Swartz assembled a crew to try to retrieve the gold, but he fell out with one man - named van Niekerk - over a woman. During the early stages of the expedition into the veld, Swartz murdered van Niekerk, and was arrested for the crime. He was executed at Johannesburg in February 1904. For his part, Hotzhausen was arrested at Kimberly in September 1905 for attempting to steal a horse and carriage, presumably to use in an attempt to retrieve the Kruger's gold. He was still in prison when we made our foray into the African interior.

"It was rough terrain, unlike anything that I had ever seen before. Under blazing skies, we walked through miles and miles of untamed wilderness. We were surrounded on all sides by some of the most dangerous predators in the world, including lions, rhinoceros, hippopotami, elephants, and cheetahs. During the ceaseless squawking of the night, we needed to barricade ourselves in thorn-bush pickets to avoid being eaten. We even were coerced into paying the local Tsonga tribesmen protection money, though whom exactly they were protecting us from was unclear.

"We finally reached the cavern described by Botha. The first hundred yards were massive open chambers, but then the way became progressively narrower. As we descended into the bowels of the earth, the temperature dropped precipitously and the chambers we entered were flooded with waters muddied by massive quantities of bat guano. Eventually the space became so constricted that we found ourselves crawling upon our hands and knees in the mud. But then we came to a crevice which contained something wondrous. Dozens of wooden boxes, carefully stacked exactly where Botha had said they would be found.

"From there, it was a relatively simple matter for us to haul the treasure out. Our guides had been carefully chosen and exceptionally well-paid to not breathe a word about the discovery of Kruger's gold. As I had promised, the remaining wealth was split between myself and the ship's captain. I used my share to travel the world, for one never appreciates the taste of freedom which travel can bring until you have been confined in one dreary spot for over seven years. Eventually, I determined that I would put my newfound wealth to another cause, a greater one. The cause of justice. I therefore turned my steps home to London. I suppose you can guess the name of the captain of the *Botany Bay*, Mr. Holmes?"[82]

"Sir Thomas Donahue," he replied.

The Marquis smiled. "Not a member of the peerage at that time, of course. However, it is a wonder what some liquid funds can accomplish in the halls of Westminster. Yes, Captain Donohue was the man who spared my life that evening. And I dare say it was a wise choice. He certainly profited well from the decision."

"And the Marquis de Loam? How did you come to be in possession of such a title?" asked Holmes.

"In the wake of the Revolution, the French aristocracy are

a pale shadow of their former selves. Men who once would never dream of such a thing are - from time to time - forced to sell their titles. It was not a hard transition. My mother was French, after all."

"So you have abandoned your English self? Does your hatred extend to all of us?" I asked.

He shook his head. "Not at all, Doctor. Paul Kruger was a rough man, but he possessed a sort of crude wisdom. He once said 'It is not the dog who should be beaten, but the man who set him on to me.'"

I shook my head. "You could have waited. Surely the men you killed would have gotten their just desserts eventually?"

"No, Doctor. I waited long enough. It has been ten years since Gloucester, Hildyard, and Chanter conspired to destroy me, solely for their venal gain. And all of that time, while I rotted in a St. Helena cell, they were enjoying the fruits of their villainy. Hildyard stole my fiancée. Gloucester and Chanter spent the wealth gained from my invention. I am afraid that the mills of the gods turned too slowly for my taste.[83] The fires of fate burned within me, calling out for revenge. I may have held the matches which helped to set the great blaze alight. But they were the instruments of their own doom."

"I have also heard it said that the evil that men do lives after them," I noted.

He frowned as he considered my words. "Are my actions truly evil, Doctor? Would you call Hamlet evil?"

I shook my head. "Fiction."

He snorted in wry amusement. "So easily you dismiss the greatest work in the English language, Doctor."

"I do not dismiss it. I urge you to study its message. If Hamlet had not sought his revenge, he would have lived."

"What is life when burdened with such sufferings as the ones I have endured?" he cried.

"It is by the tradition of such sufferings and such endurance that others are nerved to do the like," I persisted.

"Ah, so I am to inspire others then, am I? Well, I refuse such a glorious role, Doctor. Though I am happy to finally be able to tell my tale to someone. Someone who I thought might understand."

"Is that why are you telling us this?" I asked.

"Perhaps I want my story told. Not tomorrow, mind you. I have seen enough of the King's prisons to last a lifetime. But someday. For without someone to tell your story, what part of you lives on after death?"

I glanced over at Holmes. "What say you, Holmes?"

He waved his hand. "As you are well aware, I am no longer an active consulting detective, Watson. I called at this house simply to hear an account of this man's history. I have no intention of revealing my presence in London to the C.I.D. You began this investigation, my friend. You must finish it, as you will."

I turned back to the former Edgar Virgil. "And if I should swallow my tongue and let this matter pass? If I should allow Scotland Yard to close the books upon these deaths with a charge of 'will-full murders, against some person, or persons, unknown?' what will you do with your freedom?"

A faraway look came into his eyes. "That is a question I have long pondered. To be honest, Doctor, I doubted whether I could actually carry off my plot undiscovered by some clever agent of the law. Once I caught wind that you were looking into the case, I knew it was only a matter of time before Mr. Holmes appeared on the scene. I sought you out at Nevill's baths in order to gauge how long I had before the Sword of Damocles fell."

"And yet you persisted in your scheme?" I asked, astonished.

"Of course," said he, with a shrug. "The only thing that kept me alive all of those years was the thought of extracting my revenge upon those evil men. If I were to end my days back in an English prison, or dropping from a rope, I could at least die content that justice had been served. If I should be permitted to walk free, I would strive to do what any man must. Find

– and perhaps create – some happiness in my own little corner of the world. Someplace far from the painful memories of London."

"Montpellier, perhaps?"

He nodded slowly. "Yes, that might do nicely."

I looked him in the eyes for a moment before I held out my hand. "Then this is *adieu*."

A small smile lit up his face. "And to you, Doctor."

With that final parting, Holmes and I made our way outside, my friend careful to restore his old peddler disguise before he could be recognized by any passer-by.

"Do you think I am growing soft in my dotage, Holmes?"

"Not so loud, Watson," he admonished me. "Recall that I am not here. He then shrugged his shoulders. "Who is to say the right and the wrong of this matter? Not I, that is for certain. Though I admit to being curious as to why you chose to let him go free?"

"I recalled the unrestrained quality of mercy that you showed to so many throughout the years, and endeavoured to do the same."

He smiled and nodded. "Then regarding Mr. Edgar Virgil, let him remain dead. The Marquis de Loam shall do more good free than as yet another poor soul crowding Princeville. He served his time in advance, and in so doing, learned a valuable, if terrible, lesson: *la vengeance se mange très bien froide*."[84]

"If you do not mind, Holmes, I will call upon you this weekend at your villa to talk over the matter further?"

"Very good, Watson," said he with a nod, before he turned and shuffled off, his curved back and white side-whiskers seeming to belong to a complete stranger. I gazed after him for a moment, wondering if this was the last time Holmes would make an appearance in the city where so many of his great triumphs occurred? I hoped with every fibre of my being that was not the case.

§

A few words may suffice to tell the little that remains. When I returned home to Southsea, I found one final missive from Holmes waiting for me. I tore it open to read his words:

MY DEAR WATSON:
Happy to have you call this weekend. Remind me to tell you about the wonderful happening which transpired during one of my early morning walks along the cliff path. My triumph over this abstruse and unusual problem may even warrant me setting it down with my own pen, given your complete absence from the scene.

In regards to Mr. Edgar Virgil, upon further reflection, I revise my opinion about the lesson that he learned. This was not simply about revenge. It was about finding a meaning for life. For many years, revenge gave Virgil his meaning. It gave him the ability to wait and hope. Those two words contain much of human wisdom.[85]

Very sincerely yours,
SHERLOCK HOLMES.

§

LITERARY AGENT'S FOREWORD TO 'AN EAST WIND'

"There's an east wind coming, Watson... such a wind as never blew on England yet. It will be cold and bitter, Watson, and a good many of us will wither before its blast."

- His Last Bow

Sherlock Holmes did not invent the association of the east wind with unwelcome tidings. In the novel Bleak House (1852-3) by Charles Dickens, it is used as a harbinger of unfavourable events: "My dear Rick," said Mr. Jarndyce, poking the fire, "I'll take an oath it's either in the east or going to be. I am always conscious of an uncomfortable sensation now and then when the wind is blowing in the east." But, it was an inspired choice to link the east wind with the growing threat in the East of Europe, as Germany mobilized its armed forces in order to commence the Great War.

In early August 1914, Europe was a nationalistic and diplomatic powder-keg. Archduke Franz Ferdinand of Austria had been assassinated on June 28 by the Serbian terrorist Gavrilo Princip. Austria-Hungary declared war on Serbia a month later, and the Russians mobilized their army in Serbia's defence. Germany, allied with Austria-Hungary and opposed by the Triple Entente (the Russian Empire, the French Third Republic, and the United Kingdom), knew that it would be impossibly challenging to simultaneously wage a war on two fronts (on both its western and eastern borders), and therefore enacted the Schlieffen Plan. This called for a pre-emptive strike upon France via Belgium, with hopes of quickly knocking the French out of the fight so that all efforts could be focused upon the enormous threat of the massive Russian army. And thus, on August 3, the German army declared war upon France. One day later they invaded neutral Belgium, setting in motion over four years of suffering and death.

The British Empire was no stranger to war, but Holmes was presciently correct when he said that the east wind was one such as never blew on England yet. The last military action by the British was ten years earlier, the expedition to Tibet in 1903-4, where a little over six hundred men died. Before that was the 1899-1902 Second Boer War, with approximately 23,000 dead. The Crimean War of 1853-6 was still remembered by some, but even its wanton excesses only resulted in the death of a little over 40,000 British soldiers. Nothing could prepare the United Kingdom for the massive losses of the Great War, which claimed the lives of nearly a million men and women. This Lost Generation included poets such as Wilfred Owen, the brilliant physicist Henry Moseley, and Kingsley Conan Doyle, eldest son of Dr Watson's first literary agent.

In light of this devastation, one must wonder why Holmes did not do more to prevent so much tragedy and death. In his defence, one must argue that one man – no matter how remarkable – could only accomplish so much to stem the tide of the relentless drive towards self-annihilation which gripped the minds of the powers which controlled Europe. And, it should be remembered that the Allied Powers did eventually prove triumphant, in no small part due to the influx of American aid and troops, which led to the success of the 1918

Hundred Days Offensive. But who knows how different things might have turned out without the secret aid of the world's first consulting detective?

For most of the first decade of their acquaintance, Dr John H. Watson chronicled mainly domestic adventures of Mr. Sherlock Holmes. Holmes was responsible for deducing the identity of dozens of local thieves, swindlers, and murderers. But certainly, he was no stranger to international affairs. His dealings with the Kings of Bohemia and Scandinavia are testament to that fact. However, it wasn't until later that Holmes, upon occasion, began to cross the line which separated a domestic detective from an international agent.

Shortly before the Great Hiatus – during which time Holmes is suspected of travelling in Asia as part of the Great Game – Watson recorded in *The Adventure of the Naval Treaty* how Holmes' help was instrumental in foiling the traitorous deeds of Mr. Joseph Harrison, who sought to sell to a foreign power the details of Great Britain's position towards the Triple Alliance of the German Empire, the Austro-Hungarian Empire, and the Kingdom of Italy.

But it was only after the return from his falsified death in 1894, when Holmes began to take up the role of spy-catcher with more alacrity. Such was his fame as a detective that the great men of the realm routinely called upon his help. Shortly after his return to London, Watson recorded in *The Adventure of the Second Stain* that Lord Bellinger and the Right Honourable Trelawney Hope appeared in the Baker Street suite in order to engage Holmes' services to recover the Kaiser's letter, which was so inflammatory in nature that war would have broken out at once. We may also presume that there is a trace of his brother's influence in this, especially since in *The Adventure of the Bruce-Partington Plans* that Mycroft directly recruited him to solve the disappearance of the technical papers of the Government's most jealously guarded secret which would revolutionize naval warfare.

Although he had been retired from active consulting for

over ten years, Holmes was pulled from his villa on the South Downs from time to time when exceptional circumstances required. Rising international tensions must have played a role in certain of these adventures. Germany's spy ring within Great Britain, even in advance of officially-declared war, was far superior compared to England's counter-measures. And thus, in the finale of his Canonical adventures, Holmes was convinced to foil a genius who sought to steal the secrets to the British Empire's defences.[86]

Watson was an indefatigable chronicler of his friend's adventures. But only in certain instances was he permitted to publish the details of certain of these cases with international consequences. Mycroft Holmes must have suppressed the other ones. Fortunately, with the Great War now a century in the past, the Official Secrets Act has been lifted, and our recent acquisition of a large trove of Dr Watson's writings allows us to finally release these cases to the general public. These cases may now be considered in the context of the previously-published quartet of cases which dealt with international affairs. Now that these cases have been brought to light, we may finally understand the implications of the spy in the office of the Secretary for European Affairs, how warfare at sea was forever changed, how Sherlock Holmes gained the trust of one of the most astute secret-service men in all of Europe, how Holmes was involved in ferreting out German spies upon British soil, and how Holmes and Watson foiled an attempt to destroy the very foundation of Britain.

§

The Adventure of the Naval Treaty (1889)
The Adventure of the Second Stain (1894)
The Adventure of the Third Traitor (1894)
The Adventure of the Bruce-Partington Plans (1895)
The Adventure of the Unfathomable Silence (1909)
The High Mountain (1914)

His Last Bow (August 2, 1914)
**The Adventure of the Defenceless Prisoner (1915)
Their Final Flourish (1915)**

THE ADVENTURE OF THE THIRD TRAITOR

It was only with the greatest degree of pressure that my friend, Mr. Sherlock Holmes, finally consented to the publication of a carefully guarded account relating the details of the vastly important affair regarding the Kaiser's missing letter. However, that case – which I have recorded under the heading of "The Adventure of the Second Stain" – was but one supreme example of the international influences which he has exercised, and there certainly were other incidents which rivalled it in significance.

Another instance commenced mere seconds following our confidential pact with the loveliest woman in London. I may not ever secure Holmes' permission to lay this particular case before the public; however, in case he someday relents, I shall not refrain from setting it down upon paper at this time while the details are still fresh in my memory.

It was, then, in a year, and even a decade, that shall be nameless, that upon one Friday afternoon in autumn we found ourselves descending the front steps of the Whitehall Terrace residence of one of the most eminent men of the Empire.[87] With a Parthian shot regarding his own diplomatic secrets, Holmes had just taken his leave of two men of European fame, the Right Honourable Trelawney Hope, and the illustrious

Lord Bellinger, twice Premier of Britain.

Before we reached the pavement, Holmes turned to me with a gleam in his eyes.

"And now the real work begins, Watson!" he exclaimed.

I frowned in confusion. "Whatever are you talking about, Holmes? Did you not just now prevent a fatal setback to the brilliant career of the Secretary Hope while ensuring that the Prime Minister will avoid having to deal with an international complication of the utmost consequence?"

He waved his hand irritably. "Child's play, Watson. We have a far more interesting matter on our hands. Do you not recall Lady Hilda's words?"

When I shook my head in the negative, he suddenly declaimed, his voice an octave higher in pitch:

> *"Then at last I heard from this man, Lucas, that it had passed into his hands, and that he would lay it before my husband. I implored his mercy. He said that he would return my letter if I would return him a certain document which he described in my husband's despatch-box. He had some spy in the office who had told him of its existence."*

He paused and looked at me significantly. "Do you now understand the problem, Watson? There is a spy in the office of the Secretary for European Affairs! If this spy is willing to sell our empire's secrets to an international agent such as Eduardo Lucas, then he will certainly have no qualms in selling to other spies in the employ of the one of our many rivals and enemies now that Lucas is dead. No, Watson, this spy must be rooted out at once!"

"How do you propose to accomplish such a task?"

"We must first consult with the individual whose responsibilities include preventing such a thing. A visit to the Diogenes Club is overdue, don't you think?"

I frowned in incomprehension. "Whatever for?"

"Why, to see my brother, of course."[88]

Holmes led us across Whitehall and along Downing Street until he turned right at Horse Guards Road.[89] We strode along St. James' Park until we crossed the Mall and climbed the Duke of York's steps.

Holmes motioned to the mouse-coloured terraced building at No. 7. Judging by its palatial four-stories and columned entrance, I took it to be the home of some wealthy politician, for I knew that Gladstone had once lived nearby. "That, Watson, is a locale with which we someday might need to become familiar. It is the home of the German Embassy. We may find that our spy pays regular visits to its door."

He motioned for us to continue along Waterloo Place, passing the monuments to the Lords Lawrence and Clyde, until he turned right at Pall Mall, and finally stopped at the unmarked door of No. 78. Perhaps not surprising for such an unsociable and unclubbable lot, the members of the Diogenes Club did not advertise their presence. We were shown into the small chamber known as the Stranger's Room, though I was no longer unfamiliar to its walls, having been ushered in once or twice before in the company of Holmes. A few minutes later, my friend's brother appeared.

Mycroft had not lost a pound since I had seen him last, and I thought that perhaps he had even managed to put on one or two, though it was rather difficult to estimate. Nevertheless, despite the torpor of his frame, it was a sorry man who underestimated the powerful engines of his mind. It was if Mycroft's body was merely a neglected vessel for the sole purpose of transporting his mighty brain. As always, he shook my hand in greeting, engulfing it with his massive paw, like that of a brown bear.

Mycroft then turned to his brother smiled. "I trust that the Right Honourable Trelawney Hope is feeling a bit better, Sherlock?" he began.

I could not fathom how he possibly knew of our recent visit to the Secretary's home, but my friend simply returned the smile. "Of course, brother. The missing letter has made its way back into his despatch box."

"I assume this had something to do with the murder of Eduardo Lucas?"

"Oh, so you have seen the paper then?"

Mycroft snorted with amusement. "I trust you understand, Sherlock, that I was aware of it well before reports of the Westminster murder appeared in *The Times*."

"Well, only incidentally," said Holmes, airily. "Watson here can relate for you the whole tawdry tale someday, if you are truly interested. He is the narrator of the Firm."

Our host pursed his lips. "No, I am not concerned with the details, as long as you can assure me that such an incident will never repeat itself. Hope is the custodian of many important documents."

"Oh, indeed. The letter from Lord Merrow finally allowed me to understand the reason we did not participate in the Kronstadt Rapprochement.[90] And the note from Lord Flowers was rather suggestive that we might soon declare a protectorate in East Africa.[91] But it was the report from Sir Charles Hardy which really caught my eye. Tell me, Mycroft, did the Thirty really finance Bourdin's attack on the Greenwich Observatory?"[92]

"Classified, Sherlock," said Mycroft, shaking his head. "Classified."

"Well, I cannot prevent such a recurrence if you persist in allowing the spy in the office of the Secretary for European Affairs to operate freely."

Mycroft's left eyebrow rose with interest. "How did you learn of him?"

"So you don't deny it?"

"No, you are correct, Sherlock. There is a spy. I have been aware of him for some time now. I have narrowed his identity down to one of three possible men. Everyone else who is employed in the office has had access to one or two leaked documents, but not to all. They are the only three who have had access to every single one of our compromised secrets."

"So, why have you not questioned them?"

"And let them know I suspect them? That would give away the only card which I presently hold."

Holmes shrugged. "There is always brute force. Bring them in and sweat them. One of them is sure to break. Then you will not need fret that you have prematurely played your hand."

"Out of the question," snapped Mycroft. "I don't think you fully understand the implications, Sherlock. The men I suspect are no Tom, Dick, and Harry from the East End. They are members of some of the first families in the kingdom. I must have incontrovertible proof of the identity of the traitor, for if I am wrong, my position within the government would suddenly become rather tenuous."

Holmes waved his hand. "Surely you are far too indispensable for that?"

"No man is an island, Sherlock," said Mycroft, shaking his massive head. "Governments come and governments go. Only Britain herself is eternal."

"Well, then. I suppose we have only one option remaining."

"Which is?" asked Mycroft, his massive frame leaning forward with apparent interest.

"Something rather more elegant. We craft a series of three false documents, which appear to be of great importance, and provide one to each of the men. We then sit back and watch to see which one of them leaks it."

Mycroft sank back in his chair. "That has already been attempted, Sherlock," he replied, shrugging dismissively. "We employed a dramatist to craft a remarkable fake report, purporting to describe our attempts to infiltrate the staff of Count Schlieffen.[93] It was just the sort of thing that would have interested our spy. We have for some time thought that he was primarily in the pay of the Colonel Brose of the Abteilung.[94] Unfortunately, the spy must have seen through it. He subsequently went dark for some time. Only recently, with the appearance of the Kaiser's unfortunately-worded letter, did our spy re-surface in order to parlay with Eduardo Lucas."

"Then how about a real document?" I interjected.

"Too risky," said Mycroft, waving away my suggestion with a flick of his corpulent wrist.

"Hold a minute, Mycroft," said Holmes. "Watson may have hit upon an idea. You did say that your spy was too clever to fall for a fake report. However, he is clearly ready to peddle upon verifiable data, if it were to prove sufficiently explosive."

Mycroft considered this for a moment, and then turned to study me with his piercing gaze. "You are a beacon of brilliance, Doctor. Who would have thought it?"

I smiled wanly. It was not the first time – nor would it be the last, I suspected – that I received such a back-handed compliment from a son of Siger Holmes.

"Still, we have nothing of sufficient interest at the moment, I fear," continued Mycroft. "Our spy has a most discriminating taste and will not risk his neck for anything less than a document capable of inciting a war."

"What about the memorandum from Belgrade?" asked Holmes. "If that were known, the Serbs would rise up immediately against the Austrian yoke."[95]

"Absolutely not, Sherlock. Much more than my head would roll if it became known I countenanced such a stratagem. Many an English farm-boy would never return from the fields of France should I allow that news to spread."

"I will guarantee its safety," said Holmes, evenly.

Mycroft shook his head. "You have been beaten before, Sherlock. Four times by men, by my count, and then there was *The Woman*..."

"I assure you that Mrs. Irene Norton will not become involved in this matter," said Holmes, through gritted teeth.

Mycroft stared at his brother for a long minute, plainly considering whether this scheme was too rash to actually sanction. Finally, he gave a small nod. "You understand that the official forces cannot be aware of this."

"I have just the men for the job," said Holmes, a strange tone to his voice. I realized that he had been holding his breath in anticipation of Mycroft's decision.

As we departed the Diogenes Club, I shuddered to consider the risk we had just taken. It was my device which was being employed. If it went wrong, I was sure that Holmes and his brother would shield me from official blame. But what of the culpability in my heart? What if my stratagem had just started a war and consigned thousands of innocent men to their deaths?

§

The hansom cab ride back to Baker Street was a strangely silent one, both Holmes and I pensive about the enormity of our task. Once we were safely back in our chambers, Holmes threw himself into one of the fireplace armchairs. "Now, then, Watson, let us meet our potential adversaries."

He pulled from his pocket the dossiers provided to him by Mycroft, who had sent over to Whitehall for them. They were delivered sealed in a locked briefcase, which had been secured by a chain to the wrist of a lieutenant of the Royal Navy. Holmes perused the folders, carefully considering their particulars. When finished, he threw them to me, one-by-one.

The first file detailed the life and employment of Mr. Creighton Stanley, in which I read:

> **Stanley, Creighton.** *Under-Secretary for Eastern Europe Affairs, Foreign Office. Born Bombay, India, 1851. Son of Henry Bond Creighton, Companion of the Most Eminent Order of the Indian Empire, once Minister to the British Raj. Educated Harrow and St. Luke's College, Oxford. Read History and Economics. Fluent in German and Russian. Served in the Embassy in Vienna. Formerly India Office. Formerly reporter for* The Times. *Address:*

43 St. John Street, Smithfield. Clubs: The Carlton, the Oriental, the Savage.

The file included a remarkable Lippmann photochrome of Stanley, which allowed me to fully take stock of the man's measure.[96] His face was unremarkable, with straw-coloured hair, hazel eyes behind thick glasses, and cheeks which tended towards pouchy-ness. The overall effect was somewhat boyish, but also tired-appearing.

The next report contained the particulars of the Honourable Homer Durant, as follows:

Durant, the Honourable Homer. *Under-Secretary for Southern Europe Affairs, Foreign Office. Born Fitzrovia, London, 1852. Son of Sir Virgil Durant, once Leader of Her Majesty's Most Loyal Opposition (Liberal Party). Educated Radley and St. Thomas' College, Oxford. Read Modern Languages. Fluent in French, Italian, and Greek. Formerly Major, Loamshire Regiment. Formerly Colonial Office. Author of 'British Foreign Policy since Crimea' (1891). Address: 116 Sussex Gardens, Paddington. Clubs: The Athenaeum, the Baldwin, the St. James.*

Durant's file also included a photochrome, but this one showing a gaunt man. He had thin, receding light brown hair and small, deep-set blue eyes. A small moustache covered narrow lips.

Finally, the last dossier documented the essential elements of the life of Kingsford Malcolm Hicks, which were:

Malcolm Hicks, the Honourable Kingsford de Joux. *Under-Secretary for Western Europe Affairs, Foreign Office. Born Plymouth, Devon, 1851. Of Huguenot descent. Son of Sir Henry Miles Malcolm Hicks, once General and Master Gunner, 56 Regiment Royal Artillery (The Cornwall Gunners). Educated Eton and Old College, Oxford. Read History and Drama. Fluent in French,*

Spanish, and Portuguese. Formerly Commander, Royal Navy. Served aboard HMS Charybdis. Formerly Admiralty Office. Address: 16 Albemarle Street, Mayfair. Clubs: The Tankerville, the Travellers, White's.

Malcolm's photochrome revealed a most handsome man, with wavy deep brown hair, piercing brown eyes, and a clean chin.

"A pretty trio, eh, Watson?" said Holmes, when I finished reading. "As Mycroft said, it would hardly do to accuse any of them without ironclad evidence of their guilt, considering their connections. But we shall get it."

"Can you tell, Holmes, which of them is the spy?"

He emitted a barking laugh. "No, not from the files alone, Watson."

"Perhaps more study?"

He shook his head. "I assure you, Watson, that there is nothing in here which Mycroft would have overlooked. Remember, that is just the sort of thing which my brother excels at, sitting with a bunch of data and processing it in order to find the hidden strands and patterns. I freely admit that he is my superior in such matters. However, in the realm of action Mycroft is sorely lacking. And this is where I reign supreme," said he, without a trace of irony.

"So what do you plan to do? Question them?"

"No, no, Watson! My brother could have done that, but as he said, it would be tipping our hand. No, I will follow them."

"To where?"

"The spy is merely a conduit, Watson. On one end, he receives confidential material, and then he must pass it to agents in the employ of foreign powers who will pay handsomely for such information. However, herein lies the spy's fundamental weakness. For at the time of the hand-off he is vulnerable. He could take it directly to our rival's headquarters, but to leave England would be a signal-flare of guilt. In London itself, the list of foreign agents is not a long one, and

I have made it my business to become intimately acquainted with both their appearances and habits. If I see Mr. Stanley, Mr. Durant, or Mr. Malcolm Hicks in communication with any one of these agents, then my job will be done."

I shook my head. "But there are three of them. Even if you follow Stanley and I trail Durant, Malcolm Hicks will be unobserved. We cannot watch all of them all of the time."

Holmes laughed. "My dear Watson. The man in question is a spy of the highest order. He has thus far managed to escape the attention of my brother, who is one of the most brilliant men in Europe. He has not lasted this long without being extremely careful. It will require all of my stagecraft to construct a series of disguises capable of diverting our spy's suspicions." He shook his head as he studied me. "I am afraid, Watson, that your poor bones simply do not possess a sufficient degree of deception. No, I shall call upon my irregulars. They can go almost anywhere, and see almost everything, while simultaneously being utterly beneath the notice of the typical English gentleman. And they shall be glad of the work to boot."

§

The following days were filled with a rapid succession of Holmes' disguises as he attempted to dog the footsteps of Stanley, Durant, and Malcolm Hicks. Holmes said that he needed to fully understand their usual patterns so that once the Belgrade memorandum was dangled before them, he would be prepared for the deviation which signalled the identity of the traitor. I witnessed the reappearance of the drunken-looking groom, the venerable Italian priest, and the Mayfair lamplighter, while also noting for the first time a rakish young plumber and even an old woman. Each time I would have laughed with amusement at Holmes' prodigious powers of camouflage, if not for the fact that these roles were enacted in a drama with international consequences of the gravest nature.

During this time, Holmes rarely appeared at Baker Street for more than a few minutes, as he routinely changed into different costumes at the various small refuges which he had scattered about the city. He would voraciously devour some bread and cold meat which Mrs. Hudson brought up for him, while simultaneously perusing the various telegrams which had been delivered.

In addition to his usual irregulars – the street Arabs who loitered around Baker Street – Holmes brought in several of his other informants. Emmitt Vinson, a wagon driver for Harrington's Brewery, could follow the movements of three men from the safety of his perch. Mercer, a general utility man who looked up routine things for Holmes, was most useful for checking upon their shopping habits. Langdale Pike was a human book of reference upon all matters of social scandal, and he managed to unearth several interesting scraps of information which had escaped the notice of Mycroft's dossiers. Finally, Cartwright, a lad nominally employed by Wilson's district messenger service, often made a better living on the side after Holmes had discovered his abilities during the investigation which saved Wilson's good name and life. Cartwright had proven to be instrumental during the Dartmoor case, and Holmes now entrusted him with all sorts of critical tasks.

Once the Belgrade memorandum was officially leaked to by Hope at Mycroft's orders to the entire Office of European Affairs, Holmes went into a state of high alert. At any time on the day in question, one of the three men would have access to it and could – if sufficiently clever – produce a copy. Later that evening, I asked Holmes whether he particularly suspected any of the men.

He shook his head irritably. "I don't know, Watson. Each of them has points against them. Creighton Stanley has been seen repeatedly frequenting the home of a woman named Alice Coleman. Despite her English name and passport, she is suspected of originally hailing from Austria and thus travelling under an alias. It is likely that she has seduced Stanley and induced him to alter his political leanings."

"You think him capable of betraying his country for a woman?"

"Certain women are capable of exciting great passion in the hearts of men. Passion and emotion cloud men's judgment. As you know, Watson, I think women are never to be entirely trusted."

I shook my head in disappointment. "To think an English gentleman capable of such depths."

"It gets worse, Watson. According to Mercer, Homer Durant has purchased books by both Mr. Marx and Mr. Engels."[97]

"That is hardly a crime."

"No, but it might reflect a sympathy for socialist beliefs, and thus a disloyalty to the Queen. Finally, if I am not mistaken, Kingsford Malcom has proclivities akin to those of Lord Arthur Clinton."[98]

"That could cause him to be imprisoned for gross indecency!" I exclaimed.

"It is also potential leverage for blackmail. If Langdale Pike can sniff out this fact, so might an agent of a foreign power."

"Then we are no further than we started!" said I, with dismay.

Holmes nodded his head. "Indeed, Watson. Which is why I have irregulars watching all three of them around the clock. Should any of them break from their usual patterns, I shall be notified immediately."

Holmes' words were soon to prove prophetic. Not five minutes later, a telegram arrived from Cartwright. It read:

Mr. H – Stanley on the move. Told driver dest. Victoria.
– C.

"We have our man, Watson!" cried Holmes, triumphantly. "Creighton Stanley would have little reason to travel to Victoria Station at this hour of night unless he intends to hand the memorandum directly into the hands of a foreign agent. We must be on that train!"

However, before we could even reach for our coats and hats, another message came in, this time from Vinson. It read:

> *Sir – Durant is going on a trip. He just took a hansom to Victoria.*
> *– E.V.*

Rarely have I seen Holmes so flabbergasted. His face was white with chagrin and surprise. "How can this be, Watson? Why is Homer Durant also on his way to Victoria?"

I shook my head. "I don't know, Holmes. Perhaps it is a mistake?"

"How could it be a mistake?" said he, with a frown. "Well, we can stop two men as well as one, I suppose. Let us make haste, Watson. Do not forget your service revolver, Watson!" he commanded.

Again, however, our path was barred. We had no further descended the seventeen steps to the pavement when a familiar-looking street Arab approached Holmes.

"Please, sir," said the lad, touching his forelock. "Simpson said to tell you that the Mayfair swell is walking across Green Park with a valise in his hand."

Holmes staggered back. "All of them?" he cried.

"From Mayfair across Green Park is the direction of Victoria Station, Holmes," I observed.

Holmes regained his equanimity. "Yes, Watson, it is plain that all three men are headed to the main terminus of international travellers. But for what reason?"

"What do you mean, Holmes?"

"Only one can be guilty. Why are the others also travelling to Victoria? And all at the same time? What a coincidence!"

I shrugged. "The matter of the second stain proved to be a mere coincidence, Holmes. However, this might not. Why should only one be guilty? Why not all three?"

For a moment, from the look upon his face, I thought Holmes was going to embrace me. "Really, Watson, you astound me. You have seen through the layers of deceit until only the truth shines forth. This is why Mycroft could not tell which man was guilty... because none of them was solely responsible for every leak coming from the European Office! Each man sold a portion of the secrets, keeping the others safe by virtue of spreading the risk around." He shook his head with the admiration of a fellow genius. "It is brilliant!"

"Holmes, if we are to stop them, we must get to Victoria at once," said I.

This shook him from his reverie. "You are right, Watson! The game is afoot!" He swung around and signalled for a passing cab.

§

It was not until we were situated in the hansom rushing towards Victoria Station that I could ask him the reason for the precaution he bade me take. "Surely, you don't expect violence from these men, do you, Holmes?"

He shook his head. "One never knows, Watson. A traitor can be a most desperate individual. Have you forgotten Mr. Joseph Harrison, who was a gentleman to whose mercy I was extremely unwilling to trust?"

"It is a good thing that Inspector Forbes finally captured him!" I exclaimed.

"Only because I pointed him in the correct direction, Watson," said Holmes, crossly. "Now then, we must make a plan of attack for when we reach Victoria. The station is enormous and these men could be anywhere. I will inspect the ticket queue, while you check the first class lounge. You recall their pictures?"

I nodded. "As long as they have not disguised themselves, I will know them."

"I doubt that they will employ such tactics."

Holmes was proven correct, for a dirty and ragged urchin soon tugged upon my coat sleeve as I was busy studying at every face in the lounge. "Eh, mister," said the street Arab. "A tall bloke said you would give me a shilling if I asked you to return to the ticket booth."

I followed what I presumed were Holmes' orders and paid the lad before dashing back to the main concourse. There I found Holmes purchasing a pair of tickets. Turning away from the window, he handed one to me.

"I caught up with Durant just as he was asking for a ticket to Dover. I had to pay the man behind him two pounds to permit me to jump the queue, but I have now booked us on the same train. Come, Watson, let us make sure they actually board."

Holmes sprang forward and I was hard-pressed to keep up with him. His lean frame was ideal for slipping between the crowds pressing their way through the station, while I felt like I was swimming upstream. Finally, however, we managed to catch up to the three men. Although their backs were to us, from time to time one of them would turn and make a remark to the others, which allowed me brief glimpses of their profiles.

Creighton Stanley had aged since the time his file's picture was taken. He was now a middle-aged man in a rumpled coat and a cravat. However, a jovial smile would light up his face whenever he spoke. Homer Durant was grimmer, his narrow face drawn and worried. Kingsford Malcolm Hicks was even more handsome than his picture, and he appeared at ease, as if he were just about to jaunt over to Paris for a holiday.

We followed them to Platform 2 and watched as they climbed aboard a first-class Pullman coach painted blue with a white top. Its side was marked with a golden 'WL' held by two lions and yellow letters spelled '*Compagnie Internationale des Wagons-Lits.*'

"The Club Train!" Holmes exclaimed.

"The boat train to Paris?"[99]

"Indeed. They are making a run for the continent. Climb

aboard, Watson and secure us two seats in a compartment where you can keep an eye upon our friends. I will ensure this is not a diversion and that they don't disembark before departure."

Following Holmes' instructions, I proceeded to stand in the corridor outside our compartment. I slowly packed and lit my pipe with the Arcadia mixture which I favoured. The entire time I was closely watching the three men as they settled into the compartment next to ours.

Holmes stood post upon the platform, where porters scurried back and forth with baggage carts, while the stationmaster ensured that all with tickets were aboard. Once the train's whistle blew and she began to pull away from the platform, he joined me in the carriage. Holmes slid over to the side-door and motioned for me to keep an eye upon the corridor for any sign of stirring from our quarry. It would be a black eye indeed if they were to jump from the train and remain in London, while the great detective Sherlock Holmes was carried off to distant Paris.

Soon enough the train was travelling at a sufficient speed that a jump would likely prove fatal. I was not inclined to count telegraph posts, but I could estimate that we were moving at a fine clip of at least fifty miles an hour.

I turned to my friend. "We must stop them before they reach Paris, Holmes! From there, they could board the Sud Express, the Rome Express, the Train Blue, the Train Éclair, or the Orient Express and vanish to any one of the four quarters of the globe."[100]

As we passed over the Hungerford Bridge, Holmes turned to me with a grim face. "I am afraid it is much more serious than that, Watson. We have less than two hours before this train arrives at Dover. Once it loads onto the Channel steamer, we then only have three nautical miles before we leave Britain's territorial waters.[101] Moreover, once we reach the shores of France, we have no official status. Even if the document is recovered, it could fall into the hands of the French government.

I assure you that they will be most interested in its contents and my brother will be rather put out."

"So we must prevent Stanley, Durant, and Malcolm Hicks from departing the Calais Coach!"

"Or prevent them from passing the document to an accomplice on board. They will not want it found upon them if French customs decides upon a full inspection of their trunks and persons. Look!" he exclaimed, seizing my sleeve. "They are on the move."

Holmes rose from his seat and I followed. As we entered the corridor, I spotted the three men heading in the direction of the smoking car. Holmes set off on their trail, however, at the third compartment the door suddenly swung open and blocked our way. A man emerged and began to apologize to Holmes.

"Louis La Rothière!" Holmes exclaimed.

The man was of an average height, and appeared to be in his mid-thirties, with waxed black hair and a matching moustache. His eyes were alert, with small lines creasing the lateral corners of their lids. "Ah, Mr. Holmes, is it? A pleasure to run into you here! Heading to Paris, are we?"

Holmes' brow furrowed. "Indeed. And you, Monsieur?"

"Certainly. It is my home, after all. I only reside at Camden Mansions when I feel a change of scenery is needed."

"Of course," said Holmes, the scepticism plain in his voice.

"Are you heading to the smoking car, gentlemen?"

Holmes agreed and waved his hand. "After you, Monsieur."

La Rothière smiled and strode off down the corridor. We followed and I could see the wheels turning in the racing engine of Holmes' mind. However, if he produced any hypotheses as to the Frenchman's presence aboard this particular train, those were dashed to pieces when we entered the next car. This was a standard smoking car, with numerous comfortable velvet armchairs and several tables, around which convivial gentlemen could gather to discuss the news of the day. Several white-uniformed waiters carried trays, upon which they delivered spirit-filled glasses to the occupants. The three men from the Foreign Office were gathered around a far table, each with a whisky and cigar in their hands.

A dark-skinned man with a balding pate turned towards us as we entered and a smile revealed curiously animal teeth, which held a long manila cigar. He stood, revealing that he was exceptionally short. His eyes were bright with amusement. "Good day, Mr. Holmes," said he, his tone cool.

Holmes emitted a short bark of a laugh. "Ah, Signore Luigi Lucarelli of 6 Chesterfield Street, Mayfair." He then turned and addressed the other individual present, a young man with Teutonic colouring. "And here we have Herr Gephardt Bergstatt of 17 Gillingham Street, Pimlico."

Bergstatt puffed upon his cheroot and blew the smoke unconcernedly towards the ceiling. "Mr. Holmes," he replied, with a small nod of his head. "I little expected you to be taking a vacation at this time of year."

"Ah, but I hear Paris is lovely. The Prussian troops certainly felt so in 70/71," replied Holmes. Bergstatt laughed at this reference to the Franco-Prussian War, but I could see La Rothière narrow his eyes in displeasure. The wounds of that bitter defeat were still fresh in the minds of most Frenchmen. I presumed Holmes was attempting to bait the man into rashly divulging some bit of information. Holmes smiled. "Now, if you will excuse us, gentlemen."

He spun around and marched back in the direction of our compartment. As we passed back into the corridor, I asked in a low voice why we were abandoning the observation of Stanley, Durant, and Malcolm Hicks.

He shook his head. "This is a most bold plan, Watson. Feints and subterfuges everywhere."

"What do you mean, Holmes?"

"Do you not find it strange that half of the key foreign agents of London are aboard this one train? If he had not been deported for his role in the Márquez affair, I might expect Adolph Meyer to be sitting in the next compartment.

The only ones missing at the moment are Hugo Oberstein of 13 Caulfield Gardens, Kensington and Gabriel Dukas of No. 2, Eaton Square, Belgravia."

"Our spy must be planning on slipping the document to one of these agents," I ventured.

"No, Watson, it is too monstrous a coincidence that La Rothière, Lucarelli, and Bergstatt should all be on board the train at the same time. Hence, they must be present for the same reason. Each has been engaged with the belief that he will be the sole recipient of the stolen document. But I suspect that they are all distractions, paid to take this little trip for the purpose of diverting suspicion from the true planned recipient of the stolen document."

"Who is?"

He shook his head. "I do not yet know, Watson. We must investigate the other occupants of the train forthwith."

"Surely we cannot leave Stanley, Durant, and Malcolm Hicks alone with the foreign agents?" I protested.

"In fact, we are perfectly safe at the moment. For Lucarelli, La Rothière, and Bergstatt are a jealous bunch of souls. They will hardly allow one of the others to get the upper hand. Come, Watson, let us see who remains in their compartments."

However, as we entered the corridor, this plan was interrupted by the appearance of two men. The first was a dapper little man, with a curled grey moustache and green eyes covered by pince-nez. The second was a tall, thin man, with a stiff spine and curly brown hair.

"Mr. Holmes," said the first man in a strong French accent. "I suppose I should not be surprised to find you here after encountering von Waldbaum." He motioned to the second man.

If Holmes was surprised by the fact that this man knew him, he hid it well. Instead, he merely motioned to our compartment. "Gentlemen, if you would join us for a moment."

Once everyone was settled, Holmes began with introductions. "Watson, on your left is Monsieur René Dubuque of the

Paris Police. He was instrumental in helping me in '91, when I was engaged on that little matter which required my services in Narbonne and Nimes. The other gentleman is Fritz von Waldbaum, the well-known specialist of Dantzig. You may have read about the case of the councillor found hanging from the top of the Artus Court, which he so adroitly solved. Gentlemen, this is my associate, Dr John Watson."

"We are, of course, well-aware of Dr Watson," said Bergstatt. "His notes on your cases, Mr. Holmes, are most instructive. In fact, not two months ago, I was inspired to utilize your monograph on the natural poisons, and determined that Mademoiselle Boucher was given hemlock by her maid."

Holmes smiled. "I am happy to have been of service. Now, if I may ask, gentlemen, what brings you aboard the Calais Coach?"

Dubuque spread his hands before him. "The Prefecture received word from one of our paid informers that the services of Louis La Rothière had been engaged for a special service. Although he often resides in London, he is a citizen of the French Republic, and I wished to try to prevent him from causing a diplomatic incident."

"That is a noble cause," said Holmes. "And you, Herr von Waldbaum?"

The man shrugged. "It is most similar. I heard from a source that Gephardt Bergstatt was on the move, and sought to intercept him. I also saw Luigi Lucarelli climb aboard, so I assume you are on a similar mission, Mr. Holmes?"

"Indeed," said Holmes, with a slow nod. He frowned and drummed his long thin fingers on the armrest. "Gentlemen, I am afraid that we are all being played. I predict that something important is going to happen in the next few hours. However, it will not be mediated by any of the known agents. I believe that there is another – previously unrecognized – agent aboard."

Dubuque's eyebrows rose with interest. "I noted when I came aboard that the first cabin was occupied by only one individual. Fortuitously, I recognized her as the famous American prima ballerina Shevaun Wallace. I once saw her dance *Le papillon* at the Paris Opera."

"Wallace?" said I, excitedly. "I recall when she was *Giselle* at Her Majesty's Theatre. She moved like a swan across the stage."

"Oh, yes, Doctor," said Dubuque, enthusiastically. "She charmed every man in the salons of the Champs-Élysées. She was the most ravishing thing to have walked the stage in decades."

"I heard that she had retired from the stage," interjected von Waldbaum. "She is now using her considerable charms to make the acquaintance of some of Europe's reigning families, perhaps in hopes of elevating herself to royalty."

"Ah, she is an adventuress then?" said I. "Like…"

Holmes held up his hand to forestall my next words. "No need to say *Her* name, Watson. The same conclusion was plain to me. Are there any other passengers?"

Von Waldbaum jerked his thumb behind him. "I borrowed a match from the man in the compartment next to this. I am afraid that he rather mumbled as he spoke, so I could hardly make out his name. He is English, of that I am certain. And he said he was a Professor of some sort."

I shook my head. "That sounds like a disguise!"

"Possibly, Watson, though it is too early to make such conjectures."

"Well, I saw a Major of the Royal Marines come down the corridor while I was having a pipe. I didn't stop him for conversation, not wanting to be distracted…"

"Yes, very good, Watson," interrupted Holmes. "Then we have several individuals with whom we need to question."

"But, Holmes, we have less than two hours until we reach Dover." I pulled my gold watch from my waist-coat pocket. "One hour, thirty-five minutes, to be exact."

"Thirty-three, I think. Your watch must be a little slow, Watson. Nevertheless, I concur that we cannot all interview each suspect. We must divide and conquer. Gentlemen, I propose that Herr von Waldbaum re-engage in conversation with the enigmatic professor."

"I will interrogate Miss Wallace, I volunteered.

Holmes shook his head. "No, Watson. While the fair sex may be your department, I fear that the wiles of Miss Wallace may be too great for you to resist. That task will fall to Monsieur Dubuque. You shall compare experiences serving in her Majesty's forces with the Major of Marines."

"And you, Holmes?"

"I will head back to the smoking lounge, and question the three men I saw gathered therein."

"Do you mean...?" said I, before my words were interrupted by Holmes.

"While I am at it, I will also observe our trio of foreign agents and ensure that they are keeping each other occupied. Are there any questions, gentlemen? No? Then let us get to work."

§

As Monsieur Dubuque and Herr von Waldbaum set off to investigate the adventuress and the professor, I went to look for the Marines officer. However, before I could do so, Holmes took hold of my arm. "Be careful of what you say, Watson," said he, in a low voice. "Our colleagues are honourable men working on the side of the law. However, we cannot forget that they have no loyalty to the Queen. I am certain that the Third Republic and the Deutsches Reich would be very interested in the contents of the Belgrade memorandum. We must make certain that it does not fall into their hands either, for that result would be little better than La Rothière or any of the other agents."

I nodded my understanding and moved up the corridor until I found the compartment belonging to the officer. I knocked upon the door and, when it was answered, introduced myself to the white-haired man. He looked to be at least a decade older than me, his face lined by years under tropical suns. His pale blue eyes were sharp, and his mouth was covered by a walrus moustache. He sat with the rigid pose of a career soldier, despite his civilian suit. The latter was neatly pressed, though there was a bit of mud around the trouser cuffs. In his left hand, he carried a Malacca-wood cane.

"Major Gerald Kingston at your service, sir. What can I do for you?"

I suddenly realized that I had no ready story for why I needed to question the man. I could hardly just come out and ask him if he was planning to smuggle a secret document out of the country. Holmes would have had some clever subterfuge but what could I use? And then it dawned on me. "When I passed your compartment earlier, I thought you looked familiar. Did you happen to sail on the *Malabar* in '80?"

"I am sorry to say that you have mistaken me for someone else, Doctor. I have been on many of her Majesty's vessels, but none of that name."

"Ah, but you have seen action then, eh, Major?"

The man smiled wryly. "You might say that. I was a lad of eighteen when I shipped out for the Second Opium War. From there the Maori Wars, then the Abyssinian Expedition. Then the Ashantis and the Zulus. In the Egyptian Campaign on '82, I was wounded at Tell El Kebir and was invalided out."

"What have you been doing since?"

He shrugged. "After I recovered at the Cairo hospital, I naturally gravitated to London. I have kept busy with some speculations."

"And your trip to France?"

He smiled. "Some money has come through. The state of my finances are such that I thought I could spend a bit in a Paris cabaret."

"Indeed!" I exclaimed. "You sound much more fortunate than I when I first set foot in England free of my obligations to the Crown. I am afraid I was rather penniless. Eleven shillings and sixpence a day are hardly sufficient to permit a man many liberties."

Kingston shook his head in commiseration. "I concur, Doctor. It is a crying shame to see men such as yourself, your health ruined in defence of the realm, cast aside by the soft fools of Whitehall."

"I even had to take up quarters with a roommate in order to make ends meet. I tried to supplement my limited income at the Turf, but such pursuits typically left my pocket-book even more barren. Tell me, how did you manage to get by?"

"I was fortunate to come into a small inheritance. An uncle on my mother's side."

I nodded my understanding of his situation. Unfortunately, my brain was out of ideas on other topics which might reveal a secret motive for his presence on this train. Therefore, I bid him farewell, and returned to our compartment. I found that Holmes was already back in his seat, his legs crossed beneath him. His eyes were closed, and if not for the slight movement of his fingers, I might have thought him asleep. Instead, he appeared like some strange Buddha, at peace with the possibility that one little mistake would permit the Belgrade memorandum to slip from our fingers and possibly start a war.

Both Monsieur Dubuque and Herr von Waldbaum were close on my heels, and once the three of us had resumed our seats, Holmes opened his eyes.

"What did you find, gentlemen?" he asked. "Let us put our cards on the table."

The Frenchman was the first to speak. He first described the famous dancer. "Miss Wallace claims that she was invited by Miss Sibyl Sanderson to attend the premiere of Massenet's new *comédie lyrique* at the Palais Garnier."[102]

"But you do not believe her?"

"It may be true," he said, with a shrug of his shoulders. "But I doubt it is the full truth. I have it on good authority that the Prince of Transleithania, currently a guest of the Hotel due Louvre, was seen in London some four months ago."[103]

"And you believe that Miss Wallace made his acquaintance?"

"More than that," said the man, with a smile. "Her dress hides it well, but I believe Miss Wallace is expecting."

"Ah!" said Holmes. "That would be a serious indiscretion, if she could prove the involvement of the prince."

"Just so, Mr. Holmes. I believe La Rothière is attempting to intercept some document or photograph which authenticates their relationship. The prince is wooing an Imperial princess, and it would be a serious blow to that proposed marriage."

"Very good. And you, Herr von Waldbaum… did you find out anything of note regarding the professor?"

"Indeed," the German replied. He described the older professor. "His name is Kenyon Hunt Woodville. He is attached to an Institute at University College London, but has spent most of his time abroad. He is an archaeologist, and has spent time with Schliemann in Turkey and de Perthes in the Hauts-de-France. He claims to be travelling to Vienna for an international conference."

"It sounds plausible," said Holmes.

"Then why does his ticket list Budapest as his destination?" asked von Waldbaum, triumphantly.

Holmes' eyebrows rose with interest. "What do you propose?"

"There were several other peculiarities, Mr. Holmes," said the Dantzig specialist. He held up two fingers. "First, I noted that the man's luggage had a label indicating that he had stayed in the Hotel Alighieri in Ravenna. Second, he was reading a tattered copy of Jordanes' *Getica*."

Holmes shrugged. "I fail to see the significance."

Von Waldbaum shook his head. "Well, well, it appears that Mr. Sherlock Holmes has his limits! I assure you that a knowledge of literature is of the utmost use to the criminal investigator. Jordanes is the sole summary of the lost work of Cassiodorus, whose *Historia Gothica* is the definitive report on the origin and history of the Gothic people."

"Ravenna was the capital of the Ostrogothic Kingdom," I noted.

"Precisely, Doctor!" cried von Waldbaum. "What if Professor Woodville discovered a page or two of Cassiodorus' missing work in Ravenna?"

Holmes shook his head. "You mystify me, sir."

"Mr. Holmes, do you know the story of Attila?"

"Only in the most general terms."

"Know then that when Attila died, he was buried in three nesting coffins, the first of gold, the second of silver, the third of a metal stronger than iron. With him went the arms of those he defeated in battle, and many other gem-studded trappings and ornaments."

"A mighty treasure," murmured Holmes.

"That is not the half of it, Mr. Holmes! Have you heard of the Sword of Attila?"

"Should I have?"

"It was given to him by the god Mars. He who held it cannot be defeated on the battlefield."

"And you believe this sword to be buried with Attila?"

"The Habsburgs believe they have it in their *Schatzkammer*, but that blade is clearly too recent a work. No, Mr. Holmes, the sword was buried with Attila, and Professor Woodville proposes to locate it."

"I am surprised that no one has found Attila's tomb before."

Von Waldbaum smiled. "That would have been rather difficult, Mr. Holmes, as they actually diverted the Tisza River in order to dig his grave. And when they released it back to its natural course, the river ensured that Attila would be safe for centuries."

Holmes' eyebrows rose. "Even if he has learned its location, how does the professor plan to excavate this submerged tomb?"

The German shrugged. "A caisson of some sort, I presume."

"Then you believe Gephardt Bergstatt is attempting to prevent Professor Woodville from accomplishing this task?"

"I believe you would agree, Mr. Holmes, that – given the current international tensions – many in the *Stadtschloss* would be happier to see a sword with mystical powers recovered by a German instead of an Englishman."

"I am surprised that you would share this information with us," I interjected.

Von Waldbaum looked over at me. "I am a Dantziger, sir. We are a free city, or we should be, if not for the Prussian annexation. I have no love for their yoke."

Holmes nodded his head. "Gentlemen, I congratulate you. If your suspicions are correct, Herr von Waldbaum, with the information gathered by you and Monsieur Dubuque, we now have answer for why two of the foreign agents are aboard this train. But what about Lucarelli? What did you learn from the soldier, Watson?"

I related the details of my conversation with Major Kingston. When I had finished, Holmes shook his head. "You have learned very little of importance, Watson. Surely there must be some vital point which suggests an ulterior motive."

I wracked my brain, but could think of nothing.

"No matter, my dear fellow, I shall just have to see to the major myself." Holmes turned to the Paris policeman and Dantzig specialist. "It is plain that the other three gentlemen have nothing to do with Signore Lucarelli. They are merely clerks on their way to Paris for some brandy and dance. No, I think you both have – with remarkable energy – discovered the true motives for several of the train's occupants. Watson and I will endeavour to get to the bottom of the major's secret."

"I would be most interested to see your methods in action," said Monsieur Dubuque. Fritz von Waldbaum nodded eagerly.

Holmes smiled. Only I, who had known him for many years, could tell that it was insincere. "Of course, gentlemen, it would be my pleasure. First, I would sketch out the location of each person's compartment." He took a sheet of paper and a J pen from his pocket and quickly drew a rough map of the train. "I believe this is accurate." He showed us the following:

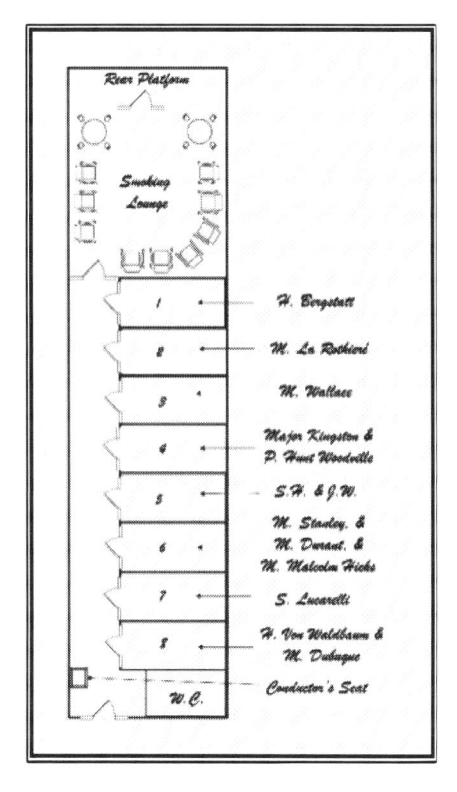

```
┌─────────────────────────┐
│  Rear Platform          │
│                         │
│   Smoking               │
│   Lounge                │
│                         │
│  ┌──┐                   │
│  │ 1│ ——  H. Bergstatt  │
│  ├──┤                   │
│  │ 2│ ——  M. La Rothieri│
│  ├──┤                   │
│  │ 3│ ·   M. Wallace    │
│  ├──┤     Major Kingston &│
│  │ 4│ ——  P. Hunt Woodville│
│  ├──┤                   │
│  │ 5│     S.H. & J.W.   │
│  ├──┤     M. Stanley, & │
│  │ 6│ ·   M. Durant, &  │
│  ├──┤     M. Malcolm Hicks│
│  │ 7│ ——  S. Lucarelli  │
│  ├──┤                   │
│  │ 8│     H. Von Waldbaum &│
│  └──┘     M. Dubuque    │
│  ┌──┐                   │
│  │W.C.│   Conductor's Seat│
└─────────────────────────┘
```

Both men nodded their agreement with Holmes' map, so he continued. "Now we may begin to see how various individuals would be able to interact with the others. It is instructive, I think."

When I admitted that I could not see how it helped, his eyebrows rose. "No? Well, then, Watson, perhaps in a little while all will be clear." He paused and reached up to press the bell for the conductor. A minute later, the man – whose name proved to be Michaels – appeared and inquired how he might be of assistance.

Holmes explained that he was on official business for Scotland Yard, and would the conductor please gather together the occupants of the coach in the dining car.

"There is no dining car between London and Dover, Mr. Holmes," said Michaels apologetically. "It is added at Calais for the final stretch to Paris."

"The smoking lounge, then," Holmes waved.

"Very good, sir. Anything else?"

"Yes, are there any railway guards aboard?"

"Yes, sir. Two."

"Excellent. Please station one upon the rear platform and one in the corridor outside the door to the smoking lounge. Once we are gathered, no one is to leave without me giving the signal."

The man's eyebrows rose at this unusual request, but agreed with impressive equanimity and set off to carry out Holmes' orders.

Holmes turned back to Dubuque and von Waldbaum. "Gentlemen, if you will prepare the lounge for a round of investigations, Dr Watson and I will meet you there in a moment."

The two men nodded and departed the compartment.

As soon as they were gone, Holmes turned to me with a smile. "This is a fine puzzle, is it not, Watson? We have less than an hour...."

"Holmes!" I protested. "How can you be so cavalier? This is no game."

"Of course it is, Watson. But it is a game with rather high stakes. For the Belgrade memorandum is invaluable, given its power to start an international incident."

"How are we to stop it? We don't know what Stanley, Durant, and Malcolm Hicks are planning!"

"If I am not mistaken, Watson," said Holmes calmly, "every passenger is lying about their reason for being aboard this train. The trick will be determining whose lie is concealing the transportation of the stolen documents. Unfortunately, based on where the compartment of our traitors is situated, it would have been possible to pass the plans to almost anyone on their way to the lounge."

I considered this for a moment and then an idea occurred to me. "What if they are all guilty, Holmes? They could be conspiring together!"

He shook his head. "Don't be absurd, Watson. Everyone on the Calais Coach is guilty? Such things only occur in the pages of fiction. Come, let us take our place for this little drama. We must both retrieve the memorandum, while simultaneously convincing our friends that we are pursuing other issues entirely. Take care to follow my lead."

§

Several minutes later, Holmes had taken his place in the middle seat along the left wall. With a wave of his hand, he bade me stand against the door to the rear platform, where I spotted a railway guard already in place. When we entered the lounge, several individuals were already within. The three Whitehall men were situated across from Holmes, while the three foreign agents were perched on stools at the small tables. Dubuque and von Waldbaum were seated next to Holmes. Eventually Miss Wallace entered, and she was directed to one of the chairs next to the door. She was even more lovely than I recalled from her time on the stage. She was followed by Major Kingston, who limped to his place next to Malcolm Hicks. Professor Woodville was last to enter, his manner furtive. He took the lone remaining seat between the former ballerina and marine.

Once all were gathered, Miss Wallace was the first to speak, "Really, sir, I must protest. By what right do you have to interrogate us so?"

Holmes smiled and leaned forward. "I apologize for the inconvenience, Miss Wallace, but I assure you that this will be brief. Most of you should make it aboard the *Guy Mannering* before the steamer departs."

Holmes first turned to the three foreign agents. "Signore Lucarelli, Herr Bergstatt, Monsieur La Rothière. I have discerned the reason why each of you are aboard this train…"

Both Dubuque and von Waldbaum looked as if they were

about to protest, for Holmes had given them no motive for Lucarelli. But he forestalled them with a raise of his hand. "Know this, gentlemen – none of you enjoy official diplomatic status on British soil. Your actions have been tolerated, but are not condoned, and should I turn my attention to you, it would mean a long stay at Wandsworth. I suggest each of you enjoy a holiday on the continent and permit me sufficient time to forget about your existence."

The three men all stared at Holmes with wary eyes. The first to rise was Bergstatt. His chin rose defiantly. "I am on my way back to Bavaria at the moment, Mr. Holmes. I do not require your permission, nor do I deserve your suspicions. Good day, sir."

The other two foreign agents made similarly feeble protests before departing. I predicted that Holmes would have little trouble from any of them in the future.

Holmes then turned his gaze to the lovely former ballerina. "Now then, Miss Wallace. Monsieur Dubuque has told me your story and I must warn you that he is aware of your intentions towards a certain august individual. You would do well to forget him and aim your gaze lower."

She stared at him, eyes blazing with anger. "I will take my own council on such matters," said she, her voice even.

"As you wish. In any case, I do not see any legal position which can be taken at the moment. You are free to go."

The former ballerina rose gracefully from her seat and strode out of the lounge. Monsieur Dubuque's eyes watched her go with interest, but Holmes had moved on.

"Professor Woodville, I believe you neglected to tell Herr von Waldbaum the full truth of your visit to the Dual Monarchy. I might suggest you reconsider the wisdom of your plan to recover that ancient weapon during these fraught times. You would not wish to incite an international incident, would you?"

The man's mouth fell open with surprise. "I had not considered the implications, sir," said the man, stammering.

"I recommend you do so while aboard the steamer. You may go now."

The archaeologist rapidly followed this suggestion and departed.[104]

Holmes saddened spun and faced Major Kingston. "Ah, Major, I had almost forgotten about you. Dr Watson mentioned that you are heading to Paris for a holiday?"

"That is correct, sir."

"And what was the purpose of your visit to Kew Gardens?"

The man's eyes widened in surprise. "How did you know that, sir?"

Holmes snorted in amusement. "It was a simple matter. The splash of dirt upon your trousers is most peculiar. In my experience, it does not exist naturally in all of London. It is a soil imported to support the growth of African plants in one of Kew's greenhouses."

The major stared at Holmes for a minute and then gave a barking laugh. "I will let you in on a little secret, sir. You and the rest of the fine gentlemen here. Perhaps some of you can put it to good use, for certainly Africa is large enough for all of us. I learned it from a Zulu whom I captured at Ulundi. Have you ever heard of a tree which I recently learned is called *Pandanus candelabrum*?"

"No," said Holmes, mildly. "Tough I am unfamiliar with most aspects of botany."

"I as well, Mr. Holmes, but this mangrove-like tree covered in thorns is one to which you should pay attention."

"Why is that?"

"I have learned that they only grow above kimberlite pipes!"

"Diamond ore?" I interjected, excitedly.

"That is correct, Doctor," Kingston said, turning to me.

"So you are travelling to Africa in order to go prospecting for diamonds?" I asked.

The man nodded, as Holmes joined in. "And now we understand Signore Lucarelli's motive for being aboard the train.

In some fashion, he had learned of the major's secret and was planning to wrest it from him. In the right hands, it could permit one to challenge the monopoly of the De Wines Consolidated company."[105]

Major Kingston smiled. "Yes, well, I would not be sad to see Mr. John Streets put out of sorts. I thank you, sir, for making me aware of the Italian's designs. I will re-double my guard."

Instead of dismissing the major, however, Holmes rose and turned to Dubuque and von Waldbaum. They also stood and shook his hand in turn, professing their admiration for his analytical methods. As they took their leave, I noticed the train slowing down and switching onto the final leg of tracks into Dover Priory station. I began to panic that Holmes had yet to reveal the location of the perilous Belgrade memorandum. Only Major Kingston and the three Whitehall men remained in the lounge with Holmes and I.

"Holmes, you have let everyone go!" I bleated. "Shouldn't we…"

"Side issues, Watson," said he, cutting me off with a wave. "Do not waste your energy worrying about such things. Stay focused on the task at hand."

As the train ground to a halt by the platform, the major rose to depart. However, Holmes forestalled him by laying a hand upon his shoulder.

"I say, sir," the major protested, "what do you mean by this?"

"You are an accomplished liar, Major Kingston. The splash upon your trousers could have been acquired anywhere, but you spun quite the tale from my suggestion that you had visited Kew Gardens. I would ask that you turn it over now. The game is up."

The man looked affronted. "I don't know what you are talking about, sir."

"I refer to the memorandum which you bought from these men. You intend to auction it to one of the great Chancelleries of Europe, where it may precipitate a war. You would rather stuff your pocket-book than protect the interests of your nation."

The man sneered. "That is a fine fable, Mr. Holmes, but a little flimsy, don't you think? Do you honestly believe that you can have me arrested on such grounds? My solicitor will have a field day with this. I hope *your* pocket-book is a deep one, for I will have you up on a charge of libel. Now if you will make way, I have a steamer to catch."

Holmes stared him in the eye, and then removed his hand and backed away. Major Kingston made for the corridor door, but he had only taken a step before Holmes reached out his foot and deliberately tripped him. As the man fell to his hands and knees, Holmes reached out and deftly confiscated Kingston's cane.

"You are sadly in need of acting lessons, Major. For your limp wanders from leg to leg. I suspect that you have little need for this cane. Ah, what have we here? Not a sword, but something mightier." Holmes twisted apart the cane, which had been cleverly hollowed out in order to conceal a roll of paper. From this compartment, Holmes withdrew the copy of the invaluable memorandum.

Holmes shook his head. "For your treason, you deserve to be hung, Major. But I suspect that the magistrate will look favourably upon your years of service. Instead, I predict you will be safely engulfed in a maximum-security prison for the rest of your natural life. I trust the thirty pieces of silver were worth it?"

Holmes waved his hand and summoned the railway guards. As they hauled away Major Kingston, Holmes sat down and turned his aquiline gaze upon Stanley, Durant, and Malcolm Hicks, who had sat mutely through the altercation with Major Kingston. "And now, gentlemen, what shall we do with you?" he asked as he drummed his fingers upon the armrest of his seat. "It is apparent that one of you is guilty of a far greater crime than receiving a foreign document. For how else would the Belgrade memorandum find its way into Major Kingston's cane? I fear the punishment for violating the trust of the Foreign Office might prove to be a capital one. If two of you were to turn upon the third and testify, you may perhaps be spared. So, who shall it be?"

Holmes paused and I watched as the three men threw shifty glances at the other. They might be old friends from Oxford, but were any of them willing to risk having their necks pulled?

"Of course, there is another option," Holmes continued. "One which you might find vastly preferable. You would continue your work in the office of European Affairs. There you will also continue your extracurricular activities in the employ of foreign powers, undertakings which I am certain are rather fiscally rewarding. However, now you will only pass on those secrets which your new master indicates."

"Triple agents!" I exclaimed.

"Precisely, Watson. What say you, gentlemen?" Holmes' gaze bore into the three men. "Disgrace to you and your families followed by probable execution, or the chance to serve your country again?"

Creighton Stanley was the first to speak. "You leave us little choice, Mr. Holmes," said he, jovially. He smiled, like a guilty boy caught red-handed stealing pudding.

Holmes inclined his head. "That was the idea, Mr. Stanley. What say you, Mr. Durant?"

The gaunt man nodded. "Tell me what I must do."

"Return to London and your job and, in the future, inform us whenever you are approached by foreign agents. It is that simple." He looked at the third man. "And you, Mr. Kingsford Hicks?"

The man grimaced. "It is not that straightforward, Mr. Holmes."

"You refer to the fact that you are being blackmailed?"

"You know about that?" exclaimed Kingsford Hicks, surprised.

"I know the reason, but not the perpetrator. If you help me, I will ensure that you are free from his power."

"And exchange one master for another?" the man replied in a bitter tone.

Holmes leaned forward, his manner grave. "Do not compare me to a blackmailer, sir! I am offering you hope and freedom and the chance to renew your Promissory Oath."[106]

The man cowered beneath Holmes' glare. "Very well. I will do as you ask."

Holmes straightened up and slowly looked at each man in turn. "Do not mistake these for empty words, gentlemen. These are binding vows, more sacred than any you have before spoken. You will henceforth work only in the service of our Queen. And should you fail, know that I will be watching."

§

It is a matter of history – the secret history of a nation which is often so much more lurid and remarkable than its public chronicles would lead one to believe – that the Oxford Three became, at the insistence of Mr. Sherlock Holmes, the most successful agents of misinformation that the world had ever seen.[107] Throughout the next two decades, innumerable rumours and leaks would emanate from their desks, some true but unimportant, others false and capable of subtly devastating the advantages of any nation foolish enough to trust them.

However, as this case deals with interests of such importance, and implicates so many of the first families of the kingdom, that I fear that even the coming of the new century will prove an insufficient period of time to allow the details to be safely shared. Like Monsieur Dubuque and Herr von Waldbaum, the public will have to be content with an expose of the side issues attached to Miss Wallace and Professor Woodville. I can only hope that some future reader, a hundred or even a thousand years from now, will appreciate the energies employed by Holmes – not just in resolving domestic matters – but also in safeguarding the interests of our worthy Empire.

§

'The July which immediately succeeded my marriage was made memorable by three cases of interest, in which I had the privilege of being associated with Sherlock Holmes and of studying his methods. I find them recorded in my notes under the headings of 'The Adventure of the Second Stain,' 'The Adventure of the Naval Treaty,' and 'The Adventure of the Tired Captain.' The first of these, however, deals with interests of such importance, and implicates so many of the first families in the kingdom, that for many years it will be impossible to make it public. No case, however, in which Holmes was ever engaged has illustrated the value of his analytical methods so clearly or has impressed those who were associated with him so deeply. I still retain an almost verbatim report of the interview in which he demonstrated the true facts of the case to Monsieur Dubuque, of the Paris Police, and Fritz von Waldbaum, the well-known specialist of Dantzig, both of whom had wasted their energies upon what proved to be side issues. The new century will have come, however, before the story can be safely told.'
   - *The Adventure of the Naval Treaty*

THE ADVENTURE OF THE UNFATHOMABLE SILENCE

T he bugle has sounded its last post. The pens have been laid down in the railway carriage at Compiègne. The eleventh hour of the eleventh day of the eleventh month has finally signalled the end of the Great War and its unspeakable horrors. Far too many loved ones forever sleep beneath the poppies and the singing larks.

But now that the Prussian yoke has been thrown off, and peace reigns upon the fields of Flanders, I can finally set down one of the stories of how my friend, Mr. Sherlock Holmes, did his part to try to stave off the madness which eventually engulfed both Europe and the world at large. In so doing, I believe that he delayed the onset of that terrible event by some five years, until the efforts of one man – no matter how brilliant – proved to be insufficient to prevent the unyielding beast from finally throwing off its shackles and catching us all up in its gaping maw.

Between the time that Holmes retired from his career as the

world's first and foremost consulting detective and the onset of the War to End All Wars, my journal entries had grown far less frequent and interesting. Hence, the events of June 1909 stand out like a supernova against the dark sky.

It began with what seemed like a simple mistake. My wife and I had travelled up from Southsea in order to take in a show at the Haymarket Theatre. Afterwards, we were dining at Simpsons, when the waiter left two slips of paper upon the table. One was clearly the bill; however, I figured the second must belong to another table. I waved the man over.

"Is there a problem, sir?" he asked.

"I think you have left one slip too many, my good man," said I.

"Have I, sir?" he replied, his voice even. "Are you certain?"

Frowning, I glanced down at the papers. One was a standard cheque; the other was something far different. It was a typewritten note, printed upon the same sort of paper as the Simpsons bill. I read:

> *Please send your wife back to Claridge's and do me the honour of joining me at No. 10, Pall Mall.*
> *– M.*

There could only be one man who would send a cryptic note in such a peculiar fashion. But what did Mycroft Holmes want of me, I wondered?

Given the quietude of my current situation, my curiosity was stoked, which made it certain that I would obey his commands. I settled my wife in a hansom cab, and took the opportunity to walk the short distance over to the Diogenes Club. The great warp-and-weft of London passed by, and for a moment, I could without difficulty imagine that I was on some errand commanded by Holmes, the dénouement of a case hanging in the balance. Once a man has lived a life filled with the most thrilling adventures, it can be a difficult thing to adjust to less-rousing circumstances.

I stopped at the familiar door, which was located some little distance from the Carlton. The door was unusual for its lack of a knocker, as the Club employed a footman to be on the constant lookout for expected visitors – all others being not welcome. The door swung open silently, and I made my way down the hall past the window overlooking the sitting room, with its plethora of little nooks. A set of double doors led into the small chamber with the sobriquet of the Stranger's Room, the only locale within the building where the sounds of the human voice were permitted. I was assured that this room possessed the thickest walls of any building in London, save only those belonging to the Old Lady of Threadneedle Street. Its bow-window gazed out over the street, which was deserted at this late hour.

Mycroft Holmes had little changed since I last encountered him. My friend might have been able to determine if his brother had added a few additional pounds to his already considerable girth, but my eyes were not up to the task. In all other aspects, he seemed remarkably like my friend, with that sharp expression in his peculiar deep-set, steel-grey eyes.

"Good evening, Doctor. A pleasure to see you again," said he, leaning forward slightly in order to shake my hand. "It's been since the resolution of the Buckland Abbey case, if I recall?"

"Likewise, Mr. Holmes. Your memory is, of course, accurate. However, I doubt you interrupted my aperitif simply in order to make pleasantries and reminisce about old times?"

He snorted and smiled. "Sherlock always said you had a pawky sense of humour. You are correct, Doctor. I have called you here upon a subject of the greatest importance."

"Unless you have a case of dropsy or of the chilblains, you might have the wrong man. You may perhaps have noted that the Firm has closed up shop? My days as unofficial biographer to Sherlock Holmes are long past."

Mycroft shook his head. "Retirement is not the end, Dr Watson. Merely the beginning of a new chapter. And when the British Government requires your assistance, it is no small matter to turn it down."

"I wouldn't dream of it. However, I think you must to take a trip down to Fulworth. If there are serious events afoot, you should speak to your brother."

"I have tried. But he will not listen. He has always had a curious stubborn streak. You are one of the few men – perhaps the only man – to whom he will, upon occasion, listen. That is why I need you to make one of your occasional week-end visits. You must incite him into looking into this problem. It won't even take him far from his magnificent Channel view. In two hours, the Southern rail will have you both in Portsmouth Harbour. No need for Sherlock to breathe the dense yellow fogs of London again."

I shrugged. "I am happy to try, of course, though I doubt that he will be any more amendable to my pleadings. He has resisted all previous attempts to pry him from Sussex."

"This is no trivial conundrum of the police court, Doctor. He might feel different if he awakens one morning only to find the southern slope of the Downs crawling with Prussians."

My eyebrows rose in alarm. "Do you mean war?"

He nodded gravely. "It is a distinct possibility, I fear. The very balance of European relations may hang upon this issue."

"Then pray tell me the details at once! I will not rest until Holmes has solved your problem."

Mycroft smiled. "I knew I could rely upon you, Doctor. Do you recall the little trouble of Cadogan West?"

"Of course," said I, thinking back to that case from a dozen or so years earlier. "Does this involve the plans for the Bruce-Partington submarine again?"

"Not the plans, Doctor. The actual submarine."

"It has been constructed?"

"Indeed. After sufficient funds were quietly snuck through the Estimates, a modified version – based on the re-designs of Mr. Holland – was built."

"So what is the issue?" I asked, slightly confused.

"The prototype submarine has gone missing."

"Missing? Do you mean, lost at sea?"

"Currently, yes."

"Mechanical error?"

"No, we believe not."

I frowned in confusion. "Based upon what?"

"An eye-witness account that suggests something far different," said Mycroft.

"Such as?"

"Well, Doctor, if you believe the report which has so riled the feathers of the Admiralty chaps, a great sea serpent is responsible for the loss of our state-of-the-art submarine."

"A Kraken," said I, evenly.

"Indeed."

"But you do not agree with the reports?"

His brows furrowed. "You accompanied my brother on some four-hundred cases over seventeen years, Dr Watson. How many spectral dogs did you encounter? How many genuine vampires? How many ghosts?"

I shrugged. "That may be true, but we should not be so rash as to suppose that we yet know all of the inhabitants of the ocean depths. Surely it is within the bounds of possibility that your witness saw some animal that has never been captured or described?"

"Fictions, Doctor."

"Not according to Aristotle."[108]

"Hearsay."

"Sir Humphrey Gilbert, half-brother of Sir Walter Raleigh, reported encountering a lion-like monster with glaring eyes upon his voyage home from claiming Newfoundland," said I, in response.

"Drink, or more likely madness," he countered. "The man had a disturbed personality."

"And Captain McQuhae of the HMS *Daedalus* who, along with his crew spotted an enormous serpent off St. Helena in 1848? Or Captain Harrington of the *Castilian*, who witnessed a monster of extraordinary length rear its head out of the same waters, not ten years later? I could go on."

Mycroft frowned and his eyes narrowed as he peered at me. "You are extraordinarily well versed in these matters, Doctor."

"I did some looking into the matter after an acquaintance from my club claimed to have seen one. He was standing on the deck of a steamer with his wife, and they were gazing at the ancient Temple of Poseidon on Cape Sounion. Suddenly, they were distracted by something swimming parallel to the ship. They saw a curious creature, with a long neck and large flippers. His belief is that it was a young plesiosaurus."

"I am hardly an expert on these sorts of things, Doctor, however, I am assured that the plesiosaurs went extinct, along with the dinosaurs, millions of years ago, Doctor."

"And yet, I have heard rumours of isolated areas of the Amazon – giant plateaus – where monsters from the dawn of man's existence might still roam, imprisoned and protected by unscalable cliffs. If possible on land, then certainty the vastness of the ocean – covering more than two thirds of the great globe, and deeper than Mount Everest is tall – could also contain such terrors?"

Mycroft shook his head. "The Royal Navy's official position – and mine – is that there are no abnormally large or dangerous sea monsters."

"Then what happened to your submarine?"

"Either the submarine has been sunk, which would be a great tragedy; or it has been captured, which would be an international incident of the most serious nature. In either case, this would require a precise knowledge of the submarine's location. And there are only two individuals in England with said information. I have had them investigated by my finest men, who have turned up nothing. From what I can gather, they both seem to be the most patriotic of men, with no skeletons in their cupboards. However, one of these men has sold our secret to the Kaiser, and I need to know which, before even more damage is done."

"And where was the submarine based?"

"At the HMS *Dolphin* which – despite its name – is actually a shore establishment located in a blockhouse at Gosport. Do you know it?"

"Across the harbour from Portsmouth, if I recall correctly."

"Very good, Doctor. The fort commands the approach to the harbour, and has stood since the days of the sixth Henry. It is commanded by Commodore Francis Shipton, and his second is Captain Elliott Urquhart. Only they were aware of the submarine's intended course. I have prepared a pair of dossiers on the two men." He indicated a pair of manila envelopes upon the table. "In those, my brother will find everything we know about them."

I picked up the envelopes. "I will ensure that Holmes receives these. Is there anything else I should know?"

"I am sending a C.I.D. man along. You and my brother will need an official voice if you are to arrest a high-ranking member of Her Majesty's Naval Service. I believe that you are familiar with him – an Inspector Hopkins? He shall meet you at Victoria Station tomorrow morning for the seven o'clock train."

§

Fortunately, my understanding wife thought that a little trip down to Holmes' villa would do me good. Therefore, as the sun began to peak out over the East End the following morn, I set out from Claridge's to see my friend again. The youthful figure and alert, eager face of Inspector Stanley Hopkins met me upon the tracks at Victoria. Hopkins was dressed in a quiet tweed travelling suit, though he retained the erect bearing of one who was accustomed to official uniform.

The trip down to Eastbourne took less than two hours, which Hopkins and I spent reminiscing about the mystery of Woodman's Lee, the killing at Yoxley Old Place, and the perplexing set-back of the Randall gang. After that, I regaled him with the story of how we had located Hatley's sunken Indiaman, the well-deserved death of the brute Giordano, the puzzling disappearance of Drake's Drum, and the horrible deeds of Dr Everhart.

From Eastbourne, we hired a trap to take us the rest of the way to Fulworth, upon whose edge Holmes' villa was situated. As Hopkins and I approached via the drive, we spotted in the fields behind his house a tall, thin figure, covered in a white one-piece jumpsuit with a veiled safari hat. He was tending to a series of boxes, which I knew from previous visits were the artificial frames for Holmes' beehives. I realized that any attempt to approach the swarms of bees would be foolish in the extreme. Therefore, we waited patiently for Holmes to finish his business. This appeared to have something to do with a small lantern-shaped item which emitted smoke, rather than light. Finally, Holmes extracted something from one of the boxes and replaced the lid.

Moments later, he was striding in our direction. Holmes removed his hat and veil as he walked, and I once more saw the narrow face and hawk-like nose of my friend. His thin lips parted in a smile as he approached. "My dear Watson, and Inspector Hopkins to boot! What a pleasure to have you drop in!"

"Feeding the bees, Mr. Holmes?" the inspector asked.

"No, no! The bees feed themselves, Inspector! Behold the plethora of wildflowers that surround us," said he, waiving his arm about. "The bees miraculous transform them into honey of the highest quality. However, harvesting honey was not my mission today." He held out a chunk of sappy-resin. "Here we have some excellent quality propolis. There is nothing quite like it to seal wood, and the old Stradivarius was looking in sorry need of a new layer of varnish. But come inside; it is time for some coddled eggs. Will you join me, gentlemen? I assure you that Martha prepares the finest in Sussex."

"Holmes, we are here on business..." I began.

"Of course you are, Watson," said Holmes, as he strode off towards the house. "The inspector here is too busy a man for jaunts into the countryside." He turned to my companion. "Still, I must say, Hopkins, that you were a tad slow in wrapping up the Merton Park case. It should have been obvious from the start that it was Chandler. The account in *The Times* – typically garbled and incomplete – was sufficient to tell me that."

Hopkins and I followed him through the French doors and into the breakfast parlour, where a fire had banished the morning's chill from the room.

"You are right, Mr. Holmes," said Hopkins ruefully. "If only I had…"

"Inspector," said I, interrupting. "We are not here to discuss old cases." I faced my friend. "Holmes, I was sent by…"

"My brother. Yes, I know."

"You do? Did he wire you?"

"There was no need." He stopped and smiled for a moment. "Surely my little devices must be evident to you by now, Watson?"

I had little time for games, but I paused to consider things. "Let me guess, Holmes. Some spot of mud upon my pant legs whose distinct colour can only be found upon Pall Mall?"

He threw his head back and laughed. "Nothing so ingenious, I am afraid, my dear Watson. However, you do have two manila envelopes sticking out of your coat pocket with a Whitehall seal. There are relatively few places where a retired former army surgeon and writer could acquire such items. Ah, here we go. Time for some eggs."

Holmes' old ruddy-faced housekeeper, her hair tucked into a country cap, entered the room carrying a large tray filled with Crown Derby china. Martha set down in front of me a white ceramic jar painted with a peach. Although time was of the essence, I lifted off the metal lid and the smell of the eggs wafted over me to the point where I realized that I was famished.

"I suppose it wouldn't hurt to eat while we talk. Thank you, Martha. Now, then, Holmes, the case concerns…."

Holmes held up a hand to forestall me. "Have you forgotten that I am retired, Watson?"

"Mycroft says this is of the utmost importance."

"Yes, yes, as were a baker's dozen other matters which have arisen over the last five years. Mycroft grew overly-reliant upon having access to my services when we resided at Baker Street. If he ever bothered to stir from his armchair, he might be able to look into things himself." He shook his head. "However, Mycroft's lack of energy now proves to be his Achilles' heel."

"But this will not require much effort, Holmes. Just a short trip along the coast."

"You know that I keep to a strict schedule, Watson. After tending to the bees, I break my fast, and then spend a solid three hours engaged in the composition of my magnum opus. A light supper is followed by a constitutional walk about the cliffs. And then I devote my time to a consideration of philosophy. I am currently most intrigued by Schopenhauer's *World as Will*. Do you know it, Hopkins?"

"I am afraid that I haven't gotten to that one yet," stammered the inspector.

"I highly recommend it. He shares certain tenets with some gentlemen with whom I became acquainted while journeying in Tibet."

"I would think, Holmes, that you might be interested in a problem which was so complex that your brother was unable to work out the explanation," said I, testily.

He waved his hand languidly in the direction of the cliffs. "I don't have to go far in order to discover cases of sufficient rarity and abstruseness, Watson."

"Oh yes, I recall you mentioning the singular case of the jellyfish," said I, my voice as even as I could maintain it.

His grey eyes narrowed and he peered at me. "Oh very well, Watson. If you are going to be so pertinacious about the whole thing, then I suppose that it will not hurt to take a quick look into the matter. Stackhurst will survive without our game of chess for one evening. Pray tell, what upheaval has so excited my brother?" He lounged back in his chair and pressed his fingertips together.

I described the case exactly as Mycroft had related it, and handed Holmes the dossiers of the two men with knowledge of the submarine's location.

"Dear me, Watson, this is really rather singular," said Holmes, when my account was complete. "Is this the work of yet another remarkable beast currently unknown to science? If so, we might have another long sea-voyage ahead of us. Don't forget how the *Friesland* affair almost turned out, mind you. However, in the case of a sea-monster, we shan't be needing these." Holmes hefted the envelopes in his hand for a moment, and then casually tossed them upon the fire.

"What are you doing, Holmes?" I exclaimed, as I leapt to my feet and vainly attempting to salvage the papers from the flames.

He shook his head. "You know my methods, Watson. I prefer to begin a case unencumbered by the hypotheses laid out by others. My mind is a *tabula rasa*. Now then, if you will reach over to that bookcase, Inspector, and pull down the Bradshaw's, we should be able to ascertain the time of the next train to Portsmouth."

§

When our train pulled into the station at Portsmouth Harbour, the first things I noted were a gentle wind blowing off the Solent – carrying with it the crisp briny smell of the sea – and the sun shining brightly off the little whitecaps in the water. We emerged next to the Gun Wharf, where lay the floating hulks that comprised the HMS *Vernon*, the Royal Navy's Torpedo Branch. Upon our right was the Royal Dockyard, from which sailed forth the ships that ruled the waves. From our vantage point, I could just make out the vast chequer-patterned bulk of Nelson's former flagship, the HMS *Victory*, now mouldering away in sad neglect, its days of glory long-forgotten.

We caught a Watermen's steam launch, which ran us across the narrow inlet over to the Gosport peninsula. This stopped at a modest marina across from a church named after St. Ambrose. Hopkins led the way from the quay, along a road which ended at the fort's gate. A guard inspected his credentials, and once satisfied, signalled to another marine. This chap motioned for us to follow, and a few minutes later, we were ushered into a plain two-story dun-coloured building, which housed the commander's office.

This proved to be an austere space, with white-washed walls, the severity broken by only a series of coloured nautical flags stained with ink, a spotted white pelt from some great cat, and a bookcase. Upon the latter, I could see a Nautical Almanac, Brassey's *Naval Annual*, Mahan's *Life of Nelson* and his *Influence of Sea Power*, amongst many others. As we entered, a man looked up from behind the desk. Although he was seated, I could tell that he was a tall man, with a sharp face – lined by years at sea – and curling hair long since passed into grey. His blue eyes were intelligent and piercing.

"Welcome to the HMS *Dolphin*, gentlemen," said he, gravely. "I am Commodore Francis Shipton. I am glad for your assistance in this matter, Mr. Holmes."

"Shipton," said Holmes, his eyes darting about the room. "Any relation to Sir George Edward Shipton, once British Minister to Nepal?"

"Indeed. He was my father."

"Ah, I thought so. A good man, your father. If memory serves, he was instrumental in securing the support of the Rana Dynasty during the Indian Rebellion. He even received a Companion of the Bath for his outstanding civil service."

"That is correct, Mr. Holmes. I hope to live up to his memory in my own way by ensuring that we retain control over the seas in any future conflict."

"We will need to ask you a few questions, Commodore Shipton, about the missing submarine," Holmes continued.

"Of course, I am happy to provide you with any information in my power. However, we will want to wait for my executive officer, Captain Elliott Urquhart, to arrive. His testimony may prove critical. Ah, here he comes now," Shipton concluded, nodding towards a man who was striding down the hall outside the office.

Once he had joined our group, Captain Urquhart proved to be a short, rather stout, Scotsman. He had eyes so dark that it was difficult to distinguish the pupils, and his face was heavily pocked. His pate was completely bald, however, a bushy moustache drooped over his lips, between which was continuously clenched an amber pipe.

After all introductions had been made, the five of us gathered about the desk, as if engaged in a convention of war. "Pray start at the beginning, if you please, gentlemen," said Holmes, instinctively taking charge over these grizzled naval commanders now that we were in his element.

"Have you been briefed regarding the Bruce-Partington submarine?" asked Shipton.

Holmes nodded. "Watson and I are well aware of its importance," said he, dryly. "I doubt that Whitehall has provided any details to Inspector Hopkins here, however, you may be assured of his discretion in these matters."

Shipton nodded. "Very good. Then you are aware that its technological advances promise to revolutionize naval warfare. For the sake of discretion, we have taken to calling them the Eques-class of ship. The plans are a carefully guarded secret, however, the actual working submarines are just as important as the schematics. Should one fall into enemy hands, it would be simplicity itself to reverse-engineer the unique aspects."

"And that is what you fear has happened?" Holmes asked.

"Honestly, Mr. Holmes, we don't understand exactly what has transpired. All we know for certain is that the captain of the HMS *Teucer* has failed to signal in at the arranged time."

"I have heard it said, Commodore, that a ship is only as good as its captain."

Shipton shook his head. "Commander White is the best man I have. His competence and loyalty to the Crown are indisputable."

"And where was the *Teucer* at the time of its disappearance?"

"The Wadden Sea."

"But that is off the Netherlands!" I exclaimed. "Can submarines travel so far? I thought that they were limited to coastal waters."

Shipton nodded grimly. "That is one of the advantages of the Eques class of submarines, Doctor. In any case, as soon as Commander White failed to report in via the wireless, we sent our swiftest boat to investigate. Captain Urquhart personally took charge." He nodded at his executive officer.

The Scotsman took over the narrative. "Aye, there was nothing to be seen at the last known location of the *Teucer*. But we spotted a few fishing boats, and these eventually led us to a pair of witnesses to the event, a Dutch fisherman and his son in a little boat they called the *Piet Hein*. It took many questions and a considerable amount of time to make sense of their account, which still seems rather extraordinary." He cleared his throat. "I shall read it for you:

> 'During the last rays of twilight, we were hauling in the nets for the night before heading back to Delfzijl. Just then, something monstrous broke the water about a hundred yards off our port side. It breathed forth an odour so foul that it seemed to come from the mouth of hell itself. The beast was longer than our ship and spindle-shaped. It was much larger and more rapid than a whale. The monster was dark grey in colour. It was silent at first, and then it growled, a noise so loud and terrible that it seemed to emanate from all around. After this roar, the beast spit a tongue of flame into the air. It was so hot, we could feel it even at our great distance. We turned

our faces away, and when we turned back, the beast had dived back down into the depths, leaving only a roiling sea in its wake. We shook out our sails and made as rapid passage back to home as the Piet Hein *would allow.'"*

Once Urquhart finished his recitation, Holmes snorted in wry amusement.

"Do you find the loss of our submarine amusing, Mr. Holmes?" said Commodore Shipton, angrily.

"No. However, I find such fairy tales to be pure lunacy."

"And do you have an alternate explanation?"

Holmes pursed his lips and shook his head. "Not at the moment. It would absurd to deny that the case is a rather abstruse and difficult one. Nevertheless, I promise to look into the matter forthwith, in hopes of determining what happened to your submarine. I have only one further question for you, Captain Urquhart."

"Name it."

"What was the weather like on the day that the *Teucer* vanished?"

"The weather?" said the man, erupting with anger. "What the devil does the weather have to do with anything?"

Inspector Hopkins held out his hand in a placating fashion. "I assure you, Captain, that while Mr. Holmes' methods may appear unusual, there is a method to them. Please answer the question."

A wave of emotion rolled over the man's features, but he finally settled down. "Very well. It was rather stormy."

"Clouds all day? No chance of a blue sky?"

The man shook his head. "Not that day."

"Very good. Gentlemen, I hope to have some answers for you shortly."

§

"Now, Watson, do you have any views upon the matter?"

asked Holmes, when the three of us had exited the building.

I considered this for a moment. "I would wager on Captain Urquhart being our man."

Holmes raised his heavy dark eyebrows. "Oh? And how did you arrive at a conclusion of his guilt?"

"The story of the sea-monster. You have yourself said – upon many prior occasions – that we must eliminate the impossible. If we are taking as our starting hypothesis that a sea-monster is impossible, then we must ask why was it mentioned at all? There is a deep lake in Scotland that is rumoured to be inhabited by just such a monster – a last remnant of earlier era. Urquhart must have gotten the idea from that legend."

"But the witness!" protested Inspector Hopkins. "How do you explain that?"

I shook my head. "Bribed, I expect. Do you not agree, Holmes?"

He shook his head. "No, no, Watson. It will not do. It could just as easily as been Commodore Shipton. Did you not notice the pelt and the flags?"

"What of them?"

"First, the pelt belongs to the fabled mountain ghost, the rarely-glimpsed snow leopard. And the flags are not nautical signals, but rather Buddhist prayer flags, inscribed with mantras which promote peace and compassion. Both items are unique to the mountainous valleys of Nepal and Tibet. Commodore Shipton was raised by his Foreign Minister father in that remote land, where he would have heard the legend of the Yeti. The legend of the wild-man of the Himalayas could have just as easily spurred the fantastic idea of a monster from the depths of time. No, I am afraid that we cannot cast aspersions upon such fine men upon the basis of such weak suspicions."

"But your brother said that only these two men knew where the *Teucer* was going to be upon that evening. It must be one of them."

"Not necessarily, Watson. In fact, I can assure you that both of those men are innocent."

"On what basis?"

"On the basis of the dossiers, of course."

"But you didn't even read them!" I protested.

"No. However, my brother did. I have told you before that Mycroft possesses even greater powers of observation and deduction than myself. If Mycroft could find no proof of their guilt, *ergo*, it is impossible for them to be guilty. Therefore, we must consider alternative explanations."

"Surely you do not subscribe to the sea-monster theory?"

He chuckled. "No, I do not."

"So, like your brother, you too doubt their existence? That all of the witnesses whom have reported seeing monsters, in every sea and ocean around the globe, were all drunk, or hallucinating, or lying?"

"Not at all, Watson. Although the great cave-bear of Castleton ultimately proved to be a hoax, not all prehistoric remnants are untrue. Take the oarfish, for example."

I shook my head. "What is an oarfish?"

"It is a most peculiar creature. I first read about it in Wood's *Out of Doors*. It looks like nothing less than a giant serpent, and can grow to great lengths. One that washed ashore upon Bermuda a few decades ago was sixteen feet, however, some have been reported to be as long as fifty. They typically inhabit the depths of the ocean, rarely appearing near the surface."

"And what does this have to do with the missing submarine?"

"Very little, Watson, save that the mind is a peculiar machine. When it sees something wholly unexpected, it attempts to construct an explanation from the bits of other ideas that it has stored away. The Dutch fisherman certainly witnessed something odd out there upon the Wadden Sea and – lacking any other frame of reference – he naturally assumed it must have been one of the mythical sea-serpents whose lore is disseminated by sailors in ports around the world."

"So what was the unexpected thing that he observed?"

"That is precisely what I am attempting to determine, Watson. I have generated several hypotheses which would serve, however, at the moment I am missing one critical piece of information."

"Which is?" I asked.

Just then, the bell began to toll in the church behind us. When it had concluded its chimes, I noted a sudden glimmer appear in Holmes' grey eyes. I could tell from our long years of association that an idea had occurred to him.

He turned to our companion from Scotland Yard. "Hopkins, we should split up. Do you see that watering hole?" He pointed to a tavern so close to the water's edge it was practically situated upon the dock itself. "The men gathered there might be a source of information about the workings of this base. Unless security is more far lax than Mycroft's information suggests, the sailors won't know anything about the missing submarine itself, of course. However, you should endeavour to see if they can shed any light upon the matter. Ask them about peculiar men seen in the area, that sort of thing."

"Very well, Mr. Holmes," answered the inspector. "But what are you and Dr Watson going to do?"

"It is difficult to work upon so delightful a day, when all of Nature is newly washed and fresh. Watson and I are going to take a little stroll along the quays in order to enjoy the exquisite air."

Hopkins briefly appeared surprised by this apparent shirking of Holmes' duty. However, the inspector hid his disappointment well and scurried off to perform the task set out for him by Holmes.

I, on the other hand, knew something was afoot. Holmes never had time for poetry when on a case, and even now that he was officially retired, I sincerely doubted that this proclamation contained any element of truth. Therefore, I watched Hopkins go for a moment, and then turned to my friend. "Alright, Holmes, what are you up to?"

He smiled. "It is good to have you by my side again, Watson. The inspector is a good man, though he still has yet to fully employ the rules of criminal investigation. Furthermore, even in his travelling outfit, Hopkins still carries himself with the air of a detective, don't you think?"

"I suppose so."

"I assure you that I am correct, Watson. Hopkins will learn nothing in that tavern, as the men within will instinctively recognize him for what he is, and will close up tighter than an oyster with a pearl. That is why I didn't wish for him to accompany us while we sought wisdom amongst the men upon the fishing boats over yonder. And yet, Hopkins will be close enough to rapidly recall should we spot something of interest."

§

We spent the next hour talking to a dozen or so fisherman about a variety of topics – including the weather, the quality of the season's catch, and the fortunes of the local rugby league – none of which, as far as I could tell, had anything to do with the Navy's missing submarine. However, each boat was rapidly dismissed by Holmes, who then moved on to the next with an ever-darkening expression upon his face.

"Our efforts have thus far been in vain, Watson," said he, grimly. "Let us hope that the next boat proves more interesting."

This turned out to be a small schooner, tied up about three-quarters of the way down one of the jetties. The name *Duke of Normandy* was painted upon its stern. As we approached, three men who had been working upon its deck turned in our direction. Two were enormous young men, both over fifteen stone of solid bone and muscle, who gazed upon us silently with faces that could have been carved from granite. The final member of the trio was an older man, with a shock of white hair protruding from beneath a nautical cap. He was much thinner than his companions, and his face was rather red from exertion and exposure to sun. He wore spectacles over intelligent green eyes, and a pair of field glasses dangled from a strap around his neck.

"I am Mr. Harris, of Bermondsey, and this is Mr. Price, of Birmingham," began Holmes. "We have been seeking a boat for hire."

"For what purpose? We run an honest operation here," answered the older man. I detected a trace of an accent in his voice, though I was unable to place its origin.

Holmes laughed. "Nothing nefarious, I assure you, sir. My friend and I are famous sport fishermen. However, we have grown tired of seeking trout and pike in the streams and lakes of England. We wish to test our mettle against some of the bigger beasts of the open water."

The older man shook his head. "I am afraid that we are simple net fishers, Mr. Harris. The *Duke* does not carry the proper equipment for line sport. I don't believe that we can be of any assistance."

"Ah, I am most sorry to hear that," replied Holmes. "My friend and I have been having the devil of a time finding someone to take us out. Do you have any suggestions for other boats at which to inquire?"

"Unfortunately not, Mr. Harris. Gosport is not our home anchorage, so we don't know the men around here well. We have merely followed the cod over to this side of the Solent."

"Ah, I see," said Holmes, disappointedly. "Very well, then. We will keep asking around." He turned to leave, and then stopped. Holmes spun back around, as another question appeared to have just occurred to him. "And if we were chasing after swordfish, where would you seek them, sir?"

The man shrugged. "Swordfish only occasionally migrate through the Channel, Mr. Harris. But I have seen them near our home isle from time to time. We hail from Guernsey. I suggest you try off its shores once you locate a boat for hire."

"Capital! I thank you for your advice, sir." With that, Holmes turned around and began to walk back in the direction of the shore. He took my arm, and muttered under his breath. "Walk normally, Watson, and don't look back. We must trust that they believe that we have been fooled by their little act."

"Is he our man?"

"Most certainly. Did you not notice, Watson, that compared to each of the other boats we inspected, their boat had brought in a rather small catch? It is as if they had other things on their minds while at sea, and the catch was merely a smokescreen. Furthermore, did you perceive his accent?"

"Of course, Holmes," I protested. "However, simply because the man hails from Guernsey hardly makes him a suspect."

"That man is no more from the Channel Islands than I am, Watson! Unless I have forgotten everything I once knew, that man's accent is from Frisia."

"Frisia?" I asked, frowning in confusion. "Aren't those islands part of Germany?"

"Precisely, Watson. And most importantly, they lie in the midst of the Wadden Sea."

"Then why are we leaving?"

"Because I can tell by the lack of bulge in your coat pocket that you neglected to bring your service revolver."

"I hardly thought it necessary for a trip to the theatre," I replied, defensively.

He waved off my protest. "And though my rheumatism is calmed by these sea airs, I don't wish to unnecessarily test my baritsu skills against those two hulking gentlemen."

"We need the inspector!" I exclaimed.

"Undoubtedly, however, if we wish to learn what happened to the submarine, we first must board that boat. They will destroy the evidence if they see us coming with a member of Scotland Yard. Did you not notice the older man's rather fine set of field glasses?"

"But how are we going to get on board the boat?" I protested.

"First, by resurrecting Captain Basil. And then, by drowning you."

§

Twenty minutes later, I found myself stumbling out of the tavern and down the pier, looking for all the world like a man who had imbibed about three shots of rum too many. Holmes had even made me exchange my regular suit for a set of rough sailor clothes, which he had purchased off of a man in the tavern. I did not bother to resist, for I knew in moments like this that Holmes could never resist a touch of the dramatic.

Long gone was the languid figure whom Hopkins and I had encountered ambling across the fields of Sussex. As he went about detailing his plans in the tavern's front room, Holmes' eager face wore that expression of intense and high-strung energy which I recognized from so many of our adventures together. It was the difference between a Thoroughbred put out to pasture, and one set loose upon the Turf of the Wessex Cup.

As I weaved and wobbled slowly towards the *Duke of Normandy*, I knew that Holmes was at that very moment situated in a small dingy, already rowing in a circuitous fashion around the marina, so as to approach the suspect's boat from the rear. Holmes was dressed in a borrowed long overcoat, with a large cap pulled down close over his eyes. He had even managed to produce a tangled, black false beard from some mysterious pocket of his coat. Even I would have had a hard time equating this salty mariner with the respectably-dressed Mr. Harris who had earlier been making inquiries upon the quays.

I knew Inspector Hopkins was watching my progress from behind a curtained window of the tavern, ready to spring into action should Holmes' plan fail to achieve its desired result. I made my way to within a dozen yards of our adversaries' boat, when I paused at the spot indicated by Holmes and leaned over the water, pretending to have a need to evacuate the contents of my stomach. I then slowly toppled into the water, attempting to make this appear like an accident and not part of Holmes' subtle plan to distract our adversaries.

The next several moments were a blur. The water was far colder than I had hoped and the immersion was a bit of a shock to my aging system. But I soon found my way back up to the surface, where I heard cries of alarm being raised. A pounding of footsteps echoed upon the wooden slats of the pier, and a kisby ring attached to a rope was tossed in my direction. I gratefully held onto it while several sets of arms dragged me out of the water.

I lay motionless upon the quay for a few moments, water dripping from my sopping outfit, hoping that my distraction had bought sufficient time for Holmes to board and search the ship. It seemed that our stratagem was successful, for I soon heard the shrill blast of Hopkins' police whistle, which he had loaned to Holmes.

That was the signal for the inspector and me to rush to Holmes' aid. With the help of some marines commandeered from the HMS *Dolphin*, it was only a matter of minutes before the three men had been secured, the leader with a pair of glittering steel handcuffs, and the others with some stout nautical rope. The three of us then proceeded to march our captives back to Commodore Shipton's office. Holmes carried with him a log-book which he had confiscated from the boat's cabin. Behind us, three marines carried a curious, heavy, round metal drum, of some two feet in diameter and less than a foot in depth. Its purpose was a mystery to me, but it was plainly not a part of the traditional gear of a normal fishing trawler.

As we approached the office, Holmes indicated that the two larger captives should be escorted to the fort's brig. The older, bespectacled man was undoubtedly the brains of the operation. This individual was forcefully seated in front of the Commodore, while Captain Urquhart, Inspector Hopkins, Holmes, and I all gathered around him.

"Now then," began Holmes. "Why don't we begin with your name, sir?"

"I am Victor Edwards, from St. Peter Port. I demand to know

the reason for this arrest!" said he, angrily. "Of what crime am I accused?"

Holmes smiled. "I asked for your name, *Mein Herr*, not your *nom de guerre*. Your accent suggests that you have never set foot upon Guernsey. It is plain that you hail from one of the Frisian Islands. Nordeney, or Borkum, if I had to guess."

The man licked his lips. "That is absurd. I am…"

"Your cover story may have been sufficient to fool the fisherman of Gosport, *Mein Herr*, but it will not stand up to any real scrutiny. A simple wire over to Guernsey will suffice to sink your little subterfuge. You can either tell me your name now, or I shall be forced to make one up. Shall we call you '*Rache*?' I have always had a fondness for that word," said Holmes, sardonically.

"Ehrenberg," muttered the man.

"Very good, Herr Ehrenberg. Now, with the help of your log-book, I shall relate to Commodore Shipton and Captain Urquhart precisely what you and your men have been up to. After that, I hope that you will find your cell at Fort Charlotte a comfortable one."[109]

"You have no grounds to hold me! This whole proceeding is outrageous," Ehrenberg protested.

"On the contrary. You are guilty of instigating an act of war."

"Pray explain yourself, Mr. Holmes," interjected Commodore Shipton. "Are you claiming that this man is responsible for the disappearance of our submarine?"

"Indeed. Not directly, of course. However, he is the facilitator of its destruction."

"Destruction!" exclaimed Captain Urquhart, his voice hoarse. "Do you mean that the *Teucer* has been lost? It carried a complement of twenty-five men!"

"I am afraid so, Captain," said Holmes, gravely. "The blood of those men is on Herr Ehrenberg's hands. It was he that tracked the submarine's movements. The recordings in his log-book confirm it."

"In a little fishing boat?" said Commodore Shipton, doubtfully. "That is impossible."

"It may have once been impossible, Commodore, unfortunately, that is no longer the case. The idea came to me like the ringing of a bell. With each technological advance we make in the science of war, a simultaneous counter-advance is made. In this case, we built the Bruce-Partington submarine, capable of long-range scouting of the German military installations in the Frisian Islands, at Wilhelmshaven, and at our former colony of Heligoland.[110] In return, Herr Ehrenberg has constructed a method with which to track our submarines. He utilized that curious drum your men left outside the office, which I have yet to closely examine. However, if you turn it over to the government's scientists, I expect that they will shortly determine that it is capable of creating underwater sounds and then picking up any resulting echoes. Given the paucity of whales or other sea-monsters in the Channel, once away from land, any echoes that his sonorous device receives must be coming from an underwater ship."

Both Commodore Shipton and Captain Urquhart had looks of horror upon their faces. "If that is true, Mr. Holmes, then the silent service has been nullified!" cried Shipton. "There is no further advantage for our submarines."

"I suspect that to be an oversimplification, Commodore. Herr Ehrenberg's device will require some experimentation, and it is likely still a rather crude affair. From an inspection of the boat's logs, it took Ehrenberg and his men several weeks in order to track the *Teucer*. And now that we are in possession of Ehrenberg's device, the Royal Navy will be able to create more. We can employ it against any German submarines sailing from Kiel. The wheel turns, gentlemen."[111]

Shipton shook his head as he mentally digested this information. "There is a major difference, Mr. Holmes, between tracking a submarine and sinking it. How do you propose that transpired?"

"A torpedo!" I exclaimed. "Ehrenberg may have wired to a destroyer, which then fired the fatal shot."

"Capital, Watson," said Holmes. "However, you are forgetting the account of the witness. Surely the fisherman would not have been so obtuse as to miss the presence of a German destroyer within torpedo's range?"

"But his account is impossible!" I protested.

"Not impossible, merely improbable. I submit that the so-called monster witnessed by our Dutch fisherman was nothing other than the submarine itself. It surfaced in order to send its nightly wireless report, not realizing that a small boat might be nearby. It also vented its black-water waste, which produced the foul smell that the man reported."

"And the loud noise?" queried Shipton. "Our submarine makes no such sound."

"Indeed not," said Holmes. "That would have come from the agent of its destruction. The engine of an aeroplane."

"Surely you jest, Mr. Holmes," objected Shipton. "Those lighter-than-air craft can barely fly a hundred yards. Mayhaps one of Zeppelin's airships?"

"Too slow," Holmes concluded. "No, it can only have been a new model of an aeroplane, capable of a long flight over water. And from that craft, the pilot dropped an explosive charge which blew open a sufficient hole to result in the sinking of your submarine. That was the tongue of fire witnessed by the fisherman."

"You horrify me, Holmes," said I, quietly. "If this is true, then soon Britain may no longer be an island."[112]

We all sat quietly for a moment and pondered the implications of this terrible news.

"This is an outrage!" thundered Captain Urquhart, finally breaking the silence. "It is worse than the Dogger Bank incident. Rather than simple incompetence, this was perpetrated as a deliberate act of war."[113]

"That is a question for men who occupy higher seats than I, Captain," said Holmes, calmly. "Herr Ehrenberg's superiors may believe that the Royal Navy was in the wrong for running a submarine so near their own bases. In any case, I think that

Inspector Hopkins will see to it that Herr Ehrenberg does not glimpse the light of day again for many years to come, until the brewing storm has cleared." Holmes paused and nodded at the men in the room before turning to me. "And now that this little business has been taken care of, Watson, I think a little stroll is in order. I have a sudden yearning to stride the boards of Nelson's *Victory*."

§

As a word of epilogue, several days later I was comfortably ensconced in my arm-chair at my little Southsea villa reading the local morning paper, when I came across a small article buried at the bottom of page five. It concerned the fishing boat *Duke of Normandy,* of St. Peter Port, Guernsey, which was tragically lost with all hands during an unexpected squall off Bembridge. I was little surprised to find that Mycroft was as equally adept as his brother at utilizing the institution of the press. Therein Mycroft could spread the supposed facts of the false narrative that he was crafting for those foreign agents inquiring as to the sudden disappearance of Herr Ehrenberg and his sonorous device.

Sadly, there was no mention in that paper, or any other, of Commander White or his twenty-five men, lost in the unfathomable deep. However, I have it upon good authority that their families were quietly presented with posthumous Conspicuous Service Crosses for their gallantry against the enemy at sea – despite the fact that we currently faced no enemy. There was only that terrible sword of Damocles hanging ominously over our heads from the East. At the moment, the only war was the secret one.... of misinformation and the shield of lies.

§

THE HIGH MOUNTAIN

I t was one sultry and stagnant afternoon early in August of the year 1914 that I received one of Holmes' typically terse telegrams:

> Bring the car round to the Portsmouth Guildhall, third pillar from the left, if feasible – if infeasible bring all the same
> – S.H.

I frowned in consternation at this unusual request. To begin with, it had been some nine months from the time when I had last heard anything from Holmes, and close by two years since I had been invited for a visit to his villa near Eastbourne. My recent letters had all gone unanswered. It was almost as if Holmes had vanished from the face of the earth.

I had, of course, kept busy in his absence attempting to do my part in maintaining a sense of sporting good will between our country and those upon the Continent. I had even participated in a tour event organized by the Royal Automobile Club to see whose entrants could drive the fastest from Frankfurt to Bremerhaven and then from Southampton to Edinburgh.[114] Secondly, Holmes had always made light of my purchase of a Model T, calling it a noisy affront to all that was graceful and civilized.[115]

Nevertheless, I sighed deeply as I realized that – no matter my annoyance – I could hardly ignore such a summon from my friend. Only a mere handful of times had we sallied forth upon an adventure since his retirement to the South Downs twelve years earlier. While I was content with my life and blessed to have my wife at my side, I could little pass up the chance for one final sail into the sunset.

I eased my frame into the small car, perhaps a stone heavier than those days when I was as thin as a lash from enteric fever. I glanced in the mirror and sighed at the sight of my moustache, now all gone to grey. Adventures were a young man's game, and thirty-three years had passed since – at the side of my new suite-mate, Mr. Sherlock Holmes – I first took up my hat and swung into a hansom cab before it drove furiously for the Brixton Road.

Fortunately, Portsmouth was very close to my Southsea home. I could have walked it in less than half an hour, if I wished. Nevertheless, Holmes had requested the car, so I acceded to his whim. When I arrived at the grand marble colonnaded neo-Grecian structure marking the indicated spot, I wondered if Holmes intended for me to park the car and meet him on foot. I glanced up at the giant clock and saw that it was still a few minutes before three. I decided to give him a quarter of an hour before I set out in search of him.

Only a few minutes had passed, however, when the passenger door opened and a tall gaunt man of sixty, with bright red hair, clear-cut features, and a small goatee beard, slid into the compartment of my car. A half-smoked, sodden cigar hung from the corner of his mouth and, as he sat down, he struck a match and relit it.

"This is not a cab for hire, sir," said I, protesting this unwarranted invasion. However, the words died up on my lips, as I finally realized the identity of the man who sat beside me. I smiled wanly. "I thought you were too old for service,

Holmes?"

"Dire straits, Watson, call for extraordinary measures."

"I presume you refer to the recent assassination of the Archduke?"

"Things are even worse than that, Watson. If I am correct, tomorrow will be the last day of peace that we shall see for many years to come."

"Is it that grave?"

"Indeed. We are ill prepared for what is to come, I fear, Watson. All of Europe is about to explode with a violence such has never before been seen upon this earth."

I sat forward at this terrible news. "What can we do?"

"I recommend putting this contraption into gear and setting out at once for Harwich. Since it is a good five-hour drive, we must hurry if we are to get there in time."

I followed his commands and embarked upon the journey that promised to take me a great deal farther than I had expected when I first set out from home that afternoon. It was fortunate that I had warned my wife I was planning to meet with Holmes. She knew from long experience not to expect an early return whenever I was in his company.

"And what are we going to do in Harwich?" I asked. "Prevent a war?"

He shook his head. "Nothing in the world can prevent it, Watson. Even if I had foreseen and forestalled the murder of Archduke Franz Ferdinand, something else would have set the fuse. No, it is widely believed in certain circles that the German Empire has been deliberately planning for a European war for some time now. To many, their special war tax of fifty million marks made that fact as plain as if they advertised it upon the front page of *The Times*. Their Kaiser wished to demonstrate Germany's new powers to the world. As you know, we have built up our own naval forces in preparation for just such a deterioration in international relations. Hence, the importance of preserving the Bruce-Partington plans from enemy hands, as well as the securing the secret activities of our forces in Bermuda.[116] All of Europe has been an armed camp for some years now, and I suspect that within days those forces will finally mobilize and commence their assaults."

"Surely there is something that can be done?" I cried.

"We cannot prevent this war, Watson, but we can ensure that England emerges triumphant. And to that end, I have been away from my bees for far too long."

"Where have you been?"

"Nearly two years ago, I received a series of visits. First from my brother, then from the Foreign Minister. When neither prevailed to move me from my humble Skyros,[117] Asquith himself made a visit and sat in my armchair."[118]

"What did they want?"

"It was clear to Mycroft that things were amiss within England. There was a secret and strong central force that was engaged in the task of ferreting out all of our military and diplomatic secrets. They have employed a clever combination of physical observation and direct theft of confidences from within our government's bureaucracy. This force has stitched all of this information into a global tapestry of our resolve and readiness. Somehow, they have learned that there is no binding treaty between the French Republic and us. They have studied our arrangement for making high explosives, and how and where we stockpile our ammunitions. They have discovered the number of our battleships and cruisers in operational shape, as well as the nature of our preparations for submarine attack. They have even fostered the Women's Social & Political Union, whose militant work – with its window-smashing and arson – have distracted both the politicians and populace from the far-greater threat abroad."

"Who could do such things?"

"In some ways, Watson, it reminded me of the late, lamented Professor Moriarty, pulling the strings from the centre of his web. As you recall, it took me many long years to follow the thread along a thousand cunning windings until I was able to finally break through the veil that shrouded the Professor's identity. However, Moriarty was the height of carelessness compared to our current quarry. There is no Greuze hanging reflectively over his writing desk, helpfully pointing to a rather large discrepancy between supposed station and tangible wealth. In this case, despite my best efforts I was unable to latch onto his trail. I had long believed that the spy reveals himself by his great politeness, his calculated self-effacement, his habit of looking at or hearing things without appearing to do so. But this one was too clever for that sort of straightforward identification to work."

"So you have become a spy yourself?"

Holmes shook his head. "Much more than a spy, Watson. That would have been simplicity itself. I was a double agent… a far more difficult role to play. Even the Prince of Denmark was less challenging. You see, to succeed in this task I would need to infiltrate the organization from the inside, until I was as trusted as the leader's own cousin or uncle."

I shook my head. "Another secret society."

"What do you mean, Watson?"

"You have battled so many over the years, Holmes. Gaelton and Lukeson's Artus Society.[119] Captain Calhoun's K.K.K. Ted Baldwin's Ancient Order of Freeman. Abe Slaney's Joint. Pietro Venucci's Mafia. Giuseppe Gorgiano's Red Circle. Even the Danites of Drebber and Stangerson, and Professor Coram's Brotherhood were peripherally involved in some of our adventures together."

"Yes, well, the Americans, Italians, and Russians have nothing on the Germans when it comes to secret societies. As far back as the fourteenth century, there were the *Vehmgericht* tribunals, and Rosenkreuz's Order also got its start there. However, we are now dealing with the ultimate culmination of those societies, backed by the full force of the German State. The machinations of the *Nachrichten-Abteilung* at the Hamilton Princess or at Portsmouth Harbour are nothing compared to their current efforts."

"How could you possibly penetrate such an organization?"

"I first asked myself, Watson, what sort of subject of the King would voluntarily work for the agents of the Kaiser?"

"A traitor, of course!" I exclaimed.

Holmes shook his head. "Yes, certainly in the eyes of the law. But not just any average traitor, selling secrets for thirty coins of blood money. No, such a greedy rogue would never be fully trusted by this organization. Only a man that did not see himself as a traitor, but rather a patriot, would be truly welcomed into the network's inner circle."

"A patriot?" I spluttered.

"Indeed, Watson. There are many a bitter Irishmen who would ne'er see the Union Jack fly over the Emerald Isle. Therefore, I dyed my hair an Irish-setter red, such that I would have vied with Mr. Jabez Wilson for a seat at the Pope's Court headquarters of the League of the Red-headed Men. My grey eyes had no need for obfuscation, but I grew a small goatee beard and when I was finished, I was certain that even Mrs. Hudson or Inspector Lestrade would have the devil's time determining I was not Mr. Carlus Altamont of Fermoy."

"Nevertheless, you do look somewhat familiar, Holmes."

"Perhaps you have finally developed the knack of seeing through my disguises, Watson?"

"No, that's not it. You resemble someone famous. I just cannot think of whom exactly. I am certain I will put my finger upon it eventually."

"Well, in any case, once my disguise was complete, I then proceeded to take passage to the New World."

"Why ever would you do that?" I protested in confusion. "I thought the threat was in England."

"Of course, Watson. However, it simply does not do to blunder in so directly. If I had tried to join straightaway this terrible organization, their agents would have quickly determined that Mr. Altamont was a fraud. I needed to establish antecedents of adamantine if I was to be honoured with their complete confidence. In short, I required an explanation as to why Mr. Altamont was not known on these shores. I determined that he must have spent much of his days in the warrens of America's great metropolises. The Irish diaspora resulting from the Penal Laws and the Potato Famine populated communities throughout the Eastern Seaboard, as well as deep into the interior.[120] They went looking for green fields, but mainly found themselves unwelcome in their new country. Therefore, they have turned inwards upon themselves, one eye always gazing eastwards towards their ancestral homeland, hoping for a day that it would be free from English oppression. Moreover, many of them are actively working towards that goal. It was these latter men whose acquaintance I was eager to make."

"So you went to New York?"

He smiled and shook his head. "I landed there, and I considered commencing my insinuation at Five Points in Manhattan, but ultimately decided that it was too close to home. There was an excessive risk of someone seeing through my disguise. Somewhere more central would better serve. My old friend Inspector Wilson Hargreave had retired some five years earlier, and although I hated to consider him untrustworthy, I decided not to test the loyalties of his Irish replacement, Inspector O'Flaherty. Instead, I called upon Mr. Leverton, of the Pinkerton Agency, who you may recall was the hero of the Long Island cave mystery. It was he who recommended I set my sights upon Chicago."

"Chicago?" I exclaimed. "I thought that city was nothing more than a miserable swamp of appalling corruption and grime, inhabited only by savages such as old Patrick's gang of crooks?"

He chuckled. "It is not quite so bad, Watson, though there is an element of truth to those horror stories. Fortunately, Mr. Leverton had a colleague in the city to whom he provided a letter of introduction. I telegrammed ahead to this Mr. Geyer, and was instructed to meet him at noon sharp in two days' time at the lobby bar of the Palmer House hotel. I therefore more-or-less immediately climbed aboard the New York Central Railroad's 20th Century Limited. Twenty hours later, this fine conveyance deposited me at Chicago's LaSalle Street Station on the morning of my planned meeting.[121]

"I had with me only a small travelling valise and a case for a battered Irish fiddle which I had picked up at a broker's in Tottenham Court Road for sixty shillings – more than I once paid for my incomparable Stradivarius! I took a cab over to the Palmer House, but one look at the structure made it clear that poor Mr. Carlus Altamont could never stay in those exuberantly ornate Italian marble-lined walls. I hefted my valise up the steps from the street level to the first floor lobby and admit to being arrested for a moment by the sight. Some thirty feet above me soared a magnificent vaulted ceiling, and the room's calcium lights shone upon its score of vibrant frescos. I had not seen its equal since I investigated the sudden death of Cardinal Tosca at the Vatican.

"I asked the barkeeper to point me towards Geyer, and he indicated a big man with a pleasant and earnest face. Geyer was roughly my age, and what were once dark brown hair and a handlebar moustache were now flecked with grey. His face was ruddy and, from the glassy look in his eyes, he appeared to be enjoying his second or third bourbon whisky of the still-early day. I sat down next to him and introduced myself as Altamont.

"He turned and studied me carefully. Despite his state of inebriation, I sensed a careful intelligence in the man's look. 'Pleased to meet you, Mr. Altamont. Angus Leverton told me you were a man to whom he owed a favour and he would be much obliged if I helped you in whatever way possible.'

"I smiled at him. 'I assure you, sir, that my request is a simple one. In fact, you hardly need leave your seat. But first, I am something of a student of crime, and I wondered if you were the same Mr. Frank Geyer who solved the Holmes-Pitezel case?'

"The man's face soured. 'Yeah, though I would be right glad if you did not speak that name in my presence. I am still troubled by the visions of that madman's deeds.'

" 'The crime of the century,' I noted.[122]

" 'Such an argument could be made,' said he, grimly.

"I nodded my head in appreciation and, changing the subject, I motioned to the luminous painting of two haystacks in a setting sun which hung behind the bar.

" 'Monet, if I am not mistaken.'[123]

"The man shrugged. 'If you say so, Mr. Altamont. Bertha Potter has festooned the whole building with artworks she has picked up in France, but it all looks rather sloppy to me. Like the man painted the whole thing in just a few hours.'

" 'I believe that is the point, Mr. Geyer. It is supposed to capture the light of a single moment in time, a brief impression which cannot be duplicated.'

"The man grimaced. 'Did you ask me here to talk about art, Mr. Altamont? If so, I must warn you that I don't know a Rembrandt from a da Vinci.'

"I smiled. 'No, in fact, I am seeking something rather more prosaic. I wish to make the acquaintance of a group of individuals from my homeland.'

"He chuckled. 'Go down to the street corner and take your pick. You can hardly spit in this city without hitting an Irishman.'

" 'Ah, but I am seeking one of a certain persuasion. One who is less than pleased that he is forced to live in exile. One who wishes that Hibernia was free of certain outside oppressors.'[124]

"At that, his eyebrows rose with interest. 'Oh, I see. A *Fenian*,' he said with interest. 'Of course, if you are a friend of Angus' then I wager you are engaged in a bit of subterfuge. It's a right good thing you came to me rather than Chicago Central, Mr. Altamont.[125] Ever since old Marvin retired, the captains over at LaSalle have become so thick with the thieves that it's tough to tell one from the other."

" 'So where might I go to meet a Fenian?'

" 'For that pleasure I would recommend you head to Bridgeport. There you will find a saloon called the Hardscrabble Hog.'

" 'A strange name for a public house.'

" 'And a strange place it is. It's a blind pig.' When he saw the look of incomprehension upon my face, he further explained. 'The proprietor has failed to properly obtain a license for the selling of alcohol. But such niceties don't stop him, or the folks which frequent the place. You would be hard-pressed to find a more diverse clientele. Behind its battered doors, you will find artists, academics and anarchists, ladies of the night, judges, and city councilmen, and a whole mess of bums and con artists.'

"I smiled. 'It sounds perfect.'

"I took my leave of Mr. Geyer and – given the fact that the sun was still high in the sky – I decided to familiarize myself with the city before heading to the indicated saloon. Many hours later, as the clock struck nine o'clock, I hailed a cab. At first, I thought the cabman was mistaken when he pulled up to the address, until I realized that the Hardscrabble Hog was located within a dilapidated former barn. When I pushed the door opened, I discovered that the place was a strange cross between a dive bar, cabaret, and social club. There was a small stage with a piano where a thin man with a pencil moustache was banging out a popular tune.

"I ordered a beer and watched the scene for a while. When the piano player took a break, I sidled up to him and offered him five dollars to fake an illness and retire for the rest of the night.[126] The man took less than ten seconds to decide. Once he made his exit, I approached the man to whom he made his excuse – presumably the club's manager – and proposed to play the fiddle for a few hours in exchange for fifty cents. The man took me up with alacrity – plainly unhappy with the thought of a music-less saloon. I forsook the use of a chair, and instead strode onto the stage with my old fiddle under my chin. The wood may have been chipped, but the catgut sang true. I first played a swallowtail jig, then the 'Boys of Malin,' and finally followed with the song I had been especially practicing for this evening. As I began to saw away upon the strings, I did something that I suspect that you have never witnessed, Watson. I sang a tune."

"I would very much like to have heard that," I interjected. I had been silently listening for some time, all the while guiding the car upon its path north.

"Desperate times, Watson," said Holmes, with a wry smile. "Well, as I was saying, in order to gain their trust, I lifted my voice, and sang:

> *Oh father dear, the day will come when in answer to the call*
> *All Irish men of freedom stern will rally one and all*
> *I'll be the man to lead the band beneath the flag of green*
> *And loud and clear we'll raise the cheer, Revenge for Skibbereen.*

"When this song was concluded, I paused to sip upon my beer, and was little surprised when one of the tavern maids whispered that a man wanted to meet me. I packed away my fiddle with care and followed her to a darkened area of the establishment. I had been unable to get a good look at that corner during my initial reconnaissance of the saloon, but there I now found a large Irishman who appeared several years past sixty. Frankness shone in his blue eyes, and good humour played round his mobile, smiling lips.

" 'My name is John Devoy,' said he.[127]

" 'Carlus Altamont at your service.'

" 'How did you hear about the Hog, Mr. Altamont?'

"I shook my head. 'I have been wandering the streets all evening looking for a place that required the services of a man with a fiddle. The barkeeper at the last place sent me here.'

" 'Well, this is a unique place, Mr. Altamont. It was founded on the principal that no man knows everything there is to know about art, literature, drama, music, science, social or political economy, or any of the many other problems confronting and bothering the human race. This is a centre where any idea or work will be given a respectful hearing.'

"I like the sound of that."

'Tell me about yourself, Mr. Altamont.'

"I shrugged. 'I was born in Fermoy. My parents perished in the *an Gorta Mor*,' said I, using the Gaelic term for the Great Hunger.[128] I was raised by the nuns and decided that I would opt for a softer life, so I joined the 117th as soon as I could pass for my majority.'

"Devoy chuckled at my small witticism. 'You saw service?'

" 'Indeed. We went out to Soudan under the Sirdar Kitchener.'[129]

" 'That must have been unpleasant.'

" 'As an Englishman's armpit,' said I, with a crassness that would have shocked you, Watson.

"Devoy smiled and licked his lips. 'And what brings you to Chicago, Mr. Altamont?'

" 'After I was discharged from the army, I tried to go back home, but it was not the same anymore. Oh, the valleys were still sweet, the hills low, and the meadows green, but there was nothing for me there. In a fit of boredom, I fell in with a lot of rough chaps who had concocted a plan to make off with the paymaster's chest at the regimental depot. We near got away with it, but most of my compatriots spent our dearly gained loot upon whisky and women at one of the local public houses. It wasn't long before the army lads put two and two together and dragged them all in. I am by nature a more temperate sort, so I managed to escape this initial dragnet. But I soon found that the countryside had become rather too hot for me, and not wanting to end up with my brothers in the Joy,[130] I rustled up seventy-five shillings and took passage aboard the SS *Cameronia*.[131] It was nothing fancy, but at least it wasn't a coffin ship.[132] I suppose you might call me a Wild Goose.'[133]

" 'A wise choice, Mr. Altamont. I myself spent five years in Portland and Millbank Prisons, and don't recommend it.' He paused for a moment, studying me. 'You strike me as a man who is good in a pinch, Mr. Altamont. I might have need of just such an individual.'

" 'For what sort of business?'

" 'Well, to tell you that, I would need to be certain of your trustworthiness.'

"I spat upon the planked floor. 'Suit yourself, Mr. Devoy, I have other fish to fry,' said I, rising to leave.

" 'Now, now, calm yourself, Mr. Altamont,' said he, his voice rising in a soothing lilt. 'Surely you can see my position? I do not know you. You do not come with endorsements from one of my associates. I might need to check your references.'

"I snorted in wry amusement. "I ain't applying for no job in a bank, Mr. Devoy. What sort of references might serve?'

"He considered this for a moment. 'Well, how about some men from the Royal Mallows?'

"I shrugged. 'Fair 'nuff. Colonel Barclay was carried off by apoplexy, but Major Murphy is still around. You could send him a wire.'

"He pursed his lips. 'You will forgive me, Mr. Altamont, if a man in my particular business is not comforted by the word of a British officer.'

" 'How about Corporal Wood, then? Henry will vouch for me, I am certain. He's a harum-scarum, reckless chap, and we got into a few scrapes together. I haven't seen him in a few years, though. Last time we met he was loafing about Aldershot.'

" 'Aldershot, eh? I know a man there in the Royal Lancers. I will wire him in the morning.'

"I sincerely hoped he would do no such thing, Watson, since his contact would surely not recall the fictional Carlus Altamont. However, I could hardly let this concern show. I shrugged indifferently. 'Whatever makes you happy, Mr. Devoy. Send word when you are ready for me to come talk with you again. In the meantime, seeing how I just arrived in Chicago this morning, can you recommend a cheap boarding house in which I may bunk down?'

"He pursed his lips and thought about this for a minute before breaking into a smile. He had plainly fallen for my bluff. 'My organization has had the occasional problem with leaks, Mr. Altamont. Why, one of our former leaders, Dr Patrick Henry Cronin, may have even been a British spy.'

"I spat. 'What happened to the bastard?'

" 'His body was found wedged into a sewer, an *Agnus Dei* wrapped around his neck and five ice pick blows to his head.'

"I shrugged. 'Such is the price one pays when consorting with the British. And what organization would that be?'

" 'Have you heard of Clan-na-Gael?'[134]

" 'Ah, you are carrying the flag of the Fenians!'

" 'Indeed.'

" 'And does that make you the leader?'

" 'I carry that honour.'

" 'Well, then, if you are in need of assistance with taking up arms in the struggle, you need only whistle.'

" 'I would need to assure myself of your bon-a-fides.'

" 'And how do you propose to establish such an understanding between us?'

" 'There might be an item I am interested in obtaining. If you were to bring it to me, I am certain that we would shortly become bosom friends.'

" 'And where might I find such a remarkable item?'

" 'The one I am thinking of is, at present, located in Jackson Park.'

" 'I will admit, Mr. Devoy, to being a relative newcomer to this neck of the woods. I am unfamiliar with that locale.'

" 'The World's Fair?' he suggested.[135]

" 'Ah, yes, of course. I read about the White City. Quite the spectacle, if I recall correctly. But did it not all burn to the ground?'[136]

"The man shrugged. "Most of it, but not all. Thanks to its brick substructure, the Palace of Fine Arts survived and is now the home of the Field Museum of Natural History.[137] The L will take you there for five cents.'

"'I suppose the item you require is not something special, which I cannot simply purchase from the gift shop?'

"'You will excuse me, Mr. Altamont, if I refrain from talking particulars. Surely you understand my caution?'

"'You are saying that, should I prove to be a copper, I could bring you up on charges of conspiring to commit a theft.'

"He spread his hands wide and nodded his head slightly to indicate that we understood each other. 'Now then, should you find yourself perusing the display cases in the museum, Mr. Altamont, I recommend you take note of one very nice piece in the Harlow Higinbotham Hall. If legend is true, it once graced the neck of Berenice, wife of Ptolemy I of Egypt. I promise you will not be disappointed in the Green Goddess.'

"With those instructions ambiguously delineated, I was plainly dismissed. Therefore, I resumed my place on the stage. I entertained the patrons of the Hardscrabble Hog for several more hours before I finally made my exit. Since the museum was long past closed, I bunked down for the remainder of the night in a rough boarding house befitting my supposed station. In the morning, as recommended, I took the L to my destination."

"What is an L?" I interjected.

Holmes smiled. "Rather than tunnelling underground like rabbits, as we have done here in London, the Chicagoans decided several decades ago to place their train tracks upon great elevated platforms over the streets. I hardly know which is worse, to be confined in those tubes, or to be subjected to the constant rattling above your head. Still, when in Rome, as they say, Watson. Therefore, I did what any local would have done.

"My train made its way south along the lake's shore close to the location of the museum and I then walked the rest of the way. I noted with some admiration the fine Athenian architecture of the front entrance, with its flanking caryatids. When I strolled through the doors, I was immediately struck by the domed rotunda soaring some six score feet into the air.

I followed the signs to the Higinbotham Hall, which proved to be the locale for an impressive collection of gemstones. After admiring some of the other stones, I finally located the item to which Devoy had referred, which proved to be a massive pear-shaped peridot. Its pale green colour sparkled in the light. I read the hand-printed card, which identified the stone as having been mined from Zabargad Island in the Red Sea, and weighing in at one hundred fifty-four carats. I carefully observed the security precautions surrounding the Green Goddess, which resided in a glass-framed case. This had a standard lock, which would be simplicity itself to open. However, the larger obstacle was the Hall itself, which was carefully watched by a quartet of guards during the day. At night, it was plain that the entire area was designed to be closed off by the lowering of a series of thick metal poles through the opening. Even the smallest urchin would have the devil of a time wiggling his way through those narrow gaps. As an interior area of the museum, the room was devoid of windows or other areas of ingress. It would be a tough nut to crack.

"I therefore spent the remainder of the morning aimlessly strolling about the other collections of the museum, searching for inspiration. There were fine natural history exhibits containing pre-Columbian gold ornaments, taxidermist-preserved animals, and botanical specimens from the far corners of the world, and ethnographic objects from a variety of both great and humble civilizations, including the pre-discovery natives of America, Africa, and the South Seas. After a spot of lunch, I departed the museum by the rear doors and strolled about Jackson Park until I came to an island that contained a peaceful garden done in the Japanese style. The Phoenix temple and graceful bridges over tranquil koi ponds were most conducive to a ratiocination session. Although I had not spotted anyone trailing me, I managed to refrain from pulling out my old black pipe in case Mr. Devoy had sent someone to monitor my actions. I did not want to break character, even for a moment. Now, here was a definite conundrum, Watson.

How was I to go about stealing the Green Goddess for Mr. Devoy? He made it clear that only by such an action could I gain his trust."

"Surely you could have simply gone to the museum's director and asked for it?"

Holmes chuckled. "I admit that I did consider that possibility. However, consider the obstacles, Watson. The director would have had to be convinced of my true identity. This would have required the cooperation of the local authorities, and how could I be certain that none of them were in the secret employ of Mr. Devoy? No, Watson, far better to actually steal the gem itself."

"But you said yourself that it would be impossible."

He shook his head. "Nothing is impossible, Watson. Merely improbable, or in this case, fairly difficult. However, as I have said before, I think I would have made a highly efficient criminal had I turned my energies against the law, rather than in support of it."

"Yes, I recall that Inspector Gregson has said as much. But to steal from a museum, Holmes! Did it not give you pause?"

"I would not hesitate to use illegal methods in the pursuit of a morally justifiable cause, Watson. Moreover, what greater cause than the defence of our nation? Nevertheless, to assuage your conscience, my friend, you will be relieved to note that I determined to follow the eventual path of the Goddess and make every effort afterwards to see it returned to its rightful place."[138]

"So, what did you do?" I asked.

"Although I devised seven separate plans, I hit upon the best solution to my plan in the hall of mammals. There I noted a stuffed ichneumon."[139]

"A mongoose!" I cried.

"Indeed, Watson. Do you recall the trained pet belonging to Henry Wood?"

"How could I forget it? But where did you find a mongoose in Chicago, Holmes?"

"Every city has its nooks and crannies, Watson, where curious wares may be located. It is merely a matter of knowing where to look. I admit that it took me the remainder of the day to uncover a naturalist shop that would serve. However, by the time I had turned in for the evening, I had found Chicago's equivalent of Pinchin Lane upon Halsted Street. There, for a certain sum of dollars, I procured the temporary service of a Mr. Johnston and his remarkable little friend.

"The following morn, I went in search of additional allies for my assault upon the Hall of Gems. Although there was no Baker Street in Chicago, along Adams Street, I recruited a gang of street Arabs who seemed right glad of the promised wages of two quarters per lad, with a dollar bonus each if the plan succeeded. Of course, for my strategy to function properly, their tattered rags would not serve. I brought the pack of them round to a second-hand store, where we scrounged through the racks of cast-off clothing until my new Irregulars were festooned in a rough approximation of schoolboy uniforms. When they were informed that, in addition to their wages, they would be allowed to keep the clothing once the mission was complete, they all beamed with pleasure. For a moment, I worried about what foolhardy schemes I had placed in their heads, but the die was cast. I could only move on with my scheme and let the future sort itself out as it willed.

"That afternoon, my new army and I paid another visit to the Field Museum. None of the Irregulars had ever been inside that edifice, and as a lot, they were rather awed by both the grandeur of the building and the vastness of its collections. I trust that I perhaps inspired some of them to dream of places beyond the gritty confines of the Chicago streets. About fifty minutes before closing, we moved from the natural history areas to the Hall of Gems. The lads gazed into the sparkling cases in wonderment. However, they eventually recalled their purpose, and in short order, a mock fight had broken out between two of them. The rest of the gang then waded into action until the entire Hall was a scene of chaos. Of course, the quartet of guards had their hands full separating the boys. This was all the distraction I required. I quickly picked the lock upon the case enclosing the Green Goddess and then turned to join the other museum patrons in enjoying the spectacle of the guards attempting to quell the fray. Of course, more guards and museum staff soon arrived, and within moments, everyone was escorted from the Hall. The museum staff made certain that none of their precious gems were missing, but – as I hoped – in their rush they failed to notice the undone lock. I watched with satisfaction as the steel bars were prematurely lowered to seal off the room for the night.

"I then turned and made my way to the Ayer collection, where several rooms from the tomb of Unis-ankh had been shipped over from Egypt and installed in the museum a few years prior. There, in a dusty corner, Mr. Johnston removed his little creature from beneath his coat. He carefully handed the mongoose – which was called Frankie – over to me. As I had worked with Frankie the night before in order to accustomate him to taking my commands, the creature came to me without qualms. Johnston then exited the museum with all of the other late visitors, while Frankie and I set about evading the guards tasked with ensuring that no one was accidentally locked in at night. Of course, my plan depended upon just such a thing, so we bunked down behind the faux spring foliage of a white-tailed deer diorama and awaited a more propitious time of night. When the luminous dials of my pocket-watch finally showed midnight, I deemed it safe to begin moving about the museum. A small dark lantern lit our way back downstairs to the barred entrance to the Hall of Gems.

"After that, it was simplicity itself. At my command, Frankie sprang from my grasp and slithered between the bars as if they did not exist. He scurried up the leg of the display case, nosed the undone lock off the clasp, and slipped under the lid. Taking up the Goddess, he quickly reversed this process and returned to my hands where he happily exchanged his shiny bauble for a bit of sugar. Given the rapidity of this process and the complete absence of any sign of a guard, I deemed it feasible to repeat the endeavour with the Goddess' neighbour. This action was also successful, and it was a contented mongoose that spent the remainder of the night curled up next to me in the shadows of the diorama.

"The following morn, we joined the ranks of early patrons of the museum, and enjoyed a few more exhibits before I deemed that it was a no-longer suspicious time to depart. On my way out, I observed a flurry of uniformed activity near the Hall of Gems, which suggested that my work had not gone unnoticed. I first returned Frankie to his owner, and then dropped by Adams Street in order to congratulate my Irregulars on their excellent work and deliver their promised payment. I finally made my way back to the Hardscrabble Hog, where I found Mr. Devoy waiting for me at his usual table.

"The man smiled when I entered, and bade me take a seat across from him. 'Mr. Altamont,' said the man. 'It has not made the papers yet, but a source at Chicago Central tells me that there is something amiss at the Field Museum this morning.'

" 'You might say that, sir.' I replied.

" 'Do you have it with you?' asked Devoy, eagerly.

"I pulled the brilliant stone from my pocket and silently slid it across the table.

"He picked it up and studied it carefully. When his inspection was complete, he looked up at me with a hint of admiration in his eyes. 'Now then, Mr. Altamont, would you care to describe how you accomplished such a wondrous task?'

"I shrugged. 'Secrets of the trade, Mr. Devoy. If I was to tell you everything, what further use would I be?'

"He studied me for a minute and then threw his head back in laughter. 'Very good, sir! You are a clever rogue, I give you that. Now, my sources claim that the Green Goddess was not the only item to have gone missing this morning. I hear that a golden pin, topped with a two-caret diamond engraved with a portrait of King William III of the Netherlands, also went missing.'[140]

"I smiled. 'It was dark and I misread the card. I thought it was King Billy and as such, that I would do him a disservice.'[141]

"Devoy chuckled. 'It will also serve our cause.' He held forth his hand for the pin.

"I shrugged. 'If I recall correctly, Mr. Devoy, the task you set for me is complete. I aim to keep the pin for myself.'

"His eyes narrowed. 'And what would you do with it, Mr. Altamont?'

"'A man must eat, sir.'

"He gazed at me for a long moment, during which time I could not tell if I had angered him or not. However, he finally smiled and shook his head. 'I suppose I cannot begrudge you that, Mr. Altamont, considering what the Goddess alone will do for us.'

"'And what is that?' I asked, with as much insouciance as possible.

"He didn't reply at first, instead, he looked down at the peridot. 'I am sore tempted to keep the Goddess, Mr. Altamont, for it is the very colour of Hibernia, it is. But a plan is a plan, and it's for the greater good. We must turn it into cold hard cash and make certain that the money finds its way into the proper hands.'

"'What did you have in mind?'

"Devoy smiled cruelly. 'Have you ever been to Buffalo?'"

"Didn't Birdy Edwards once live there?" I interjected.

"Your memory is, as usual, impeccable, Watson." Holmes continued. "And so, that is how I found myself that afternoon aboard the Empire State Express, pulled by the magnificent black steel engine no. 999. Some fifteen hours later, we arrived at the City of Light. It is a remarkable city in which to walk about, Watson. In preparation for the 1901 Pan-American Exposition, they have harnessed the power of a nearby massive waterfall in order to generate amazing amount of electricity, and every street it brightly lit. You would also appreciate that half of the vehicles upon the smooth roads are horseless carriage, which are manufactured in great numbers at Buffalo."[142]

"It's not all light, Holmes. Was not an American president assassinated there a dozen years ago?"

Holmes nodded gravely. "Indeed, Watson. The work of a former steel worker turned mad anarchist.[143] And there are many more such desperate men to be found in Buffalo's notorious Canalside District, as I was soon to discover. But first, John Devoy had sent me to see his compatriot, Joseph Loggins, who - I was informed - headed a secret splinter of the famous Saturn Club.[144] As I learned from Devoy, this faction is called the Enceladus Club, and is involved in secret negotiations with Imperial Germany to supply rifles to Irish revolutionaries in exchange for money."

"An apt name," I remarked.

Holmes frowned at my interruption. "How so, Watson?"

I had momentarily forgotten my friend's limited grasp of astronomy and literature. "Enceladus is one of Saturn's moons. He was also the Titan of volcanos and earthquakes," I explained. "And to Longfellow, he was a symbol of a struggle for independence." I declaimed:

'And the nations far away
Are watching with eager eyes
They talk together and say
To-morrow, perhaps to-day
Enceladus will arise!'[145]

Holmes eyed me for a moment, before shaking his head in disdain at my poetry recitation. "May I continue, Watson?"

"Pray do so, Holmes."

"As I was saying, I met the next day with Mr. Loggins, who was a black-maned man, bearded to his cheek bones. This contrasted greatly with his vivid blue eyes, which peered out from behind thick spectacles. Loggins was quite impressed with the gift that I bore him from Devoy. I handed over the

Goddess, and he assured me the money it generated would be well spent.

" 'Are we resuming the Dynamite War, then?' I asked.

" 'Oh, yes, Mr. Altamont. And this time we will win. Ireland will be free of the English once and for all. For the first time since the Normans set foot upon our shores, we shall rule ourselves.'

" 'But why pay for guns?' I asked.

" 'What do you mean?' replied Loggins, surprised by this odd question.

" 'The Germans need steel to make their guns, do they not?'

" 'Yes,' agreed Loggins, slowly.

" 'Well, last night, I noticed a lot of steel being loaded into ships down at the harbour.'

" Loggins frowned in confusion. 'Those ships are destined for England.'

" 'But they don't have to be, do they, Mr. Loggins? What if we hijacked one and steered it for Hamburg? What if instead of that steel being turned into more rifles for the English occupiers, we traded it to the Germans?' "

"Holmes, really!" I interjected in protest. "Say you did no such thing! Even for the sake of your cover, such an action could never be justified!"

Holmes chuckled. "Calm yourself, Watson. I assure you that Mr. Loggins was just as taken aback by this audacious plan. However, after more persuading, he began to see the logic of it. For my part, I needed both a ride back in the direction to England and a reason to have my name passed further up the ladder to the Rebellion's leaders in Ireland. For only from the Emerald Isle did I have a hope of catching the eye of one of the mastermind's agents.

"As it turned out, Loggins eventually embraced my plan, and as a reward for suggesting it, he put me in command of twelve of his best men from the Canalside alleys. The lot of us proceeded to get ourselves hired as seamen aboard the SS *Dante*, sailing for Liverpool.[146] We waited until we were far out to sea to make our move, which was accomplished with nothing more than a bruised head of one sailor. I persuaded the Irishmen under my command that the American captain and the non-mutinous sailors should not be harmed, so they were safely locked up in the cargo-hold for the duration of the voyage. As the unofficial captain of the hijacked ship, I spent most of my free hours in the bridge. Of course, as a relative stranger to the Buffalo ruffians, I was never left completely alone. Loggins was not a stupid man, and he set his men to watch me constantly. Fortunately, they were a dull lot. If they had been more observant, perhaps they might have noticed that – whenever he was not playing his fiddle – Carlus Altamont was in the habit of idly drumming his fingers. One day, without anyone noticing, I turned on the ship's Marconi system. In plain view of one of Loggin's men, I then drummed out the following words in the code system developed by Mr. Morse: '*Hijacked Fenians Dest Hamburg.*' I trusted that one of the Royal Navy's vigilant patrols would receive my surreptitious communication.

"Fortunately, my plans came to fruition. Later that night, the unarmed *Dante* was surrounded by a small flotilla of our frigates. Anticipating just such a thing, I had taken the night shift on the bridge. I grabbed the one man who was still awake - an impressionable lad named Sean McAdams – and pulled him towards one of the lifeboats. We climbed aboard and slipped past the Royal Navy ships. These had boarded the *Dante* and – as I later discovered – freed the crew before sailing the ship successfully for Liverpool. The eleven remaining mutineers from the Buffalo secret society were taken into custody for the remainder of the war.

"McAdams was a fresh-complexioned youth and it was a good thing that his arms were fresh. He and I pulled for the coast of Ireland. I will admit, Watson, there was a moment when I began to doubt the wisdom of my plan. For the great ocean can seem merry during a summer day, when viewed from the comforts of a pleasure craft cruising near to shore.

Nevertheless, alone in the midst of nowhere, the wind whipping up great heaving waves and howling in my ears, being out on the ocean was another matter indeed. I will not look at the sea the same again, I fear. Perhaps the Pacific may be as peaceful as legends hold, but the Celtic Sea is like a great wild beast of uncertain temper and immeasurable strength. For many hours, it was touch-and-go whether the two of us would ever again set foot upon dry land.

"By the time we pulled into the harbour of Skibbereen, McAdams and I were near spent. However, once the lad had a few glasses of whisky poured down his throat, McAdams could do little but sing my praises. For even if the *Dante* had been retaken, it had still been a bold plan. And was Carlus Altamont still not the liberator of the famous Green Goddess? After a few evenings spent in the public houses, my legend continued to grow. As such, it was little wonder that I was soon introduced to Mr. Robert Popper, editor of the *Northern Star* newspaper.

"Popper was an older man not far, one would guess, from his sixtieth year. He had small, shrewd, humorous green eyes. However, there was a certain firmness of jaw and grim tightness about his lips which warned that there were unfriendly depths to the newspaperman. 'I am impressed by the things I hear about you from Mr. McAdams,' said he. 'I even wired to my good friend Joseph Loggins, who confirmed them.'

"I smiled at the small man. 'You are very careful, Mr. Popper.'

" 'It is how I have managed to live a long life, Mr. Altamont. Now, what are your future plans?'

"I pretended to consider this for a moment. 'Well, I would like to continue to sting the English in some way.'

" 'And how would you propose to do that?'

" 'I wouldn't say that I have a fully mature plan as of yet, Mr. Popper. The Royal Navy rather upset my last endeavour.'

" 'Yes, that was most unfortunate. But there are many other things that could be done by an enterprising individual.'

" 'Such as?' I asked.

" 'Have you heard of the Sack of Baltimore?'

"I frowned as if affronted. 'What Irishman hasn't?' I asked. But in truth, Watson, it took all of my effort to drag the history of that event from the deep recesses of my brain-attic. I finally recalled that, in the early seventeenth century, Barbary pirates had attacked a small Irish village and a hundred or so villagers were hauled off to a life of slavery in North Africa.

" 'Would it surprise you, Mr. Altamont,' continued Loggins, 'if I told you that those pirates did not attack Baltimore without reason? They were hired to do so by an Englishman who orchestrated the raid in order to consolidate control over the area.'[147]

"I spit upon the ground. 'Nothing would surprise me, when an Englishman is involved.' I considered what he was saying for a moment. 'I suppose it would put a right wicked thorn in the English Government's side if a strike was made upon the English coast by German-marked boats? Say, at St. Ives or Newquay.'

" 'Indeed it might. If an English town was attacked, it might induce the English Army to stay closer to home in order to defend their citizens. They might withdraw troops from Irish garrisons to accomplish such a task.'

" 'That would be lovely. But I would need many men for such an enterprise.'

"Popper smiled. 'I think the men of the Phoenix Society would be happy to assist you.'

" 'The Phoenix Society?' I asked. 'I thought they were absorbed into the Fenians?'

" 'True, but like our namesake, we rise again. It is a lesson that the English refuse to learn.'

"I grinned cruelly and stuck out my hand. 'We'll stir up a devil's brew!' "

"But, Holmes, I heard of no such attack," I interjected, interrupting his narrative.

"Of course not, Watson. The escapade with hijacking the

ship was risky enough. I could hardly control all of the variables of a full-out assault upon a Cornish town. Civilians might be hurt. No, all I could do was fall in with the scheme and, at the proper time, move to betray it to the local constabulary.

"That proved to be harder than it looked, for despite the growing trust I had developed with Popper and his confederates, I was still an outsider. If the scheme were found out, I would obviously be suspected of being the squealer. Moreover, I had little doubt of how Popper and his ilk would deal with informers.

"At this point, I deemed it was time to take a risk and finally contact Mycroft. We had communicated very little in recent months, as a safeguard against any potential breaches in my secret identity. Before my departure, we had determined that a book cipher, such as once used by Porlock, seemed the strongest option. We had chosen a recently published collection of short stories by a minor Irish writer named Joyce, which would not be looked at askance if found in Altamont's possessions.[148] Via this method, I informed my brother of what we were planning, and let him take it from there.

"In the meantime, I threw all of my energy into helping Popper's men disguise a couple of old fishing boats as the above-water sections of German U-boats. In such fashion, I explained, the inhabitants of the fishing village we raided would blame enemy combatants and we would deflect any repercussions from falling upon Ireland. In order to accomplish this task in secrecy, we moved our base of operations from the town of Skibbereen to a remote cove along Roaringwater Bay.

"Everything seemed to be progressing according to plan, and on the calm night of the fifth of May, our flotilla set out in hopes of raining fire and destruction down upon the coast of England. Of course, that was not to be, for we sailed right into a pack of Acheron-class destroyers of the Royal Navy. The lead faux U-boat and all hands aboard were quickly captured by the HMS *Lurcher*, but I managed to get our rear vessel turned around. We headed back for Skibbereen post haste, the

HMS *Firedrake* close on our heels. We managed to beach the 'U-boat' in a deserted stretch between Glandore and Rosscarbery, and all of the Phoenix Society members aboard melted into the countryside. I hid out with one lad, named Jim Connolly, near a remote megalithic stone circle until the pursuit of the Skibbereen constabulary had died down. I had decided to help Connolly evade pursuit because his father seemed highly placed in Republican circles, and I supposed that he might have other contacts of which I could make use. We eventually made our way to Dublin, judging Cork County to be too hot for us, and from there, I made clear my plans to sail for London. By this time, Connolly trusted me implicitly, for I too had been nearly caught up in the U-boat fiasco. I had even managed to convince the simple lad that Mr. Popper – who had not sailed with us – was the most likely source of the leak. For surely there must have been a traitor, or why else would the Royal Navy have been waiting in St. George's Channel? I later heard that the Fenians took care of Popper after their own fashion. I lost little sleep over such matters, given that the seemingly placid newspaperman had cheerfully suggested bringing the war to peaceful English civilians.

"For his part, Connolly decided to not accompany me on the ferry to Holyhead, where I could catch the Irish Mail boat train. However, he suggested that once I reached London, I meet with a man named Hollis who could often be found enjoying tea in the lobby of the Grand Hotel. Intrigued by this tip, I followed Connolly's advice, and a few days later presented my card to Mr. Hollis. He proved to be a small, sharp-faced, nervous, brown-eyed man. Hollis certainly did not appear to be the mastermind whom I was seeking.

" 'I hear you are a gentleman who might have use for an individual like me,' said I.

"Hollis smiled thinly. 'Oh no, Mr. Altamont. Not I. But I know people.'

" 'I hope they are trustworthy. Several of my last attempts have plainly been betrayed by informers and I only escaped the last one by the skin of my teeth.'

"He laughed nervously, and gestured for me to keep my voice down. 'Please do not forget, sir that we are just around the corner from Whitehall and Scotland Yard,' said he, explaining his anxiety.

"I looked about, as if I could determine by glance alone which of our neighbouring diners were in fact secret agents. 'Then why do you take tea here? Or does it amuse you to do so at the epicentre of the enemy's power?'

"He smiled. 'Something like that. But I can assure you, Mr. Altamont, that the man you are about to meet will never betray you.'

"I shrugged, as if only mildly interested. 'I will be the judge of that, pal, mark my words. And who is he?'

" 'His name is Von Bork. You can find him at the George and Dragon. It is a public house a few blocks from Carlton Terrace. I will let him know you are expected.'

"Von Bork! The name ran though my brain like electricity, Watson. I knew that I finally had my man. I took my leave from Mr. Hollis. He seemed a nice enough chap, and a small bit of me was pained that I would have to expose his traitorous activities to Mycroft. Hollis would surely hang. I had clearly been playing this part for too long. It was time to put an end to things. It was time to meet the puppet-master.

"I will admit, Watson, that I was unhappy to not have access to my Index, for I was certain that I knew the name Von Bork. Eventually I recalled that I was peripherally acquainted with the man. For don't you recall, Watson, that we once saved his uncle, the Count Von und Zu Grafenstein, from an assassination attempt by the Nihilist Klopman?"

"Oh, yes, from the upper window at the Great Northern Hotel?"[149]

"Very good, Watson, your memory is as sharp as ever. In any case, it was high time that Altamont met with Von Bork. I made my way to Regent Street, and loitered in the vicinity of the aforementioned locale until I saw my quarry enter. There was little mistaking him. His eyes were like those a rapacious eagle, and his face sunburned and aquiline. He had the stride of a born sportsman, and he was constantly puffing on an expensive hand-rolled cigar. He looked for all the world like one of those knock-about-town, devil-may-care squires with far too much inherited wealth. No one would have studied him and conceived of the possibility that he was in fact the greatest spy in Europe!

"I posed as a motor expert in order to approach him, though it was evident from the gleam in his eyes that he had already received word about me from Mr. Hollis. 'I hear you keep a full garage, sir,' said I.

" 'That's right, Mr. Altamont. Do you know anything about German automobiles?'

" 'Of course, sir.'

" 'Well, I have a Mercedes Simplex which is in need of some work. Can you help me?'

" 'If it needs new sparking plugs, a radiator, or an oil pump, I am your man. Where is the car?'

"He gave me an address at Holbein Place and I met him at his residence there later that evening. I shared with him Carlus Altamont's feelings about the English and over a high glass filed with Imperial Tokay we sealed our business compact. I would provide him with information regarding the varied defences and strategies that protect what he termed 'the docile and simple' Englishmen. In return, he would provide Carlus Altamont with a regular salary, bonus cheques in exchange for certain high-risk jobs, and the satisfaction of seeing Ireland finally break free from the English yoke.

" 'I have taken a fancy to this Tokay, Von Bork,' said I, after shaking his hand. 'I wouldn't mind drinking this again.'

" 'Well, it's a rare vintage, Mr. Altamont, and I have only one more bottle left. But I tell you what – upon the day that we finally accomplish our great task, I will open that bottle and share another drink with you.'

" 'Sounds fine,' said I, agreeably. 'You will get the goods, I can promise you that.' I then slapped the German upon the shoulder with the rough familiarity of co-conspirators."

Holmes fell quiet for a moment. On any other day, I would have enjoyed the scenery of the drive. There was much around of interest, for we were passing through as flat and as green a countryside as any in England, filled with a few scattered cottages and enormous square-towered churches, which bristled up to defend old Essex from the pillaging Norsemen. I remembered passing through it many years before, aboard a horse-drawn carriage bound for Ridling Thorpe Manor. I silently hoped our mission was a more successful one this time, for poor Mr. Hilton Cubitt was killed before we could help him. At long last, the violet rim of the German Ocean appeared over the green edge of the Essex Coast. In the Harwich harbour, innumerable boats were making their way in and out of the port.

Holmes broke his silence and pointed. "There is Parkeston Quay, Watson, our destroyer and submarine base. That is the sole reason for Von Bork maintaining quiet villa in this particular area. Back to our story we must go, for time is drawing short.

"Carlus Altamont was true to his word, and before Von Bork could count to *zwanzig*,[150] all sorts of useful information was flowing into his ears. I provided him with statistics on the various Royal Navy bases, from Rosyth to Sheerness and all of the others in-between. There was data on harbour defences and shore fortifications. The strength of our expeditionary force was to him an open book, as were our plans to counter Zeppelin attacks via the use of aeroplanes. He wished to know about all of our colonies, from Canada to Egypt, from Bermuda to India, from Gibraltar to South Africa, from Valetta to Australia, and beyond. And most of all, he devoutly desired to learn everything about the Channel, which has preserved out island for almost a thousand years. Van Bork's appetite for information was boundless and as I also began to visualize the connections that he was drawing, I became exceedingly concerned. For his intellect was a formidable one, and the threat he posed to England was most grave indeed.

"But in turn, I found out everything there was to know about Von Bork and his activities. Because of his vigour and genial nature, he was constantly being invited to yacht, play polo, race, and even box with our Governmental ministers and military officers. I despaired over what secrets were accidentally being spilled within range of his hearing.

"Why did you not have him arrested at once?" I inquired.

Holmes shook his head. "If we prematurely arrested Von Bork, we would never learn the identities of his agents. He is far too cagey ever to reveal that information to his enemies. Only by becoming his ally could I learn about the entire network. For left in place, even with Von Bork neutralized, it would simply resume transmitting our secrets to a new master.

"Over time, Von Bork began to fully trust and rely upon me. He even went so far as to ask me to help him locate a quiet servant for his country house – the very one we are about to visit, you and I. I hope that you will be pleased, Watson, to see old Martha again, who was a little lonely watching over my Downs villa during my long absence."

I shook my head in admiration. "I cannot believe that you managed to engender such a degree of confidence, Holmes."

"It is all a matter of inhabiting a part, Watson. One must put every bit of one's soul in to the expressions, mannerism, and patterns of speech of the person you wish to be. I *was* Altamont, so there was never any reason for Von Bork to doubt me. Still, I suppose the men I turned in to the authorities will be rather displeased to someday learn of how exactly they were found out. For, like Hercules at his labours, I have cut off every head from the hydra. Shortly after I first signed on with him, I learned that Von Bork had recruited the five premier agents in England.

"The first I learned of was Clyde Abraham. He was a postmaster at Devonport in Plymouth, where he watched and collected information about the activities at HMS *Vivid*. A dedicated Marxist, he betrayed his country to the Hun over hopes that the capitalist state would be replaced with a worker's utopia. I turned him in first and you may guess, Watson, at his ultimate fate.

"Wilcox Hamilton was the next to go. He was a barkeeper based near Chatham Dockyard. I could never figure out the motive of that strange man, though he possessed a deadly and malignant hatred for the land of his birth. I was not sorry to hear that he had vanished in the night, and I sincerely doubt that he will ever again see the light of day.

"Jack James was a supplier of goods to the Aldershot Garrison. Given my professed backstory, I did not want to grow too close to him. Scotland Yard was tipped off that he was collecting restricted information while on base, and they promptly brought him in. However, as an American citizen, he has been safely stashed away at Portland Prison for the unforeseen future.

"Poor, anxious Mr. Hollis was also recently snatched up by Scotland Yard. I had learned that he was employed at the Admiralty Arch as a clerk, and had for years been surreptitiously been selling secrets to Von Bork.

"And last night, after I alerted them, the authorities carted off Von Bork's final agent – excepting Altamont, of course – a Portsmouth storekeeper named Max Steiner. He had supplied Von Bork with a massive trove of information regarding the activities at Gunwharf Quays. Moreover, he had blackmailed one of the signal operators to pass him a copy of our Naval Signals book. Although of German extraction, Steiner is a British citizen, and I fear that he too will hang for his treason.

"However, even as all his agents fell about him, Von Bork never suspected that Carlus Altamont could possibly be responsible. For that great feat, I may have to take a bow."

"But with no one left, who else would he suspect, Holmes? What if he turns violent? Surely a sportsman and spy has a plethora of firearms from which to choose!" I shook my head in frustration. "And I never thought to bring my old service revolver!"

Holmes smiled and patted my shoulder. "Is it still oiled and ready after all these years? Unless you have engaged in some adventures without me, Watson, your Eley's no.2 has not been fired in quite some time. But it is no matter. Von Bork will be taken down by a simpler stratagem than the end of a pistol. Do you recall my long-ago demonstration to Dr Roylott? Well there is still some strength left in these hands. And I have in my pocket a phial of chloroform, a sponge, and a strong strap with which to secure him."

"And why do we strike tonight, Holmes?"

"I have finally determined that the fruits of Von Bork's labours are stored in one of the most advanced safes ever constructed. Despite my best efforts, I have been unable to open it."

"You have picked safes before, Holmes."

He shook his head. "Not like this, Watson. It is really quite a wonder. The key alone is insufficient. Around the keyhole is a double-radiating disk with both letters and figures, which must be aligned before the key can be placed into its hole. The possible combinations are infinite."

"He may have written it down somewhere?"

"Not likely. Von Bork is far too careful to make such a simple mistake. He has not utilized the name of his wife, nor any of his close relatives or acquaintances. I have even tried the name of his favourite hunting terrier, all to no avail."

"Cut into it."

"I considered this possibility. However, it is a special tungsten-steel alloy from the Hemerdon mine. With sufficient time, the metal might be able to be cut, but it would require an industrial-level effort, and is not something I could have done in the small hours of the night. I would require the safe to undergo official confiscation. This, of course, cannot occur until I have sufficient proof of Von Bork's guilt. Such is the magnificent fair play of British Law, Watson. Unfortunately, the only such proof is stored in the safe."

"That sounds like a double bind, Holmes."

In the dash mirror, I saw a small rise to his lips.[151] "Precisely, Watson. It is just the sort of paradoxical and apparently unsolvable logic puzzle which I so prize."

"So what did you do?"

"I have not done it yet, Watson. It is what I plan to do tonight. What I have been planning for two long years. I will employ Alexander's solution in Gordia."

I raised my eyebrows. "I do not see a sword in your possession."

"Metaphorically, Watson, metaphorically. In short, I will get Von Bork to open the safe himself."

"And how do you intend to accomplish that? Are you armed?"

He shook his head. "Brute force would never work on Von Bork, Watson. The man is far too resilient for such crude methods. No, he will open the safe because he trusts me. For I am not Sherlock Holmes tonight. I am Carlus Altamont."

"He trusts you that much?"

"He will when he sees what I have in my possession."

"Which is?"

Holmes held up a small brown-paper parcel. "I slipped into a telegraph office shortly before you arrived, Watson, and informed Von Bork of my intention to deliver to him tonight a copy of the entire Naval Signals code-book, newly-changed after I alerted Mycroft that Von Bork had obtained a copy of the prior version from Steiner. Should Von Bork deliver this to Carlton Terrace, and from there to his ultimate masters in Berlin, our fleets in the North Sea and beyond will be laid defenceless before the might of the German Imperial Navy. I suppose I need not relate to a student of history such as you, Watson, in what grim straits England will find itself should it no longer rules the waves."

As we were talking, I noticed the sun slip beneath the distant horizon and the stars began to appear in the firmament, like beacons of hope. "Then this is the week of our destiny."

Holmes smiled. "I suppose a little poetry is in order, Watson." He pulled out his pocket-watch. "Ah, nearly nine o'clock, I see. Von Bork is even now meeting with Baron von Herling and planning his escape from England. Time for us to be on our way."

"Where are we headed?"

"Up the Main Road through the village. At the top of the great chalk cliff, near the old Fort, you will find a long low, heavily gabled house with a stone parapet along its garden walk. As we get close, dim your headlights and then wait."

I followed his commands, and cut the engine. Half an hour passed, each ticking of my pocket-watch like a shot in the darkness. Suddenly, from the house above us a lamp was put out.

"There, Watson!" Holmes exclaimed. "That is Martha's signal. The game is afoot! Fire up the engine, my dear lad, for we risk all upon this toss. Take care to watch for Von Herling's departing Benz, Watson. It may require your excellent driving in order to avoid that juggernaut. If we carry the pitch, I think it not unlikely that we may be called to Westminster by a grateful Premier and King in order to take one final ovation."

§

NOTE: The story ends abruptly here...

LITERARY AGENT'S NOTES ON 'THE HIGH MOUNTAIN'

Upon the story 'His Last Bow,' and the Relationship of this Unearthed Tale to that Account of the War Service of Mr. Sherlock Holmes

As all readers of the Strand Magazine well knew from the 1917 Preface by John H. Watson, M.D., Mr. Sherlock Holmes had been permanently retired to the South Downs for several years until: "the approach of the German war caused him, however, to lay his remarkable combination of intellectual and practical activity at the disposal of the Government, with historical results which are recounted in His Last Bow."

However, the aforementioned story is a very odd one indeed for – save only the equally mysterious *The Adventure of the Mazarin Stone* (published in 1921) – it is unique in that Dr Watson did not narrate it. Indeed, it has a strangely omniscient understanding regarding the dealings of Von Bork and Baron Von Herling. Unless Von Bork later confessed all of these details, upon further consideration we must consider the story to be more fiction than fact. So the question remains, who wrote *His Last Bow* and is it an accurate account?

The recently unearthed fragment, festooned by this literary agent with the sobriquet *The High Mountain* may finally shed some light upon the matter. It has been speculated by some historians that *His Last Bow* was written by none other than Mycroft Holmes, who certainly would have had the clearest understanding regarding the details of Holmes' Foreign Office role masquerading as Carlus Altamont. However, now we can plainly see that Dr Watson did indeed pen a tale regarding Holmes' (pre) War Service. For reasons which remain unclear but which likely have to do with the vagaries of the editing process, the tale was severely truncated and compressed into a brief retelling set after an imagined conversation between those two famous Germans. We may speculate that Dr Watson's first literary agent, Sir Arthur Conan Doyle, decided that the story would work best as a short and simple patriotic tale, and thus he must have significantly rewritten Watson's original manuscript.

Sadly, the concluding part of this original manuscript is still missing, so we may never know the truth regarding the last words between Holmes and Watson before the outbreak of war. We must take it on faith that the latter half of *His Last Bow* is both a faithful recounting of Holmes' confrontation with Von Bork and of the two friends' final recorded conversation, in which Holmes both claimed that an east wind was coming, and that Dr Watson was the one fixed point in a changing age.

In any event, one cannot argue with the success of the final product. Published in September 1917, over a year before the end of the Great War on 11 November 1918, *His Last Bow* gave a sliver of hope to the millions of English-reading people that the long-desired peace was, in fact, possible.... for Sherlock Holmes himself was on the case.

§

THE ADVENTURE OF THE DEFENCELESS PRISONER

In the face of the national emergency engendered by the German Empire's declaration of war, Mr. Sherlock Holmes has hardly been idle. I have already recorded how Holmes returned from retirement in order to infiltrate the various associations of the Fenians and utilized this connection to bring down the extensive spy network of Herr Von Bork. Unfortunately, not even Holmes' prodigious powers were sufficient to forestall the coming madness.

Shortly after the war broke out, Holmes and I crossed the channel in order to meet with our allies in Paris. From our base in the Hotel Lutetia, Holmes first conferred with General Dupont, head of the Deuxième Bureau, France's military intelligence, assisting his team with the decryption of the German's diplomatic cryptographic system. He also worked with Commissioner Hennion, head of the Interior Ministry's mobile counter-espionage brigades, helping revolutionize their use of homing pigeons to carry messages swiftly from their border patrols to a centralized office. Finally, he located the Rue d'Astorg print shop of the German forger Helmut Schuhl, who had been flooding the Eighth Arrondissement with counterfeit francs intended to destabilize the country's economy.

Meanwhile, carrying out the dastardly plan of Count Schlieffen, the Imperial German Army rolled through Belgium and the French countryside. They rapidly advanced towards Paris, as the Republic's government decamped for Bordeaux. While there were many French reinforcements stationed at Paris, these men were prevented from reaching the front by both a severe lack of official transport vehicles, and – for those other vehicles that were actually available – a shortage of competent drivers. Therefore, under the cover of darkness one night early in September, I volunteered to drive a Renault taxi loaded with troops to the banks of the Marne River, where they assisted in a decisive repulsion of the German advance and turned the tide of the war.[152]

Upon our eventual return from London, Holmes vanished into his work. He would tell me little of it, though I routinely saw him meeting with a trio of men he introduced as Sir Mansfield, Sir Vernon, and Basil Thomson of the CID.[153] Other than knowing that it must have something to do with the war effort, I was kept largely in the dark, under the executive decision that their discussions were classified as 'Most Secret.' I kept myself busy, of course, but was rather dismayed to realize that someone within the ranks of the British Government felt my discretion could not be fully trusted.

Therefore, it was with some surprise when, one day in the middle of March 1915, Holmes knocked upon my door. He was looking a bit more gaunt than usual, and I thought I detected some silver strands appearing at his temples, but his grey eyes retained their sharp and piercing nature.

After I warmly welcomed him into my parlour, per his typical practice, Holmes discarded the usual societal niceties and launched directly into the matter at hand. "I have been asked, Watson, to investigate the case of Captain John Fowler," said he.[154]

"The officer accused of killing his fiancée, Miss Ena Garnier?"

"The very one. So you have read about it in the papers?"

I nodded. "Yes, the case has roused a very general interest. I heard that he has withheld his defence, which has caused much speculation. Either he is guilty or he is not."

"Perhaps not, Watson. There may be rather more to this case than first meets the eye."

"What do you mean?"

"On first glance, the case appears a simple one. I shall recite the facts, as currently known. On one hand, we have Miss Garnier, aged twenty-five. She was a Frenchwoman working as a tutor in Radchurch, Essex, at the home of the local squire.[155] By all accounts, she was both exceptionally intelligent and a great beauty, blonde and tall, with delicate features. On the fourth day of March, she was riding her FN Four motor-cycle along the Pedley-Woodrow Road when the accused – who appears to have been lying in wait for her to pass by – sprang up from the side of the road and fired two bullets into her.[156] One penetrated her brain, killing her instantly."

"That seems rather straightforward, Holmes."

"Perhaps, Watson, perhaps. On the other hand, we have Captain Fowler. Witnesses have come forward who have reported that the accused was subject to fits of jealousy, and that he had already been guilty of some violence owing to this cause. His defence has been exceptionally limited due to the fact that he collapsed after the event in question. The squire, a Mr. Murreyfield, found him raving like a maniac over her body. This has progressed into a full-blown episode of brain-fever, and the man has alternated between unconsciousness and fits of madness for the last two weeks. Does that match with your understanding of the case, Watson?"

"It does," said I. "Are you suggesting that he is feigning his brain-fever?"

"Not at all! Dr Trevelyan was called in and confirmed that the man is genuinely stricken. However, there has been a suggestion that Miss Garnier may have well-deserved the bullet which killed her."

"You horrify me, Holmes!" I exclaimed. "How could any woman deserve such a cruel attack?"

"That is what I intend to discover. Here," said he, handing me a military dossier he pulled from his coat-pocket, "take a look at Captain Fowler's career."

This is what I read:

Fowler, John Morgan *(commonly called 'Jack'): Captain, Second Breconshire Battalion. Born Newtown, Powys, Wales, 1877. Educated Harrow and Selwyn College, Cambridge. Served in the South African Campaign. Mentioned in despatches after the Battle of Diamond Hill (12 June 1900). Seconded from his regiment in September 1914 and appointed adjutant to the First Scottish Scouts, newly raised.*[157] *January 1915: Appointed to War Office, London. Clubs: United Service, Army and Navy.*

"Does he appear, Watson, to be a man capable of killing his fiancée in cold blood?"

I shrugged. "Who knows what evil lurks in the hearts of men, Holmes? Do you remember when you told me the harrowing tale of the most winning woman you ever knew?"[158]

"You may be right," said he, with a nod. "That is what we must determine. Fowler has since been moved to Queen Alexandra's Military Hospital in Millbank, where he is under close guard."

"Will we try to question him?"

"Not as of yet. It would be easy to obtain the necessary permits, however, if his mental state is as dire as it is made out to be, there will be little to learn there. Instead, I thought we would start with his barrister, Mr. Joyce Cummings, King's Council."

I was surprised to recognise the name. "He who defended Miss Grace Dunbar from a charge of murder?"

"Indeed. He has risen far in the fourteen years since we crossed paths. I am told he maintains a nice set of chambers off

Brick Court. Shall we?"

As Holmes remained generally averse to travelling in the Underground Electric Railways, we took a hansom cab along Knightsbridge across the southern edge of Hyde Park. As we passed the Wellington Arch, I silently hoped that the spirit of the Iron Duke would inhabit Field Marshal Haig so that he too would lead our boys to victory in the fields of Belgium.

Twenty minutes later, Holmes was knocking on the door of the barrister's chambers. The sound boomed through halls that had stood since the days of Elizabeth. A clerk received Holmes' calling card and promptly showed us into the presence of Mr. Cummings, who was a comfortable middle-aged man, with a receding hairline and intense blue eyes.

Holmes began with an explanation for the reason for our visit. Cummings nodded his understanding and motioned for us to sit in chairs across from his desk. Holmes then began to question the lawyer. "I understand, Mr. Cummings, that Captain Fowler had a brief moment of lucidity upon his fifth day at the hospital?"

"Your understanding is accurate, Mr. Holmes."

"And you were present for this?"

"I was."

"And based on his words to you, you subsequently asserted before the proceedings of the police-court that the answer to the charge cannot yet be given."

"That is correct."

"So he has refused to defend himself? Some might argue that is a proof of his guilt."

"I did not say that he would never defend himself."

"Ah, then you suggest that an answer to the charge may eventually be possible?"

The lawyer shrugged. "Perhaps. He implied that an answer will be available before the Assizes at Chelmsford in six weeks' time."

"Do you know the nature of the answer?"

"I do not."

"Because he lapsed back into madness?"

"No, because he has refused all offers of legal assistance from this counsel."

"You astonish me, Mr. Cummings," said Holmes, leaning back in his chair. "Who then will undertake his case?"

"You misunderstand me, Mr. Holmes. Captain Fowler did not refuse my aid in favour of another barrister. Rather, he is determined to conduct his own defence."

"Then why did he retain your services in the first place? Surely his means are rather limited, and you are reputed to one of the first talents of the Bar, with a matching remuneration."

"He did not. I was engaged by a group of his fellow officers who generously pooled their resources so as to afford my fee."

"A strange action if they thought him guilty."

"The entire thing is strange, if you ask me, Mr. Holmes. However, now that I see that you are involved, I am rather less surprised. After our last interaction, I made England ring with the vindication of Miss Dunbar. I find that you are stormy petrel of the *outré*, sir."

Holmes chuckled ruefully at this not-unreasonable charge. We bid farewell to Mr. Cummings. Departing the Middle Temple via the Devereux passage from Fountain Court, we emerged onto the Strand next to the tearoom. Despite my thirst, Holmes immediately hailed a hansom cab and instructed the driver to take us to Liverpool Street Station.

"Where are we going, Holmes?" I asked.

"It is time to inspect the scene and question the direct witnesses, Watson. We will get on to Radchurch via the next available train."

§

The station at Radchurch junction was livelier than I suspected it had been in many years, for it was now the closest locale to the newly established Army camp.

Despite the fact that our rapidly growing troops had commandeered much of the local transport, Holmes eventually managed to engage the services of a passing farmer who took us in his trap the five miles from the station to the house of the Squire Murreyfield. Holmes was usually impatient on such rides, but he actually seemed to be enjoying the views of the passing countryside with its scattered cottages and groves of trees. He hardly drummed his fingers upon the seat once. Eventually, an ivy-covered two-storied house with brick and timber gables came into view.

Mr. Murreyfield came out of the manor at the noise of our approach. He proved to be a genial man of some fifty years, with a kind smile and a widening girth. His wife was at least a dozen years younger than he was, but seemed more careworn, such that they appeared to be a well-matched pair.

At the presentation of Holmes' card, Murreyfield warmly welcomed us into his parlour. He and his wife sat across from us on the settee. Holmes and I took chairs separated by a small table, which held a tea set brought to us by the maid.

Holmes explained that he had come to investigate the death of Miss Ena Garnier. "Mr. Murreyfield, would you please describe your relationship with her?"

The man cleared his throat and shook his head sadly. "Well, she came to us in September of last year from Montpelier, in the south of France."

Holmes nodded. "I am familiar with it," said he, dryly. "Go on."

"We had placed an advertisement for someone to teach French to our children, Edward, Sarah, and Lucy. Miss Garnier said that she had always been fond of the English and desirous to live in England, but the outbreak of the war had quickened her feelings into a passionate attachment for her nation's ally."

"Was she a good tutor?"

"Oh, yes, excellent. She and the children would go over their lessons all day in her little study."

"And her personality?"

Mrs. Murreyfield answered this question. "Well, she had some strange moods and fancies, on account of her being French and all. She could be tender, and then suddenly aloof and even harsh. This often occurred after a letter from home, and I thought it might be due to worry over her brothers. When I asked her about them, however, she always assured me that they were fine. She became very popular amongst the officers at Chelmsford and Colchester. She was never without a partner for one of the dances."

"And then what happened?"

"Well, once Captain Fowler was billeted out to reside with us," said Mr. Murreyfield, "he and Miss Garnier quickly became intimate. When I first met the Captain, he seemed a reserved and cool sort. However, I believe that Miss Garnier incited a feverish passion in him."

"And she returned his attention?"

"Yes, I believe that she was not insensible to the advances which he made to her."

"Oh, more than that, my dear," interjected Mrs. Murreyfield. "His wooing was not a difficult one. When Captain Fowler proposed to her, she accepted on the condition that they would only marry after the war finally ends, so that he could go out to Montpelier and meet her people. She was most insistent that the French proprieties should be observed."

"But he was jealous of her?" asked Holmes.

"Well, there was one episode," said she, slowly, "which I hesitate to even mention, Mr. Holmes. You see, Captain Fowler had gone into her room to look for her and found a photograph of a man upon her table. When he asked her who this individual was, she refused to give him any information. In fact, she said that it was a man whom she had never seen in her life. Captain Fowler thought this explanation incredible and he raised his voice."

"What did he say?"

"He declared that she must tell him more about her life or he would break with her. I happened to be passing along the corridor outside her room and heard him."

"Passing along!" guffawed Mr. Murreyfield. "More like standing outside with a glass pressed against the door!" He turned to Holmes. "My wife took a most sympathetic interest in their romance."

Mrs. Murreyfield raised her chin and stoically refused to respond to this accusation. "I knocked upon the door, Mr. Holmes, and reproved the Captain for his jealousy. I told him that women must have their little secrets and that if a man learned everything there was to know about his bride before the marriage, what remained for the rest of their life together? I finally persuaded him that he had been unreasonable, and they reconciled."

"That's right," said Mr. Murreyfield. "She was quite proud when the Captain was appointed to his post at the War Office in London."

"That is because she hated the Boches," interjected Mrs. Murreyfield.[159] "Her grandfather had been killed in '70 under very tragic circumstances at Sedan, and her two brothers are both currently in the French army.[160] Her voice vibrated with passion whenever she spoke of the infamies of Belgium. Why, once she became acquainted with Captain Fowler, I even saw her kiss his sword and revolver because she hoped that they would one day be used upon the enemy. That is why I cannot credit Captain Fowler's assertion that she was a German spy."

"What?" I cried.

"Yes, Watson," said Holmes. "This is the reason why I was asked to investigate her murder. I must ascertain whether Captain Fowler was telling Mr. Murreyfield the truth when he said that Miss Garnier was a spy."

"I see," said I. "So you were tasked to look into this by your bro…"

"By someone who shall remain nameless," Holmes quickly interjected. "Now, Mr. Murreyfield, tell me everything which transpired on the day of her death."

"Well, Captain Fowler had previously written to say that

he planned to return from London for a few day's leave of absence. Richard, the coachman, had taken Miss Garnier over to the station to meet him there. According to Richard, the two seemed overjoyed to have been reunited and they spent the ride back to the house closely huddled together in the cabin. After they returned, Captain Fowler paid his compliments to Mrs Murreyfield and I, and then he went out on military business for a span of about two hours."

"You are certain of the time?" asked Holmes.

"Oh yes, I recall glancing at the clock when I heard him come back into the house and inquire after Miss Garnier."

"What happened then?"

"Perhaps twenty minutes went by. I was sitting in the parlour, reading the news from the Continent when I heard the bell ring in Miss Garnier's day study. A few minutes later, the maid came in, looking rather flustered, and told me that Captain Fowler desired to see me at once on a matter of grave urgency. I promptly rose and made my way there, where I found Miss Garnier slumped on the sofa, softly rubbing a redness of the skin at her wrist. I could hardly credit my eyes, for it looked as if the Captain had assaulted the young woman who I had come to think of as part of our family. Glancing over at the Captain, I was shocked to see the horror-stricken look upon his face."

"What did he say?" asked Holmes.

"I can remember the whole thing like it was yesterday, Mr. Holmes. As she sat there, watching him, Captain Fowler spoke. 'She is a German spy, Mr. Murreyfield,' said he, hoarsely.

" 'I am aghast, Captain,' said I. 'What proof do you have for such a terrible accusation?'

"He waved a letter before me. 'I cannot show it to you, on account of the secret that it contains. However, it tells her Berlin masters of plans the BEF has made to strike a blow at the Western Front.[161] I can show it to my superiors and they will concur with my judgement. You must understand, sir, this is of desperate importance.'

"The look in his eyes convinced me of the truth in his words. 'What are we to do?' I asked. 'I never could have imagined anything so dreadful. What would you advise me to do?'

" 'There is only one thing that we can do,' he answered. 'This woman must be arrested, and in the meanwhile, we must so arrange matters that she cannot possibly communicate with any one. For all we know, she has confederates in this very village. Can you undertake to hold her securely while I go to Colonel Worral at Pedley and get a warrant and a guard?'

" 'We can lock her in her bedroom,' I suggested.

" 'You need not trouble,' said she. 'I give you my word that I will stay where I am. I advise you to be careful, Captain Fowler. You have shown once before that you are liable to do things before you have thought through the consequences. If I am arrested, all the world will know that you have freely given away the secrets that were confided to you. There is an end of your career, my friend. You can punish me, no doubt. But what about yourself?'

" 'I think,' said the Captain, coolly, turning to me, 'you had best take her to her bedroom, Murreyfield.'

" 'Very good, if you wish it,' said she, and calmly followed us to the door.

"When we reached the hall, however, she suddenly broke away and dashed through the front entrance. In the yard, she made for her motor-cycle, which was parked off to the side. Fortunately, before she could start it, we had both seized her. During the struggle, she even stooped and bit my hand. With flashing eyes and tearing fingers, she was as fierce as a wild cat at bay. It was with rather some difficulty that we mastered her, and dragged her back inside, almost carrying her up the stairs. We thrust her into her room and turned the key, while she screamed out abuse and beat upon the door from the inside.

" 'It is a forty-foot drop into the garden,' said I to the Captain, as I tied up my bleeding hand. 'I will wait here until you come back. I think we have the lady fairly safe now.'

" 'I have a revolver here,' said Fowler, taking a gun from his pocket. 'You should be armed.' He slipped a couple of cartridges into it and held it out to me. 'We can't afford to take chances. How do you know what friends she may have?'

" 'Thank you,' said I, with a shake of my head. 'However, I have a stick here, and the gardener is within call. Hurry off for the guard now, and I will answer for the prisoner.'

"Captain Fowler ran off to the camp at Pedley, which is some two miles from here. He had been gone a long time, and all was quiet in my prisoner's room. Then suddenly, I heard the whirr of the cycle coming from the front of the house. As fast as I could, I bounded down the stairs and out into the yard. In the distance, I could see Miss Garnier furiously riding away down the Pedley-Woodrow Road, hatless, her hair streaming in the wind. Flabbergasted, I turned about and looked up. The window to her room was open, and only then did I comprehend that – with great courage and activity – she must have scrambled down the ivy of the wall.

"I set off down the road, running as fast as these old legs would carry me. I hardly knew what I intended to accomplish, for I surely could not possibly hope to catch a woman riding upon a motor-cycle. I had gone about half-a-mile when I heard two pistol shots ring out from the twilight ahead. This was followed by a scream and a noise that could only have been made by the crashing of her cycle. All was then still. I continued my sprint and was nearly out of breath when I came upon Captain Fowler standing by the side of the road. His pistol was in his hand and he was looking down into the ditch, where I spied the body of Miss Garnier. It was obvious that she was dead.

"I tried to explain to the Captain how she had escaped, but he seemed in a daze. By the time the police and soldiers arrived and arrested him, Captain Fowler's behaviour had degenerated into a full fit. He seemed out of his mind with anguish that he had been forced to kill the woman that he loved.

That is all, gentlemen," the squire concluded.

"So you believe his story?" asked Holmes.

"That she was a spy? Yes, I do, Mr. Holmes. Why else would she bite my hand? Moreover, why else did she try to flee? If he had made up the contents of the letter, why not just patiently wait for the Colonel to exonerate her?"

Holmes nodded. "I agree those are valid points against her, sir. But where is the letter?"

"What?" Murreyfield exclaimed. "Why, Captain Fowler had it."

"No such letter was found on his person, Mr. Murreyfield. And you never saw it. Hence the difficulty. I wonder if you could show us Miss Garnier's study?"

"Of course, Mr. Holmes," said our host, rising to his feet. "Follow me."

He led us along the hall passage, and waved his hand to one of the doors. Holmes opened this, revealing a small room, which contained little more than a chair, and a wooden writing desk tucked up against the window. A lock had once secured a small drawer, but this had plainly been forced open.

Holmes studied this with interest. "Ah, what have we here!" exclaimed Holmes. He held up the blotting paper from her desk. "Do you see it, Watson? There is a name there, reversed. It looks like 'Hubert Vardin.'"

"Who is Hubert Vardin?"

"If Captain Fowler's story is accurate, I suspect that it is the name of the man to whom Miss Garnier was passing our military secrets. It appears to be part of the address of an envelope, for underneath I am able to distinguish the initials 'S.W.' Unfortunately, the actual name of the street has not been clearly reproduced."

"The South Western postal division is enormous, Holmes. It stretches from Whitehall to Merton. How will we ever find him?"

He inspected the remaining contents of her desk. "Sadly, the picture discovered by Captain Fowler is gone. I wager that she burned it shortly after that confrontation. Should the Captain recover from his illness, he might be able to describe the man well enough to reproduce his likeness in a sketch."

"So, we are at an impasse until he awakens?"

"Not necessarily, Watson." He turned to our host, who was waiting in the hall. "Mr. Murreyfield, you have been extraordinarily helpful. I wonder if you would do me one last favour?"

"Name it, Mr. Holmes," said he with feeling. "My wife and I must know what really happened here. In either case, we have been greatly fooled, either by a devious spy or by a violent murderer. We cannot rest until you tell us which was the true culprit and which the victim."

"I hope to be of assistance to you, sir. If you would be so kind as to take up your walking stick, I wish to be guided to the site where Miss Garnier met her tragic end."

Murreyfield nodded and followed Holmes instructions. He led us along the lane by which we came. He stopped a short way from the point of junction with the high road to Colchester. "It was right over there, Mr. Holmes," said he, pointing with his stick.

Holmes carefully made his way over to the indicated spot and proceeded to inspect carefully the ground all about the site of the crash. He kept his peering eyes riveted upon the trampled grass as he looked at the area from every angle.

"Can you make anything of it, Holmes?" I asked.

He shook his head dejectedly. "Well, the rains three nights ago did little to improve this area. In addition, there are so many footstep marks that it appears as if the German army has made its way along here. So... wait, what have we here?" he exclaimed.

He bent and carefully extracted a sodden mass from the ground.

"What is it?" I cried.

"If I am not mistaken, Watson, it is a letter, albeit one very much the worse for wear."

"We already knew that there was a letter, Holmes. Mr. Murreyfield noted that much. But it won't do us much good now."

He shook his head. "Do not give up so easily, Watson." He turned back to Murreyfield. "Do you have an ice-house, sir?"

The man looked confused, but nodded. "Of course."

"I am most desirous of seeing it."

"As you will, Mr. Holmes." Murreyfield led us back to his house and around to the back. There he indicated a domed structure of thick stones, the entrance to which was secured by a stout wooden door.

Holmes asked Murreyfield to wait outside and then led us inside the brick-lined house, where he proceeded to brush away the straw from the top of one of the blocks of ice. He gently placed the sodden mass onto this, and extracted a pair of tweezers from his breast pocket. Despite the chilly temperature, with infinite patience – like a surgeon removing every last bit of shrapnel from a wound – Holmes carefully pulled the edges of the letter apart.

"The cold inhibits the bleeding of the ink," he explained, as he completed his task.

I leaned over and stared at the blurry words, but as it had obviously been written in considerable haste, I could not read much beyond the name 'Vardin' and that it was signed with a name other than that of Ena Garnier. Here is a reproduction of the letter:

"Can you make anything of it, Holmes?" I finally asked
He studied it for a moment and pulled out his note-book and pen. He began to jot down words as he answered me. "It was written in French and many words have been lost to the damp, making it a difficult task, Watson. Fortunately for us, she was too rushed to utilize a cipher. Given the ruined state of the original, if she had bothered to encrypt it with key text from a certain book – like our friend Porlock once did – or with one of the German army's codebooks, I likely would not have been able to make heads or tails of it. But, permitting me a few guesses, here is what I believe it likely once said." He handed me a sheet of paper in which he had scribbled the following:

MURREYFIELD HOUSE, RADCHURCH.
Dear M. Vardin,
Stringer has told me that he has kept you sufficiently informed as to Chelmsford and Colchester, so I have not troubled to write. They have moved the Midland Territorial Brigade and the heavy guns towards the coast near Cromer, but only for a time. It is for training, not embarkation. And now for my great news, which I have straight from the War Office itself. Within a week there is to be a very severe attack from Vimy Ridge, which is to be supported by a holding attack at Aubers Ridge. It is all on a very large scale, and you must send off a special Dutch messenger to Von Starmer by the first boat. I hope to get the exact date and some further particulars from my informant to-night, but meanwhile you must act with energy. I dare not post this here you know what village postmasters are, so I am taking it into Colchester, where Stringer will include it with his own report which goes by hand.
Yours faithfully,
SOPHIA HEFFNER.

"So she was a spy after all," I surmised. "Her real name was Heffner."

"Indeed. Moreover, it appears that Captain Fowler was rather indiscrete with whom he shared his confidential knowledge. He must have told her of the upcoming combined British and French attacks in Artois."

"But that is tantamount to treason!" I exclaimed.

"Hence his attack of brain-fever, Watson. Like your friend Phelps."

I shook my head. "I can hardly imagine it, Holmes. To learn, within a matter of moments, that you have both shamefully, hopelessly ruined your career, and have been betrayed by the woman you loved would bring any man to his knees."

He smiled wryly. "Almost any man, Watson. It goes to show the dangers of emotion. Cold reason is the only approach which lends itself to a life of equanimity."

"Well, that solves things, then. Captain Fowler discovered she was actually a German spy and shot her. As you said, Holmes, she deserved it. Probably a quicker death than even the long drop."[162]

Holmes looked at me with astonishment. "Watson, do you realize that we are at war? The treacherous Miss Heffner may have gotten her just due, but what of her handlers? Can we let them run loose in the country, continuing to transmit our secrets to Colonel Nicolai and the Abteilung?"[163]

"I thought we had already dealt with all the spies in England, Holmes?"

"Just because we arrested von Bork and rounded up his little ring of Steiner, Abraham, Hamilton, Hollis, and James, does not mean, Watson, that we have located everyone who wishes to see us defeated."

"So what are we to do?"

"London is a vast metropolis, Watson, but Colchester is not. If we make inquiries there, I am certain that someone will recall a tall, beautiful blond woman riding a FN Four motor-cycle. When we learn whom it was that she regularly visited, we shall have located the mysterious Mr. Stringer. From there, we merely need trail him upon his next hand-delivery to Mr. Vardin."

Holmes was soon proven correct. We took our leave of the Murreyfields and made our way to Colchester. There, we were quickly pointed to the chemist store belonging to a Mr. Gilbert, outside of which the motor-cycle was often found parked. Holmes paused outside and grabbed my arm. "I trust, Watson, that you will not think me guilty of arrogance when I suggest that my undisguised visage is far too familiar for me to just stroll into Mr. Gilbert's emporium. His hackles would be immediately raised, and we will never learn the location of Monsieur Vardin, who is, of course, the bigger fish that we wish to catch."

"So what are we to do?"

"I believe Dr Hill Barton is in need of re-stocking his medical bag. Be so good as to go inside and reconnoitre the place. It would behove us to learn whether it is Mr. Gilbert himself or some assistant whom we need to watch."

I followed Holmes' instructions to the letter and, if modesty permits, I rather think that I conducted this interaction with considerably more success than I once did when trying to fool Baron Gruner that I was a connoisseur in Chinese pottery.

Gilbert appeared to be a few years over forty, with close-cropped brown hair and soft green eyes behind thick glasses. He little looked like a master spy, though I supposed that was rather the point. Over the course of the next few minutes, while Mr. Gilbert located the various agents and medicinals for which I asked, I learned that Gilbert operated the business by himself. He went into London every Sunday to take personal delivery of new items for the store. It was with great difficulty that I managed to refrain from smiling as I watched Mr. Gilbert tie up my brown-paper wrapped package of drugs with a neat white string. 'Stinger' indeed!

Once outside, I gave my report, and Holmes, typically restrained in doling out praise, was effusive in his congratulations of my success. As it was now Friday evening, we took the next train back to London. When we parted at the station, Holmes promised to call upon me as soon as the identity of Monsieur Vardin was determined.

§

I had not long to wait. The following Monday, a terse note arrived from Holmes:

Meet me at Queen Alexandra's at noon.
-S.H.

I supposed that he referred to the hospital at which Captain Fowler was being treated and held, so I made my way by cab through Belgravia and over to Millbank. I found Holmes waiting for me under the bow window and decorated gable of the brick-fronted stone building's entrance bay.

I raised my hand in greeting. "I presume that we are visiting Captain Fowler, Holmes? Has he recovered his wits?"

"Indeed, Watson. So I learned this morning. I plan to inform him that the matter is resolved."

"It is?"

"I spent Saturday morning inquiring into the affairs of Mr. Gilbert. He is a widower with one son, Virgil, aged twenty. It seems that last year Virgil joined the Second Battalion of the King's Own Yorkshire Light Infantry. You may recall, Watson, that this unit was part of the rear-guard covering the retreat from Mons, and it appears that Virgil was captured at Le Cateau."[164]

"A brave boy, Holmes," said I, "but what does that have to do with his father's treachery?"

"Everything, Watson. I suspect that Mr. Gilbert is being blackmailed. As long as he follows Vardin's instructions, his son will be spared. If he disobeys, they will execute him."

"That is barbaric!" I exclaimed.

He shook his head sadly. "The German gaolers are most cruel, Watson. Reports suggest that – unlike how we treat our German prisoners with honour and respect – they kick, beat, free, and stave our men."[165]

"Better, then, to die on the field than fall into their hands."

"It does not excuse Mr. Gilbert's actions, Watson, but it does mitigate them somewhat. He was in a most difficult position. Betray his country or sacrifice his son. Once I learned this, I returned to Colchester on Saturday evening, Watson, so that I could be in place when Mr. Gilbert departed for London. Little did he know that the asthmatic master mariner sitting behind him on the train was none other than yours truly. At Liverpool Street, I followed his hansom cab across town to no. 37 De Vere Gardens, where the landlady informed me that indeed one of her rooms was kept by a man who calls himself Monsieur Hubert Vardin. Vardin himself turned up after a short while, and when eventually he left, I followed him to his place of work. Monsieur Vardin proved to be the pseudonym of Henk Veenhuis, a minor diplomat attached to the Dutch embassy."

"The Dutch? But they are neutral!"

"The Dutch queen may be sympathetic to the plight of the Belgians, Watson, but her German prince-consort is openly on the side of his former countrymen.[166] Therefore, it takes little to convince certain Hollanders to operate on their behalf."[167]

"It is a shame that Veenhuis will go free."

"What do you mean, Watson?"

"Well, he is a diplomat. He has immunity."

Holmes smiled. "Technically, yes. But have you forgotten the little mission which I once so delicately and successfully accomplished for the reigning family of Holland?"

"Of course not. Though you never confided to me the details. I only recall that they gave you a brilliant ring as payment for your services."

"Yes, well, I called in a favour, Watson. Let us just say that the queen will ensure that Veenhuis will soon be recalled home, where he will not see the light of day for many years. And we now have men in place at Rotterdam in order to watch Count von Starmer. He may soon find himself the recipient of some classified information regarding which the details will prove to be rather incorrect."

I smiled. "Then what is there left to do?"

"We only need hear the final details from Captain Fowler himself."

Making our way inside, we found that two soldiers from the 117th Foot guarded Fowler's room. Holmes showed them an official-looking letter, such that we were soon permitted to pass. The white-washed room beyond was completely devoid of windows or other forms of exit and was Spartan to an extreme, containing only a metal bed and small side table.

When we entered, Fowler was sitting in bed reading *The Morning Post*. He was wearing a hospital gown, but even in his weakened state, he was a man of striking appearance, swarthy, black-moustached, nervous, and virile, with a quietly confident manner.

"Captain Fowler," said Holmes. "My name is Sherlock Holmes and this is Dr Watson. We have come in an official capacity to hear your words on what happened at Radchurch."

"Good day, gentlemen. I hear that Neuve Chapelle was a success," said he.[168]

"Yes, such as it was," Holmes agreed. "We proved that trench defences can be breached if the attack is carefully prepared and disguised in order to achieve local surprise. I fear, however, that the German army will quickly amend its defensive tactics. It may be a long time before such a stratagem works again. You were successful in preventing Fraulein Heffner from leaking word of the attack and spoiling the surprise."

He nodded. "So you know all?"

"Almost all. We have visited Radchurch. We have read her letter to Hubert Vardin. He has been dealt with most severely, and Mr. Stringer will be passing along no further information."

"Then what have I to tell?"

"I would know exactly what you told her and why it was that you did it."

He sighed. "So be it. If you, my fellow-countrymen, think that I did wrong, I will make no complaint, but will suffer in silence any penalty which you may impose upon me."

"Very good," said Holmes, severely. "Pray proceed."

"It may not seem proper at such a time and place as this that I should describe Miss Ena Garnier. Let me only say that I cannot believe that Nature ever put into female form a more exquisite combination of beauty and intelligence. I have read of people falling in love at first sight, and had always looked upon it as an expression of the novelist, like something from Hugo.[169] And yet from the moment that I saw Ena Garnier, life held for me but the one ambition that she should be mine. I had never dreamed before of the possibilities of passion that were within me. I will not enlarge upon the subject, Mr. Holmes, but to make you understand my action for I wish you to comprehend it. However much you may condemn it, you must realise that I was in the grip of a frantic elementary passion which made – for a time – the world and all that was in it seem a small thing if I could but gain the love of this one girl."

"And what of your honour as a soldier and a gentleman?" I interjected. "Did that count for nothing?"

"I trust, Dr Watson, that this is the one thing which I placed above her. You will find it hard to believe this when I tell you what occurred, and yet though for one moment only did I forget myself; my subsequent actions speak to my desperate endeavour to retrieve what I had done.

"If you have already spoken to the Murreyfields, then you know the history of our time together. I never understood her fondness for long, solitary rides upon her motor-cycle. After our engagement, I was occasionally allowed to accompany her. However, more than once she had refused my company with no reason given, and with a quick, angry flash of her eyes when I asked for one. Then, perhaps, her mood would change and she would make up for this unkindness by some exquisite attention, which would in an instant soothe all my ruffled feelings. It was the same in the house. My military duties were so exacting that it was only in the evenings that I could hope to see her, and yet very often she remained in the little study, which was used during the day for the children's lessons, and would tell me plainly that she wished to be alone. Then, when she saw that I was hurt by her caprice, she would laugh and apologise so sweetly for her rudeness such that I was more her slave than ever.

"Of course, gentlemen, with the wisdom of hindsight, the reasons for these behaviours is now crystal clear. I will admit that I was a fool. I should have seen the signs. However, I chalked it up to simple jealousy. When a man loves with the whole strength of his soul it is impossible, I think, that he should be clear of jealousy, and I was absurdly jealous. The girl was of a very independent spirit. I had heard that she knew many officers at Chelmsford and Colchester. She would disappear for hours upon her motor-cycle. There were questions about her past life, which she would only answer with a smile unless they were closely pressed. Then the smile would become a frown. Is it any wonder that I, with my whole nature vibrating with passionate, whole-hearted love, was often torn by jealousy when I came upon those closed doors of her life, which she was so determined not to open? Reason came at times and whispered how foolish it was that I should stake my whole life and soul upon one of whom I really knew nothing. Then came a wave of passion once more and reason was submerged.

"There were doors of her life that were closed to me. I was aware that a young, unmarried Frenchwoman has usually less liberty than her English sister. And yet in the case of this lady it continually came out in her conversation that she had seen and known much of the world. This was all the more distressing to me, as whenever she had made an observation which pointed to this she would afterwards – as I could plainly see – be annoyed by her own indiscretion, and endeavour to remove the impression by every means in her power. We had several small quarrels on this account, the most serious of which arose from my finding the photograph of a man upon her table. She displayed evident confusion when I asked her for some particulars about him. The name 'H. Vardin' was written underneath – evidently an autograph. I was worried by the fact that this photograph had the frayed appearance of one that has been carried secretly about, as a girl might conceal the picture of her lover in her dress. She refused to tell me whom he was, and made up an outrageous lie. And yet, my eyes could still not see the truth of the adder which I nestled to my breast.

"Ena was so madly fascinating and I so hopelessly her slave that she could always draw me back, however much prudence and reason warned me to escape from her control. I tried again and again to find out about this man Vardin, but was always met by the same assurance, which she repeated with every kind of solemn oath, that she had never seen the man in her life. Why she should carry about the photograph of a young, somewhat sinister man – for I had observed him closely before she snatched the picture from my hand – was what she either could not, or would not, explain.

"Then came the time for my leaving Radchurch. My post at the War Office was exceptionally demanding. Even my weekends found me engrossed with my work. Nevertheless, every night when I laid my head upon my pillow and closed my eyes, I saw her face before me. I suppose I always will.

"When I finally secured a few days for a leave of absence, I had only one thought of where I would go. However, gentlemen, it is those few days which have ruined my life, which have brought me the most horrible experience that ever a man had to undergo, and have finally placed me here in the hospital, pleading as I plead to-day for my life and my honour.

"It was the first time that we had been reunited since I had put all my heart and my soul upon her. I cannot enlarge upon these matters, gentlemen. You will either be able to sympathise with and understand the emotions which overbalance a man at such a time, or you will not. If you have imagination, you will. If you have not, I can never hope to make you see more than the bare fact. That bare fact, placed in the baldest language, is that during this drive from Radchurch Junction to the village I was led into the greatest indiscretion, the greatest dishonour, if you will, of my life. As you have already divined, Mr. Holmes, I told Miss Garnier a secret, an enormously important secret, which might affect the fate of the war and the lives of many thousands of men.

"It was done before I knew it, before I grasped the way in which her quick brain could place various scattered hints together and weave them into one idea. She was wailing, almost weeping, over the fact that the allied armies were held up by the iron line of the Germans. I explained that it was more correct to say that our iron line was holding them up, since they were the invaders.

" 'But is France, is Belgium, never to be rid of them?' she cried. 'Are we simply to sit in front of their trenches and be content to let them do what they will with ten provinces of France? Oh, Jack, Jack, for God's sake, say something to bring a little hope to my heart, for sometimes I think that it is breaking! You English are stolid. You can bear these things. But we others, we have more nerve, more soul! It is death to us. Tell me! Do tell me that there is hope! And yet it is foolish of me to ask, for, of course, you are only a subordinate at the War Office, and how should you know what is in the mind of your chiefs?'

" 'Well, as it happens, I know a good deal,' I answered. 'Don't fret, for we shall certainly get a move on soon.'

" 'Soon! Next year may seem soon to some people.'

" 'It's not next year.'

" 'Must we wait another month?'

" 'Not even that.'

"She squeezed my hand in hers. 'Oh, my darling boy, you have brought such joy to my heart! What suspense I shall live in now! I think a week of it would kill me.'

" 'Well, perhaps it won't even be a week.'

" 'And tell me,' she went on, in her coaxing voice, 'tell me just one thing, Jack. Just one, and I will trouble you no more. Is it our brave French soldiers who advance? Or is it your splendid Tommies? With whom will the honour lie?'

" 'With both.'

" 'Glorious!' she cried. 'I see it all. The attack will be at the point where the French and British lines join. Together they will rush forward in one glorious advance.'

" 'No,' I said. 'They will not be together.'

" 'But I understood you to say… of course, women know nothing of such matters, but I understood you to say that it would be a joint advance.'

" 'Well, if the French advanced, we will say, at Vimy Ridge, and the British advanced at Aubers Ridge, even if they were dozens of miles apart it would still be a joint advance.'[170]

" 'Ah, I see,' she cried, clapping her hands with delight. 'They would advance at both ends of the line, so that the Boches would not know which way to send their reserves.'

" 'That is exactly the idea: a real advance at Vimy Ridge, and an enormous feint at Aubers Ridge.' Then suddenly a chill of doubt seized me. I can remember how I sprang back from her and looked hard into her face. 'I've told you too much!' I cried. 'Can I trust you? I have been mad to say so much.'

"She was bitterly hurt by my words. That I should for a moment doubt her was more than she could bear. 'I would cut my tongue out, Jack, before I would tell any human being one word of what you have said.'

"So earnest was she that my fears died away. I felt that I could trust her utterly. Before we had reached Radchurch I had put the matter from my mind, and we were lost in our joy of the present and in our plans for the future.

"You must know the rest, gentlemen. After I returned from my military errand, I had gone into her little study to seek her. She was not there, but rather than traipse around the house looking for her, I decided to wait in the study, for it opened on to the hall passage, and she could not pass without my seeing her.

"There was a small table in the window of this room at which she used to write. I had seated myself beside this when my eyes fell upon a name written in her large, bold handwriting. It was a reversed impression upon the blotting-paper which she had used, but there could be no difficulty in reading it. The name was 'Hubert Vardin.'

"Then I knew for the first time that she was actually corresponding with this man whose vile, voluptuous face I had seen in the photograph with the frayed edges. She had clearly lied to me, too, for was it conceivable that she should correspond with a man whom she had never seen? I do not desire to condone my conduct, Mr. Holmes. Put yourself in my place. Imagine that you had my desperately fervid and jealous nature. You would have done what I did, for you could have done nothing else. A wave of fury passed over me. I laid my hands upon the wooden-writing desk. If it had been an iron safe, I should have opened it. As it was, it literally flew to pieces before me. There lay the letter itself, placed under lock and key for safety, while the writer prepared to take it from the house. I had no hesitation or scruple. I tore it open. Dishonourable, you will say, but when a man is frenzied with jealousy, he hardly knows what he does. This woman, for whom I was ready to give everything, was either faithful to me or she was not. At any cost, I would know which.

"A thrill of joy passed through me as my eyes fell upon the first words. I had wronged her. 'Cher Monsieur Vardin.' So the letter began. It was clearly a business letter, nothing else. I was about to replace it in the envelope with a thousand regrets in my mind for my want of faith when a single word at the bottom of the page caught my eyes, and I started as if I had been stung by an adder. 'Aubers' that was the word. I looked again. 'Vimy' was immediately below it. I sat down, horror-stricken, by the broken desk, and I read this letter in full.

"I was stunned at first, and then a kind of cold, concentrated rage came over me. So this woman was a German and a spy! I thought of her hypocrisy and her treachery towards me, but, above all, I thought of the danger to the Army and the State. A great defeat, the death of thousands of men, might spring from my misplaced confidence. There was still time, by judgment and energy, to stop this frightful evil. I heard her step upon the stairs outside, and an instant later she had come through the doorway. She started, and her face was bloodless as she saw me seated there with the open letter in my hand.

" 'How did you get that?' she gasped. 'How dare you break my desk and steal my letter?'

"I said nothing. I simply sat and looked at her and pondered what I should do. She suddenly sprang forward and tried to snatch the letter. I caught her wrist and pushed her down onto the sofa, where she lay, collapsed. Then I rang the bell, and told the maid that I must see Mr. Murreyfield at once.

"Murreyfield surely told you of what we did next, Mr. Holmes. We secured her in her room, then, having taken, as it seemed to me, every possible precaution, I ran to give the alarm. At Pedley, I found that the colonel was out, which occasioned some delay. Then there were formalities and a magistrate's signature to be obtained. A policeman was to serve the warrant, but a military escort was to be sent in to bring back the prisoner. I was so aggravated with anxiety and impatience that I could not wait, but I hurried back alone with the promise that they would follow.

"By this time, it was evening and the light was such that one could not see more than twenty or thirty yards ahead. I had proceeded only a very short way down the road from the point of junction when I heard, coming towards me, the roar of a motor-cycle being ridden at a furious pace. It was without lights, and close upon me. I sprang aside in order to avoid being ridden down, and in that instant, as the machine flashed by, I saw clearly the face of the rider. It was she, the woman whom I had loved. Her face glimmered white in the twilight, flying through the night like one of the Valkyries of her true native land. She was past me like a flash and tore on down the Colchester Road. In that instant I saw all that it would mean if she could reach the town. If she once was allowed to meet her agent we might arrest him or her, but it would be too late. The news would have been passed on. The victory of the Allies and the lives of thousands of our soldiers were at stake. The next instant, I had pulled out the loaded revolver and fired two shots after the vanishing figure, already only a dark blur in the dusk.

"Honestly, gentlemen, I have little memory of anything else. I am told that my brain cleared long enough to refuse to defend myself. I have been informed that I am to be charged with murder on account of jealousy. However, it is not murder that I committed. I should have thought myself the murderer of my own countrymen if I had let the woman pass. But I am glad that the hour of the combined British and French advance has finally passed. Now that it is over, my lips may be unsealed at last. I confess my fault, my very grievous fault."

Holmes shook his head. "She was a magnificent actress, Captain," said he. "She fooled many more men that just yourself. Your guilt is evident, but perhaps understandable."

Fowler nodded. "Thank you, sir. These are the facts, gentlemen. I leave my future in your hands. If you should absolve me, I may say that I have hopes of serving my country in a fashion which will atone for this one great indiscretion, and will also, as I hope, end forever those terrible recollections which weigh me down. If you condemn me, I am ready to face whatever you may think fit to inflict."

Holmes stared at him for a moment and pursed his lips. "You will understand, Captain Fowler, that your post at the War Office is no more. You cannot ever again be entrusted with military secrets. However, you are undoubtedly a brave man. It would be foolish of me to deprive our troops of such a leader. As soon as you have recovered your strength, I will see that you are sent to the Front. I trust that your future actions will justify this decision?"

§

And they did. For it was three years later when I learned that Captain Fowler had been killed leading his battalion across the Sambre-Oise Canal. His sacrifice helped ensure our victory at one of those final conflicts which sealed the fate of Kaiser Wilhelm and the German Empire.[171]

We had stepped back out of the hospital and begun to stroll northwards along the Thames, when Holmes finally spoke. "Such are the dangers of love, Watson. As I have said before, women are never to be entirely trusted."

I shook my head. "I cannot agree, Holmes. Surely, you cannot condemn the whole on the account of one woman's treacherous action? And, in the end, what do we really know of Miss Sophia Heffner? Perhaps, like poor Mr. Gilbert, she too was forced into this role of deception?"

"Perhaps, Watson, perhaps. I doubt we will ever learn her true motivations. We can only be on guard. For there may be more just like her even now walking the streets of London."

"I trust not!" I cried.

"One never knows, Watson. The machinations of Colonel Nicolai and his superiors are appalling. War was never as clean and filled with honour and mutual respect as the writers of historical fiction would have you believe. However, the Germans have sunk to new lows with their current methods, from the sinking of innocent merchant steamers, to the bombing of simple country villages. We can only hope that we have seen the worst of their crimes."[172] He shook his head sadly. "It would be unwise, Watson, to publish our involvement in this case. That would only serve to alert the Germans that I am actively engaged in seeking out their spies upon our soil. Far better for them to think that I am still smoking my pipe and tending my bees down at Eastbourne. You might let them know that I do not get around well anymore. Perhaps I am even crippled from attacks of rheumatism?"[173]

§

THEIR FINAL FLOURISH

September 1915 was a dark time for the British Empire. The prophecy that Sherlock Holmes had spoken some six years earlier, during the case of the vanished submarine Teucer, had finally come to pass. England was no longer an island. The skies had become filled with invaders and death struck from above.

When the first Zeppelin appeared high up above us, amid a gleaming of clouds, it seemed quite small, like the bright golden finger of an angel. Then came the flashes near the ground and the shaking noise. It was then that Milton's prophetic words rang true, for there was a war in the heavens.[174] Once, it seemed to me that the moon was Queen of the Night, and the stars were the lesser lights. However, they have now been displaced by the monstrous invention of Graf von Zeppelin, whose airship steals the light of the moon and drops bursting shells, dealing out a devastation that displaces the benedictions of the stars.[175]

I was back in London, for I could not sit idly by in Southsea while the bloom of our youth was spilling its blood upon the fields of Flanders. I had applied at the War Office, intending to re-join my old service in the Royal Army Medical Corp and utilize my skills in some needy field hospital. However, despite my protests, I was instead assigned to my old stomping grounds at Barts. Most of its attending staff and dressers had long since been shipped over the Channel, such that very few qualified surgeons remained in London to deal with the usual litany of ailments that refused to pause their scourge against civilians during this time of War. It was not glamourous work. However, I felt that I was, in a small way, doing my part by allowing other, younger men to help across the Channel.

As for my friend, Mr. Sherlock Holmes, the official word reported that he was too old to serve. Nevertheless, I knew better. He had boarded up his villa on the South Downs and embarked on a series of dangerous tasks put forward by his brother. For Mycroft Holmes, though no warmonger himself, had set his magnificent brain to the great work of bringing this terrible conflict to a swift and victorious conclusion. It was Holmes who discovered the gap in the German defences at the Marne, which General Joffre and Sir John French exploited to such brilliant effect.[176] It was Holmes who learned the terrible details of the Schlieffen-Moltke plan and ensured that the German Race to the Sea would be successfully countered.[177] It was Holmes who turned the police onto the tracks of the German spy Carl Hans Lody, who had been observing our naval movements and coastal defences.[178] And it was Sherlock Holmes who prevented the traitor Merryweather from selling the plans to the Tritton Machine, an impressive invention which would eventually help turn the tide of the war for the Allies.[179]

As my wife and I had sold our Queen Anne's Street home when we left London in 1904, I took a small flat on Lucerne Mews, just around the corner from where Louis La Rothière once lived. I had suggested that my wife remain in Southsea for the duration of the War, but she would not hear of such a thing. She volunteered as a nurse at St. Mary's, a task that she learned as a duck takes to water.

To brighten our temporary home, my wife had brought with us the gramophone from Baker Street, which Holmes had generously gifted to me upon his retirement. She loved to play patriotic music on it. When I came down for my coffee on the morning in question, '*The Bugle Calls*' from Wood's Sea Songs was spinning, and when I kissed her goodbye for the day it was a newly recorded song called '*Keep the Lamp Lit ('Till We Come Home)*.'[180] While this last tune was rather sentimental, it had already become exceptionally popular. For all Englishmen and women were constantly filled with dread that some poor lad for whom they cared would never return from the Western Front. It was one of the few times in my life when I did not regret my lack of a son. For what father could possibly bear to see his child struck down by such madness?

Shaking off these morbid thoughts, I took the Central London Underground line from Notting Hill Gate to Post Office.[181] I found the Tube rather efficient and no longer unpleasant, now that the coal engines had been replaced with electric motors. In this opinion, I rather differed from my friend. For I could count on one hand the number of times that Holmes had voluntarily ridden the Underground. In fact, he had once said to me that: 'a journey from Baker Street to King's Cross is a form of mild torture which no person would undergo if he could conveniently help it.' Of course, he was not sympathetically disposed to the transformation of the roads of London either, where the horse-drawn hansom cabs of yesteryear were rapidly vanishing in favour of various automobiles and motorcycles. Since its appearance in 1908, the petrol-fuelled Unic taxi had proliferated to such a degree that I had read there were now over two thousands of them competing for business with the long-accustomed horse-drawn hansoms and four-wheeled growlers. Despite my fondness for my Model T, as well as an appreciation for the general diminution of wayward horse droppings, I suppose I agreed with Holmes that this conversion had robbed London's streets and alleyways of a certain air of romance that they once held. The times were changing and I was, perhaps, a relic of a bygone era.

As I travelled along the Underground, I studied a poster

plastered to the side of the carriage. It depicted a Zeppelin, illuminated by a spotlight as it soared over Big Ben and the dome of St. Paul's Cathedral. The words beneath read:

*IT IS FAR BETTER
TO FACE THE BULLETS
THAN TO BE KILLED BY A BOMB*

*JOIN THE ARMY AT ONCE
& HELP TO STOP AN AIR RAID*

GOD SAVE THE KING

It was a sentiment with which I heartily concurred. I wished, not for the last time, that my request to cross the Channel had been accepted.

When I arrived at Barts, I found myself instantly occupied by an acute case of appendicitis. I stabilized the poor soul, and raced off to the chemical laboratory to look for a new supply of tincture of iodine. I was rummaging through the supply cabinets when I heard a familiar voice behind me.

"How are you, Watson?"

I turned and gazed upon my old friend. The advancing years had added some grey to his hair, but could not alter his tall and lean frame, or dull his sharp and piercing grey eyes. When he held out his hand for me to shake, I found that it still possessed that same iron grip for which I should hardly have given him credit had I not seen it in action so many times. In a moment, some thirty-four years seemed to vanish and it was as if I was meeting him again for the first time. Only Stamford was missing from the scene.

"Whatever are you doing here, Holmes?" I finally managed.

"It is about the Zeppelin raids."

"The Huns have made a grave error if they think to terrorize us into surrender!" said I, with heat. "I read in today's *The Times* an editorial which said that: 'if it were possible for the enemy to increase the utter and almost universal detestation in which he is held by the people of this country, he did it yesterday.' I cannot agree more!"

"Yes, yes, Watson. Even some of the Germans agree with you. I have it on good authority that the Chancellor himself warned General von Hindenburg that the anger of the British public would be so great over these attacks that a negotiated peace will become impossible.[182] However, the foolish man did not listen. Still, there is something odd about the most recent raid, Watson. I am headed to investigate it now and – as I knew that you were in the neighbourhood – I thought that you might wish to accompany me. I will admit that, upon occasion, you have been of some assistance with helping me see a light where all else is dark."

"It is good to know that you still value my efforts, Holmes," said I, warmly. "For it has been quite some time since we dealt with the case of Captain Fowler."

I hurriedly informed my dresser that I had been called away, and when I re-joined Holmes outside the Henry VIII Gate, I found that he had engaged a hansom cab. Once we had boarded, I leaned back and asked him to tell me of the current problem.

"Yes, well, as you know, Watson, when we rounded up Herr Von Bork, we also rolled up his entire operation. Most of the men are now safely ensconced in various of His Majesty's prisons, though we did leave one or two of the less-clever ones in place as a conduit for passing along misinformation whenever we so desired. Moreover, we recently made certain that Monsieur Vardin would give us no further trouble. However, I am now concerned that there may be another agent roaming free in London."

"Why?"

"Because of the path of the bombs."

"I do not follow you, Holmes."

He shook his head. "I forget sometimes, Watson, that not everyone carries a map of London in their head. Let me draw it out for you." He withdrew his notebook from his breast-coat pocket and sketched a sinuous line, which I recognized as the path of the Thames through London.

"The first bomb fell here on Bartholomew Close, near Smithfield Market, at twenty to eleven," said he, marking an 'X' upon the paper. "Then more bombs fell on the textile warehouse north of St. Paul's." He marked several additional 'X's. The pilot must have then turned his monster to the east, for several additional bombs fells on Liverpool Street Station." He marked a large 'X' in the appropriate spot on his rough map.

"The last bomb was noted here." He marked another 'X' at a location far to the southeast in relation to the others. "The Zeppelin was spotted by the searchlights, even if our anti-aircraft guns fired in vain. There is no chance that it could have altered course and managed to drop this particular explosive."

"Perhaps there was a second Zeppelin?"

"There was. One of our aeroplanes saw it as it dropped its bombs on Dereham before turning back across the Channel. It never came close to London."

"So what are you proposing, Holmes?"

"It is too soon to theorize, Watson. I only note an anomaly. And this is an ill time for such irregularities. Ah, here we are." He motioned out of the window.

The cab turned on Cannon Street and pulled up in front of a church, which lay across the street from the now-shuttered train station. I recognized St Swithin's, one of Wren's works from the rebuilding after the Great Fire of 1666.

Once we departed the cab, Holmes motioned for me to wait while he inspected the area. I was not sure how he intended identify any clues, given the massive damage induced by the bomb. Chunks of stonework littered the ground and the pavement sported a gaping hole some five feet deep.

After a few minutes, Holmes turned to me, his face grim. "It is as I thought. This is not the work of a German incendiary, Watson. I have made a study of the various high explosives, and I recognize the distinctive handiwork of nitro-glycerine.

THE GATHERING GLOOM

It was packed in a wagon, which was itself obliterated in the blast. So why, pray tell, did a bomber set off his charge at this spot last night?"

"To damage the station? To prevent goods from being sent from here to the docklands?"

"Hardly. The Germans are not as obtuse as that. If they have an agent moving about freely in London, surely he would have selected his target with more care. Cannon Street Station has been closed for several months. Moreover, they would have parked their incendiary wagon on the south side of the street. Instead, it was situated here, nearer to this church," he concluded, turning his head.

I followed his gaze. St Swithin's was about forty feet wide on its southern side. I knew it had a tower and spire on the northern side. However, from our current vantage point, these were not visible. Instead, there was an elliptical pediment over the central of three windows. This was decorated with a carved wreath, flanked by festoons in high relief, while the heads of the flanking windows were decorated with stone drapery. The explosive had heavily damaged the wall, such that a new aperture had been opened. Through the wreckage, I could see the reredos behind the altar.

A dim remembrance tickled my brain and my legs began to pull me towards the church. I was drawn to an alcove in the centre of the south wall. At that spot, there was once a circular opening with a protective metal grille, through which the object inside the alcove could be viewed. However, this had been ripped out, and the item – which once rested within a stone frame atop a plinth – was missing. The only thing that remained was the decorative plaque above, which read in both Latin and English:

LONDON STONE
Commonly believed to be a Roman work long
placed abovt xxxv feet hence towards the Sovth
West and afterwards bvilt into the wall of this

Chvrch was for more carefvl protection and
transmission to fvtvre ages better secvred by the
Chvrchwardens in the year of ovr Lord MDCCCLXIX

Holmes had followed me over to the spot and studied the vacant alcove with interest. "The London Stone?" he asked. "Why would someone steal a block of stone?"

"I have read about this, Holmes," said I, excitedly. "It is a stone from the very beginnings of Roman Londinium. Brutus of Troy laid it here as a Palladium, the object in which the city's safety and well-being are embodied.[183] Much later, the Medieval Kings would strike it with their swords after their coronations, in order to signify the City's submission to their rule. Do you not recall Jack Cade in *Henry VI*?"[184]

"Yes, of course, Watson, but why steal it? If one were to use the cover of an air raid to make off with something in this neighbourhood, the Old Lady of Threadneedle Street, or Silvester's Bank, seem far more likely targets."

"Do you not know the ancient proverb, Holmes?"

He shook his head irritably. "No," said he, gruffly. "But I suppose you are about to inform me?"

I puffed out and declaimed, as if I was Irving himself:[185]

"So long as the Stone of Brutus is safe
So long shall London flourish."

"Nursery rhymes, Watson." He waved his hand dismissively.

"Perhaps. But there is power in belief, Holmes. Do not forget about Drake's Drum, or the Angel of Mons."[186]

He peered at me. "And what, pray tell, is the Angel of Mons?"

"You recall the battle last August, of course. It was the first major engagement of the BEF. Our heavily outnumbered men initially turned back the German advance, until the sudden retreat of the French Fifth Army exposed our flank and forced our own retreat. Shortly afterwards, a Welshman reported in the *Evening News* that phantom bowmen from the

Battle of Agincourt, summoned from the reaches of the past by a soldier calling upon St. George, had destroyed the German host."[187]

"Balderdash!" Holmes exclaimed.

"True or not, it gave hope to the reading public that, during our hour of greatest need, our heroes would not fail us."

"What is your point, Watson?"

"A German agent could cause great loss of morale if he were to destroy the Stone. Spirits in London are already perilously low on account of the Zeppelin raids and the lack of progress in France."

Holmes pondered this for a moment and finally nodded. "There may be truth in what you say, Watson. The raids have resulted in limited military advantage, as their aim is far from precise. They have killed as many children as they have knocked out our military supply depots. However, if destroying the stone were their purpose, they would have detonated their nitro-glycerine much closer to their target. No, I think they intended to carry off the stone, perhaps to Germany itself, in order to demonstrate their dominance over us."

"It would have been quite a feat to carry off the stone," I opined. "It must weigh three-hundred pounds!"

Holmes shook his head. "A little more, I think, Watson. Three-hundred and seventy-five to four-hundred and twenty-five, depending upon the density of this particular specimen of limestone."

"You seem rather certain," said I, a hint of peevishness creeping into my voice.

"The calculation is a simple one, not unlike that of calculating the speed of a train by watching the telegraph posts."

"I fail to see it."

"The vacated space is roughly twenty-one inches wide, by seventeen inches high, by twelve inches deep. That suggests a volume of some two-and-a half cubic feet. Moreover, the density of limestone is typically between one hundred-fifty and one-hundred seventy pounds per cubic foot. This fact suggests that multiple individuals were responsible for the theft of the stone, unless the sole culprit is both exceptionally strong and well-used to lifting heavy objects."

"A stevedore!" I ventured.

"Perhaps, Watson, perhaps. It is a theory worth exploring. However, for our next task, we will require rather more man-power. It is time for us to pay a visit to Scotland Yard."

§

Both Lestrade and Gregson were still with the C.I.D., of course, though – with both the passing of years and the successes gleaned from their long association with Holmes – they had risen to more sedentary positions. Therefore, Inspector Stanley Hopkins was the man whose assistance Holmes sought out.

Holmes' name had certainly not been forgotten at Scotland Yard, and we were promptly shown into the tidy office belonging to Hopkins. The Inspector was still fairly youthful and alert, though his once-eager face was now beginning to show lines of care and strain. Few Englishmen had been untouched in some way by the War, even if they did not serve in the trenches.

"What can I do for you, Mr. Holmes?" said Hopkins, warmly, as he welcomed us in.

Holmes explained what we had discovered at the St. Swithin's bombing site.

As Holmes was talking, Hopkins had leaned back in his chair, and wrapped his hands behind his head. "That is very interesting, Mr. Holmes. Very interesting, indeed," said he, when my friend had concluded. "I think it might explain this." He leaned forward and plucked a report from his desk. Holmes took it from him and rapidly flipped through the file.

When complete, he glanced over at me. "It seems, Watson, that your theory was correct. A pair of burly lascars were found in a Deptford alley this morning, each with a bullet in

THE GATHERING GLOOM

their heart."

"Were there any witnesses?" I asked.

Hopkins shook his head. "Unfortunately not. We were about to chalk it up to some rival gang, but now I wonder if they might have been hired help for the theft of the Stone. I suppose we could ask around, and see if any of their mates know who employed them?"

Holmes shrugged. "That is unlikely to be enlightening, Hopkins. Our mysterious agent surely would have ensured that strict secrecy was a required part of their engagement."

"But what sort of cold-heated monster would then shoot them dead?" I protested.

"Indeed, Watson. This is a most dangerous adversary with whom we are dealing."

"But if none of the other lascars know his identity, then we are in a pickle, Mr. Holmes," said the inspector, his brow troubled.

"Not exactly, Hopkins. There are several essential elements required in the production of nitro-glycerine. You must combine eight parts sulphuric acid with four parts nitric acid and one part pure glycerol. These must be mixed with a long glass rod by a man with iron nerves, for it is not uncommon to stir too quickly and make the entire brew explode. Of these, the most difficult upon which to lay hands is certainly the nitric acid. Glycerol is common. Any Tom, Dick, or Harry can walk into their local chemists and purchase a pint of sulphuric acid by claiming they need it for cleaning. However, the non-explosive uses of nitric acid are far fewer, and the Government maintains a tighter supply of this substance. If we can find the chemist who has recently sold a supply of nitric acid, we might be able to trace the man who purchased it."

The man nodded his understanding. "Very good, sir. I will put my best men on it. We will knock on every door in London if need be."

"Capital," said Holmes. "When you have found the establishment, I would be grateful if you would notify Watson and me forthwith. You will find us at the National Gallery."

Taking our leave of Hopkins, Holmes led us out of the Norman Shaw North Building and along the Victoria Embankment. We went some ways, until we had passed the Hungerford Footbridges and reached Cleopatra's Needle. From this particular vantage point, I could take in the whole sweep of the Thames in both directions.

Holmes, however, stared out at the water towards the east, his eyes fixed on the austere spans of the Waterloo Bridge. "It is funny, Watson, to stand here and consider the bridge which commemorates a battle that transpired barely a century ago. There, by the side of our current enemy, Prussia, we fought against our current ally, France. How things change."

I shook my head. "It is sheer madness, Holmes, but what can you and I possibly do about it?"

"We can ensure that we win," said he, simply, without turning to look at me.

I stood there silently, agreeing wholeheartedly with this sentiment, but unable to think of anything else to say on the matter. "And why are we headed to the National Gallery?" I finally asked.

"Why not?" said he, with a shrug. "It is in times like these that we must remind ourselves that beauty still exists in the world, and that there are places well worth protecting."

Some two hours later, after appreciating when Holmes finally stopped before Turner's *Téméraire*. Something about the painting clearly called to him. I stood by his side and admired this great masterpiece of British Romanticism, the old warship rising in stately splendour against the triangle of blue sky and rising mist, while the sun set into the estuary. Next to the ghostly-outline of the obsolescent vessel, a little black tugboat heralded the onslaught of a less glorious age. I wondered if, like Turner when he set down this picture, Holmes was now contemplating his own inevitable mortality.

I was eager to remind him that the curtain had not yet fallen upon us, nor upon Great Britain. As long as we had hope, we would fight on. In a low voice, I began to sing:[188]

*"And she's fading down the river;
But in England's song for ever;
She's the Fighting Téméraire."*

Holmes did not acknowledge my words; however, we were still standing there when Hopkins came to find us. His face clearly showed that the Yard's inquiries had borne fruit.

"We found a man named Leonard, owner of a shop on Chalk Farm Road near the Regent's Canal, who recently sold a considerable quantity of nitric acid."

"Excellent!" exclaimed Holmes. "Then a trip to Camden Town is in order."

When we arrived at Leonard's establishment, we found a building that was a little rough around the edges, but carefully maintained. A constable stood watch outside, as if the chemist was considering fleeing from the reach of Scotland Yard. Once we saw the man, however, we realized that nothing could be furthest from the truth. For Leonard was a mild-appearing man of some sixty years, with a pate covered by only a few wispy strands. He wore the typical white jacket of a chemist.

Holmes had requested that Hopkins allow him to do the talking, and the inspector kindly agreed. So, Holmes launched into questioning of the man.

"I understand, Mr. Leonard, that you admitted to the constable selling some nitric acid recently?"

"That is correct, sir. I sold four pints to a man about two weeks ago. I can look up his name if you wish?" said he, waving towards a large red account book.

"Please do so," said Holmes, tersely.

Leonard settled a pair of glasses on his nose and proceeded to flip through the pages for a few minutes. "Ah, here we go," he exclaimed. He swung the book about, facing Holmes and I, and stabbed his finger at one line, which read: "3 Sept '15: Nitric acid. 4 pints. 4s5p. Bottles refundable. Purchaser: Mr. Owen Glendower, No. 1 Borough High Street, Southwark."

"We have him!" I cried.

But Holmes only shook his head. "I think not, Watson. Does the name ring any bells?"

"Owen Glendower? Well, it is Welsh name…"

"It is not just Welsh, Watson. Have you forgotten your Shakespeare? Henry IV, Part One? It is the name of a very famous Welshman, more properly called Owain Glyndŵr, the last native Prince of Wales and famous leader of the Welsh Rising against King Henry IV.[189] It is an allusion to the rebeller Jack Cade and the London Stone. This pseudonym is a little joke by our adversary, should anyone have followed him this far."

"So the address is…"

"Also a fake and not worth our time." He turned back to the chemist. "Can you describe him?"

Mr. Leonard pursed his lips and considered this. "Well, sir, he was a middling height with a pleasant and cultured face. Perhaps fifty years of age, I recall that he had a confident manner. He was carefully dressed, with clothes of the current fashion."

"Not a poor man, then," said Holmes. "Anything else?"

The chemist shook his head. "No, sir, not that I can recall."

"Tell me, Mr. Leonard, the sale of nitric acid is restricted, is it not?"

"Of course, sir."

"Then why, pray tell, did you sell it to him?"

"I broke no laws, sir, I assure you!" Leonard exclaimed. "I am permitted to sell for legitimate artistic purposes."

"Such as?"

"Etchings, sir, for printmaking. He said he had a commission to create posters for the war effort."

Holmes' eyes narrowed. "Are you telling me the man was an artist?"

"Yes, sir. He had a note from Sir Cecil, the Director of the V&A."

"Presumably forged," said Holmes, irritably. "Anything else which would prove his bona-fides?"

"Yes, sir. He had a lovely copperplate with him which he had etched before the war."

"Of what?"

"I am not certain, sir. I only saw it for a moment, but I suppose it looked like a Last Supper scene."

"Anything else?"

Leonard considered this for a moment. "Well, now that you mention it, sir, I did think it odd that everyone around the table was holding an egg."

Holmes looked up with a startled expression. "Eggs? Are you certain?"

"Yes, sir," said the man, emphatically.

Holmes smiled and turned to me. "I know this engraving, Watson, and I know who might have sold it."

§

Holmes stepped outside the shop and, after promising to keep Hopkins up to date on the investigation, he hailed a passing hansom cab for the two of us. He instructed the driver to take us to Piccadilly, before he leaned back and explained. "I believe that our man has finally made a mistake, Watson."

"How so?"

"Our man should have better covered his tracks. If it had been I, engaged in such activities in Berlin, I would have burned the chemist's shop down rather than let someone trace me via it."

I was momentarily taken aback by this ruthless vein, but pressed on. "Yes, there cannot be that many engravers active in London."

"Don't be absurd, Watson. The man is not an artist himself. He merely pretended to be one so as to disarm Mr. Leonard's suspicions."

"But the engraving...."

"Something our man purchased in order to complete his feigned personae. The engraving of several men sitting about a table holding eggs can only be Hogarth's *Columbus*. Do you know it?"

I shook my head. "No."

"It is an old work, dating from circa 1750, by the artist William Hogarth. I only learned of it because of a recent editorial in *The Times* complaining that most of Hogarth's original copperplates were being scrapped in order to produce material for munitions and aircraft. They were asking at what price comes our victory over the Huns if our culture is lost in the process."

"A valid concern," said I, with warmth.

"Fortunately, Watson, the paper output of a copperplate engraving can survive long after the prime source is gone. Furthermore, in this case, the former owner of several of the plates was permitted to keep one. This is a Mr. Russell Trefoil, an antiquarian of Shaftesbury Avenue. We must determine whether Mr. Trefoil has recently sold his *Columbus*. This only goes to show, Watson, the utility of carefully filing away facts in one's brain attic, for who can say when such a thing may prove to be of use?"

Our hansom drew up in front of the Criterion, and we crossed the road to the shop at No. 15, which was marked by stacks of books in the windows and a nice marble relief of heraldic lions. Inside, the antiquarian's rooms were just as one might imagine. The walls were lined with floor-to-ceiling bookshelves, which themselves were overflowing with musty tomes. A few easels held old prints, and several tables and benches were scattered about. The distinctive grass and vanilla smell of old paper lingered in the air.

When we entered, a man who was standing halfway up a ladder on rails turned to greet us. He was still young, such that I was surprised that he had not yet joined the Army. It was only when he stepped down from the ladder and made his way over to us that I was able to discern that his right leg was no longer made of flesh and bone. I had little doubt that the original now resided in the Flanders earth.

Holmes introduced us and asked after Hogarth's engraving.

"Ah, yes," said Trefoil, "the *Columbus Breaking the Egg*. My favourite. Do you know the legend, sir?"

"No," said Holmes, his tone implying that he little cared.

However, that did not dissuade the bookseller. "It is perhaps apocryphal. When Columbus returned to Europe, his detractors began to suggest that his feat of discovering the New World was actually unremarkable because of its utter simplicity. Columbus retorted that it only appeared straightforward now that he had demonstrated how it was done. By way of an example, he challenged anyone present to stand an egg on its end. After all those attempting the feat had admitted defeat, Columbus demonstrated the ease of the challenge by crushing one end of the egg against the table, thereby allowing it to remain upright."

Holmes smiled. "The Gordian Knot."

"Precisely," said Trefoil, happily, not understanding the stakes of this particular game.

"And do you still have it?"

"I am afraid not, sir. The recent editorial in *The Times* stirred up interest in the last of Hogarth's plates. I sold it about a fortnight ago."

"To whom?"

"Sir Ethan Hillcroft."

I knew that Holmes possessed a remarkable ability to maintain his facial composure when confronted with surprising information, but this name was sufficient to bring a brief look of shock to his grey eyes. He quickly thanked the antiquarian and we departed the store.

Once outside, Holmes stopped in the street and appeared lost in thought. The afternoon was getting on, and a dense drizzly fog had descended upon the great city. The street lamps were dark, in order to avoid marking a route to any potential aerial invaders. Avoiding Holmes as if he were a statue, the people of London filed past, oblivious to the fact that his great brain was occupied in the consideration of something that might spell the doom of our glorious Empire.

I finally could no longer take the suspense. "Who then, is Sir Ethan Hillcroft?"

Holmes looked up with a grave expression upon his face. "Sir Ethan is an MP, and the Second Secretary to the Admiralty. More importantly, he is one of only a handful of men who are privy to one of our greatest secrets."

"And he is a traitor?" said I, aghast at the thought.

"It appears so. This is grave news, Watson. We must consult with Mycroft at once."

As it was but a brisk ten-minute walk along Haymarket and Cockspur, we abjured the use of a cab. As we walked, Holmes shook his head. "I cannot fathom why Hillcroft would have made his move now. The only possible explanation is that he – or his masters in Berlin – must have realized that the war in Belgium and France has bogged down into an interminable stalemate. They saw only one possible solution – the swift crushing of the English will. However, if we move quickly enough, we can ensure that their plan never comes to full fruition."

Once we reached the unassuming door on Whitehall, a uniformed lieutenant promptly showed us into the office belonging to Holmes' brother. Mycroft seemed even more worn and weary than the last time I had seen him, like a massive boulder sitting upon a bleak hillside. His role in the government had been a heavy one for some time now, but even more so while the terrible War raged. Only his deep-set, steel-grey eyes were unchanged. As we entered, he was studying some files and taking notes upon a yellow legal pad, though he soon set down his pen and looked at us with interest.

"Good evening, Sherlock. I expected to see you round last month, to consult with me over that little matter regarding the Partridge handbag.[190] Other than the fact that you have been inspecting a bomb site and a visiting a bookshop, I cannot fathom what you are working on at the moment."

I attempted to follow his chain of logic, but to no avail. Holmes, however, smiled thinly. "This is no time for petty games, Mycroft. I have come to ask you about Sir Ethan Hillcroft."

Mycroft's eyes narrowed dangerously. "What of him?"

"What do you know of his history?"

He frowned. "Everything. A man does not rise to his position without a careful vetting."

"Not careful enough."

"What do you mean?"

"I suspect that Sir Ethan is a spy for the German government."

"Impossible!" exclaimed Mycroft.

"Is it? Have there been no unexplained leaks from Whitehall?"

The elder Holmes narrowed his eyes and pursed his lips. Without a word, he then rolled his chair over to a large wooden filing cabinet. Unlocking this with a key that hung about his neck, Mycroft said, "All of those with Most Secret clearance have full files of their antecedents stored in this cabinet. Even you, Sherlock. Given certain events in your past, brother, I must say it required rather a great deal of difficulty to secure you such clearance."

"Am I in there?" I asked.

"No," said he, simply.

Holmes reached out his hand for Sir Ethan's file, which Mycroft handed over. "I doubt that you will find anything of note."

Instead of answering, Holmes studied the pages carefully. "It is a rare day, indeed, Mycroft, when I can say that you are wrong. I suppose, however, that hindsight is always more clear."

"Whatever are you referring to?" said Mycroft, his brow furrowed.

Holmes passed the file back to him. "On the first page, note his mother."

"Lady Gertrude? She has been dead for years. What of her... oh!" exclaimed Mycroft.

"What is it?" I asked.

"Sir Ethan's mother was German. Her maiden name was von Dönhoff."

I shook my head. "There are many fine Englishmen with German blood, Holmes, not the least of which is our King. How does that fact alone make him a traitor?"

"The German blood is not the issue, Watson. If I had to guess, I would wager that the bigger fault lies with the quality of the English stock in his veins."

"How so?"

"His father was Sir Charles Hillcroft, Baronet. He died while I was living at Montague Street. I recall the case, because he was at the time under a cloud of suspicion."

"Regarding what?"

"The death of one of his servants. It seems that Sir Charles was rather prone to violent outbursts and one of these episodes went too far. It was rumoured that his own passing was self-inflicted. Sir Ethan's mother died early, and he was sent off to a boarding school, where he studied under a kindly German master. It looks as if he also belonged for a time to the German Gymnasium at Charing Cross."

"That is all rather circumstantial, is it not?"

"Imagine, if you will, Watson, what it must have been like to be Sir Ethan. Bullied and neglected by his father, he would have grown to hate Sir Charles, and so – in turn – he grew to identify with his German mother. He would have been the perfect target of the Abteilung."

Mycroft shook his head, his massive face livid. "This is terrible, Sherlock. I should have seen it. It explains much. We never understood how our reports of the Ottoman's troop strength at the Dardanelles, or the mobility of their batteries, could have been so wrong.[191] However, now I see that the First Lord of the Admiralty was purposely misinformed. We must stop Sir Ethan at once."

He leaned over and spoke into a voice-pipe. "Perkins, will you come in here?" He then proceeded to jot a note upon a piece of paper. When the lieutenant entered the room, Mycroft handed him the note, and nodded for the man to depart.

When we were again alone. "You said that Hillcroft was privy to one of our greatest secrets?" I asked.

Mycroft swung his gaze upon me, but remained silent.

"You can count on Watson's discretion, brother," said my friend.

"Can I? I seem to recall, Doctor, that in October 1893, you revealed the nature of our secret treaty with Italy. In December 1904, you told the world that our statesmen cannot be trusted with important despatches. And in December 1908, you divulged the secret of the Bruce-Partington Plans."

"All true, Mycroft," said Holmes. "Though all of those were old news by the time Watson released the details. In his defence, Watson never told of our double agents in the Office of European Affairs. Or, how we captured Herr Ehrenburg's oscillator device in 1909. Or, how I infiltrated the spy network of Von Bork. Or, the indiscretions of Captain Fowler. Moreover, and perhaps most importantly, he has already been to the place in question. Room 40 is no secret to him. I trust you have not forgotten the aftermath of the murder of Mr. Horace Brownlow?"[192]

"Of course not, Sherlock. But he does not need know about Room 42."

"What is in Room 42?" I asked.

Holmes turned to me. "You are one of only a handful of people, Watson, who is aware of the fact that in Room 40 sits a team of the best cryptographers ever assembled. There, they decode all of the wireless transmissions that we intercept. Do you recall our great victory at Dogger Bank in January? Yes? Well, it is because we knew ahead of time that the German raiding squadron would be found there. However, the

Germans are not slow-witted. Surely, they must suspect that we are attempting to break their codes, just as they are likely doing to ours. Moreover, they are constantly at work at creating new ciphers, which they hope will be completely unbreakable. To counter this, we have been working in Room 42 to construct a fully functional difference engine."

This meant nothing to me. "And what, pray tell, is a difference engine?"

"It is more properly termed an analytical engine, Doctor," interjected Mycroft. "The mathematician Babbage first conceived of it, but he ran into issues with the engineers and funding.[193] Those are no longer barriers to us in this time of great need. The engine is a machine that is capable of tabulating complex mathematical functions, an essential role of the modern code-breaker. I cannot impress on you strongly enough that the existence of a functional analytical engine is the highest secret of the war effort, Doctor. It will give us the permanent upper hand on the Germans' plans. If they were to become aware of its existence, they would immediately cease to transmit any critical information over the airwaves."

"But surely Sir Ethan has told them by now?"

Mycroft glanced over at Sherlock before speaking. "One might think so, Doctor. However, as you are fundamentally an honest and decent man, you have little understanding of the mind-set of the spy. Sir Ethan may have betrayed England out of some perverted feeling for his mother's homeland. However, surely he is smart enough to realize that their affections will only be returned as long as he is useful to them. Therefore, he will have retained some critical information as his ace card. At least until he has made his final move."

"I believe that he has now done so," said Holmes.

"He must have sensed, Sherlock, that your ongoing efforts to unearth German spies on our soil was about to lead to him."

"We must arrest him at once!" I exclaimed.

"I have already sent some of my most trusted men to Half Moon Street, Doctor, to carry out that very task."

Holmes shook his head, his face grim. "You will not find him at home." He sat down in one of the chairs and proceeded to fill his pipe. It was clear that he believed that a ratiocination session was in order.

§

Holmes was proven correct. Lieutenant Perkins soon returned with another man. This latter individual never gave his name, though from his mannerisms and words, I took him for a member of one of those shadowy organizations dedicated to the pursuit of espionage.

"No sign of him, sir," said the man to Mycroft. "His servants report that he never returned home last night. He went out for dinner and a show around six o'clock."

"Why did they not report this?" asked Holmes.

The man shrugged. "They say that it was not unusual. In any case, we searched the house from loft to cellar and found no signs of bomb-making equipment."

"Very good," said Mycroft, dismissing the man with a wave of his massive hand.

"This is terrible!" I cried. "How else are we possibly to locate him?"

"Sir Ethan must have a bolt-hole somewhere in London," said Holmes. "It was never very likely that he would construct a bomb in his Mayfair town-home under the watchful eyes of all of his servants. No matter how loyal they may be, I doubt that they would ignore such a thing."

"But how are we to find it?"

Holmes smiled and turned to his brother. "His file indicated that Sir Ethan was not married, but he went to dinner and the theatre with someone. With whom was he close?"

Mycroft considered this and then nodded slowly. "It is unspoken knowledge that he keeps a woman in Marylebone, around the corner from the Langham. Her name is Miss Lydia Peele. Once this liaison became known, she was investigated, of course, but was deemed to have no links to Germany."

"We shall see about that," said Holmes, grimly.

He motioned to me, and I followed him out to the street, where he waved down a passing cab. Ten minutes later found us knocking on the door to Miss Peele's flat. At the presentation of Holmes' card, we were showed in by a maid. Although hardly located in the finest part of town, the reception room was decorated with an array of elegant furnishings and artwork. Sir Ethan may not have been willing to wed Miss Peele, but he certainly spared no expense upon her. As we waited for the lady to appear, I studied her bookshelf. I have found that one can learn much about an individual by their taste in books. In Miss Peele's case, that ran to Austen and Bronte. I also noted a fondness for games, for she owned a finely carved backgammon set, though it was folded and tucked away. While I was engaged in this task, Holmes had swept his eyes over her Chippendale writing desk before settling onto the sofa.

Miss Peele swept into the room in a rustle of silk. She was an exceptional beauty, with a graceful figure and perfect complexion to match her golden hair and blue eyes. She was shrouded in a loose dressing gown of green and black, her feet covered by dainty slippers. She lay back upon a couch, apparently unconcerned by a sudden visit from London's premier detective, though I thought I detected a hint of alertness in her eyes.

"What can I do for you, Mr. Holmes?" she asked.

"Merely a few routine questions, Miss Peele."

"Regarding?"

"All in good time, Miss Peele. Your name is familiar to me. Are you not the same Lydia Peele who once enraptured the critics with her portrayal of Casilda in the 1908 revival of *The Gondoliers* at the Savoy?"

She smiled thinly. "That is correct, Mr. Holmes. Though I am now retired from the stage."

"May I ask from where you originally hale?"

She shrugged. "I cannot see the relevance to anything. But if you must know, I was born in Aldershot."

"Very good," said Holmes. "I wonder if you have recently seen Sir Ethan Hillcroft?"

Her eyes tightened slightly. "Yes. If you must know, we had dinner last night. Then we caught *Robinson Crusoe* at the Lyceum. Does this have something to do with Sir Ethan? Is anything wrong?"

"As you must know, Sir Ethan is a highly placed member of His Majesty's Government. He failed to return home last night and has not been heard from all day. I was asked to inquire as to his whereabouts."

"Oh!" she exclaimed, leaning forward. "Anything I can do to help, of course! His carriage dropped us here around ten o'clock. He then stayed for coffee until eleven or so. I have not seen or heard from him since. Have you asked his driver, Smithson?"

"No," said Holmes, with a smile. "That is an excellent suggestion. I wonder if you know of any other locale in London where Sir Ethan might stay the night?"

She shrugged. "His club, perhaps? It's the Carlton."

"What about the countryside?"

"Well, there is his estate near Cromer. He did mention over dinner last night that he needed to look in on it sometime soon, for most of the men are away at the War. Perhaps he suddenly decided that he needed to do so?"

"Perhaps. And there is nowhere else?"

"No."

"You are certain?"

"Positive."

"Then I thank you for your time, Miss Peele."

"Please find him as soon as possible, Mr. Holmes. I can hardly bear the thought that he is missing. Oh!" she exclaimed. "Perhaps he was injured in one of the Zeppelin attacks? He could have amnesia! You must check the hospitals!"

"A capital thought. You have been most helpful," said

Holmes.

We then took our leave of Sir Ethan's mistress. When we reached the pavement, Holmes began to chuckle softly. "Well, I can see why Miss Peele retired from the stage, Watson. She is a terrible actress."

"You believe that she was lying?"

He began walking down the street. "Of course. Miss Peele may not be fully informed of Sir Ethan's plans, but she was not surprised to hear that he was missing. Ask yourself, Watson, why Sir Ethan never married her. Even I will admit that she has a certain beauty. The only possible reason could be that her social station is too far below his."

"She said she was from Aldershot, near the garrison. Is she the daughter of a common soldier?"

"Or worse, an illegitimate one. Such a thing might be sufficient to engender in Miss Peele a hatred for English soldiers, as the careless action of one prevented her from ever achieving such a desired position in society. A mistress is never as secure as a wife, Watson. But perhaps, far from London society, she believes that he might marry her. Moreover, I am certain that she knows the location of his bolt-hole. However, she rather did her best to induce us to follow up a bunch of false trails. A jaunt to Norfolk, indeed!"

"So, what are we to do, Holmes? Wait for her to leave and follow her movements? Perhaps she will try to find him at the bolt-hole?"

"No, she is far too clever for that. Now that she knows that we are on his tracks, she will purposely stay away from the bolt-hole for at least a few days."

"Then what?"

"Fortunately, I noted a receipt on her desk from Lincoln's draper shop, which I know to be situated on Evelyn Street."

"I do not recognize it."

"I have made it my business to be familiar with all of greater London's byways. Evelyn Street is located in Deptford."

"The lascars!" I exclaimed.

"Precisely, Watson," said Holmes, grimly. "There is no good reason for Miss Peele to be shopping in that locale, when there are plenty of closer options. She must have been visiting Sir Ethan in his bolt-hole. We have significantly narrowed the search area."

He turned into a telegraph-office and used their telephone to ring up Inspector Hopkins. Holmes instructed him to send the closest set of constables to canvas Evelyn Street with descriptions of Sir Ethan.

We set out to cross the heart of London. As Deptford was beyond the reach of the Underground, we took a hansom cab to the Westminster Wharf, where Holmes' name was sufficient to procure us a berth upon a green-lamped police-boat. This launch carried us swiftly down the river until it turned up the Deptford Creek and deposited us very near to our destination. It was not long before a constable appeared and Holmes flagged him down.

"Yes, Mr. Holmes. The scrivener's shop down the way said that a man matching Sir Ethan's description has been seen turning into an alleyway off Tidemill Way. I can show you."

Holmes waved for the man to proceed with all haste, and so we followed the constable to the spot. There we found Inspector Hopkins standing with a group of men outside of a seemingly abandoned warehouse.

"You are too late, Mr. Holmes," called Hopkins. "It's Sir Ethan's bolt-hole, that for certain, but I am afraid that he has already fled."

"Let me see," said Holmes.

Hopkins led us up a flight of rough wooden stairs to what had once been the overseer's office. By the sight of the various items lying about, it was plain that this had been converted to a bomb-making factory. However, it was also evident that Sir Ethan spent some more leisurely time here, for one corner had been furnished with a comfortable chair, scattered about which were several books and a cigar case. On a nearby side-table sat a backgammon table, interrupted in the midst of a game, with pieces dispersed about the board."

"Hannibal and his elephants would have caused less damage in this room then your men, Hopkins," said Holmes, acerbically. "I suppose you found nothing of note?"

The man looked chagrined. "No, I am afraid not, Mr. Holmes. There is evidence in the grate that bunches of papers have recently been burnt, but they are too far gone to make out anything. Sir Ethan did a rather thorough job of it."

"Then we will never know where he went!" I cried.

Holmes pursed his lips and tapped his foot irritably. His eyes darted about the room, studying everything within view and cataloguing its role in Sir Ethan's life. "Hold!" said Holmes, suddenly. "The backgammon board. Miss Peele had one too."

"What of it?" I studied the old, battered board. A Latin inscription circled its edge. *"Ita in vita ut in lusu alae pessima jactura arte corrigenda est."* I read.

"How would you translate that, Watson?" he asked.

My schoolboy-Latin was rusty, but thanks to its use in medicine, not completely atrophied. I studied it for a moment. "As in life, so in a game of hazard, skill will make something of the worst of throws."

"Yes, it is something very close to that. A wise motto. So what game is Sir Ethan playing?"

"What do you mean, Holmes?"

"I put to you, Watson, the incongruity of this partially-played game of backgammon. First, the positions of the draughts are most unusual. And more importantly, with whom, pray tell, was Sir Ethan opposing?"

"Anyone, I suppose."

"No. Look about you. There is evidence everywhere of his bomb making. It would have been far too risky to bring someone else into his plan. The lascars were hired help, unaware of the mythological significance of what they were stealing. But where else would Sir Ethan find a man that he could fully trust?"

"So he was playing against himself. I have known men to do

that with chess. Yourself, for instance."

He shook his head. "Nonsense. Chess is a game of pure strategy, not unlike the manoeuvres on a battlefield. Backgammon – while requiring a certain degree of mathematical acumen from its aficionados – relies too much upon the luck of the dice to make for a satisfying game of solitaire."

"What are you suggesting, Holmes?"

"I am suggesting that the board is a code. Sir Ethan has made another critical mistake by leaving it."

"A code? How can that be?"

"I have something of its like before. Have I ever told you the case of Miss Marguerite Marceau?"

"No, I would have recalled that name."

"She was an Alsatian actress living in Paris. She befriended, if you follow me, Mr. Niels Jensen, who was an attaché in the Danish embassy. One day, she asked him whether he knew any authority on chess in his home country. He did not, but he knew of a famous chess club in Copenhagen. When he asked why, Miss Marceau admitted to being an enormous aficionado of the game. She was particularly interested in puzzling out the strategy of various attacks. She was stuck on a problem, and was unable to locate anyone in Paris willing to help her solve it. Mr. Jensen kindly offered to forward the problem to the club via his embassy mail. She gratefully sketched out a chessboard and then asked what opening had been used in order to leave the various pieces on the board in the indicated positions?

"Fortunately, the French Government had gotten into the habit – rather illegal, but who can blame them under the circumstances? – of intercepting and reading the mail of the various neutral embassies. Having gotten hold of the letter, they brought it to me and began to keep a tab on Miss Marceau, of whom they now had some reasonable degree of suspicion. They soon discovered that on the day before the sketch was made Miss Marceau had kindly visited one of the field hospitals. This happened to hold a German aviator who had been shot down behind the French lines, and who would have been kept in a prisoner-of-war camp if not for his fractured legs.

"It was plain to me what had transpired. You see, Watson, the German military is nothing if not incredibly precise. When they were marching through in 1870, they carefully surveyed and mapped out the entire eastern portion of France. In so doing, they laid out the country in squares. Fortunately, the French Government had managed to obtain a copy of the German survey. When I suggested that they lay the sketch of the eight-by-eight chessboard over the military survey, all became clear. For the two corresponded precisely.

"By taking into consideration the known character of the armed forces occupying these sections behind the French lines, I was able to determine what each chess piece stood for. Pawns represented infantry; rooks were field artillery; bishops were heavy artillery; the queen was an air division; and the king was military headquarters. So, Watson, the sketch of the chess problem was, in fact, a map showing the exact position of the whole French reserve forces massed behind the lines, as seen from the air by the captured German aviator."

"And you think this is the same sort of thing?"

"I am certain of it."

"But why would he leave a code?"

"We know that Sir Ethan did not destroy the London Stone. Therefore, he must be planning to take it to Germany. There are very few places in England, Watson, where a man can find a boat willing to take him to a neutral country, such as the Netherlands or Denmark. Hillcroft must have been informed regarding the location of a man willing sell his loyalty for price, likely in one of the historic smuggling villages of the southern coast. However, he was unwilling to trust the entirety of his plan to Miss Peele ahead of time, for who truly understands the heart of a woman? Nevertheless, he likely told her that he would leave behind directions for her to follow, should she so desire. And there are those directions."

THE GATHERING GLOOM

"How so?"

"Note the twenty four triangles at which the draughts can be based. That, plus the two home positions, gives us an interesting number, does it not, Watson?"

"The number of letters in the alphabet!" I exclaimed.

"Precisely. If we were to write a letter above each spot, as so, it would look something like this," said he, hurriedly sketching out what he meant upon a piece of paper, which I reproduce here:

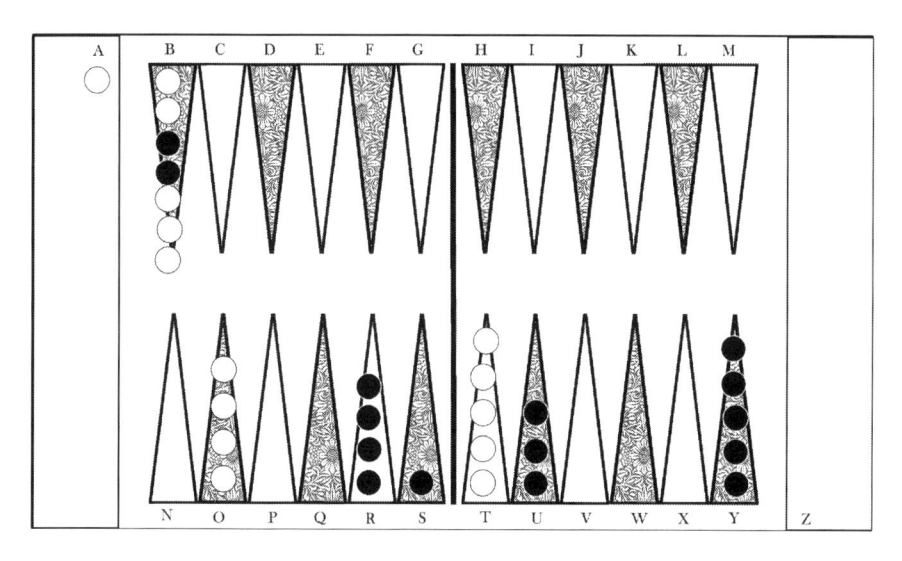

"We have ten groupings; therefore, I suspect that we are dealing with a word of ten letters. The red draughts are grouped from one to five, and the same for the black. If red represents the first five letters and black the second, we would take an 'A' for the one red draught. Next would be 'B' twice, for both the two red draughts and three red draughts are on that triangle. Next would come 'O' at the position of the four red draughts, and so on until we have spelled out: 'A – B – B – O – T – S – B – U – R – Y.' I believe that is an old fishing village in Dorset. Not as prominent a smuggling spot as Purbeck or Fleet, and therefore not as closely monitored, it would be a wise choice by Sir Ethan's German masters."

"What an ingenious code," said I, somewhat admiringly.

"You could leave it out for anyone to see and no one would ever know that it was anything other than an innocent game."

"Yes, however, it is also one rather susceptible to accidents," said Holmes, his smile somewhat unkindly. "I imagine from our conversation with Miss Peele today that she will be rather upset to learn that Sir Ethan never intended to leave her a message. Who knows how that might loosen her tongue and induce her to tell us of his other activities?"

I frowned. "What do you mean, Holmes? The message is right here," said I, motioning to the board.

Instead of answering, he reached out and slammed the board closed. I heard the draughts rattling about inside and knew that the message was lost forever. "Is it?"

§

After that, it was a relatively simple matter. Holmes relayed to Inspector Hopkins his theory as to the location from which Sir Ethan was attempting to flee England's shores. Within minutes, a flurry of instructions were passing along the wires to the Royal Navy base at Portland Harbour.

I later learned that a series of cruisers were quickly sent out and intercepted a fishing boat belonging to a local drunkard and ne'er-do-well named John Dockery, who was later hung under the Defence of the Realm Act for his intent to assist the enemy in exchange for money. A German U-boat had been spotted in the area earlier in the day, and it was determined that Dockery's boat was attempting to rendezvous with this, rather than carry its precious cargo all of the way to the continent.

Of Sir Ethan himself, there was no sign. However, after some rather aggressive questioning, Dockery eventually admitted that Hillcroft had thrown himself overboard once it became clear that the HMS *Adventure* was going to reach Dockery's boat before it could close with the U-boat. His body was never located, and for the sake of public morale, it was quietly put about that Sir Ethan had tragically perished in the successful act of preventing a German spy from escaping. This report was not entirely inaccurate, I suppose. As for the London Stone, it was found carefully packed in a crate sitting in the cabin of Dockery's boat, awaiting its transportation to Berlin. The captain of the *Adventure* made certain that it was quietly returned to agents under the command of Mycroft Holmes, who saw to its safekeeping for the remainder of the war.

Unfortunately, none of these actions prevented the German air raids from coming. Not three mornings later, I read that the famous American lyricist Elizabeth Graves Horne and her son Daniel had been killed by a bomb that had fallen on St. John's Wood, not a mile north of our former flat in Baker Street. No more would we be treated to her comforting words.'[194]

As much as it pained me to admit, I thought the only possible response to these aerial murders of our civilians was to deal the same back upon the Germans. If a small avenging squadron of swift British aeroplanes were stationed in Eastern France, and if it were announced by the Government that every raid upon a town in Great Britain would automatically and remorselessly cause three similar raids on German towns, I thought it probable that we should soon bring them to reason. Of course, it is undeniable that our airmen would find such work repugnant. However, innocent women and children have been, for a long time, sacrificed in England, and we have shown all forbearance. Therefore, I could think of no other methods but those of harsh reprisal, which would offer a modicum of assurance that we could hope to save our civilians from these murderous outrages of the German military.[195] With these thoughts, I paused for a moment to consider the fact that at times, it seemed as this war had stripped away all of the centuries of civilization until we were back in the age of Hammurabi.[196]

It was with such grim and uncharitable notions in my brain that I went to work at Barts. The day passed as any other, as I engaged in my humble task of healing the sick. Once the darkness descended upon the city, I began to make my way back home along the crowded Strand, intending to do some shopping. As I had not seen Holmes for the greater part of a week, it was with some surprise when he suddenly appeared by my side.

"Holmes!" I exclaimed. "What a coincidence!"

He shook his head. "It is no coincidence, Watson. I knew that your post-work habits often take you along this route."

"Do we have another case?"

"Not as of yet, Watson. Though, who knows what the future may hold? No, I merely wished to let you know that I might be away for some time. I have something I need to accomplish upon the continent which is best done alone, for you will admit that your skills with disguises are rather limited."[197]

"Is there nothing I can do?"

"No, my dear fellow. You should continue your work here, knowing that it too is a vital contribution to the war effort. Please give my greetings to Mrs. Watson, will you?"

From the way Holmes spoke these words, I feared that he was setting forth on a journey from which he thought he might not ever return. I was suddenly reminded of his terrible letter at Reichenbach. I could only hope that, as then, he would again reappear after facing terrible odds. I swallowed heavily and cleared my throat. "Well then, in regards to the London Stone case, I believe that congratulations are in order, Holmes. You have foiled a terrible plot."

We had reached the end of the Strand, and Holmes stopped at the great square in the centre of London and shook his head gravely.

"This was only the narrowest of victories, Watson," said he, standing in the shadow of Admiral Nelson. "We have been humbled, both here and in the fields of Flanders. I fear that the sun is finally beginning to set on our Empire. But the German High Command has made a terrible mistake; one which I predict will eventually spell their doom."

"What is that, Holmes?"

"They have forgotten their own myths. They have forgotten that Charlemagne waits inside the Untersberg near Salzburg for the last great battle. And that Frederick Barbarossa sleeps under the Kyffhäuser hills, ready for the ravens to circle its summit and signal their country's hour of greatest need.[198] However, our American cousins, so fresh and full of vigour, have no such legends. They have only Mr. Van Winkle, the faithful subject of King George III, who awoke one day long after the Revolution, wondering why they had ever separated from us."[199]

"But the Americans have not come yet!" I cried.

Holmes shook his head. "Every man is the best judge of his own honour, and so is every nation. I appreciate how complex and difficult is the American situation. But rest assured, Watson, I predict that they will eventually act in such a way that they can justify their position to succeeding generations of Americans. It is inevitable that they shall soon reunite with us, in spirit if not in law. Yes, the folly of a monarch and the blundering of a minister in far-gone years have prevented our peoples from being citizens of the same world-wide country, under a flag which might have been a quartering of the Union Jack with the Stars and Stripes. Nevertheless, England and America are eternally linked. They shall soon wake from their slumber, outraged if not by the death of Miss Horne or the sinking of the RMS *Lusitania*, then by some other German atrocity.[200] And when they do, I promise you now, Watson, the Huns will break, and our trumpets will sound their final flourish."

§

After I returned home to the tender embrace of my wife, I considered Holmes' words. With his eminently rational mind, he would have scoffed at the idea that had sprung into my mind. For I thought about Arthur – asleep under Sewingshields – and Drake – waiting for the sound of his Drum –

and realized that England had another guardian, ever ready to rise to her defence from his final refuge on the South Downs. And his name is Sherlock Holmes.

§

APPENDIX: ON DATES

A CHRONOLOGIC ORDER OF SHERLOCK HOLMES ADVENTURES (CANONICAL & NON-CANONICAL)

How best to read the various tales of Sherlock Holmes? The most obvious answer to that question is "the order in which they were written and published, beginning with A Study in Scarlet." However, Sir Arthur Conan Doyle, the first literary agent for Dr John H. Watson, did not publish the stories in a strict chronologic order, with many stories told primarily as flashbacks. Therefore, for the reader, either new to these wondrous tales or seeking to read them all again, I present the following option. By following this list, the reader is able to see for themselves the maturation of Holmes and Watson, from relatively young lads with all of London at their fingertips, to the mature gentlemen reflecting upon a lifetime of adventure.

I generally follow the dating laid out by the great Sherlockian editors William S. Baring-Gould in *The Annotated Sherlock Holmes* (1967) and Leslie S. Klinger in *The New Annotated Sherlock Holmes* (2005-6), which are themselves the product of consensus of other Sherlockians. These have often followed the vaguest of clues in the stories themselves in order to come to their conclusions. Dr Watson, for all his excellent qualities, was never his best with dates (he was known, from time to time, to even be off by a year or more). For point of reference, it is generally considered that Sherlock Holmes was born in 1854 (6 January, to be precise) and John Watson in 1852 (7 August, to be precise), making them at the time of their meeting in January 1881, approximately twenty-seven and twenty-nine years of age, respectively.

At the risk of being accused of vanity, into the list this literary agent interjects the timing for those stories (in bold) that I have been so fortunate as to unearth and publish.

Before 221B Baker Street (1874 – 1880)
- July 12 – September 22, 1874: The *'Gloria Scott'* (from *TMSH*). Recounted to Watson c. February 1888.
- April 4–22, 1875: **The Lost Legion** (from *TTI!*). Recounted to Watson c. December 1894.
- December 28 – January 7, 1875-76: **The Father of Evil** (from *TSS*). Recounted to Watson January 6, 1903.
- October 2, 1879: The Musgrave Ritual (from *TMSH*). Recounted to Watson c. February 1888.
- July 27 – December 4, 1880: **The Isle of Devils**

A Suite in Baker Street (1881 – 1889)
- March 4–7, 1881: A Study in Scarlet
- August 25, 1881: **The Adventure of the Tragic Act** (from *SAO*)
- December 3, 1881: **The Adventure of the Double-Edged Hoard** (from *FMFL*)
- April 6, 1883: The Adventure of the Speckled Band (from *TASH*)
- May 5-12, 1883: **The Adventure of the Monstrous Blood** (from *TFC*)
- August 23 – September 10, 1884: **The Gate of Gold**
- October 6–7, 1885: The Resident Patient (from *TMSH*)

- November 3-4, 1885: **The Adventure of the Mad Colonel** (from *TFC*)
- October 8, 1886: The Adventure of the Noble Bachelor (from *TASH*)

The Well-Remembered Door (The First Desertion) (1886 – 1888)[201]
- April 14–26, 1887: The Reigate Squires (from *TMSH*)
- May 20–22, 1887: A Scandal in Bohemia (from *TASH*)
- June 2–4, 1887: **The Adventure of the Dawn Discovery** (from *FMFL*)
- June 18–19, 1887: The Man with the Twisted Lip (from *TASH*)
- June 19-21, 1887: **The Adventure of the Missing Mana** (from *APRT*)
- September 29–30, 1887: The Five Orange Pips (from *TASH*)
- October 18–19, 1887: A Case of Identity (from *TASH*)
- October 21–22, 1887: **The Adventure of the Queen's Pendant** (from *TTI!*)
- October 29–30, 1887: The Red-Headed League (from *TASH*)
- November 19, 1887: The Adventure of the Dying Detective (from *HLB*)
- December 27, 1887: The Adventure of the Blue Carbuncle (from *TASH*)

The Return to Baker Street (1888 – 1889)
- January 7–8, 1888: The Valley of Fear
- April 7, 1888: The Yellow Face (from *TMSH*)
- April 14–15, 1888: **The Red Leech** (from *Assassination*)
- August 30-31, 1888: **The Adventure of the Loring Riddle**
- September 12, 1888: The Greek Interpreter (from *TMSH*)
- September 18–21, 1888: The Sign of Four

- September 25 – October 20, 1888: The Hound of the Baskervilles
- March 24, 1889: **The Adventure of the Pirate's Code** (from *TTI!*)
- April 5–20, 1889: The Adventure of the Copper Beeches (from *TASH*)

The Second Desertion (1889 – 1891)[202]
- June 15, 1889: The Stockbroker's Clerk (from *TMSH*)
- July 30 – August 1, 1889: The Naval Treaty (from *TMSH*)
- August 31 – September 2, 1889: The Cardboard Box (from *TMSH*)
- September 7–8, 1889: The Adventure of the Engineer's Thumb (from *TASH*)
- September 11–12, 1889: The Crooked Man (from *TMSH*)
- September 21–22, 1889: **The Adventure of the Fateful Malady** (from *TFC*)
- March 24–29, 1890: The Adventure of Wisteria Lodge (from *HLB*)
- June 8–9, 1890: The Boscombe Valley Mystery (from *TASH*)
- June 20 – July 4, 1890: **The Oak-Leaf Sprig** (from *ARW*)
- September 25–30, 1890: Silver Blaze (from *TMSH*)
- December 19–20, 1890: The Adventure of the Beryl Coronet (from *TASH*)
- December 25, 1890: **The Adventure of the Spanish Sovereign** (from *TSF*)
- April 24 – May 4, 1891: The Final Problem (from *TMSH*)

The Great Hiatus (1891 – 1894)
- August 1-8: 1891: **The Harrowing Intermission** (from *FMFL*)

The Great Return (1894 – 1902)
- April 5, 1894: The Adventure of the Empty House (from

TRSH)
- October 7-9, 1894: **The Adventure of the Boulevard Assassin** (from *APRT*)
- October 20 – November 7, 1894: **The Adventure of the Double Detectives** (from *RTW*)
- November 14–15, 1894: The Adventure of the Golden Pince-Nez (from *TRSH*)
- September 18–22: 1894: The Adventure of the Second Stain (from *TRSH*)[203]
- September 22–25, 1894: **The Adventure of the Third Traitor** (from *AEW*)
- December 23, 1894: **The Adventure of the Manufactured Miracle** (from *TSF*)
- January 13-14, 1895: **The Adventure of the Dishonourable Discharge** (from *TSS*)
- February 13-15, 1895: **The Adventure of the Secret Tomb** (from *APRT*)
- April 5–6, 1895: The Adventure of the Three Students (from *TRSH*)
- April 13–20, 1895: The Adventure of the Solitary Cyclist (from *TRSH*)
- June 23-25, 1895: **The Problem of the Black Eye** (from *SAO*)
- July 3–5, 1895: The Adventure of Black Peter (from *TRSH*)
- August 20–21, 1895: The Adventure of the Norwood Builder (from *TRSH*)
- November 21–23, 1895: The Adventure of the Bruce-Partington Plans (from *HLB*)
- December 22, 1895: **The Adventure of the First Star** (from *TSF*)
- October 28, 1896: The Adventure of the Veiled Lodger (from *TCBSH*)
- November 19–21, 1896: The Adventure of the Sussex Vampire (from *TCBSH*)
- December 8–10, 1896: The Adventure of the Missing

- Three-Quarter (from *TRSH*)
- January 23, 1897: The Adventure of the Abbey Grange (from *TRSH*)
- March 16–20, 1897: The Adventure of the Devil's Foot (from *HLB*)
- May 2–3, 1897: **The Adventure of the Fatal Fire** (from *TSS*)
- July 7, 1897: **The Adventure of the Sunken Indiaman** (from *FMFL*)
- September 4-5, 1897: **The Mannering Towers Mystery** (from *SAO*)
- July 27 – August 13, 1898: The Adventure of the Dancing Men (from *TRSH*)
- July 28–30, 1898: The Adventure of the Retired Colourman (from *TCBSH*)
- January 5–14, 1899: The Adventure of Charles Augustus Milverton (from *TRSH*)
- February 2, 1899: **The Adventure of the African Horror** (from *RTW*)
- June 8–10, 1900: The Adventure of the Six Napoleons (from *TRSH*)
- October 4–5, 1900: The Problem of Thor Bridge (from *TCBSH*)
- November 4, 1900: **The Adventure of the Awakened Spirit** (from *TSS*)
- May 16–18, 1901: The Adventure of the Priory School (from *TRSH*)
- June 20-23, 1901: **The Adventure of the Fair Lad** (from *RTW*)
- May 6–7, 1902: The Adventure of Shoscombe Old Place (from *TCBSH*)
- June 26–27, 1902: The Adventure of the Three Garridebs (from *TCBSH*)
- July 1–18, 1902: The Disappearance of Lady Frances Carfax (from *HLB*)
- September 3–16, 1902: The Adventure of the Illustri-

ous Client (from *TCBSH*)
- September 24–25, 1902: The Adventure of the Red Circle (from *HLB*)

The Final Desertion (1903)[204]
- January 7–12, 1903: The Adventure of the Blanched Soldier (from *TCBSH*)
- May 26–27, 1903: The Adventure of the Three Gables (from *TCBSH*)
- June 28, 1903: The Adventure of the Mazarin Stone (from *TCBSH*)
- August 2, 1903: **The Adventure of the Silent Drum** (from *TTI!*)
- September 6–22, 1903: The Adventure of the Creeping Man (from *TCBSH*)
- December 20-21, 1903: **The Adventure of the Barren Grave** (from *TFC*)

Retirement (1904 – 1918)
- January 6-18, 1904: **The Adventure of the Dead Man's Note** (from *APRT*)
- July 3–5, 1907: **The Cold Dish** (from *TSS*)
- September 2, 1907: **The Adventure of the Twelfth Hour** (from *SAO*)
- July 25 – August 1, 1907: The Lion's Mane (from *TCBSH*)
- June 21, 1909: **The Adventure of the Unfathomable Silence** (from *AEW*)
- October 31 – November 1, 1909: **The Adventure of the Pharaoh's Curse** (from *Assassination*)
- November 2–5, 1909: **The Problem of Threadneedle Street** (from *Assassination*)
- November 30 – December 1, 1909: **The Falling Curtain** (from *Assassination*)
- August 2, 1914: **The High Mountain** (from *AEW*)
- August 2, 1914: His Last Bow: The War Service of Sherlock Holmes (from *HLB*)

- March 19-22, 1915: **The Adventure of the Defenceless Prisoner** (from *AEW*)
- September 17, 1915: **Their Final Flourish** (from *AEW*)
- October 22, 1917: Preface (from *HLB*)
- December 22, 1918: **The Grand Gift of Sherlock** (from *TSF*)

THE COLLECTIONS

Literary Editor, Sir Arthur Conan Doyle (56 cases & 4 novels)
- *TASH: The Adventures of Sherlock Holmes* (12 cases; published 1891-92)
- *TMSH: The Memoirs of Sherlock Holmes* (12 cases; published 1892-93)
- *TRSH: The Return of Sherlock Holmes* (13 cases; published 1903-4)
- *HLB: His Last Bow: Some Reminiscences of Sherlock Holmes* (7 cases & 1 preface; published 1917)
- *TCBSH: The Case-Book of Sherlock Holmes* (12 cases; published 1921-27)

Literary Editor, Craig Janacek (45 cases & 2 novels)
- *The Assassination of Sherlock Holmes* (4 cases; published 2015)
- *Light in the Darkness*, comprising:
  - *TSF: The Season of Forgiveness* (3 cases & 1 letter; published 2014)
  - *TFC: The First of Criminals* (4 cases; published 2015-16)
- *The Treasury of Sherlock Holmes*, comprising:
  - *TTI!: Treasure Trove Indeed!* (4 cases; published 2016)
  - *FMFL: Fortunes Made and Fortunes Lost* (4 cases; published 2018)
- *The Gathering Gloom*, comprising:
  - *TSS: The Schoolroom of Sorrow* (5 cases; published

2018)
  - *AEW: An East Wind* (5 cases; published 2019)
- *The Travels of Sherlock Holmes*, comprising:
  - *APRT: A Prompt and Ready Traveller* (4 cases; published 2019)
  - *RTW: Round the World* (4 cases; published 2020)
- *The Chronicles of Sherlock Holmes*, comprising:
  - *SAO: Seen and Observed* (4 cases; published 2020)
  - *TDC: Their Dark Crisis* (4 cases; published 2021)

§

ALSO BY CRAIG JANACEK

THE DOCTOR WATSON TRILOGY
THE ISLE OF DEVILS
THE GATE OF GOLD
THE RUINS OF SUMMER*

THE MIDWINTER MYSTERIES OF SHERLOCK HOLMES)[205]
(alternatively known as THE SEASON OF FORGIVENESS)
THE ADVENTURE OF THE MANUFACTURED MIRACLE
THE ADVENTURE OF THE FIRST STAR
THE ADVENTURE OF THE SPANISH SOVEREIGN
THE GRAND GIFT OF SHERLOCK

THE FIRST OF CRIMINALS[206]
THE ADVENTURE OF THE MONSTROUS BLOOD
THE ADVENTURE OF THE MAD COLONEL
THE ADVENTURE OF THE BARREN GRAVE
THE ADVENTURE OF THE FATEFUL MALADY[207]

TREASURE TROVE INDEED![208]
THE LOST LEGION
THE ADVENTURE OF THE PIRATE'S CODE
THE ADVENTURE OF THE QUEEN'S PENDANT
THE ADVENTURE OF THE SILENT DRUM

FORTUNES MADE & FORTUNES LOST[209]
THE ADVENTURE OF THE DOUBLE-EDGED HOARD[210]

THE ADVENTURE OF THE DAWN DISCOVERY
THE HARROWING INTERMISSION[211]
THE ADVENTURE OF THE SUNKEN INDIAMAN[212]

THE SCHOOLROOM OF SORROW[213]
THE FATHER OF EVIL
THE ADVENTURE OF THE FATAL FIRE
THE ADVENTURE OF THE DISHONOURABLE DISCHARGE[214]
THE ADVENTURE OF THE AWAKENED SPIRIT[215]
THE COLD DISH

AN EAST WIND[216]
THE ADVENTURE OF THE THIRD TRAITOR[217]
THE ADVENTURE OF THE UNFATHOMABLE SILENCE[218]
THE HIGH MOUNTAIN
THE ADVENTURE OF THE DEFENCELESS PRISONER
THEIR FINAL FLOURISH

A PROMPT AND READY TRAVELLER[219]
THE ADVENTURE OF THE MISSING MANA
THE ADVENTURE OF THE BOULEVARD ASSASSIN
THE ADVENTURE OF THE SECRET TOMB
THE ADVENTURE OF THE DEAD MAN'S NOTE

ROUND THE WORLD[220]
THE OAK-LEAF SPRIG
THE ADVENTURE OF THE DOUBLE DETECTIVES
THE ADVENTURE OF THE AFRICAN HORROR
THE ADVENTURE OF THE FAIR LAD[221]

SEEN & OBSERVED
THE ADVENTURE OF THE TRAGIC ACT
THE PROBLEM OF THE BLACK EYE
THE MANNERING TOWERS MYSTERY
THE ADVENTURE OF THE TWELFTH HOUR

THE ASSASSINATION OF SHERLOCK HOLMES

THE ADVENTURE OF THE PHARAOH'S CURSE
THE PROBLEM OF THREADNEEDLE STREET
THE FALLING CURTAIN
(THE RED LEECH)

OTHER STORIES OF MR. SHERLOCK HOLMES
THE ADVENTURE OF THE LORING RIDDLE[222]

SET EUROPE SHAKING: Volume One of 'The Exploits and Adventures of Brigadier Gerard'
(Compiled and Edited by Craig Janacek, with Three New Tales)
HOW THE BRIGADIER WRESTLED THE BEAR OF BOULOGNE
HOW THE BRIGADIER FACED THE FIRING SQUAD
HOW THE BRIGADIER DUELLED FOR A DESPATCH

A MIGHTY SHADOW: Volume Two of 'The Exploits and Adventures of Brigadier Gerard'
(Compiled and Edited by Craig Janacek, with One New Tale)
HOW THE BRIGADIER COMMANDED THE EMPEROR

OTHER NOVELS
THE OXFORD DECEPTION
THE ANGER OF ACHILLES PETERSON

*Coming soon

§

FOOTNOTES

---

[1] Before 1888, Holmes had made a study of the Buddhism of Ceylon (*The Sign of Four*, Chapter X) and in c.1891-4 travelled to Lhasa, Tibet to study with the lead Llama himself.

[2] Browner's case (*The Adventure of the Cardboard Box*) was removed from *The Memoirs* due to its controversial subject matter. While it appeared in *The Strand* in 1893, it was not republished in book form until 1917, when it was included in *His Last Bow*. Watson withheld the facts of Dr Purcell until his speech at the University of London Medical School in 1904 (eventually published in 2015 as *The Adventure of the Fateful Malady*). Amberley's case was not published until 1926. These clues, as well as later evidence, suggest that Watson penned this tale sometime between 1902 and 1904.

[3] In the Canonical adventures, Holmes quotes twice from Shakespeare's *Twelfth Night, or As You Will*, suggesting that is birthday may have fallen on 6 January.

[4] Millbank was closed in 1890, and the Gallery opened in 1897. Renamed the Tate Gallery in 1932, since 2000 it has been known as Tate Britain.

[5] This appears to be a reference to *The Vale of Rest* (1859) by John Everett Millais, presented to what is now the Tate in 1894. The painter gave it the subtitle 'Where the weary find repose,' which sounds peaceful enough, though the subject matter is ripe with deep and dark allegory.

[6] The case of Phineas Gage occurred in 1848 in Cavendish, Vermont. It is believed that damage to his frontal lobe was responsible for his change in personality.

[7] The repulsive case of Mrs. Kirby was eventually published as *The Red Leech* (2015).

[8] Aphorism 146 of *Beyond Good and Evil* (1886).

[9] I am unable to trace a religious order by this name, and it is suspected that Watson changed it to avoid any charges of libel.

[10] The *Historia Ecclesie Cippus* ('History of the Landmarke Church') appears to have been a medieval chronicle, but it no longer in the possession of the Bodleian, making this the only surviving mention of its existence.

[11] Stonyhurst is notable for being the school attended by Sir Arthur Conan Doyle, Watson's first literary agent, from 1868-75. There is no Landmark Priory in Oxfordshire, though elements of its history appear similar to that of Abingdon Abbey.

[12] Written in 1854 by Alfred Charles Hobbs (1812-1891).

[13] The philosopher and cosmological theorist Giordano Bruno (1548-1600) was tried in a kangaroo court by the Jesuit Cardinal Bellarmine and sentenced to burning at the stake in the Campo de' Fiori for the so-called crime of challenging the Church's teachings.

[14] It is not clear who this man is. There were no formal relations between England and the Vatican from 1801 to 1914, as England feared excessive German and Austrian influences over Vatican policies.

[15] Pius IX died in 1878, and he was replaced by Leo XIII, who lived until 1903.

[16] Holmes is referring to the Explosives Act of 1875, which was set out the laws pertaining to 'manufacturing, keeping, selling, carrying, and importing Gunpowder, Nitro-glycerine, and other Explosive Substances.'

[17] It seems likely that the monograph referred to was *On Explosive Agents*, written in 1872 by Sir Frederick Augustus Abel.

[18] Sadly, Holmes' wish went unheeded. Mass graves of children have been found in other orphanages, such as Smyllum Park in Lanark, Scotland (discovered in 2017), and Tuam in County Galway, Ireland (discovered in 2014).

[19] A reference to a thought by Henry James, written into one of his *Notebooks* in 1869, though not published until 1947. Where Watson and Holmes would have heard it is unclear.

[20] Thomas Campion (1567-1620) was an Elizabethan composer. Holmes' *Variations* have sadly never been recovered.

[21] There is no 'Gleannlaithe Castle' near Loch Arkaig. The name ap-

pears to be a contraction of the Scottish Gaelic words for Valley and Fowl.

[22] Presumably a reference to William III of Orange, who along with his wife, Mary, usurped the throne of England from James II in 1688 during the so-called Glorious Revolution. He was not popular amongst the Scottish.

[23] There is no such regiment listed in the British Army.

[24] *Elephantiasis tropica*, now known as lymphatic filariasis, is caused by parasitic worms spread by the bites of infected mosquitos. In the era before the development of anti-parasitics it could be a very debilitating affliction.

[25] A reference to the Medical School at Teviot Place, part of the University of Edinburgh, from where Watson's first literary editor, Sir Arthur Conan Doyle, obtained his MD in 1885.

[26] An Antimony pill is made from the metal antimony. It was designed to be swallowed, passed through the intestines, and then recovered for reuse, thereby giving rise to the name of the 'everlasting pill.' It was thought to have purgative effects, as well as having some anti-protozoal effects on infections such as leishmaniasis. Unfortunately, filarial worms are not protozoa. Such were the perils of 19th century medicine!

[27] Bacterial meningitis has a terrifyingly high mortality rate in the pre-antibiotic era, and for those fortunate few who did recover, hearing loss, cognitive impairment, and epilepsy were common sequelae.

[28] Sheridan Le Fanu (1814-1873) was an Irish writer of Gothic tales, including the story 'Green Tea,' from the collection *In a Glass Darkly* (1872), wherein such visions were recounted.

[29] In 1839, Dr George Sigmond published a lecture regarding the 'Effects, Medicinal and Moral' of green tea. This describes the risk of becoming 'hysterical' after drinking green tea on an empty stomach, with possible 'fluttering of the heart.'

[30] As described in the non-Canonical tale *The Adventure of the Fateful Malady*.

[31] Treasure Trove laws in Scotland are clear that: '*bona vacantia quod nullius est fit domini regis*' ('vacant goods [objects which are lost, forgotten, or abandoned] that which belongs to nobody becomes our Lord the Queen's').

[32] Lestrade must have seen that the treasure was recovered with

great secrecy, for it officially remains unfound to this day.

[33] For reasons which remain obscure, Watson failed to have this adventure forwarded to *The Strand*. Instead, from June to December 1897, that august journal ran an edited version entitled '*The Tragedy of the Korosko.*' This was attributed to Watson's first literary editor, Sir Arthur Conan Doyle who later adapted this version into a play which he called '*Fires of Fate*' (first performed at the Lyric Theatre on 15 June 1909).

[34] The pejorative term 'Dervishes' was generically used during the Victorian era to denote Islamic forces opposed to the colonial powers. In this particular case, it was the Mahdist State which ruled the Sudan from 1885 to 1899. The Madhi was the term for Muhammed Ahmad bin Abd Allah (1844-1885), a messianic religious leader, who died of typhus. His bones were later thrown into the Nile by General Kitchener.

[35] The pulpit rock of Abousir (also spelled Abusir) is a sloped outcropping in Upper Nubia near the Second Cataract.

[36] The Khalifa, Abdullah Ibn-Mohammed (c.1846-1899) was the Madhi's successor. He was killed by forces under Sir Reginald Wingate while hiding after his defeat at the Battle of Omdurman.

[37] Now commonly spelled 'Aswan.'

[38] Shellal is a small village south of Aswan that was the site of an important granite quarry. The First Cataract was located at Aswan, but was eventually replaced by the Aswan Low Dam (constructed 1899-1902). Aswan's famed Cataract Hotel did not open until 1899.

[39] There is no longer a town of this name, though it may be an Anglicized name for Al Balyana, which lies downstream of Dendera.

[40] This passenger card closely matches that reported in *The Tragedy of the Korosko*, with one exception. In that novel, Colonel Egerton is called Colonel Cochrane Cochrane. The reason for this name alteration is not fully clear.

[41] Wimbledon Common was the headquarters of the British Rifle Association. It held a competition every July. In 1890, the National Shooting Centre was moved to Bisley, a village in Surrey, where it remains to this day.

[42] The Radicals were a loose parliamentary grouping which was in favour of universal suffrage, lower taxes, and the abolition of sinecures. It was dissolved in 1859 and merged into the Liberal Party.

[43] Walter Pater (1839-1894) was an English essayist and art critic. His most famous work was *Studies in the History of the Renaissance* (1873). The conclusion of this work would have much appealed to Holmes, as it discusses how our perceptions, feelings, thoughts, and memories are always in flux, such that, to get the most from life we must learn to discriminate through 'sharp and eager observation.'

[44] Korosko was a modern settlement which served as a departure point for caravans heading to Abu Hamad in the Soudan. It was flooded after the construction of the Aswan High Dam.

[45] Wady Halfa (also spelled Wadi Halfa) is a modern town built as a port for troops headed south into the Soudan.

[46] Now spelled Thutmose III.

[47] Herodotus (c.484-425 BCE) was a Greek historian. Giovanni Battista Belzoni (1778-1823) was a pioneer archaeologist (read 'tomb raider'). Charles George Gordon (1833-1885) was a British general who had recently been killed by the Madhi at Khartoum.

[48] Trachoma is a bacterial infection which, to this day, spreads in crowded areas of poor sanitation. The purulent discharge attracts flies, which then further spread the disease. Left untreated, it results in blindness.

[49] A *khor* is a Middle Eastern watercourse or ravine, usually dry except during the wet season.

[50] These are excerpts from Canto 55 of 'In Memoriam A.H.H,' in which the great poet rages against the cruelty of nature and mortality upon the death of his friend Arthur Hallam.

[51] Colonel William Hicks (1830-1883) was a retired British Army officer who entered the service of the Khedive. His men first defeated a force of Dervishes at Sennar, but the Egyptian ministry greatly underestimated the strength of the Madhi and his troops were later obliterated. He was to be revenged by General Gordon, who instead also fell to the Madhi at the Siege of Khartoum in 1885. They were both eventually avenged by Earl Kitchener at the Battle of Omdurman in 1898, where the army of the Khalifa was finally destroyed.

[52] Bimbashi is a term derived from the Ottoman army, which signified the rank of Major in the Khedival Egyptian army. The identity of Bimbashi Mortimer has been lost to history.

[53] The Khedive is an Ottoman word roughly equivalent to 'viceroy' and indicated the ruler of Egypt and the Sudan. The first to take

the title was Muhammad Ali Pasha (1769-1849), and his great-great-grandson Abbas II held the title from 1892-1914.

[54] Egyptian for 'There is no more; I have nothing.'

[55] Evelyn Baring, 1st Earl of Cromer, was the Consul-General of Egypt during the British occupation prompted by the 'Urabi revolt.

[56] The Embassy of the United Kingdom in Paris is the Hôtel de Charost at 39 Rue de Faubourg Saint-Honoré. The building was purchased in 1814 by the Duke of Wellington from Pauline Borghese, sister to Napoleon.

[57] Shawish is a term derived from the Ottoman army, which signified the rank of Sergeant in the Khedival Egyptian army. The Sirdar was General Lord Kitchener.

[58] This is a matter of considerable debate. Much damage to the Library has already been caused by a fire set by troops of Julius Caesar (48 BCE), fighting between Queen Zenobia and Emperor Aurelian (c.274 CE), and especially by the orders of Theophilus, Bishop of Alexandria (391 CE). The Muslim conquest of Egypt did not occur until 642 CE, though they undoubtedly finished the job.

[59] Tel El Kebir was an 1882 British victory against the Egyptian Army led by Colonel Ahmad Ourabi (1841-1911). It consolidated British power in Egypt.

[60] These battles took place in 1896, on June 7 and September 23, respectively.

[61] There is no Barclay Square in London, though Admiral Sinclair is also said to have a home at that locale (*The Adventure of the Bruce-Partington Plans*).

[62] All Soul's Day is celebrated on 2 November.

[63] Unfortunately, Watson neglected to write up any cases which included a Gascon lieutenant, someone dying at the Great Geysir of Iceland (upon land owned by Lord Craigavon), a Ghazi's scimitar-like weapon, or a cipher belonging to one of the rival factions in the politics of medieval Italy.

[64] The Cock Lane ghost was mentioned in both *Nicholas Nickleby* (1839) and *A Tale of Two Cities* (1859).

[65] The Fox Sisters were American girls who began to report ghostly rappings in 1848, when they were twelve and fifteen years of age. They eventually became spiritualist mediums, eventually confessing

to faking everything in 1888.

[66] The Davenport Brothers were American magicians who claimed to possess a cabinet filled with musical instruments which were played by spirits of the dead. They were debunked in the 1860's while touring in England. The ghost of Lady Dorothy Walpole (1686-1726) has been reported by many individuals to wander the halls of Raynham Hall since as early 1835.

[67] The South Sea Bubble (1720) was one of the earliest stock market crashes, and the Railway Mania (1846) was another collapse which occurred closer to the Victoria era. Various witch trials, such as the one in Salem (1692) resulted in the deaths of some forty-thousand women over a period of three centuries; the last 'witch' in Scotland was executed in 1727.

[68] Clearly a reference to his 1866 short story, *The Signal-Man*, about a railway monitor who is haunted by a phantom warning him of impending disasters.

[69] Montague Rhodes James (1862-1936) was an English author, most famous for his ghost stories. The first collection, *Ghost Stories of an Antiquary*, was published in 1904. He lived for many years, as an undergraduate, don, and provost, at King's College, Cambridge.

[70] "Angels, and ministers of grace, defend us! / Be thou a spirit of health, or goblin damn'd. / Bring with thee airs from heaven, or blasts from hell. / Be thy intents wicked or charitable. / Thou com'st in such a questionable shape, / That I will speak to thee." (*Hamlet*, Act I, Scene IV).

[71] The Marsh Test (1836) detected arsenic, the Marquis (1896) detected alkaloids, and the Mandelin (c.1880's) detected strychnine.

[72] Presumably a reference to Dame Clara Ellen Butt (1872-1936), a renowned contralto.

[73] The details of this case have clearly yet to come to light.

[74] Watson would later write up this case as *The Adventure of the Awakened Spirit*, though it was not published during his lifetime.

[75] Baku is an Azerbaijani town on the Caspian Sea. At the time, it was the site of a massive oil boom.

[76] The adventures referred to by the Marquis were published in 1891, 1892, 1893, 1904, and 1904, respectively.

[77] Meaning, beyond the extents of limits of morality or acceptable

behaviour.

[78] French for 'open sesame', a magical phrase from Antoine Galland's French translation of *A Thousand and One Nights* (1704-17).

[79] The Black Hole of Calcutta was a small prison in Fort William where many British prisoners of war were suffocated in 1756.

[80] The Second Boer War lasted from 1899-1902. Sir Arthur Conan Doyle, Watson's first literary editor, was knighted for his account of it, entitled *The Great Boer War* (first published 1900, and constantly revised).

[81] Estimated to be worth $500 million to $1 billion in today's terms. In comparison, the Great Agra treasure was 'only' worth about $75 million in today's terms.

[82] If Botha's tale is true and he and Donahue successfully removed the Kruger millions, this could explain why so many people searching for them to this day have done so in vain.

[83] This Greek proverb referring to the notion of slow but certain divine retribution was first quoted in Plutarch's *Moralia* (c. 100 CE). It later underwent appropriation by Christian writers, and was finally popularized by Henry Wadsworth Longfellow in 'Retribution' from *Poetic Aphorisms* (1846).

[84] Revenge is very good eaten cold. This term has been in the English language since the 1846 translation of the novel *Mathilde* (1841) by Marie-Joseph Sue, who in turn appeared to be quoting a proverbial saying.

[85] Although Virgil professes to have been inspired by *A Study in Scarlet* (1887), it seems likely that he would also have been familiar with the true tale of the shoemaker Pierre Picaud, published in 1838 by Jaques Peuchet, a French police archivist. Picaud plotted a meticulous revenge upon the three men who falsely accused him of being a spy for England, and killed them in a fashion most similar to that carried out by Virgil. Alexandre Dumas was also inspired by Picaud's revenge, using it as part of the basis of *The Count of Monte Cristo* (1844).

[86] *His Last Bow* (subtitled, *The War Service of Sherlock Holmes*).

[87] Watson has taken unusual pains to obscure the date of this adventure, which follows directly upon the heels of *The Adventure of the Second Stain*. One clue comes from the beginning of *The Adventure of the Naval Treaty*, where he claims it took place in 'the July which immediately succeeded my marriage,' which most scholars believe took

THE GATHERING GLOOM

place in late 1888. However, other internal evidence suggests a date of 1894 for this adventure.

[88] The careful reader may wonder if there is an anachronism in this adventure. For it was not until *The Adventure of the Bruce-Partington Plans* in 1895 when Holmes revealed to Watson that Mycroft was so critical to the British Government's War Office and Admiralty. However, since Watson did not have Holmes' permission to publish the current adventure, we can assume that he feigned his ignorance in that account for the sake of explaining Mycroft's role to the reading public.

[89] Downing Street was not gated off to public passage until 1920, after which date a series of increasingly secure barriers were erected at either end.

[90] Also known as the Franco-Russian Alliance, formed against Germany. Negotiations began in 1891 in Kronstadt, and were formalized on 4 January, 1894.

[91] The East Africa Protectorate, also known as British East Africa, was formed in 1895 and roughly covered the territory of present-day Kenya.

[92] Martial Bourdin died on 2 February 1894 when chemical explosives he was carrying to destroy the Royal Observatory in Greenwich Park. The Thirty was an association of anarchists in Paris who were rounded up in a series of raids and put on trial beginning on 6 August 1894. All but three were acquitted due to lack of evidence.

[93] Alfred Graf von Schlieffen was a German General and Chief of the Army General Staff from 1891 to 1906.

[94] Also known as Division IIIb, the Abteilung was the military intelligence branch of the Prussian/German army from 1889 until 1918.

[95] The precise contents of the Belgrade memorandum are never fully explained. In 1894, Belgrade was the capital of the Kingdom of Serbia, and was ruled by an increasingly authoritarian young king who was closely allied to Austria-Hungary. This small nation would later be at the centre of the 1914 powder-keg when its Black Hand secret society assassinated Archduke Franz Ferdinand.

[96] A photochrome was an early colour photographs invented in 1891 by the Luxembourgish physicist Gabriel Lippmann.

[97] Karl Marx wrote *Das Kapital* (1867-83) in the reading room of the British Museum. Friedrich Engels wrote *The Condition of the Working*

Class in England (1845).

[98] Lord Arthur Pelham-Clinton (1840-1870), third son of the 5th Duke of Newcastle, committed suicide before facing a trial for violation of the 'Offenses Against the Person Act 1861' with Boulton and Park, two Victorian cross-dressers.

[99] The Club Train was introduced of 4 June 1889, with service from either Charing Cross or Victoria via Dover and Calais to Paris. The service was discontinued on 1 October 1893, making the dating of this adventure a difficult one.

[100] The Sud Express began in 1886, running to Madrid and Lisbon. The Palatino Express began in 1890, running to Florence and Rome. The Train Blue began in 1886, running to Nice. The Train Éclair began in 1882, running to Vienna. The Orient Express began in 1883, running to Istanbul.

[101] The Strait of Dover is the narrowest part of the English Channel at 18 nautical miles (which are 1.151 standard miles) wide. Until 1982, maritime territories have been defined by international law as extending three nautical miles from shore, which is the distance a standard cannon could fire.

[102] Jules Massenet premiered *Thaïs* at the Garnier on 16 March 1894 with American soprano Sibyl Sanderson in the title role.

[103] Transleithania is an unofficial term for the 'Lands of the Crown of Saint Stephen.' This included Hungary, Transylvania, Serbia, Croatia-Slavonia, and the free port of Fiume. It was part of the Austro-Hungarian Empire, and did not have a separate prince, making the identity of this individual unclear.

[104] Either Professor Kingston followed Holmes' advice, or was he incorrect in his theory as to the location of Attila's tomb, which – to this day – has yet to be discovered.

[105] As there is no De Wines company, this appears to be a thinly-veiled reference to the De Beers Company, founded by Cecil Rhodes.

[106] The Promissory Oaths Act 1868 sets forth the following: 'I, (Insert full name), do swear that I will be faithful and bear true allegiance to Her Majesty Queen Victoria, her heirs and successors, according to law.'

[107] The careful reader may quibble with Watson's choice of title for this continuation of *The Adventure of the Second Stain*, as a simple count reveals that Stanley, Durant, Malcolm Hicks, <u>and</u> Kingston

were all traitors, making a grand total of four. Watson must have felt that the alliteration was worth being a bit imprecise.

[108] "In Libya, the serpents are very large. Mariners sailing along the coast have told them how they have seen the bones of many oxen which, it was apparent to them, had been devoured by the serpents. And as their ships sailed on, the serpents came to attack them, some of them throwing themselves upon a trireme and capsizing it" (*Historia Animalium*, 4th Century BCE).

[109] Fort Charlotte is an artillery fort in Shetland, Scotland. There are no records that it was ever used as a prison, however, here Holmes appears to be implying that it was used for the detainment of top-secret military prisoners.

[110] Heligoland is a small archipelago in the North Sea which came under British control at the end of the Napoleonic Wars. It was traded to Germany in 1890 in exchange for the protectorate over the Zanzibar archipelago.

[111] Ehrenberg's device sounds very similar to a Fessenden oscillator, the first successful acoustical echo ranging device, and a precursor to sonar. Although invented by the Canadian Reginald Fessenden (1866-1932), the German physicist Alexander Behm (1880-1952) obtained a patent for an echo sounder in 1913, so we know Germany was also working on such a device at this time. British H-class submarines, first launched in 1915, were equipped with Fessenden oscillators.

[112] The first known heavier-than-air aeroplane to cross the English Channel was the Blériot XI in July 1909. Another early aircraft was the Voison II plane bought by Armand Zipfel and flown in Berlin in January 1909. The Farman III, which began to be manufactured in Germany in December 1909 under the name Albatros F-2 flew the first known military mission in Europe in October 1912. However, the earliest recorded use of explosive ordnance dropped from an aircraft occurred in November, 1911, when the Italian pilot Giulio Gavotti dropped several grapefruit-sized grenades upon Ottoman positions in Libya.

[113] The Dogger Bank incident occurred in 1904, when the Russian Baltic Fleet mistook a British fleet of fishing trawlers for an advance force of the Imperial Japanese Navy (with whom the Russians were at war). The Russian ships fired upon the British fishermen, killed three and wounding many others.

[114] Further details of this tour have been lost to history, though some aspects appear similar to the 'Prince Henry Tour' from Bad Homberg to London in July 1911. Sir Arthur Conan Doyle raced as No.52 for the British team, which won the race.

[115] Dr Watson's notes never adequately explain why he purchased an American car, rather than a British car, such as a Vauxhall (released 1903) or a Morgan Runabout (released 1909).

[116] The machinations of the German Naval Intelligence Department at Hamilton, Bermuda were detailed in the non-Canonical tale *The Adventure of the Dead Man's Note*.

[117] Skyros was the island where Achilles had been hidden by his mother, in hopes that he might avoid being pulled into the Trojan War by Odysseus.

[118] The Right Honourable Herbert Henry Asquith (1852-1928) was Prime Minister of England from 1908-16. While he may have been prescient in engaging Holmes' service before the start of the war, he ultimately proved to be a weak war leader and was replaced by David Lloyd George.

[119] The misdeeds of the Artus Society were chronicled in the non-Canonical tale *The Lost Legion*.

[120] The Penal Laws were a serious of misguided laws from the 1660's which were imposed in an attempt to force Irish Catholics and Protestant dissenters to conform to the state-established Church of Ireland, a branch of the Anglican Church. These laws were not repealed until 1920. The Potato Famine lasted from 1845-9.

[121] The 20th Century Limited debuted in 1902, running from Grand Central Terminal in New York to Chicago. It was targeted to upper class travellers and had an understated but spectacular style that suggested exclusivity and sophistication. Passengers walked to the train on a crimson carpet, from which the term 'getting the red carpet treatment' originated. At its peak, it was called the 'Most Famous Train in the World,' but it succumbed to the age of aviation and was eventually discontinued in 1967.

[122] Holmes is referring to the foul deeds of Herman Webster Mudgett (aka Dr H.H. Holmes), a serial killer who operated the 'World's Fair Hotel' as a 'murder castle.'

[123] This appears to be Claude Monet's *Wheatstacks (End of Summer)* from c.1890. Bertha Potter befriended Monet and eventually accu-

mulated the largest collection of Impressionist art outside of France. This now forms the core of the Art Institute of Chicago's Impressionist collection.

[124] Hibernia is the classical Latin name for the island of Ireland.

[125] 'Chicago Central' refers to the Central Division of the Chicago Police Department. Its headquarters were located in City Hall on LaSalle Drive.

[126] In 1914, $5 would have had the same buying power of about $120 in 2019 money.

[127] John Devoy (1842-1928) was an Irish rebel leader who was called 'the greatest Fenian of them all.' He worked with the traitor Roger Casement and the German Diplomat Count von Bernstorff to sell guns to Irish rebels, thereby diverting English troops from the war with Germany.

[128] The Great Hunger was a period of mass starvation, disease, and emigration lasting from 1845 to 1852. Holmes was born in 1854; however, it is possible that 'Altamont' disguise caused him to appear a few years older.

[129] The Sirdar was the title of the British Commander-in-Chief of the Egyptian Army between 1883 and 1937. Earl Herbert Kitchener (1850-1916) was one of the great British Field Marshalls. He was known for his exploits during the Battle of Omdurman, where he reconquered the Soudan from the Madhis (who had killed General Gordon), and during the Boer War. He was Secretary of State for War in 1914 and was one of the first to realize the full extent of the Great War. He began a massive recruitment campaign and deployed the British Expeditionary Force to France. He was killed when the cruiser HMS *Hampshire* was sunk near Orkney, Scotland by a mine laid by a German U-boat.

[130] Presumably a reference to Montjoy Gaol in Dublin, built in 1850 and still operating today.

[131] The SS *Cameronia* was converted to a troopship during the Great War, and was sunk by a German U-boat in 1917, thereby proving the importance of obtaining the upper hand in submarine warfare.

[132] Coffin ships carried Irish fleeing the Great Hunger and Scottish fleeing the Highland Clearances across the Atlantic. The owners provided as little food, water, and living spaces as possible such that the disease-ridden ships resulting in so many deaths that it was said

sharks followed them across the waves, feeding upon the corpses thrown overboard. By 1867, regulations were enforced to the degree that crossings became relatively safe, if not comfortable.

[133] The Wild Geese were Irish Jacobite soldiers who left to serve Continental armies beginning in the 1580's. Holmes is obviously speaking metaphorically, since the Flight of the Wild Geese ended shortly after 1745.

[134] Glan-na-Gael was founded in 1870 by Sam Cavanagh, who was known for having killed the English informer George Clark in Dublin after Clark exposed one of their operations to the police. Informers had successfully penetrated it in the past. One of its former leaders, Michael Boland, was later pointed out as a British spy, which might have explained why the majority of its bombers were caught and jailed before they could strike.

[135] Devoy is referring to the famous 1893 World's Fair; where a team of architects and sculptors created the 'White City' of plaster buildings and artworks in a Beaux-Arts style.

[136] Less than a year after the fair closed, a terrible fire ravaged the majority of the buildings and sculptures of the World's Fair.

[137] Rather confusingly, the Field Museum is no longer located in Jackson Park, having moved to the area south of Grant Park in 1921. The building visited by Holmes now houses the Museum of Science and Industry.

[138] How and when Holmes did just that is uncertain, but it must have eventually transpired, since the magnificent Green Goddess can be viewed to this day in the Museum's renamed Grainger Hall of Gems.

[139] The ichneumon was the enemy of the dragon in medieval literature. The mongoose's natural enmity for snakes has led some to call it by that archaic name.

[140] Because only other diamonds can engrave diamonds, it took the DeVries diamond cutters of Amsterdam five years to complete this portrait. It was first displayed at the 1878 Paris Exposition Universalle, where the head of the Statue of Liberty was also first showcased.

[141] King William III (1650-1702), widely known as William of Orange, assumed the crown of England with his wife Mary after the Glorious Revolution deposed King James II. He was known disparagingly as 'King Billy' to the Irish and Scottish, for he effectively ended the pro-Catholic reign of the Stuarts by winning the Battle of

the Boyne in County Meath, Ireland (1690).

[142] Indeed, Buffalo once was the epicentre of the American automobile revolution during the Brass Era (1896-1915). However, the city fathers refused to give Henry Ford any incentives, so he took his method of mass production to Detroit, from where he proceeded to put all of the Buffalo companies, such as Pierce-Arrow, out of business.

[143] Leon Czolgosz shot William McKinley (1843-1901) in the abdomen during the Exposition. He died eight days later and was succeeded by his Vice President, Theodore Roosevelt.

[144] A private social club founded in 1885.

[145] The third stanza of *Enceladus* (1859) by Henry Wadsworth Longfellow, written about the Second Italian War for Independence from the Austrian Empire, fought that same year.

[146] Although we can find no historical record of the SS *Dante*, many such attempts were made to smuggle guns from Germany to Ireland during World War I, in order to aid the Easter Rising of 1916.

[147] This theory is, at best, unproven and most likely inaccurate. The probable culprit was Sir Walter Coppinger (d.1639), who sought to gain control of the village and its fishery. Coppinger was Irish, not English.

[148] It seems likely that this is *Dubliners* (published June 1914) by James Joyce.

[149] Sadly, the details of this lost adventure have yet to be unearthed. Given its prime overlook onto people entering or departing both King's Cross and St. Pancras, it seems an ideal spot for an assassination attempt.

[150] Twenty, in German.

[151] Although not patented until 1921, a primitive mirror was in use in automobiles as early as 1908.

[152] General Joseph Gallieni gathered the famous Taxis of the Marne on 7 September 1914 at Les Invalides. About six hundred taxicabs carried five soldiers each, four in the back and one next to the driver, fifty kilometres to the front. This act quickly became a symbol of the sacred unity of the French people in response to an invader.

[153] Sir Mansfield Cumming (1859-1923) and Sir Vernon Kell (1873-1942) were the first directors of MI6 and MI5, respectively.

Basil Thomson (1861-1939) was the head of the Criminal Investigation Department of Scotland Yard, which acted as the enforcement arm for the various intelligence bodies.

[154] For reasons explained later in the tale, Watson never published this case. Instead, he must have related the major details to his first literary editor, Sir Arthur Conan Doyle, who adapted them and published in Collier's on 8 January 1916 as 'The Prisoner's Defence.'

[155] There is no town of Radchurch in Essex. We may presume that this is actually the town of Witham, which lies between Chelmsford and Colchester.

[156] The Fabrique Nationale Four was a Belgian motor-cycle produced from 1905 to 1923, capable of speeds up to 40 miles per hour.

[157] I am unable to find any details of the First Scottish Scouts, suggesting that Watson obscured the name.

[158] The most winning woman Holmes ever knew was hanged for poisoning three little children for their insurance-money (as noted in *The Sign of the Four*).

[159] 'Boche' was a derisive term used by the Allies for their German enemies. It is an abbreviation of a French word meaning 'head of cabbage' or 'imbecile.'

[160] The Battle of Sedan (1-2 September, 1870) was the decisive battle of the Franco-Prussian War at which Emperor Napoleon III was captured and forced to abdicate.

[161] The British Expeditionary Force was the Army originally sent to the Western Front in 1914. Its first battle was at Mons (23 August 1914).

[162] William Marwood (1818-1883) invented the 'long drop' method of hanging, which ensured the prisoner's neck was broken instantly. This was considered more humane than the 'short drop' where prisoners slowly strangled to death. The technique was used up to 1965, including upon several Nazi war criminals.

[163] Walter Nicolai (1873-1947) was the head of the Abteilung IIIb, the German military secret service.

[164] The Battle of Le Cateau (26 August 1914) was part of the retreat from Mons. The Germans were victorious, but the majority of the BEF was able to escape to fight again another day.

[165] '*The Story of British Prisoners*' was published by the Foreign Office

(The Central Committee for National Patriotic Organizations) in May 1915. It included a vitriolic preface and annotations by Sir Arthur Conan Doyle, who was appalled by the actions of the German Army during the War.

[166] Queen Wilhelmina (1880-1962) was officially neutral, but her husband Duke Henry (1876-1934) was from Schwerin in Mecklenburg.

[167] Several months after this adventure, two Dutch spies, Haicke Janssen and Willem Roos, were arrested under suspicion of espionage against the United Kingdom. They were executed by firing squad at the Tower of London.

[168] The Battle of Neuve Chapelle (10-13 March 1915) was a British victory in the Artois region intended to cause a rupture in the German lines. They captured about two kilometres of ground. However, the planned simultaneous French attack at Vimy Ridge was cancelled, and ultimately the battle had little overall strategic effect.

[169] Marius and Cosette fall in love at first sight in *Les Misérables* (1862) by Victor Hugo, but of course, the notion goes back as far as ancient Greece.

[170] The two ridges are approximately nineteen miles apart. Aubers Ridge is now the site of a small British Cemetery constructed after the armistice. Vimy Ridge is now the site of a war memorial to the Canadian Expeditionary Force who fought there in the spring of 1917.

[171] The Battle of the Sambre (4 November 1918) was the final British offensive of the war. The victory there allowed Allied troops to cross the cancel, after which they advanced relentlessly through Belgium. The armistice was announced a week later.

[172] Holmes must have been livid a month later to hear news of the Germans' perfidious deployment of chlorine gas at the Second Battle of Ypres (22 April – 25 May 1915), the first mass use of chemical warfare.

[173] Watson perpetuated this myth in his 'Preface' to the collection *His Last Bow: Some Reminiscences of Sherlock Holmes* (published 22 October 1917).

[174] From the sixth book of *Paradise Lost* (1667) by John Milton.

[175] The first Zeppelin raid in central London took place on 7 September 1915, though earlier strikes had affected the outlying areas beginning in April. Eventually the fledgling Royal Air Force began to

shoot down the invaders, such that further raids effectively ended by September 1916, though they continued sporadically until 1918.

[176] General Joseph Joffre was Commander-in-Chief of the French Army and Field Marshal John French of the British Expeditionary Force. Together, they won of the First Battle of the Marne on 10 September 1914.

[177] The Schlieffen-Moltke Plan was a German strategy centred on the goal of a single-front war, while the Race to the Sea was an attempt from 17 September to 19 October 1914 to envelop the flank of the Franco-British armies.

[178] During his public trial, Lody freely admitted to being a spy. He was shot at dawn by a firing squad at the Tower of London on 6 November 1914.

[179] The Tritton Machine was the first prototype of the tank, which would eventually see action at the Battle of Flers-Courcelette on 15 September 1916. The particulars of the traitor Merryweather have sadly been lost to history.

[180] I cannot find a historic reference to this song, though it sounds very much like the tune 'Keep the Home-Fires Burning ('Till the Boys Come Home).' Ivor Novello composed this in 1914, with words by Lena Guilbert Ford.

[181] The Post Office Station was renamed St. Paul's in 1937.

[182] Paul Von Hindenburg (1847-1934) was one of Germany's premier field marshals, eventually taking the place of Erich von Falkenhayn as Chief of the General Staff in 1916.

[183] This is only one theory of the origins of the London Stone. It has also been proposed to be a Roman milliarium, the central stone from which all distances in Roman Britain were measured, as well as a terminus, the stone sacred to Jupiter which stood at the centre of every Roman city. The stone originally was in the centre of the street and it was damaged in the Great Fire of 1666. It was moved to the east end of the church's south wall in 1798 and set into the protective alcove. Although St. Swithin's escaped the Zeppelin raids of World War I relatively unscathed, it was heavily damaged during the Blitz of World War II and was demolished in 1961. Excepting a brief stint in the Museum of London from 2016-18, the London Stone has remained located in specially constructed niches in the various replacement buildings that have occupied the site.

[184] Jack Cade was the leader of a popular revolt in 1450 against Henry VI. His followers were defeated at a battle on London Bridge and he fled but was later killed in a minor skirmish. They brought his dead body back to London for trial, beheaded it at Newgate, dragged his body through the streets of London, then quartered it and sent the limbs about the locations in Kent where his rebellion had begun.

[185] Sir Henry Irving (1838-1905) was the greatest actor – save perhaps Sherlock Holmes – of the Victorian era.

[186] Holmes and Watson encountered Drake's Drum in 1903, as recounted in the non-canonical *The Adventure of the Silent Drum*.

[187] Written in the false document style, the common reaction to Arthur Machen's story 'The Bowmen' (1914) was to assume that it was an authentic recounting.

[188] Joseph M.W. Turner (1775-1851) painted *The Fighting Temeraire tugged to her last berth to be broken up*, in 1838. It was kept it in his studio until his death, after which it has hung in the National Gallery. Sir Henry Newbolt was so moved by the painting that he wrote a ballad to it in 1897, from which Watson quotes.

[189] Owain Glyndŵr (c.1359-c.1415) instigated the unsuccessful Welsh Revolt of 1400 against English rule in Wales. He was never captured and is now considered the national hero of Wales.

[190] Sadly, we have no record of this case.

[191] The Dardanelles Campaign (1915-1916) was a long, failed attempt by Britain to take control of the connection to the Black Sea, thereby weakening the Ottoman Empire, a key German ally. The defeat was a major humiliation to Winston Churchill, the First Lord of the Admiralty and the major architect of the attack.

[192] The murder of Mr. Horace Brownlow was documented in the non-Canonical story, *The Adventure of the Dead Man's Note*.

[193] Charles Babbage (1791-1871) was a mathematician and engineer who is considered by some to be the 'father of the computer.'

[194] I have been unable to find any records of Miss Horne. Her story fits well with that of Lena Guilbert Ford, writer of the famous song 'Keep the Home Fires Burning.' However, Mrs. Ford and her son Walter were not killed until 7 March 1918.

[195] Watson's first literary editor, Sir Arthur Conan Doyle, shared his views regarding reprisals for the German air raids on civilian targets.

For both men – normally the kindest of individuals – to suggest such a terrible counter-strike upon innocent Germans was a sign of their deep disturbance by these war crimes. Despite these suggestions, outside the battlefield of World War I, the Allies would not descend to the level of bombing civilian targets until the next war several decades later.

[196] Hammurabi (c.1810-c.1750 BCE) was the sixth king of Babylon and famous for his Code, which is the oldest set of laws in the world. It is famous for its strict punishments.

[197] Sadly, Holmes never related to Watson what this task entailed.

[198] Charlemagne (742-814) was the Holy Roman Emperor and legends of his eternal sleep have been circulating since the Middle Ages. Jacob and Wilhelm Grimm in *Deutsche Sagen* (1816) first documented the Barbarossa myth.

[199] *'Rip Van Winkle'* (1819) is a short story by Washington Irving.

[200] A German U-boat sank the RMS *Lusitania* on 7 May 1915. Over a hundred US citizens were killed. However, it was not until the release of the Zimmerman Telegram that President Wilson and Congress finally declared war on 6 April 1917. The American Expeditionary Force arrive on the Western Front on 25 June 1917 and within six months, the US was represented in full force. Less than a year later, Germany capitulated in a railway coach at Compiègne, France.

[201] The first desertion refers to the period of time when Watson married his first wife and returned to practice. During this time, some evidence suggests that he resided on Cavendish Avenue in St. John's Wood.

[202] The second desertion occurred when Watson wed Mary Morstan in the spring of 1889, approximately six months after the adventure they shared together. During this time, Watson's practice was reportedly located at Crawford Place in Marylebone (approximately May 1889 to May 1890), followed by Earl's Terrace (which backed up to 'Mortimer Street') in Kensington (approximately May 1890 to April 1894).

[203] The dating of *The Adventure of the Second Stain* is one of the most controversial of the entire Canon. Watson himself deliberately attempts to obscure the date: "It was, then, in a year, and even in a decade, that shall be nameless, that upon one Tuesday afternoon in autumn we found two visitors…." Baring-Gould places it on October 12–15, 1886 under the very reasonable hypothesis that it must have

occurred during a year when two different men held the offices of Prime Minister and Foreign Secretary.

[204] While the identify of Watson's third wife is unclear, it is apparent that he wed her in late 1902, from which time, he practiced out of rooms at Queen Anne Street until his own eventual retirement to Southsea.

[205] Collected in paperback as *Light in the Darkness;* independently published by The New World Books (2017).

[206] Collected in paperback as *Light in the Darkness;* independently published by The New World Books (2017).

[207] First published in *The MX Book of New Sherlock Holmes Stories, Part I: 1881 to 1889;* David Marcum, Editor; MX Publishing (2015).

[208] Collected in paperback as *The Treasury of Sherlock Holmes;* independently published by The New World Books (2018).

[209] Collected in paperback as *The Treasury of Sherlock Holmes;* independently published by The New World Books (2018).

[210] First published in *The MX Book of New Sherlock Holmes Stories, Part IV: 2016 Annual;* David Marcum, Editor; MX Publishing (2016).

[211] First published in *Holmes Away from Home: Tales of the Great Hiatus;* David Marcum, Editor; Belanger Books (2016).

[212] First published in *The MX Book of New Sherlock Holmes Stories, Part VI: 2017 Annual;* David Marcum, Editor; MX Publishing (2017).

[213] Collected in paperback as *The Gathering Gloom;* independently published by The New World Books (2019).

[214] First published in *The MX Book of New Sherlock Holmes Stories, Part XI: Some Untold Cases;* David Marcum, Editor; MX Publishing (2018).

[215] First published in *The MX Book of New Sherlock Holmes Stories, Part VIII: Eliminate the Impossible;* David Marcum, Editor; MX Publishing (2017).

[216] Collected in paperback as *The Gathering Gloom;* independently published by The New World Books (2019).

[217] First published in *Sherlock Holmes: Adventures Beyond the Canon, Volume II;* David Marcum, Editor; Belanger Books (2018).

[218] First published in *Tales from the Stranger's Room 3;* David Ruffle, Editor; MX Publishing (2017).

[219] Collected in paperback as *The Travels of Sherlock Holmes;* independ-

ently published by The New World Books (2020).

[220] Collected in paperback as *The Travels of Sherlock Holmes;* independently published by The New World Books (2020).

[221] First published in *The MX Book of New Sherlock Holmes Stories, Part XVIII: Whatever Remains... Must Be the Truth;* David Marcum, Editor; MX Publishing (2019).

[222] First published in *The MX Book of New Sherlock Holmes Stories, Part XXIII: Some More Untold Cases 1888-1894;* David Marcum, Editor; MX Publishing (2020).

ACKNOWLEDGEMENT

First and foremost, I must give a grateful acknowledgment to Sir Arthur Conan Doyle (1859-1930) for the use of the Sherlock Holmes characters. Without his words, this could not have been written.

For reference, I consider Leslie S. Klinger's 'The New Annotated Sherlock Holmes' (2005 & 2006) to be the definitive edition, which builds upon William S. Baring-Gould's majestic 'The Annotated Sherlock Holmes' (1967). I also frequently consult Jack Tracy's 'The Encyclopedia Sherlockiana, or A Universal Dictionary of the State of Knowledge of Sherlock Holmes and His Biographer John H. Watson, M.D.' (1977), Matthew E. Bunson's 'Encyclopedia Sherlockiana, an A-to-Z Guide to the World of the Great Detective' (1994), and Bruce Wexler's 'The Mysterious World of Sherlock Holmes' (2008).

Finally, many of these stories owe a massive debt to David Marcum, author and editor of several wonderful compilations of Sherlockian tales, whose praise and encouragement prompted me to continue unearthing these lost cases of Mr. Sherlock Holmes, written long ago by his biographer Dr John H. Watson.

§

ABOUT THE AUTHOR

Craig Janacek

In the year 1998 CRAIG JANACEK took his degree of Doctor of Medicine of Vanderbilt University, and proceeded to Stanford to go through the training prescribed for paediatricians in practice. Having completed his studies there, he was duly attached to the University of California San Francisco as Professor.

The author of over a hundred and fifty medical monographs upon a variety of obscure lesions, his travel-worn and battered tin dispatch-box is crammed with papers, nearly all of which are records of his fictional works. These include several collections of the Further Adventures of Sherlock Holmes ('Light in the Darkness', 'The Gathering Gloom', 'The Treasury of Sherlock Holmes', 'The Travels of Sherlock Holmes', & 'The Assassination of Sherlock Holmes'), two Dr Watson novels ('The Isle of Devils' & 'The Gate of Gold'), the complete and expanded Adventures and Exploits of Brigadier Gerard ('Set Europe Shaking' & 'A Mighty Shadow'), and two non-Holmes novels ('The Oxford Deception' & 'The Anger of Achilles Peterson').

His short stories have been published in several editions of 'The MX Book of New Sherlock Holmes Stories, Part I: 1881-1889' (2015), 'Part IV: 2016 Annual' (2016), 'Part VI: 2017 Annual' (2017), 'Part VIII: Eliminate the Impossible' (2017), 'Part XI: Some Untold Cases' (2018), 'Part XVIII: Whatever Remains Must be the Truth' (2019), and 'Part XXIII: Some More Untold Cases' (2020). Other stories have appeared in 'Holmes Away From Holmes: Tales of the Great Hiatus' (2016), 'Tales from the Stranger's Room 3' (2017), and 'Sherlock Holmes: Adventures Beyond the Canon' (2018).

He lives near San Francisco, California with his wife and two children, where he is at work on his next story. Craig Janacek is a nom-de-plume.

ABOUT THE AUTHOR

Sir Arthur Conan Doyle

In the year 1885 ARTHUR CONAN DOYLE took his degree of Doctor of Medicine of the University of Edinburgh, and (after diversions in Greenland, West Africa, and Southsea) proceeded to Vienna and Paris to go through the training of an ophthalmologist in practice. Having partially completed his studies there, he was duly attached to a consulting physician at 2 Devonshire Place, London. The patients were few in number and, to bide his time, he turned his attention to the writing of fiction.

The author of twenty-four novels, some two-hundred odd other fictions of all genres, and more than a thousand other works (including plays, poems, essays, pamphlets, articles, letters to the press, and architectural designs). Although he personally preferred some of his other works, he has been forever immortalized as the creator of one of the greatest and most famous characters to ever be set down in print – Mr. Sherlock Holmes.

In 1902, he was made a Knight Bachelor by King Edward VII. He is buried in Minstead, New Forest. The epitaph on his gravestone reads simply: 'Steel true / Blade straight / Arthur Conan Doyle / Knight / Patriot, Physician and Man of Letters / 22 May 1859 – 7 July 1930.'

PRAISE FOR AUTHOR

" 'The Watson style is deceptively difficult to imitate. Good practitioners include….' I'm now adding the stories in Craig Janacek's series, 'The Midwinter Mysteries of Sherlock Holmes' as well."

- DAVID MARCUM, EDITOR OF 'THE MX BOOK OF NEW SHERLOCK HOLMES STORIES', IN 'THE DISTRICT MESSENGER' (JANUARY 2014)

"Craig Janacek combines the puzzle mystery and the paranormal brilliantly in 'The Adventure of the Fair Lad.' "

- 'PUBLISHERS WEEKLY' (DECEMBER 2019)

THE FURTHER ADVENTURES OF SHERLOCK HOLMES

A large cache of manuscripts by the biographer of the world's first consulting detective, Mr. Sherlock Holmes, has been found! Restored, edited, and compiled into thematic collections, these tales augment and expand upon the Victorian world so vibrantly laid forth in the 60 original adventures. Setting forth from their base at 221B Baker Street, herein, Holmes and Watson come upon friends – old and new, and villains – both cunning and tragic. Fully annotated, these editions contain a cornucopia of scholarly insights which compare these newly unearthed tales by Dr John H. Watson to the classic adventures from the Canon of Sherlock Holmes.

Light In The Darkness

Sherlock Holmes returns! He must deal with a series of cases which encompass the broad range of the human experience, from the grim workings of physicians who have violated their oaths, to the magnanimous moods which every man – no matter how cool and emotionless – feels at the time of Christmas. Comprising the collections 'The First of Criminals' and 'The Season of Forgiveness,' all seven recently-unearthed adventures in this volume are narrated by Dr Watson in the in the finest tradition and spirit of such classics as 'The Adventure of the Speckled Band' and 'The Adventure of the Blue Carbuncle.'

THE FIRST OF CRIMINALS: Descend into the horrors that lurk in the minds of doctors who have gone terribly wrong in this quartet of stories featuring the world's first consulting detective, Sherlock Holmes, and his able assistant, Dr John H. Watson. This collection includes the tales 'The Adventure of the Monstrous Blood,' 'The Adventure of the Mad Colonel,' 'The Adventure of the Fateful Malady,' and 'The Adventure of the Barren Grave.'

THE SEASON OF FORGIVENESS: Celebrate the spirit of the season with the world's first consulting detective, Sherlock Holmes, and his able assistant, Dr John H. Watson. This collection includes the tales 'The Adventure of the Spanish Sovereign,' 'The Adventure of the Manufactured Miracle,' and 'The Adventure of the First Star.' It also includes 'The Grand Gift of Sherlock,' a final letter from Holmes to Watson at the very end of World War I, which is sure to delight bibliophiles with its depiction of Watson's bookcase and its moving testament to the enduring power of friendship. Also published as 'The Midwinter Mysteries of Sherlock Holmes.'

The Gathering Gloom

Embark on an exploration of the darker corners of the human experience with the world's first consulting detective, Sherlock Holmes, and his able assistant, Dr John H. Watson. Comprising the collections 'The Schoolroom of Sorrow' and 'An East Wind,' all ten recently-unearthed adventures are narrated by Dr Watson in the in the finest tradition and spirit of such classics as 'The Problem of Thor Bridge' and 'The Adventure of the Bruce-Partington Plans.'

THE SCHOOLROOM OF SORROW: Dive into the deepest abysses of the human soul with Mr. Sherlock Holmes and Dr John H. Watson. From the days before his career as a consulting detective to years of his restful retirement, Sherlock Holmes has all too often encountered terrible events that served to shape his philosophy. To Holmes, every adventure holds the possibility of teaching an earthly lesson regarding the nature of good and evil. This collection includes the tales 'The Father of Evil,' 'The Adventure of the Dishonourable Discharge,' 'The Adventure of the Fatal Fire,' 'The Adventure of the Awakened Spirit,' and 'The Cold Dish.'

AN EAST WIND: In the time of England's greatest need, Sherlock Holmes and Dr Watson stand ready. A great and awful war is brewing in the East, and foreign agents will do everything in their power to see England brought to its knees. Only the swift actions of Sherlock Holmes can prevent the empire's secrets from being sold to its enemies, thereby dooming thousands of brave young men to terrible deaths upon the fields of Flanders and in the frigid waters of the North Sea. This collection includes the tales 'The Adventure of the Third Traitor,' 'The Adventure of the Unfathomable Silence,' 'The High Mountain,' 'The Adventure of the Defenceless Prisoner,' and 'Their Final Flourish.'

The Treasury Of Sherlock Holmes

Embark upon quests for buried treasure with the world's first consulting detective, Sherlock Holmes, and his assistant, Dr John H. Watson. Comprising the collections 'Treasure Trove Indeed!' and 'Fortunes Made and Fortunes Lost,' all eight recently-unearthed adventures are narrated by Dr Watson in the in the finest tradition and spirit of such classics as 'The Musgrave Ritual' and 'The Adventure of the Six Napoleons.'

TREASURE TROVE INDEED!: Things get lost very easily in England. Across the realm, from the remote Peak District to the sea-faring shores of Bristol, from the ancient manors of Devonshire to the warrens of London, Sherlock Holmes is faced with a series of challenging cases. Ranging in time from his days at university until shortly before his retirement, these adventures span the gamut of Holmes and Watson's time together. This collection includes the tales 'The Lost Legion,' 'The Adventure of the Pirate's Code,' 'The Adventure of the Queen's Pendant,' and 'The Adventure of the Silent Drum.'

FORTUNES MADE & FORTUNES LOST: The pursuit of fortune may lead a man to riches or to ruin. From Cambridge to Scotland to London, Sherlock Holmes and Dr Watson must face the darker side of treasure hunting, as they contend with criminals driven mad by their quest of fortune and glory. The full brilliance of Sherlock Holmes is on display as he solves an ancient curse, the singular adventures of the Grice Patersons in the island of Uffa, and a mysterious cipher. Meanwhile, with Holmes thought lost over the Reichenbach Falls, Dr Watson must attempt to employ his methods in the solution of an exotic tragedy. This collection includes the tales 'The Adventure of the Double-Edged Hoard,' 'The Adventure of the Dawn Discovery,' 'The Harrowing Intermission,' and 'The Adventure of the Sunken Indiaman.'

The Travels Of Sherlock Holmes

Embark on a series of journeys with Mr. Sherlock Holmes and Dr John H. Watson. Although Holmes was at his best amongst the ghostly gas lamps and swirling yellow fog of London's streets, he was occasionally willing to venture forth to strange locales whenever a sufficiently-interesting adventure called. Comprising the collections 'A Prompt and Ready Traveller' and 'Round the World,' within are eight recently-unearthed cases which induced Holmes to set forth to the Continent, the Colonies, and even the Americas. All are narrated by Dr Watson in the finest tradition and spirit of such classics as 'The Disappearance of Lady Frances Carfax' and 'The Adventure of the Devil's Foot.'

A PROMPT & READY TRAVELLER: While Sherlock Holmes protested leaving London for too long, for fear of causing an unhealthy excitement among the criminal classes, Dr Watson was always a prompt and ready traveller, who could be counted upon to encourage his friend to take up a peculiar case, no matter where it might lead them. From a spiritual visit to the exotic Kingdom of Hawai'i to the dangerous boulevards of Paris, from to the dark catacombs of Rome to the posh resorts of Bermuda, Holmes and Watson must deal with private revenges and matters of grave international importance. This collection includes the tales 'The Adventure of the Missing Mana,' 'The Adventure of the Boulevard Assassin,' 'The Adventure of the Boulevard Assassin, 'The Adventure of the Secret Tomb,' and 'The Adventure of the Dead Man's Note.'

ROUND THE WORLD: Sherlock Holmes would recommend rejuvenating trips round the world for certain of his clients, but it took a strong force for him to do the same. And yet, occasionally, he would don his travelling cloak and ear-flapped cap and set forth to deal with challenging cases. These adventures include a faerie kidnapping in Ireland – featuring one of the most fantastic deductions of Holmes' career – and a trip to the American South to face the return of a terrible enemy – the K.K.K. Closer to home, the return of a tragic adversary – Dr Leon Sterndale – coincides with the emergence of a new horror. Finally, we learn the true story of whether or not Holmes ever visited the silver fields of California, as previously reported by an American author of some repute. This collection includes the tales 'The Oak-Leaf Sprig,' 'The Adventure of the Double Detectives,' 'The Adventure of the African Horror,' and 'The Adventure of the Fair Lad.'

The Assassination Of Sherlock Holmes

Embark on an epic adventure featuring the world's foremost

consulting detective, Sherlock Holmes, as told by Dr John H. Watson in the finest tradition of the Canonical stories. Comprising three parts, 'The Adventure of the Pharaoh's Curse,' 'The Problem of Threadneedle Street,' and 'The Falling Curtain,' these tales relate one of Holmes' final and most gripping adventures. This special Collected Edition also contains the previously unpublished tale 'The Red Leech.' For the first and only time, rather than a stranger, it is a desperate Dr Watson himself that is sitting in the client chair at 221B Baker Street. Can Holmes help save him from the clutches of the repulsive Red Leech?

THE ADVENTURE OF THE PHARAOH'S CURSE. October, 1909. Sherlock Holmes has been retired to the South Downs for six years, resisting all entreaties to return to his career as the world's foremost consulting detective. But the brutal murder of one of his former colleagues from Scotland Yard has finally galvanized him back into action. Dr Watson at his side, Holmes journeys to London's British Museum, where a series of singular disappearances have taken place. With the museum staff convinced that the curse of a four thousand year-old pharaoh is emanating from the Egyptian Gallery, it is up to Holmes to prove that the worst horrors come from the minds of men. But will the echoes of the past prove to be his undoing?

THE PROBLEM OF THREADNEEDLE STREET. November, 1909. Sherlock Holmes has been called out of retirement to successfully solve the mystery of the British Museum's Pharaonic curse. But while he longs to return to his villa on the South Downs, a new threat has arisen. A twisted riddle of the sphinx suggests that Holmes and Dr. Watson are wading through deep waters. And when the main vault at the Bank of England is inexplicably plundered, Holmes realizes that his enemies may be trying to bring down the nation itself. Only the piercing acumen of the world's foremost consulting detective could see that this theft was but the first blow, and that the villain is certain to mount another daring robbery. From a baffling series of seemingly unconnected events, Holmes must make the brilliant leaps of deduction required in order to determine where his adversary next plans to strike. Only then can Holmes set his own traps and turn the tables on his foe. But will Holmes be able to anticipate all of the forces that are aligning against him?

THE FALLING CURTAIN. November, 1909. Sherlock Holmes has successfully prevented further robberies of England's greatest institutions and captured one of his most dangerous enemies, but something is still rotten in the streets of London. A series of attacks threaten not only his life, but the lives of those few individuals that he calls 'friend.' With Dr. Watson injured, his defenses crumbling, and Scotland Yard deaf to his appeals for succor, Holmes must call upon some irregular help and use every means at his disposal to determine what adversary is stalking him from the mists of the past. From the cells of Wandsworth to the heights of Tower Bridge, Holmes is once more on the hunt. But is he willing to make the sacrifice required to put a final end to this monstrous menace?

Printed in Great Britain
by Amazon